Domestic Enemies
Kent Wyatt

<u>If cited as GNT:</u>
GNT

Scripture quotations marked (GNT) are from the Good News Translation in Today's English Version-Second Edition Copyright © 1992 by American Bible Society. Used by Permission.

<u>If cited as GW:</u>
GOD'S WORD is a copyrighted work of God's Word to the Nations. Quotations are used by permission. Copyright 1995 by God's Word to the Nations. All rights reserved.

Book Cover: Cover design by Kent, Calista, and Rebekah Wyatt. American flag background photo by Aaron Ahlquist on Freerange stock photos. Airliner and sunset photo from stock photos on Freerange stock photos. People and fire photo by Alex McCarthy on Unsplash. Photo compiling and modification by Kent Wyatt. Font design by Kent and Rebekah Wyatt. Author photo by Rebekah Wyatt.

Internal art: Section break image of jetliner by Icons 8 from Ouch!

Winged Publications
PO Box 8047
Surprise, AZ 85374

ISBN: 978-1-0881-6245-3

Dedication

To our more recently acquired daughter, Calista, who so kindly agreed to our son's proposal a few years back. You might not have known the strange world you were stumbling into, but you have graciously allowed yourself to be absorbed into our family, and we are grateful. Your forbearance with the Wyatt eccentricities has sealed you in our hearts. We prayed for someone who would be perfect for our son. We prayed for someone who would encourage him and help him be an even better man of God. We prayed for someone who would complement our family so we could grow together. I selfishly prayed for someone who could help me in my writing ministry. How did God manage to give us all that and more? Boy, He's good.

To our new granddaughter, Avery. We welcome you into God's world. No matter what it may look like in this hour, He knows what He is doing. You can trust Him with all things in all times. He is our only hope, but He is all the hope we need. Listen to the call of His purpose for your life and every evil stumbling block thrown in your path will form the steps that lead you upward in the Lord's plan. May your joy be full so that you might overflow with Living Water for a dry and dying world so ravaged by the cost of sin. Live truth and speak life so those you touch might feel the reality of the One True God revealed in Jesus Christ.

Prologue

JULY 3, 1988
Bandar Abbas, Iran

Alireza Hamadani glanced at his watch, his hatred toward the Turk festering. He had hoped to test his bomb at the hotel, but he had to make the flight to Dubai. *If I wait any longer, I'll miss it.* He contemplated what to do. *I can't cancel with this client. It will set the release back at least another week, maybe longer depending on scheduling.* Large banks didn't like last minute changes. Neither did the Imam.

"Imam." Alireza used the term out of respect for Islam, but he had seen that the man the rest of the world knew as Ayatollah Khomeini was not infallible as the Imam title was supposed to denote. *The old fool has no respect for the scientific community and no concept of the time required to create a masterpiece like this.*

Alireza patted the case on his belt to reassure himself. He needed a success and he needed it soon. Grabbing his bag, he jerked open the door. A dark face made him jump.

Whenever Alireza looked at the Turk, he found himself staring at the scar that crossed his hooked nose and ran down past his mouth. He glanced away as he stepped back so the Turk could enter, but the casual expression on the craggy face angered Alireza.

"This was supposed to happen last night." Alireza clenched his teeth and glared at the floor.

"Yes, it was." The Turk entered the room carrying two identical nylon bags and kicked the door shut with his foot. "You were late."

"Fifteen minutes? You couldn't wait fifteen minutes?" Alireza's eyes connected with dark circles gazing at him over the scar, which lifted at the volume in Alireza's voice.

Alireza's gaze retreated to the carpet.

"Sadly, no. Not in this business." The dark man dropped the bags on the other side of him, away from Alireza. "Two Compaq SLT/286 computers. Not scheduled to be released to the public until September. No extra charge for early delivery."

The thump the cases made hitting the floor made Alireza cringe. "Please don't damage them." It was all he could do to restrain his anger. *I doubt he could even operate a computer.*

The Turk let go of the smile that he held for a moment. "I hear the Compaq company has a very good warranty." Holding out a waiting hand, he reminded Alireza, "You were in a hurry, were you not?"

Alireza knew the hazard of asking the taxi driver to get to the airport as fast as he could, but he had no choice. When the cab screeched to a stop in front of the terminal, he was grateful to be the one sliding himself across the seat instead of the inertia. He paid the driver for the abuse and hurried into the building.

Loaded down with the three bags, Alireza glanced at his watch again. No time to test it before boarding. He moved toward the line for the Iran Air counter.

Alireza carried the newly acquired computers and pushed his carryon bag with his foot. After a few minutes, the line stopped moving. Around the heads of the people ahead of him, he could see a man gesticulating in front of a stone-faced official who stood behind the counter. The whispered information made its way down the line, informing Alireza there was an immigration issue. He knew the flight would be delayed.

Wiping sweat from the back of his neck, Alireza used the motion to mask a look around. There was no better place to find out how well his bomb would work. Slipping out of line, he moved to a vacant set of seats in an out-of-the-way part of the terminal where he could still watch the progress of the line.

On each of the seats beside him, Alireza set up one of the portable computers he had obtained from the Turk and turned them on. When Windows 3.1 finished booting on both machines, Alireza took out the disks he had in his case. He inserted one into the computer on his right and ran the program.

Calling up the timer setting, he saw the default of a three-month delay before detonation. He hoped that length would be right for the bomb he would plant at the client's location in Dubai. He wanted the bomb to do the most damage and not be traced back to him.

Looking to the check-in line for Iran Air, Alireza saw there was no movement and some of the customers were sitting on the floor. But that could change any moment. He needed to shorten the time to detonation as low as he dared. He erased the three-month entry and typed in one minute. The default was for his program to keep everything it was doing concealed, but Alireza changed that setting so a countdown timer would be displayed.

Pressing the start button, Alireza drew in a breath. The numbers denoting one minute appeared on the screen and started reducing by seconds…59…58…. Would his bomb work the same with this new breed of portable? Alireza would soon find out.

As the numbers on the screen clicked by, Alireza second guessed himself. He had initially wanted to wait a year before the big detonation, but he had decided on three months to make sure his bomb wasn't discovered before it could go off.

The timer reached 30 seconds.

The earlier version that Alireza had planted in Jerusalem had been found too quickly to have the impact for which he had hoped. *I need things to work this time.*

20 seconds.

Everything was a calculated risk. The longer he waited to detonate, the more widespread the damage—wait too long, and the bomb might be found before it went off.

10…9…8…

He had worked hard to make his bomb undetectable, but he didn't want to be so short sighted as to underestimate the pace of development of the new virus scanners that were starting to appear… Alireza looked at the timer.

3…2…1.

It was done. The timer went back to one minute and displayed another start button.

To check the files on the computer, Alireza used a separate disk that he had designed to get past the masking features and find the subtle changes his program caused in certain files.

Alireza disliked the word "virus" to describe what he had made. It sounded small and inconsequential. He also did not like that the term had been coined by an American Jew. He preferred to call it his "bomb." This was no ordinary virus. His latest version was invisible and devastating.

Alireza regretted that the Zionists would not be the first to feel the explosion, but it was too risky to go back to Israel. But Dubai, the largest city in the United Arab Emirates, was only a 28-minute flight away. *The spoiled rich Emirates are always flirting with the infidels. They will spread it all over the world.* At the speed Alireza had calculated his new program could reproduce itself, months should be enough. *Let's see what it did in one minute on a portable computer.*

In the minute that had elapsed, his bomb had attached itself to every program. Alireza took another disk containing financial software and loaded it on the computer. His check program verified that the financial disk was immediately infected. He then inserted a game disk and checked it to find the same result.

Alireza was pleased. The new portables were just as vulnerable as the other computers he had tested. "Laptops," as they were being called, were the future of computing, and people would be connecting them to everything.

Even though it altered files on the computer, his program had the traits of what some were calling a "worm." If a computer was attached to a communications port of any kind, including a modem, his creation would silently, aggressively try to contact other computers to link with them and duplicate itself onto the new machine. His bomb attached itself to everything that it touched, and then it waited. The detonation was yet to come.

Alireza switched to the timer window, changed the time to ten seconds and pushed start. At the end of those ten seconds, the timer would simulate what would happen across the world, three months after the bomb's release. As he watched the screen, the time elapsed and the timer reset to five minutes and began counting down again.

Alireza smiled. The bomb had armed itself for the actual detonation. He quickly created a file in the word processor and saved it. Typing rapidly, he created small documents, spreadsheets, batch files—as much as he could in the five minutes he had. He searched for the files and they were all there where he had saved them. Everything looked normal. Then he waited again.

The five-minute timer was the default time he had preprogramed for the detonation on the portable. 3...2...1. The screen went blank.

The beauty of his bomb was that there was no visible explosion. But, once armed, the bomb would surreptitiously begin deleting files. In the version he was going to release in Dubai, the files would vanish one hour after they were created. He had set the five-minute delay for the simulation on the portables to speed up the test.

Alireza searched for the files. The first document he created was gone. Another search a few seconds later showed more of the files were gone. He ran the search program repeatedly, ever more satisfied. Whenever a file reached the five-minute mark, it vanished, its data completely overwritten and irretrievable.

None of the virus scanning software created so far would detect his bomb, and if the computer techs got too aggressive in their effort... From another disk, Alireza loaded a high-level diagnostic and repair tool and ran the program. Though it occurred invisibly, Alireza knew that his bomb was reacting to the deep scan program by replicating itself over and over and each time it was 100% larger. Within seconds it would fill all available memory.

The computer crashed.

Alireza tried to reboot it, but it would always die at the same point. He tried every method he knew to get it going again but nothing worked. It was sweet failure.

If the computer had been connected to other computers in any manner, it would have sent the detonate command to them. Whole networks would go down. Alireza also designed the bomb to immediately digitally shred any backup. The backup data would appear normal until it was used to restore the computer. Then the only thing it would do was reload his bomb.

Alireza eyed the check-in line—no movement yet. He switched to the second portable on his left. *I still have time to test the defusing program.*

He inserted a different disk that contained the protection software and let the program load. When it was complete, he put in the disk containing his bomb and ran it. Using the unmasking disk, he searched for evidence of his bomb attached to the programs on the portable computer—nothing. His defusing software had prevented the bomb from loading. It was the same protection program that was being loaded on all of Iran's major computer networks.

Alireza set the computer aside. He would use it to tie into a phone line in some out-of-the-way office or conference room when he got to his client's headquarters in Dubai and make the release there. He glanced across the expanse of the airport lobby. The line was moving.

Approximately fifty miles south

The boom of the deck gun reverberated through the hull of the USS Vincennes, a Ticonderoga-class, Aegis, guided-missile cruiser. The barrel recoiled into the mount housing, and the spent casing ejected onto the deck with a metallic clank.

A young seaman, barely out of high school, pushed his way into the group of crew members gathered on the deck. He had been in the head when all the excitement started. The young man was proud to be part of the fleet of US Navy ships cruising the waters of the Strait of Hormuz, protecting cargo vessels going in and out of the Persian Gulf from both sides of the war between Iran and Iraq. He didn't want to miss a minute. "What's going on?"

The slap of the sea against the ship was overwhelmed by the sound of the next round from the gun. Smoke from the five-inch round barrel followed the faster-than-sight projectile like an old dog after a rabbit but abandoned the chase and dissipated into the hazy atmosphere. The rabbit, a deadly explosive shell, whistled through the air toward its target.

"Boghammers were hassling an oil tanker again." Another seaman, only a couple years older, pointed across the sea toward a group of small Iranian gunboats weaving through the water. "They went too far this time. They fired at our helicopter that was monitoring them."

"They hit it?"

The older crew member shook his head. "Nah, our bird bugged out before they could. But I think the captain's had enough. We're hit'n 'em and so's the Montgomery." The crewman dipped his head toward the other U.S. ship that was also in pursuit of the boghammers.

The young crew member licked his lips and strained to see the action. It was the first time any of them had experienced live combat. He tapped the shoulder of another young man who held binoculars pressed hard against his eyes. "Let me take a look."

The other man glanced at him with a wrinkled forehead then handed over the binos. "Take a quick look and then I want 'em back."

Through the lens the first crew member focused on the enemy boats. One of the large shells fired at the boghammars found its mark.

An equally young-sounding voice from the Montgomery came over the radio, "Hey, all stations, I think we just smoked that guy."

The other man grabbed the binoculars with a scowl. "You made me miss it."

The first young man resumed his bare-eyed watch, listening to the rapid overlapping voices around him as some called out details of the engagement and others commented.

Below, in the dark of the Combat Information Center (CIC) of the ship, where the row of computer monitors gave the commanders their view of the action, the mood ran more toward tension than excitement. The skipper of the Vincennes, Captain William Rogers, mulled over the situation. He had taken the plunge and ordered the attack on the Iranian boats. *They're getting bolder. Someone has to put a stop to it. I can't let them take a shot at our bird and get away with it.*

The captain focused on how the Iranians might respond. *We can handle the boghammars. Not much of a threat there, but that P3 is still out there.* Earlier Rogers had his radio man give a warning to one of Iran's long-range surveillance aircraft. The pilot had agreed to keep his distance, but he was still in the area. *He'll have us on his radar. It wouldn't be much for him to call in an airstrike. I'm not going to let this end up like the Stark.*

Rogers remembered how thirty-seven sailors had died when an Iraqi jet hit the USS Stark with two Exocet missiles a year earlier. The Stark's captain was retired under the cloud of not acting to defend his ship. *I'm not going to let my career end that way.*

Alireza sat in the first-class section of the airliner designated as Iran Air 655. Even his anger at the Turk had subsided. He let a smile form and took a minute to let the stress roll off. *The bomb works. That's all that matters.*

Alireza imagined what it would be like to watch an average office setting on the day that his digital bomb *detonated*. Despair and suspicion would run wild through the organization as more and more critical files disappeared. In the banking industry, a customer would deposit money in an account, and one hour later all record of it would be wiped away. People would flood the bank, waving receipts for transactions that could not be verified, demanding their money in cash—far more than the bank would have on hand.

People would be fired, departments reorganized, new security put in place, all on a quest to find who was deleting files. Trust would be gone as the bomb used every weakness and back door to spread itself from computer to computer and organization to organization. Businesses would fail with no knowledge of the program that could hide in the latent memory of every floppy disk and tape drive. Only Iran's technology was protected.

Alireza envisioned the effect on the wealthy westerners and Europeans that presumed to dictate what his country could do right down to denying import of the two portable computers that he now possessed. In less than a year, the world would bow under his electronic jihad, and Iran would hold the keys to power. *The Imam will be pleased. He already likes Failak, and this will secure a place for the boy. We can outlast the old man.*

His thoughts turned to Failak. *One of the portables will make a nice gift.* Alireza would give it to his son on his upcoming sixteenth birthday—after he reformatted it and wiped it clean of any evidence of what he was about to do. *He's earned it.* Alireza knew that he pushed the boy too hard, even with his son's natural aptitude for math and computers.

I need him to be ready, just in case. Not that Alireza took the Imam's veiled threats seriously. He was too important to them. So many intelligent people had left Iran since the revolution. It made Alireza valuable.

Only he and Failak understood the computer code and knew the location of his notes and backups. He needed to maintain his value to the Imam until he passed it on to his son. Someday, Failak would be that "arrow" that his name suggested, piercing retribution even further into the world of their enemies.

Alireza's daydreaming was interrupted by the captain's voice over the speaker. "Our flight has been cleared for departure. Please fastened your seatbelts."

Soon, the plane was under way. As it lifted off, Alireza thought about his next steps. *I'll soon be in Dubai, and I need to be ready.*

Petty Officer Andrew Anderson, the identification supervisor on duty aboard the USS Vincennes, jerked his head to the top of his screen when the dot appeared – a new aircraft contact that the Aegis computer had designated as 4474. The designator then switched to 4130. For a second, he thought he had another plane on the screen, but then he realized that the computer was communicating with another US ship's computer that had already assigned the same aircraft the 4130 number. The computer had settled on using that number to track this particular aircraft and had deleted the 4474 designator—the Aegis was a very smart machine. It was the most sophisticated mix of computer and radar deployed by any military in the world, yet it still couldn't ID the plane. Anderson knew that was up to him.

The aircraft was moving at over 300 knots, so it was something powerful, but beyond that it was just another blip on the radar screen. It had apparently lifted off from Bandar Abbas Airfield. That could mean it was commercial, but the Iranian Air Force also flew out of there. He was fairly sure he remembered that one of the many recent intel warnings the Vincennes had received talked about the Iranians moving F-14 fighters to that field. One thing was certain. the new contact was heading right for them.

The forward five-inch gun on the deck of the Vincennes boomed, and the lights in the CIC flickered off and on as they did each time the gun fired. It irritated Anderson. They were in a battleship after all. You would think that they would have designed the lighting system to take a little pounding.

Anderson moved his cursor across the screen and onto the dot which represented the new contact. He pressed the button, triggering the IFF (Identification/Friend or Foe) radio frequency squawk that went out from the ship, requesting an identification signal from the plane. Another round from the deck gun caused another flicker of the lights. Anderson made a growling sound in his throat. *Come on. I've got to see what I'm doing.* He waited for the lights to settle so he could verify what the IFF was telling him.

The digital display showed the plane responding on Mode III, a designated commercial frequency. That should mean it was a civilian airliner not a warbird. The frequency was 6760. As Anderson checked his reference to identify the particular aircraft that used that code, the lights flickered with the next round.

"New bird on the scope," Anderson called out. "It looks like COMAIR. Working on an ID now." He fumbled with the notebook in his hands, turning past the place he needed to be. "Come on." He flipped the pages back the other way. The aircraft identification was crucial. The captain was waiting. Another vibration – another flicker of the lights.

Captain Rogers gritted his teeth in frustration. The last round had jammed the forward gun.

A voice called out. "Captain, topside reports the boghammars are returning fire and heading our way."

Rogers contemplated the risks. The two things the boghammars had in their favor were acceleration and maneuverability. With the forward gun out of commission, even temporarily, the relatively tiny crafts gained a new advantage. He didn't want to underestimate them.

He also had this new radar contact. He could hear the radio operator transmitting on various frequencies, requesting the new contact identify itself and state its intention.

Rogers prioritized. He was waiting on an identification on the aircraft. *The boats are the more immediate threat.* He wanted to be sure he could fully engage them, so he ordered the Vincennes into a high-speed turn. He needed to get it done while the boghammars were still a distance away. "I want rounds in the tray on the rear gun," he snapped, as the ship was swinging around. "We'll show 'em our good side."

Petty Officer Anderson was frantically trying to decipher a copy of the Iranian commercial flight schedule in the dark of the CIC. At least the lights had stopped going out, but he was wishing he had learned how to read the civilian flight schedule prior to that moment. To make matters worse, there were four different time zones used in the Persian Gulf, and Anderson was trying to decide which zone the schedule was based on, but he wasn't sure. He imagined the captain staring his direction, still waiting. So far, he had not found any flights scheduled for that time.

Anderson routinely pressed the IFF again to verify the contact. A rapid turn of the ship sent his papers and reference binders sliding onto the floor, and he scrambled to retrieve them. As he came back up with the bundle of items, he noticed something new on the IFF. A second frequency was squawking on Mode II—that was definitely a military aircraft. Was it a new bird or the same contact now identifying as military? There was nothing else close.

Anderson slid his chair back up to the console as he deposited the armload of paper and binders onto the workspace. What should he do? The plane looked a lot closer on the screen than it had. Was it speeding up? Speeding up and diving would indicate an attack profile. He was trying to remember how high the plane was before and determine its present altitude, but he decided that he should be identifying this new IFF code.

Anderson tried to calm his mind and focus on what he was trained to do, but none of this fit the training scenarios. The IFF indicator said 1100. Anderson began digging through the pile on the workspace until he found the binder that contained the IFF codes.

Apprehension began to give way to fear. If this was a fighter attacking, Anderson needed to get that information to the captain before it was too late.

He ran his finger down the columns of numbers until he found 1100. As he moved his finger to the column that indicated the aircraft that used those numbers, he was incredulous as he read, "Iranian F-14." He quickly ran his finger back, making sure he was on the right column.

Anderson pressed the transmit button and practically yelled into his headset. "All stations. I have a possible Mode II on track 4-1-3-1, 1-1-0-0 which breaks as an F-14."

Anderson had everyone's attention. "You got an F-14?" one of the other crew members asked in disbelief.

Anderson was shaking as he searched the radar screen, not really seeing the activity he thought he saw before. The CIC began to crackle with the news.

"Possible Mode II, breaks as an F-14," was repeated throughout the Command Center.

Captain Rogers looked away from his screens to the sound of the voices that were transmitting the ominous announcement. All eyes were on him.

Shifting back to the monitors, Rogers saw the tactical display in front of him had changed. The contact "blip" had been relabeled as an F-14. The title moved with it as the dot advanced, bringing potential destruction with every refresh of the screen. Rogers was not a man who hesitated.

"Radio command," he ordered the operator. "Tell them what we have and request permission to engage the aircraft if it crosses within 20 miles."

In a moment, the radio operator gave the response. "Theater commander concurs. Warn the aircraft first and then fire on it if it continues."

And continue it did. The dot moved, but the crew was fixated on the "F-14" trailing along with it. With every rotation of the radar, it closed in on the circular display now encompassing the Vincennes indicator on the screen—the ominous twenty-mile radius.

The officer standing behind Rogers called out, "Sir, possible Comair." He pointed at the IFF squawk that had changed to the civilian frequency.

What was going on? Rogers considered what it meant. *It might be a warbird masked as a commercial flight.* The missiles that hit the Stark were fired from a retrofitted civilian jet.

The radio operators in the CIC were again calling out warnings to the aircraft, but it was not responding. The lieutenant sitting next to Rogers announced that the aircraft had crossed the twenty-mile boundary.

Rogers inserted his launch key into the slot on the console in front of him but didn't turn it. To fire his deck guns on the boghammars was one thing, but to launch the deadly SM-2 missiles at a plane that was now identifying as "civilian" was beyond frightening. He could feel his hand shaking on the key, and he hoped no one else could see it in the dim light. Moments passed.

Beside him, the lieutenant was poised. "Captain, do you wish to engage the target at twenty miles?"

Rogers deliberated. *Would they really risk an attack like this?* He wondered if the Stark's captain had thought the same thing.

"Captain, do you wish to engage the aircraft?" The Lieutenant's voice made it sound like a plea.

If the contact was an Iranian fighter, it would soon be able to launch its own missile first. Still, Rogers…hesitated. "Negative." *What if it's a civilian aircraft? How many people would be on board a jet like that?* He needed more than what he had. Why weren't they answering?

The buzz from the earlier information was still moving through the crew. Inside the command room, someone called out, "Altitude declining!"

Declining? The word was like a slap to Rogers. All indication was that the plane had just taken off from the Bandar Abbas Airfield. There would be no reason for it to decrease altitude unless it was a fighter diving to attack.

Rogers realized he wasn't breathing and took a deep inhale. It was much louder than he intended. His priority was to his crew. He grabbed onto that thought and his mind used it to push confusion aside.

Rogers turned the key. He had never done anything so simple and yet so difficult. "Take order on track 4131." Rogers pronounced the fate of the unidentified aircraft that was now within eleven miles. The captain's words set the CIC in motion.

Rogers thought about the possibility of dying. The dot had moved far inside the circles surrounding the Vincennes indicator. It was close enough to accurately fire a missile.

The activity buzzed around Rogers along with the deep metallic thumps and vibrations of the missiles moving into firing position. The missiles launched – first one, then the other.

"Birds away. Rails clear."

When Rogers heard the verification called out, he was both relieved and petrified. The object the missiles were streaking toward had better be an F-14.

Hovering his finger over the hold fire button, Rogers considered the reality of the situation. If he pushed the button, the missiles would self-destruct before they reached the target. The button represented his last chance to stop what he had done. He wanted to push it, but he dared not.

The missiles also represented the last chance for him to protect his ship from the potential enemy that was closing on them.

The radio operators were yelling warnings to the plane on all the frequencies they had available to them.

"Come on. Respond, you idiots." Rogers was immersed in contradicting emotions. Everything else faded into the background. All he knew was fear and resolve crashing against each other like the sea against the hull of the ship.

So many apprehensions were running through Alireza's mind as he stared out the window and watched the water widen below the airliner as it climbed out over the Persian Gulf. He went over what he remembered about the client in Dubai, strategizing about the best place to make the release undetected.

Suddenly, there was a flash of light, the entire plane shuddered, jerking him hard against the seat. His body lurched sideways, following the radical bank of the aircraft. His hands were clamped onto the armrests, gouging deep indents as his face was pulled against the clear plastic window. In milliseconds, he processed changes, more sky, a mass of jagged metal and broken hydraulic hoses sticking into the open air back where the wing had been. Thin streams of oil stretched out toward the tail of the plane. He had no time to realize the significance of the sight.

The second missile slammed into the tail of flight 655 ripping it apart with a shock wave so strong it blew the clothes from Alireza's body, tore the seat belt from his waist, and crushed the two computers under his seat. Naked and lifeless, Alireza fell through the hazy Persian Gulf sky, unaware of the triumphant cheer that went up from the young men on the deck of the Vincennes in celebration of a direct hit.

It did not take long for the mood to change on the Vincennes as they began to pick up the traffic on the distress frequency indicating that a civilian jetliner had crashed in the Strait.

Ironically, but certainly to be expected, the Vincennes was the first on the scene of the disaster. The enthusiasm on deck was gone. The young seamen stared in shocked disbelief as the Vincennes slowly moved through the macabre scene of floating bodies and debris. They watched like wide-eyed children, aged in moments. The horror would be the subject of many nightmares to come, both asleep and awake.

The inquiry into what happened would go before the military court, Congress, the United Nations and the media. In the end, it would be ruled a horrible, perhaps preventable, accident by most of the United States. The strange events in the CIC that day would be explained as human error brought on by a combination of lack of training and misinterpretation of data in the stress of the event. "Scenario Fulfillment" the psychologists called it—fear so strong that it caused crewmembers to see what they feared they would see even in the face of conflicting data. The event would eventually fade in the memory of most. But some would not forget.

JULY 7, 1988

Iranians poured through the streets of Tehran like blood in an artery, separate corpuscles, unique but mingled and adhering into a flowing unit where all personality was lost. Failak's right hand was raised above his head as he partially supported his father's coffin. There were so many others assisting in carrying his father's remains that he hardly felt the weight. People moved in from all around just to touch the box, people he did not even know, as if the physical contact would somehow establish a connection with the unknown man inside, entitling them to a share in the outrage.

The coffin he carried was one of many, draped in honor and lifted up on the flow of people. Failak struggled to keep pace, fearing that the simple wooden box would be carried away from him on the throngs of uplifted arms. Only the slow movement of the masses allowed him to stay with it. The noise from the shouts, the wails, the hate-filled chants, was so extreme that it became a feeling as much as a sound. Failak knew he could not escape it even if he wanted. The people were packed so closely around him that he, along with the others, had no choice but to gradually flow down the street wherever the current took them. His body was pressed on all sides by other bodies, but the crowd was connected even more by the emotion than the proximity.

Yet Failak felt detached. The ones around him did not know what he knew. Even in his grief, the knowledge lifted him up above the crowd, much like his father's coffin. The Imam had honored him, but it must be in private. No one else must know. He was not part of this group, but Failak had no desire to escape the scene. He wanted to hear the crowds pay tribute to the martyrs. He wanted to think of his father that way—to feel something besides the ache inside. He needed somewhere else to channel his feelings. The horror of it was too much to contain. It was easier to blame and to hate. So that is what he did.

KENT WYATT

Chapter 1

Colorado Springs, Colorado
Autumn, 2001

"Tac One in place," came over the earpiece Darrell wore as Pete brought the undercover Celica to a stop.

Dark houses lined the street, tidy yards faintly illuminated by streetlights, except for one. At the far end of the block, light blazed from a dwelling like fire in a jungle. The splinters of illumination left by the careless hanging of a blanket over a large window lit up the front yard, showing the outline of a broken-down Mazda Miata. Darrell was glad that he wouldn't have to be walking around the car to get to Dashawn's front door anymore. He felt sorry for the aging neighborhood that had been desecrated by Dashawn's drug house, but his undercover buys were about to bring the operation down.

Pete keyed the mic attached to his vest. "Hold there until Tac Two is in position, then we'll move."

Darrell smiled to himself. Instead of the ripped jeans, T-shirt, and backward "Raiders" ball cap that he normally wore when he stopped by Dashawn's place to pick up the latest batch of weed or cocaine, he had on a ballistic vest that said "Police" and a matching ball cap that he wore facing front with his long brown hair tucked up inside. Dashawn always gave him trouble about the "Raiders" hat, telling him white boys didn't get to wear those in the hood. Darrell wondered if he would like this one any better.

"You got the warrant?" Pete gave him a hopeful glance.

Darrell reached down the front of his tactical vest and took out the folded paper he had tucked there. He had made sure he brought a copy this time—he wasn't making that mistake again.

"See," Pete grinned. "You're learning."

Darrell grimaced. "How long is it going to take me to live that down?"

His sergeant looked across the car at him with a good-natured smile.

"Until we get a new rookie on the team."

"I'll let you know tomorrow who I'm going to kill to make an opening," Darrell shot back.

Pete smiled again. "Make it Schafer. He's a pain in my butt. Or better yet, just shoot me in the leg and I'll retire on a medical and won't have to wait another fifteen years. Then you can have this job."

Darrell shook his head. "I don't think I'm ready to take your place."

Pete gave him a look of admiration. "It won't be long. We've been trying to make buys from Dashawn forever. You did it inside of two months. You'll be sitting on this side before you know it."

Darrell let his face display gratitude at the compliment. "I just wish the Middle Eastern mystery man would have shown up. It's the right time for him. You don't suppose he spotted Jay watching the house?"

"Naw. I've got him hid too well. You said the guy was unpredictable."

"He is, but he always shows up not long after the dope arrives."

"Well, it's been there for a while, and we can't wait any longer. We're going to be on overtime finishing up this search and all the evidence the way it is. If we wait any longer, the Lieutenant is going to be all over me." Pete looked toward the house. "So, the rooms go living room, dining room, kitchen and two bedrooms on the other side of the house with a bathroom in the middle." Pete pointed his finger, tracing the various sections of the layout that Darrell had gone over in the briefing. "And the basement goes laundry, TV room and two bedrooms at the front end."

"Right." Darrell nodded as his gaze followed Pete's finger. "Atari sleeps in the north room, and his computer set up is in the south room. I only got a glimpse of that when Crystal was showing me around."

Pete snickered. Darrell hung his head and shook it slowly back and forth, sorry he had brought up the tour of the house that Dashawn's "main squeeze," Crystal, had taken him on.

"I'm sorry," Pete said. "I can still remember your voice on the wire when that was going on. You trying to keep her off you and still get a look around the house." He mimicked Crystal's voice. "You have such beautiful brown eyes, Darrell. Don't you like me, Darrell?" Pete laughed harder.

"Please don't remind me." Darrell hoped Pete would let it go. But his sergeant was against the car door holding his stomach as he guffawed uncontrollably.

"Sure, I like you..." Pete parroted Darrell between gasps. "I just...don't like...to mix business...with pleasure."

Darrell looked out the window while Pete whooped it up on the other side of the car. "I was so glad to see Atari come down even when he got all mad about us being down in his space. So then I have this little nerd yelling for us to get out and Crystal trying to put her arms around me and saying, 'Don't let him hurt me' - like the little weasel could." Darrell looked over at Pete who was using his Crystal voice again.

"Save me, Darrell, save me."

"Oh, stop already. She didn't even say that. That's what I wanted to say," Darrell pointed at himself. "Save me, Sarg, save me. You still owe me for that."

"Hey," Pete blurted out, trying to twist his smiling face into a distressed look. "It wasn't easy for us listening to it out in the van, either." He held the mock remorse for as long as he could and then burst into laughter again. "I 'bout wet my pants."

Darrell looked in disgust at his supervisor. "Yeah, I'm sure it was a real hardship for you."

After a few more moments, Pete got himself under control. "Well, tonight we'll finally see what's so important down in that basement. This Atari guy will probably crack and tell us what he and your mystery man are up to." Still chuckling a little he asked, "Speaking of romance, how are you and Jodi getting along?"

"Great." Darrell was thankful for the subject change. "I really like her."

"Who doesn't?" Pete shrugged and raised his hands as if he was saying something that was obvious. "I think that is part of the reason Shirley was so eager to get you two set up. The Bible study was going a little off track with all the new single guys we were attracting. Especially since they all seemed to be coming for something other than the lesson or the chip dip. I was getting tired of hearing, 'Wow Jodi, that was so insightful.' Pete mimicked and gestured derisively. "Shirley is usually not the jealous type, but even she asked me to maybe not talk to Jodi so much—so people don't get the wrong idea. But it's hard, I don't want to just ignore her and she's easy to talk to."

Darrell wrinkled his brow. "I have to admit, that part is a little intimidating—having every man staring at us everywhere we go. Sometimes I almost want to ask her, 'could you wear something that doesn't look so good on you?'"

Pete smiled mischievously. "That might be a challenge for her. Oh well," he said reaching across and giving Darrell a fist bump on the shoulder, "it's a burden you're willing to bear, right?" Then he added, "If anybody deserves her, you do."

The radio interrupted their conversation. "Tac Two in place."

Pete gave Darrell an unusual look as he spoke into his radio. "Copy that. All units start moving up. Nora Twelve meet me in the yard of the house just south of the target. Nora Fifteen will keep watch out here."

Darrell snapped his head around when Pete said his radio designator. "Hey, I want to go in. This is my bust."

Pete was nodding. "I know, it's definitely yours, but I don't want to burn you. Dashawn will probably be out on bond before we get this evidence processed. But he won't get a lawyer until the court appoints him one at his first hearing. You know how it is, poor little dope dealer with no documented income. You and I and every other taxpayer are going to foot that bill.

"But the beauty is that, on his own, Dashawn won't be asking the prosecutor's office for any police reports for his defense case. It will be quite a while before he knows how we got the warrant. He'll think it was that chick you said has been coming over to visit Crystal. Guys like Dashawn think they're too smart to get burned, so they're always looking for a way to blame their old lady. If he doesn't see you on the bust, he won't know. You might be able to go right back in after a couple days and ask why all the cops were over here. We can start all over—stack the charges so we can put Dashawn away for a while, see if we can get the mystery guy the next time."

"Sure you're not just trying to pacify me because you don't trust me to go in with you?"

"I'm sure. I meant what I said. You're probably gonna take this spot someday if you want it. But until then you're going to make me look good by reeling in a boatload of dope. So keep your head down. I don't wanna ruin my best man when he's just starting."

Darrell could see no insincerity on Pete's part. "Well, if you're placating me, at least you made it sound good."

Pete smiled and slapped him on the chest with the back of his hand. "See, that's why Dashawn thinks you're his college connection. You're always using those big words. As soon as we get everybody cuffed and stuffed and on their way to jail, I'll call you in so you can join us."

"Right when the fun ends and the work begins."

Pete grinned. "Hey, you don't think I'm gonna write this report, do you? And don't worry; I won't be moving in on your girlfriend, Crystal, while I'm in there." He was still smiling as he opened the door and got out. "Bring the car up when I call for you."

Darrell moved over to the driver seat.

Pete slipped across the street and into the dark along the tree lined yards, drawing his gun as he went.

Darrell had trained with the Tac team. He knew that as they were moving up on the house, they would limit their radio traffic, keeping the air clear for any last-minute emergencies.

There was a streetlight about a half a block behind Darrell, and it gave enough light that he could barely see Pete's shadow moving quickly toward Dashawn's. He thought he could make out movement just past the house, and he suspected it was Tac One moving in as well.

Darrell glanced back to where he had last seen Pete, but he was lost in the darkness. He must have stopped, holding just south of the house, waiting for the Tac unit to take the lead. Silhouettes moved under the cover of the trees on the north side of the house. The Tac team was setting up, making preparations to hit the front door.

Darrell caught movement with the corner of his eye. A long shadow wavered on the sidewalk across the street. He heard footsteps coming closer. Darrell froze. *We don't need some civilian getting in the middle of this.*

He doubted if the person had seen him in the car. The vehicle interior was even darker than the street, so Darrell decided to let the person go by without revealing himself. If they kept going toward Dashawn's, he might have to stop them.

As the footsteps got closer, Darrell considered the possibilities. *They're probably going to our dope house. It's that time of night. That could be the mystery man.*

Darrell allowed himself just enough adjustment to position his hand on his gun, ready for a quick draw. He inched his other hand to the door handle, taking care not to let the motion transfer to his upper body.

The footsteps stopped. Darrell felt vulnerable with whoever it was still behind him. Had the person spotted him? *Don't panic. More likely they saw something they didn't like down by Dashawn's.* That could be worse. *I can't let them get on a cell phone and give us away.* Darrell was almost ready to throw open the door with his gun drawn, when the footsteps resumed. The figure came into blurry perspective in Darrell's peripheral vision. Was that the long coat the man always wore?

As the individual moved into better view there became no doubt. Darrell recognized the Middle Eastern features.

The mystery man halted; his eyes locked on the activity outside Deshawn's.

The man was so close that if Darrell got on the radio, he would hear him. He had nothing to arrest him for, but he needed to do something. He made a quick glance up the street. The shadowy Tac team moved up on the porch.

Mystery Man caught his attention again by reaching into the pocket of his overcoat while still fixated on Dashawn's. Darrell didn't wait to see what he was reaching for. He pulled the handle and threw his well-muscled, six-foot frame into the car door, popping it open. Jumping out of the car, he drew his gun. "Police. Don't move."

The man whirled Darrell's direction but never stopped moving. He bolted down the sidewalk back the way he had come.

Darrell almost shot him from the sheer surprise of the move. He came to himself and was after the man, feet beating hard against the pavement.

Mystery Man used a driveway to get to the open street where there were fewer obstacles. He sprinted, the open coat flapping like a wild goose trying to take off.

Darrell managed to get his gun back in the holster as he ran, grabbed his radio and yelled his radio designator into the mic. "Nora Fifteen. I'm in foot pursuit." He panted. "I'm—" *Oh blast, what street am I on.* The natural pursuit reflex of his body had pumped more blood to his legs and away from his brain. He couldn't remember the street name. Then he recalled typing the address on the warrant – "southbound on Sunview Dr…the 600 block."

The man had reached the end of the street and turned west. Darrell was close behind, but his chest was hammering to escape the constriction of the ballistic vest as it swelled with each gasp of air. As he rounded the corner, headlights came on about a block down the street. The lights belonged to a van that was lurching away from the curb and heading their way. He guessed the van was the mystery man's ride. Darrell put on a burst of speed to catch him before the van could intercept them.

As he closed the distance, he grabbed onto the collar of the man's coat. The steam-engine puffing emitting from the man's mouth was suddenly restricted, and the mystery man twisted around and batted Darrell's hand away with his arm. The movement, combined with the momentum of the run, threw his opponent off balance and Mystery Man stumbled sideways, falling hard on his left hip.

Darrell resisted the temptation to go hands on with the man. He was confident in his skills. Few people could match up with him on the mat. But the van was coming too fast. He had no backup, and it would be foolish to try handcuffing a man with a van load of who knew what bearing down on them. He drew his gun and leveled it at Mystery Man. "Don't move." He still didn't know what the man had been reaching for back on the sidewalk. "I don't know what you have in your pocket, so keep your hands where I can see 'em."

The man spat a string of foreign words at Darrell that needed no translation, but he kept his hands in sight.

As the van advanced, Darrell sidestepped putting the mystery man between him and the vehicle. "I hope these guys are friends of yours, otherwise, we're both in trouble."

The van showed no signs of stopping. Darrell made a show of

presenting his handgun. Still, the vehicle was headed right for them and coming fast. He scanned for cover—behind the cars at the side of the road. But he also had his prisoner to worry about. Surely the van was not going to run the man down.

Darrell was just about to open fire when the van swerved to the right and spun around so the driver's side rear corner was facing him. He heard the passenger door open on the opposite side of the van. Heavy boots hit the ground. At the same time, he recognized another sound—someone pulling back the slide on an assault rifle.

Darrell headed for the cars. Out of the corner of his eye, he saw Mystery Man roll away toward the van as Darrell headed in the opposite direction. Behind him, the man yelled something in the foreign language.

Darrell was almost to the cars when he heard the rifle booming, louder than he had ever heard gunshots before. Everything slowed down. The bullets parted the air near him, making a singing tone in his ear. He gradually closed on the nearest vehicle when one of the bullets found him. It burned through his right buttocks, jerking him off balance. He fell across the back of the car as another round ripped across the back of his ballistic vest, yanking him again. The surface in front of him began erupting. It seemed like he could see the bullets coming in as they hit the trunk of the car, leaving behind holes and long gashes in the metal.

As he pushed off the trunk to propel himself behind the vehicle, his left arm shuddered. He tried to use it to move behind the car, but nothing worked as it should. It was not pushing right, like it was asleep. He couldn't feel what he was touching, no grip. Sliding across the trunk, he finally dropped behind the car. Rounds pounded the other side.

There was a reverberating explosion. It came from the direction of Deshawn's house, and vibrated in the asphalt beneath Darrell. The rounds hitting the vehicle stopped. He could still hear gunfire but not as loud. It was coming from the area as the explosion. The shooter must be moving around the car - coming for him.

He raised his gun in his right hand, pointing it at the corner of the car. The gunsights waivered with the shaking of his hand. He brought up his left hand to steady the weapon, but there was nothing to grip with. His hand was not there. He stared, not comprehending. Something dangled from an exploded mass of flesh—fingers. *Those can't be my fingers. What—?*

He felt the first deep, burning, pulsating pain coming up through his hip and back. He tried to ignore it, his trembling handgun at the ready. The man might be coming to finish him. *I need to get help for my hand.*

Darrell heard his name. The man was after him, calling out, "Darrell, Darrell, stay down. I'm coming for you."

The man was coming for Darrell. He couldn't let his guard down. But the floodgates of pain had opened. What he felt was indescribable. It clouded his vision. Bile rose in his throat causing him to cough and gag. He dropped his gun, no longer caring about his attacker. He just wanted the pain to stop.

Darrell heard the voice, closer now. "Darrell, stay still. Oh, no, please no." Pete's face floated in front of him, blurry and indistinct. He was talking into a handheld radio. "We've got an officer down and a house explosion and fire. Send me everyone you've got and start calling out units. We've got officers still in the house. We need every medical and fire unit we have. Get 'em here fast. Darrell, it's gonna be okay. Hang in there." He was on the radio again, "Jay, stay out of that house, I know you want to help them, but wait for the fire units. Stay with me, Darrell." Pete was wrapping something around Darrell's arm. It made the pain worse, and Darrell tried to push him away, but the mist closed in.

There was light, sometimes right in Darrell's eyes, sirens and voices, hurried, urgent, and pain, plenty of pain. He felt his body being moved more than once. That brought more agony. Coherence was a fleeting thing, not that he desired it. He was half aware of a needle being inserted in his arm, someone squeezing a syringe, and he was spared the burden of consciousness.

Chapter 2

Besides the aching, Darrell was first aware of a clicking and humming. He concentrated and his mind identified it as the sound of an IV machine. He opened his eyes and struggled to get them to focus. There was a white wall. He perceived he was in a bed. A plastic siderail with markings blocked part of his view…it was a hospital bed. The shoulder and hip of the side he was lying on felt like it had hardened to concrete. Trying to change position brought pain, especially in his left hand. He groaned. It was all he could do.

A man in scrubs came and talked to him, asked him how he was doing and said something about rating his pain. Darrell moaned and made a little nod with his head. The man left for a few minutes and returned with a syringe that he injected into the IV in Darrell's right hand.

Darrell licked his dry, cracked lips. The nurse must have noticed and came over with a rough, wet sponge on a stick and scrubbed out his mouth. He tasted mint. Some of the water dribbled onto his chin. Because of the IV in his right hand, Darrell reached with his left to try to wipe it away. Pain shot through his hand and into his arm, causing him to whimper.

"Hey, don't try to move that arm." The nurse frowned. "It can be very painful at first. It will get better though."

Darrell looked down at his hand. He stared at the bandage. It was rounded where his forearm ended. It couldn't be his arm. Where was his hand? It was some trick his mind was playing. "I can feel it."

"I know it hurts." The man's voice was sympathetic. "But I can't give you any more pain meds for a while."

He hadn't meant to speak to the nurse. He must have said what he was thinking out loud. Darrell looked up at the man. "Is my hand gone?"

The nurse nodded weakly. "I'm sorry, it is. Remember the conversation you had with the doctor earlier today?"

Darrell had no idea what he was talking about. "But I can feel it."

"That's pretty common. Listen, I know it's shocking, but it will be okay. There are lots of things they can do. Right now, it feels like this is the end of the world, but we're gonna get you through this."

My hand can't be gone. Darrell squeezed his eyes shut. "No. It…I'm a cop." Darrell began to wade through his drug impaired mind and comprehend what the nurse had said. Panic set in. "I need to speak with someone about my hand." He was desperate. "Someone has to do something. I can't lose my hand."

The nurse looked at him in confusion and that panicked Darrell more. "What happened…how did…?" He had foggy images of something happening on a street somewhere. "Someone needs to come in and fix it. I can't work without my hand."

The nurse came closer with sympathy on his face. "Remember, the doctor told you there was nothing else they could do. They tried everything."

"I want to talk to the doctor." There was hesitation on the man's face and Darrell added, "Right now!"

The nurse hurried out of the room and returned with a tall thin man with white hair.

Darrell raised his arm despite the pain. "Doctor, please, you have to fix my hand. I have to have it. I can't be a cop without a hand."

"Who says?" The older doctor lifted his head and gazed down his nose and through his glasses at Darrell.

Darrell didn't understand. He had to get through to the man. "Please."

"Let me just talk to you straight." The doctor leaned closer. "The nurse said you don't remember the talk we had about what happened to your hand. It's not surprising. This is a big shock, and you have a lot of narcotics on board."

Moving his finger toward Darrell's arm the doctor narrated without emotion. "Someone shot you with a rifle. The bullet entered at your upper forearm, here." The doctor pointed in a manner that told Darrell he wasn't planning on touching the sensitive appendage. "It hit the bone here. Fortunately, it glanced off and only took out a little chunk."

The doctor's face got even more serious. "But then it got ugly. It began to tumble and tear apart as it went." He spun his finger in a spiral along Darrell's forearm to illustrate his explanation. "It ripped open your hand and tore up a lot of the bones in there, then took them with it as it left you. The surgeon tried to fix it, but you lost so much bone, nerves, tendons and blood vessels that there was nothing left to build on. It would have threatened your life because of all the destroyed tissue with no blood flow. Infection would have set in as that tissue rotted away. We had no choice, son. It had to come off."

Darrell squeezed his eyes shut again. Breathing heavily, he shook his head.

The doctor shifted gears. "Now, about this business of you not being able to work. Not only can you work, but you have a lot of it ahead of you. First, you are going to work in here. You're going to do your therapy, so you will be stronger than when you came in. You're going to work at learning how to do the same things you did before only in different ways. Then you are going to work on getting back to your old job by being better with one hand than the other guys are with two. We will just see about this not being a cop issue. The only person that is going to stop you is *you*. So, *you* better start working on *you* right now. That hand was only a little part of *you*. So you need to let it go and rest up the rest of *you* because that part of *you* has a lot of *work* ahead. You don't have time to look behind."

The doctor ceased his lecture and his face softened. "Sorry, kid," He laid a light hand on Darrell's shoulder. "But when you are as old as I am, you don't have time to beat around the bush. Now get some sleep. That is what your body needs right now." He smiled. "That and a good attitude." The doctor stood and looked at the nurse, "Take care of him, Dave," With that, he walked out.

Members of the Narc unit came in and out, but Darrell did not feel up to talking. After three days, he looked at Pete sitting in a chair next to the bed. "What happened?"

Pete appeared mournful and shook his head. "You just get better."

"Pete?" Darrell looked in the sergeant's eyes. "Please, come on."

Taking a deep breath and letting it out, Pete acquiesced. "We still don't know for sure. You came on the radio and said you were in a foot pursuit. Jay and I left the Tac guys as they were securing the house, and we went to help you. We started hearing shots; some guy by a van was firing at a car. Jay and I laid down some fire at the shooter and got him to duck behind the van. Then I saw you down behind the car. I couldn't see well, but I knew it was you. You started moaning and rolled over. I could tell something was wrong, that you must have been hit."

Pete's face said the discussion wasn't easy. "There were at least a couple of other guys in the van, and they were moving around like they were doing something inside. Then we heard this explosion behind us. One of the guys in the van started yelling something foreign. The shooter jumped back in the van, and they tore out of there. I couldn't get a plate in the dark – don't even know if it had one. We still have no idea who they were or if they blew up the house, but the bomb guys say it was a remote detonation. We figure that was what they were doing in the van. They brought in the FBI, and they said it was pretty sophisticated explosives. This was definitely more than just gang violence."

"Was anyone inside the house?"

Pete's voice came as almost a whisper. "Yeah."

Darrell leaned heavily back on the pillows and winced when the weight transferred to his tail bone. He shook his head. "I can't remember it."

"It's better."

"No, it's not." Darrell almost snapped at Pete. He paused to regain control. "I remember the briefing. Raul, Frazier, and Steve were going in the front. Were they…?"

"We left them to secure the house," Pete's voice went up a notch and caught at the end of the statement. He sniffed. "They didn't suffer. Raul and Frazier were just going downstairs when we left to cover you. So, I guess you saved Jay and me's life. John, Montie and Rod were still in the back yard. They didn't want to shoot that stupid dog Dashawn had tied up there. I guess he saved their lives. They took some hits from debris when the back wall blew out, but they're going to be okay. The explosion started in that downstairs computer room. Raul, Frazier and that Atari guy were down there. It blew right up through the floor where Steve had Dashawn and Crystal cuffed and sitting on the floor."

Darrell squeezed his eyes to hold the tears.

After a while, he asked, "Who was I chasing?"

"We were hoping you would remember."

"I remember the briefing." Darrell's mind was foggy, probably from the morphine. "It's just bits and pieces after that." Darrell remembered a Middle Eastern face. It was dark and in shadow. He wouldn't forget it, but he didn't know why.

Chapter 3

Colorado Springs, Colorado
Summer, 2014

For Cissy, there was something about having her hands in the warm soapy water that made her think of family times. She needed the comfort, especially tonight. She knew Tom was probably right. Just because the police hadn't made any arrests didn't mean they were in danger. The Montebello Drive area of Colorado Springs was a safe neighborhood. She was glad he agreed to purchase the new security system, just the same.

Could there really be a serial killer in the city? She wished she had never listened to all the gossip at the Iris Society meeting. They should have stuck to talking about the new bulbs they were going to plant at the library.

Cissy turned from the sink and peered out the sliding glass door that led from the second story kitchen of their bi-level home. Was that a noise outside or just her imagination again?

Easing across the kitchen, Cissy looked through the glass, past the deck and to their yard below—no movement. It looked empty.

Lights were on in some of the windows of the small apartment complex that butted up to the right half of their back privacy fence. Darkness had moved in leaving just a silhouette of Pikes Peak visible through the open expanse to the left, above the strip malls and office complexes that backed up to Tomah Drive further down the hill.

Click, click, click. Cissy stiffened and then relaxed in recognition of the noise—canine toenails on tile. She glanced down at the curly haired face. Cissy beckoned toward the door. "Tripsy, you want to go outside and look around?" The animal took off for the living room. *Maybe we need a braver dog.*

Cissy pulled the cord that closed the vertical blinds and went back to her dishes. She wished she felt better about the new security system. She had to force herself not to check the alarm panel again.

Taking in a cleansing breath, Cissy tried to clear her head. The image of the large man with the security company's installation team came into her mind. The memory of how he had stared at her was affecting the peace she should be feeling about having the house more secure.

A scream from the living room made her jump. Shaking her head, she grabbed a glass off the counter and shoved it into the suds. She wished Tom hadn't chosen a horror show to watch.

"How's it going in there?" She called over her shoulder. She could hear sinister background music playing. Someone must be getting murdered on the screen, with all the screaming going on. The new video system enhancement must be a hit. The sound certainly was realistic. "Are you liking it okay?"

She heard a noise behind her. Tom was always bringing in some last-minute plate from the living room before she finished the dishes. Cissy turned with a smile. Her mind could not react quickly enough, and the smile was still half frozen on her face when she realized the knife was not going to stop as it plunged toward her.

Neighbors watched from their windows and front porches. Darrell examined the groups gathered on the sidewalk surrounding the crime scene tape. Using his prosthetic hook in the spinner ring attached to the steering wheel, Darrell guided the car to the curb. Surveying the area to see what commanded so much attention, he held the radio mic in his right hand and told the dispatcher that he had arrived.

Everyone in view was riveted to a scene playing out on the lawn. Across the street, a television camera operator was also zoomed in on the drama while a reporter was narrating beside him.

Two uniformed officers stood on either side of a woman who looked barely out of high school. She was on her hands and knees, screaming and rocking back and forth. Her face, arms, and clothes were covered in blood.

Darrell assessed the scene. *Where's medical?* There they were. Two male paramedics leaned against a rolling stretcher at the back of an ambulance that sat next to the curb. A third sat in the open back door of the medical vehicle.

The woman was apparently not a victim, or the EMS crew would be taking her to the hospital. The blood must be someone else's.

The cops stood stiffly, looking around and then back at the woman. Darrell recognized the younger officer from the last academy class when

Darrell taught them crime scene investigations, but he couldn't recall the name. Gill Wengert, the older of the two cops, was usually good with people.

Gill reached down and said something to the woman, putting his hands on her shoulders, trying to get her up. She batted his hands away, yelling an anguished, "No, no, get away from me!" Standing up again, Gill looked around, hands at his sides, trying to appear professional. He shifted from one foot to another, a lost public servant with no clue how to serve at the moment.

Shawn Davenport, Darrell's sergeant on the Major Crimes team, was not watching. He was at one of the cars, talking to a man. His yellow notepad lay on the trunk, already a ream of pages flipped behind the pad, creating a large roll at the top. Shawn nodded as the man spoke, occasionally writing on the pad.

Darrell looked at the woman again. The cops were still having no success. Darrell did not mind the bodies, the dead of the crime. He had often heard other cops say, "Kids are the worst." To Darrell, they were all just bodies, lifeless things, as much so as the dust on the floor where they were laying. At a death scene, the fundamentals of what was left of his faith always came out. Darrell still believed in something beyond this life, even believed in God—they just were not usually on speaking terms.

No, it was not the dead that affected him. It was how the dead affected those around them. Perhaps not all of them. Some people might be truly cold. Others put on a brave face and kept themselves busy helping everyone else. They would probably break down later and grieve in private.

But some were totally unprepared for that kind of twist in life. The day-to-day routine of interaction with their loved ones was so ingrained in them that the concept of life without them came through like static to their consciousness, leaving them with nothing to broadcast but senseless noise. Like the woman that the cops were trying to console. "What's Your reason for this?" Darrell directed the question to the Heavens, expecting only silence, as usual.

He looked at Shawn again as the other detective flipped another yellow page to the back. The man that was talking to Shawn was distracted, glancing occasionally at the wailing woman. Darrell had taken his own yellow pad out of his briefcase. Breathing deeply and then letting the air out, he flung the pad onto his dash. Getting out, he walked over to the ambulance attendants. "Can't you guys do something with her?"

One of the men came off the stretcher and raised his hands in a defensive gesture. "We tried. We were able to examine her enough to know that she's not injured. The problem is she doesn't want to leave her little brother. That's his blood, probably some from mom. We coaxed her that far and then she wanted to go back for the kid. When the cops wouldn't let her…well, you can see for yourself."

"Why don't you take her to the hospital so she can talk to a counselor or something?"

The man was shaking his head the moment Darrell began asking the question. "We can't transport anyone unwillingly. Only you guys can make that decision." The look on Darrell's face must have been obvious because the man quickly added, "I know, I know, we feel the same way, but it would be our jobs. If she were in police custody…but your guys said that if they can't show that she is an immediate threat to herself or others, they can't take her in either."

"Okay," Darrell told him, even though it wasn't. "I guess I'll have to take care of it." He took a moment to smooth down his short haircut. He knew he was about to be on TV

Walking from the ambulance, he began making his way up the sidewalk. The reporter jumped to life and began calling out trying to get his attention. He put her off with, "Can't talk now," and headed to the nearest group of bystanders.

"Listen, we need to get this poor woman to someone that can help her, but as you can see, she does not want to go. I don't want to, but I am going to have to get her into a car. She will probably fight me, so don't be alarmed. Try to give her as much privacy as you can." Darrell looked right at the news team. The cameraman kept the lens aimed his way, and the reporter continued holding her microphone toward him.

The group glanced at each other and slowly began to spread out and pretend they were leaving. Darrell knew they wouldn't. He continued up the sidewalk, giving each gaggle of onlookers the same talk. He needed them to understand what he was about to do. Most people weren't prepared for this. Half of them would still think whatever the police did was wrong, not even considering whether they could do any better. But with a little prep work, maybe some of them would at least keep their mouths shut and just be glad it was not them that had to do it. As he came back down the walk, he noticed that the first group had gone no further than across the street and had already reformed.

Darrell stepped over the yellow tape that surrounded the sloping yard and finally left the news behind. He headed directly to where the cops watched over the woman.

The young one straightened at his presence. "Good afternoon, Lieutenant Jacobs."

"Sorry, Darrell." Gill's face emphasized the apology. "We're trying."

"Isn't there a chaplain?" Darrell searched the area with his eyes.

"He gave up. He's in the car over there with the neighbor. At least she'll talk."

Darrell made eye contact with the younger officer, "Go open your car door for me."

The woman was on her knees, now, rocking backward with her arms drawn up to her chest, sucking air through her clenched teeth and moaning.

Nodding at Gill, Darrell moved beside the woman. "Grab her under the arms and lift her up even if she fights you. I'll take her after that."

When the officer took hold of her, she screamed and wailed—nothing but noise.

Gill raised her up enough that she put her feet on the ground, but she would not support herself, trying to wiggle away. Darrell scooped his real hand under her knees as they came up and wrapped his prosthetic around her back. With his arm stretched out, the two sides of his stainless-steel hook came open. He gently cupped her tiny shoulder with the two smooth rounded ends and easily lifted her.

The young woman began to beat on Darrell with her fists, screaming, "No! Let me go! Let me go!"

He took off walking toward where the younger officer held the car door. She tried to squirm away, but Darrell rolled her into his chest and held her firmly. She struck at his head and shoulders. Darrell tucked his chin and kept going. She tried to grab his hair, but his detective haircut was too short for her to be effective. Gill hurried ahead and lifted the crime tape as Darrell continued toward the car.

The woman's attack slowed to the point she was just thumping on his back and chest. Then her arms went around his neck, and she hugged him, burying her face in his shoulder. When he got to the car, he tried to set her on the seat.

The woman gripped his neck and would not let go.

Darrell was off balance and went sideways. He pivoted and landed with his back against the car, the girl still in his arms. Gill was there, grabbing Darrell's shoulders to steady him.

The woman clung to Darrell. He collected himself, carried her back to the open door and dropped onto the seat of the car with the woman on his lap. "It's going to be all right. We are going to take good care of your family. It's going to be okay. You can see them later after we get them cleaned up. We're going to help you. We'll take care of everything. You don't worry. Just cry."

And she did – great sobs and tears that wet his shirt. She gripped him so tight it constricted his throat, but he held her like he would his own daughter.

After several minutes, he began to pry her arms from around his neck.

She shook her head and whispered, "No. No."

"It will be all right. Just lay down here and cry and rest. It will get better."

Better, maybe, Darrell thought, *but you will live with it for the rest of your life. And later, it might get worse.*

Darrell laid the girl onto the seat and eased himself out from under her legs. She curled up into a ball and whimpered. Darrell told the young cop, "Crawl in beside her and make sure she doesn't slide onto the floor."

The young man looked petrified but complied immediately. Darrell turned his attention to Gill. "Take her down to one of our interview rooms, and get her someone that can talk to her. Don't leave her until you know she is going to be all right. Get some family for her if you can." Darrell paused then added, "Maybe someone from her church or something. We'll interview her later, but we're going to need her clothes as evidence because of the blood on them." Darrell turned away from the you're-kidding-me look on Gill's face. "I'll have Christie, from our team, come down to help."

On the way back to his vehicle, he called Christie and arranged for her to meet Gill at the detective office. Retrieving the crime scene bag from his car, Darrell headed for Shawn.

"Okay, thanks for taking the time to talk to me," At six three, Shawn dwarfed the man he had been interviewing. The guy gave a shocked glance at Darrell, and then moved off as if he was in a fog.

"Who was that?" Darrell watched the man walk toward a utility van down the street. Normally Shawn's good-natured humor relaxed people. *Not today.*

"Repairman who was next door and heard the little gal screaming..." Shawn eyed Darrell in the same way the man had. It drew Darrell's attention to the front of his shirt and pants, which were now blood stained. "...the one you were carrying around. I remember my training detective, guy named Darrell, telling me to let the patrol officers worry about those things. Stay detached, objective, focus on the investigation."

"It wasn't happening," Darrell said. "Somebody had to do it." *Like everything else. It might as well be me; one more thing to absorb.* Even though the thought was unspoken, his tone must have come through.

"Oookay..." Shawn said shifting his body weight away from Darrell.

Darrell regretted his attitude. His life was full of so many regrets anymore, but he did not seem to be able to stop himself. He wondered how many times the news would play the scene of him carrying the girl. What parts would they show? What would they leave out? Tomorrow he might be a hero, or he might be typing another I-messed-up letter for his file. In police work, one never knew.

"It is definitely good not to have her screaming." Shawn was continuing as they both started walking toward the house. "Not that I don't understand. I guess the man found her sitting in a pool of blood, holding her little brother. That must have been a sight, but hey, these days you can see worse on television. The mom's been moved around also – postmortem. The girl probably did that as well. She didn't seem to touch the man. I guess someone said it was her stepdad. She's a college student living in a dorm, and she just stopped by to see the family, is about all I could get so far."

"Three dead, all stabbed?"

"Well…four if you count the dog."

"You're kidding me."

Shawn shook his head. "Little wire-haired terrier-looking thing."

Darrell and Shawn made it to the crime scene tape that was surrounding the house. Shawn lifted it as they both ducked under. Darrell stretched trying to get a kink out of his neck. They had three previous murder scenes. Each case with no suspects and no real leads, and everyone was looking at him to make it stop. He could dodge the press, but the chief would also be expecting an update. The public was coming to the conclusion that the crimes were connected simply because the department was not denying that they were.

Shawn gave just a hint of a smile as he looked around to see who might be watching. "We need to catch this clown. He's making us look bad."

"You think?" Darrell did not mean to put so much edge on his sarcasm and quickly tried to correct it. "Sorry, bud. Just tired."

"I know. We're all tired and you have the worst of it." Shawn gave a sympathetic smile, making Darrell feel like even more of a heel.

As they came to the front door, Darrell lowered the bag that he held with his hook. "The killer locked up the house when he left, just like the others?"

"We've got a wrinkle in this one," Shawn leaned his head Darrell's way and gave a thin smile.

"I don't think I even want to hear this. We don't need any more wrinkles."

"The house has an alarm system; real nice one. Goes off if any door or window is opened. Glass break sensors too. The house was locked like the others, only this time the alarm was also armed. The daughter set it off when she came in." Shawn pointed to a set of keys that were still in the lock on the door. "The officers were en route before the repairman ever called. The neighbor said they just had the alarm installed after all the news reports about the other murders."

Darrell shook his head. "I'm sure it won't be long before the news interviews the neighbor and reports that the alarm was on. Just what the town needs to hear, a killer that can get past alarms. You're sure it was working right?"

"Since the family was home, the inside motion detectors were off, but the perimeter was armed. No signs of any tampering. No indication that the alarm was set off prior to the daughter entering. She apparently couldn't remember the code because Gill had to get dispatch to call the alarm company to figure out how to shut it off. The killer had to get around the alarm somehow."

Darrell held up his hand and Shawn stopped. "And then rearm it." Darrell bowed his head to the side in thought. After a moment, he motioned to Carlos, a junior detective who was coming from the next-door neighbor's house. Darrell turned back to Shawn, "This could be a good thing."

"Did they have anything?" Darrell addressed Carlos as the rookie hurried up to the other two.

"Nothing." Carlos had a frustrated wrinkle to his forehead. "I checked with every neighbor, nothing new."

Darrell engaged him with direct eye contact. "Okay, I want you to find out who installed this alarm and interview them. I want to know when it was put in, who knew the code, how it all works. Talk to every employee. Don't work on anything else until you can tell me everything about this system, okay?"

"Got it." The young man pointed to a sign in the yard, boasting the name "Deepclad Security" and a phone number.

Darrell thought he knew all the security companies in town, but the name was new to him. "That's a good start. Now get me the rest."

The young detective was nodding as he wrote down the number from the sign. He headed toward his car, already pulling out his cell phone.

There was a plastic tote full of latex gloves and shoe covers at the front door. Both detectives leaned against the house to put on the booties. They stuffed gloves in their pockets.

Shawn wiggled his hands into a pair.

Darrell only needed one. His hook he could sanitize.

Shawn opened the door and took a giant step over the threshold and to the side to avoid bloody shoeprints just inside the door.

Darrell eyed the prints as he avoided them as well. "The daughter's?"

Shawn nodded. "The officers did a good job. They stayed out of the blood themselves, but when they brought her out…you saw how covered she was."

The house was a bi-level. The door opened onto a small linoleum entry with a set of stairs in front of them leading down to the lower level and a short set to their left leading up to the living room. Both he and Shawn climbed the stairs to the living room by placing their feet on the very outside edges of the steps, avoiding the middle area where they could see blood stains.

A DVD menu was playing on the TV, but there was no sound. Darrell didn't recognize the title, but he could tell it was some kind of horror show.

Shawn motioned toward the screen. "Hey, that's Final Death. I've been waiting for that to come out."

They stood for a moment surveying the room. The soundless images of a woman screaming filled the television. It made Darrell think of the screams that must have filled the house earlier as real people lost their lives. He imagined the news release, "Another senseless killing…" As if murder made sense sometimes.

In his mind, Darrell heard the girl's cries as he had carried her to the car. He tried to suppress the thoughts. Human pain and fear were things to be analyzed to reconstruct the scene and nothing more. He knew that to let himself think of them beyond that were sure routes to more depression and burnout…like he hadn't already gone down that road.

Every cop had to find a way to detach. But the girl's cries wouldn't leave him. He had touched the case too closely and now it was touching him.

The show's menu was repeating the scenes, and every minute or so the face of the screaming girl would return. A feeling of dread passed through Darrell. He suddenly had the impression of someone else in the room. Jerking his head around, he scanned the area behind them.

"You okay?" Shawn asked.

"Has this place been searched good?"

Shawn gave him a quizzical look. "I kinda thought that's what we were doing."

Darrell didn't smile. "I mean for people." Before Shawn could smart off again, Darrell added, "live people."

Shawn looked around. "I am sure they did. Why, you hear something?"

"I don't know, maybe…no, just a feeling."

Shawn walked around the room and glanced in all the doorways, looking and listening.

He had his hand on his gun as he talked. "Never known you to get rattled for nothing." He returned to Darrell. "I don't see anyone. You want me to get a unit to come over and go through it?"

Darrell shook his head. "Just my imagination, probably lack of sleep," He turned his attention back to the TV. "Were they watching television when it happened?"

"Possibly. Oh yeah, I know the house was searched because the officers told me they turned the TV down so they could hear better while they cleared the place."

Darrell turned off the TV. "I don't need distraction."

Shawn shrugged. "I can understand. Looks like a good show." With a gloved hand, he flipped through the stack of DVD cases at one end of the TV stand. "They've got a lot of good ones here, lots of blood and guts. I've been meaning to see this one. Hey, let's just order Chinese and watch a flick. These bodies ain't goin' anywhere. We can call it research."

Darrell let himself smile and shook his head at his partner. "You do know what you do for a living don't you?"

"Yeah, but a guy gets tired of all this amateur stuff we investigate— he wants to see what real murder looks like once in a while."

Sick humor, the cop's stress reliever. Darrell checked the other end of the entertainment center. Lying on the stand was an instruction manual. "I recognize this emblem." He picked up the pamphlet. "There was one of these in the last scene, remember?" Darrell's brow was furrowed. "MEamp - Media Experience amplification," he read and peered at the new black electronic case that sat on the stand. Clean black cables came out of the back and snaked through a hole in the entertainment center. "Another recent installation. These guys come into some money or something?"

"They really aren't that expensive."

Darrell examined where the cables disappeared behind the entertainment center. "You got one? I never heard of it."

Shawn gave a guilty dip of his head and grinned. "I got the number off the brochure from the last scene and had Sandy call for me."

Darrell shook his head and chuckled.

Shawn held up the brochure and pointed at it. "Hey, I wanted 'The next generation in entertainment.' It's like '3D for television only better. People are calling it 4D' Says so right here."

"How do you like it?"

"Don't know yet. They had her fill out a survey of my movie preferences and said they would try to get to us this month sometime. They must be pretty hot to afford to put a customer off for that long. That says more than the brochure."

The front door opened, and Darrell turned toward the sound.

Fritz from the lab, clothed in disposable white coveralls, hauled in evidence bags.

"Hey, Fritz." Darrell pointed at the media enhancer. "Package this up carefully and see if we can get prints off it. Don't fume it though. I want it to be usable in case it has some log-in identifiers in the memory that might tell us who was using it or who set it up."

He turned back to Shawn. "When Christie gets through with the girl, I want her on this. We may have our break here somewhere. We always knew our killer had to have some inside knowledge of the homes he's entered and how they work. In this case he had to know how to rearm the alarm. We know these aren't domestic violence cases since there are multiple family groups with no connection that we can find. Maybe this is the connection. Have you ever heard of that alarm company before?"

Shawn shook his head. "But the other houses didn't have alarms."

"But maybe it was a salesman. Either from the alarm company in which case they might have gotten inside the other homes and gained enough information but never made the sale or they never had a chance to install it. If not the alarm people, maybe these TV enhancer installers.

"Do me a favor and keep on top of Carlos and Christie's investigations from an overarching perspective. Let's focus on the idea of a salesman, or installer, handyman…someone or some service that has been in all of the neighborhoods. If nothing comes from the alarm company or this electronic gadget, I want us to go back and canvas all of the neighborhoods again with the specific purpose of looking into any company that has had people in the area. Maybe something else will show up when we go back with this specifically in mind. These killings don't feel random to me. There is a link somewhere."

The two detectives spent the next four hours in the house, processing the scene. Darrell and Shawn walked through with Fritz and another lab tech, telling them about specific things they wanted them to do. Then they left them to it.

As they walked back out to their cars, Darrell remembered what he had to do the next day. "Listen, can you head this thing up tomorrow? I think we have some good leads that might help us focus in on some suspects for the first time."

"You not coming in tomorrow?"

"No, I have a doctor's appointment. I got a letter from HR that the chief told me to be expecting. They want me to look at something new. I hate to take the time, but the worker's comp calls the shots when it comes to my friend here." Darrell held up his prosthesis. "I'm happy with what I've got, but the chief says this is something new that I might like. I'm going to take the rest of the day to catch up on yard work. My neighbors are going to call code enforcement on me if I don't mow my lawn."

"Why don't you come over to the gym with us one of these days? You used to be pretty handy with that thing." Shawn motioned toward the hook.

"Thanks. I'll see if I can make it." Darrell walked away knowing neither one of them believed that.

The sidewalks had cleared. The show was over. Reporter and cameraman had moved on, no doubt to roam the neighborhood getting the obligatory "man on the street" quotes, the part where they find some idiot who knows nothing about the situation but is not afraid to say something outrageous or emotional.

Darrell sat in his car. With the distraction of work over again, for the moment, he sank into his own thoughts. He found himself focusing on the part of the lawn from which he had taken the young woman.

In the quiet of the car, the memory of the girl came back – clinging to him, face buried in his chest. It mingled with another memory, one far and away, another girl, another time. It seemed important, like something he wanted to remember. He had the feeling come and go for years, but it had been a while since he experienced it. The deja vu feeling persisted until he gave a shake of his head and shoulders. Too many hysterical family members over the years. They were running together.

You are really tired. Maybe a break tomorrow might be good. *See what the doctor has to offer, turn 'em down, and then go home and take a nap. Forget the lawn.* Good idea…if he could finally sleep, which he doubted.

Chapter 4

"Finally," Darrell said to himself when he saw the number
he had been searching for on a decorative stone sign in front of a building
at the corner of Garden of the Gods Road and Arrowswest Drive. The sign
sat in the middle of a perfect green grass border surrounded by a circular
drive leading up to a large building boasting reflective windows and
shining chrome architecture. "Advanced Trans-Human Solutions" was on
the sign above the number. *Doesn't look like a medical building.*

In the large foyer, a stylish woman sat behind an impressive reception
desk. She seemed to brighten when she saw him.

"I'm Darrell Jacobs. Sorry, I'm a little late. I didn't expect to have an
appointment out in this area of town."

The woman smiled pleasantly, "Not a problem, but I am glad you're
here. Now maybe a certain someone will stop ringing my phone." The
woman's comment did not diminish her smile; if anything, it brightened
it. "Ms. Williams will be right with you."

Ms. not *Doctor* Darrell noted. Of the many appointments he had been
to since he was released from the hospital, this one had a different feel.

The receptionist called to announce him. In a few moments the door
burst open, and a woman came out. The expanse of her smile wrinkled her
nose and formed dimples that raised the cheeks of her lovely chocolate
brown face. She wore a brightly colored blouse that floated loosely to her
mid thighs, which were covered by coordinating orange slacks. "There you
are, Lieutenant Jacobs. I'm so glad to see you."

Before Darrell could respond, the woman had closed the distance
between them. He started to reach out to shake her hand, but she grabbed
him in a hug. Darrell stood rigidly, his face engulfed in the woman's soft,
dark, afro that smelled of strawberries and machine oil. The feeling of déjà
vu swept over him like it never had before. His impulse was to wrap his
arms around the woman and hold her, clearly not appropriate. He stiffened
even more as he fought the urge. *What's wrong with me?*

Perhaps she felt his awkwardness because she broke the embrace quickly. She used a finger to push her wide, thick glasses back into place, her smile still peeking out on either side of her hand. She looked in his eyes for a moment as if waiting for something. Could she tell what he was thinking?

The smile dimmed for a heartbeat then resumed. "Oh, forgive me, I just can't believe you're here," The woman's voluptuous figure curved in all the right places, causing the softness of her hug to linger in his senses. Her face glowed with such inviting friendliness that, in afterthought, the hug did not seem so out of place. The strange familiarity also lingered, to the point that it unnerved him. He mentally shoved it down, reminding himself that this was a medical visit concerning his prosthetic. He forced himself to focus professionally on what the smiling face was saying.

He hoped he hadn't freaked her out. Perhaps he was projecting what he was feeling because there was a hint of nervousness in the woman's voice. "Ever since I've known you, I have been wanting…I mean it's not like I've really known you…since we just…but it's like we've…I hope you feel the same way…ooh, forget I said that." The woman waved her hands back and forth in front of her like she was erasing a chalkboard. "I mean you don't have to feel any certain way, it's just…anyway, since I read your story, I have been waiting to meet you. You are a hero, Lieutenant Jacobs. I am honored."

The words relaxed Darrell's guilt but made him self-conscious. "Well, I don't know about—"

"Oh, but you are. It must have been horrifying to have someone trying to kill you and to know that he's still out there somewhere."

"I don't really remember much about—"

"But how hard you worked to get back to being an officer again, that's the hero part. I want to tell you that you have inspired me. I loved how you said that God helped you get through the rough times. I feel the same way. The Lord helps me like that, but I haven't been through anything as tough. There is something about a man...person… that can keep a good attitude through something so awful."

Darrell cringed mentally and hoped it didn't show. There was no reason he should dampen someone else's exuberance with his issues. The woman's kind eyes reddened as she talked, and she began to wipe them with the sleeve of her blouse before the tears could escape. Again, Darrell thought that she might be seeing inside him, but her smile never dimmed.

"But look at you now, a lieutenant in the detective bureau. I see your name in the paper all the time." The woman twisted her head slightly sideways and raised her eyebrows. "Highest case clearance in the history of the department." The tears were gone as soon as they came. She narrowed her eyes in seriousness and pointed her finger at him. "If you hadn't been in the hospital so long, I know you would have caught that guy." The serious look was washed away by a thoughtful head cock. "But they probably don't let you work on your own case, kind of like a doctor not operating on himself and all. But, anyway, that's why I told Raji that I wanted you… I mean, I didn't say that I *wanted* you… I mean it's not that I don't want you… for my project, I mean." She stopped and took a deep breath and drew her open hands across her chest and threw them down to her sides as if clearing away the confusion. "Anyway, he wanted to go military again, but I told him that nobody would work as hard as Lieutenant Jacobs to make this a success. But it's okay, I convinced him that we needed something more 'out-in-the-open' so we can get public approval generated, and that you would really help us."

Looking into Darrell's face, she pushed her glasses up again. She drilled him with a fascinated stare, using her hand to pat the air between them for emphasis. "I saw the video on YouTube that they made of you doing all those martial arts takedowns with your hook and it was so cool."

Darrell started to say, "There's a video on YouT—?"

But the woman scurried around to his left side. "Oh, and let me see it." She took hold of the hook prosthesis that was attached to his arm. With clinical intentness, she began to inspect the hook design and narrated as she went. "I see how this part is longer than usual and has a little different bend than normal so you can do those joint locks with it."

Darrell was mentally disarmed. The woman handled his prosthetic with such freeness. Usually, people were embarrassed to even look at his arm, let alone touch it and talk about it. As her fingers moved over the mechanics of his artificial appendage, he felt a thrill to have her so close. There was no pretense in her. Jodi was the last woman that touched his arm and…she had left an unseen scar that was just as ugly as his amputation.

The young woman moved to the cable system that operated the opening mechanism. Her nimble fingers traced the prosthesis sleeve up his forearm. "Okay, I get it. I was wondering how you could keep the sleeve in place during those dynamic moves."

Darrell could easily see the difference in the hands that touched him. He had wondered if he would ever feel a woman's touch, again, a real touch.

"You have metal reinforcing it, and it is all one piece here where it is secured around the back of your elbow and up around…" she finger-walked up to where his arm expanded his short-sleeve shirt, and she gave his bicep a squeeze. "Oooo, Lieutenant Jacobs." She gave an exaggerated lean backward and rocked her head and shoulders causing curly strands of hair to sashay back and forth across her pretty cheeks. "You have got some guns."

Darrell liked her fun manner, but he didn't know how to respond. He gave a smile that he feared looked stupid and was glad the woman turned toward the receptionist.

"Peggy, you should see what he can do – and it takes a whole lot more strength to operate a prosthesis than it does your own arm."

The lady behind the counter was watching the interaction, her chin propped up with two outstretched fingers and a smirk on her face. "You showed me the video, remember. Me and everyone else."

Darrell didn't have time to be embarrassed by the comment. The woman that was apparently Ms. Williams turned back to him with a dismissing wave toward the receptionist. She wrapped her right arm around the bicep she had admired and rested her other hand on the sleeve of his prosthetic. "Come on in and I'll show you what I have been working on for you."

"Mr. Jacobs."

Darrell glanced back at the sound of the receptionist's voice.

The woman took her fingers out from under her chin and pointed one at Darrell. "You have just met your biggest fan. If you go through that door, I cannot guarantee you will ever come out again."

Ms. Williams turned and apparently gave the receptionist an accusatory look, judging from the mock look of innocence that she responded with.

"Peggy, don't tell him that, you'll scare him off." She turned her attention back to Darrell. "My name's Callie."

Darrell continued his smile - it was a rare event anymore, but he had hardly stopped since the hug from this woman named Callie.

The card clipped to Callie's blouse must have signaled the card reader on the wall next to the door as the woman moved him to it. The red light on the scanner turned green, and there was a click from the locking mechanism. Callie hip-bumped the door, not letting go of his arm, and then pulled him through with her.

Conflicting thoughts warred in Callie's mind as she walked Lieutenant Jacobs down the hallway and explained the work she was doing. She had envisioned the reunion so differently. He would say, "It's you." She imagined the things they might say to each other. She had not considered him not remembering.

It wasn't his fault. It had been dark, and she had been so traumatized that night she kept her face buried against the chest of his uniform shirt. But she remembered there had been another reason. She had feared if she moved, he would stop holding her. His embrace had represented someone stronger than the evil she had experienced. It was like her father used to hold her before everything changed. In her young heart, she had hoped she could feel that for the rest of her life. She had hoped that he might feel the same.

Why did you hug him today? It had been a spontaneous thing. A person didn't just shake the hand of the man who saved her life.

Time had passed, but she thought he would remember. She should have said something but when she realized he didn't recognize her, she was too embarrassed. She was so nervous anyway. Everything was going wrong. Why had she taken his arm? If she let go now, it would look so awkward. He didn't seem to mind but maybe that was her wishful thinking. Why had she thought he would still know her?

Callie had also been skinny when she was eighteen. She had filled out late in life. When she looked at pictures from back then, she hardly recognized herself. She hoped she didn't look fat to him.

The horrible thought crossed her mind that maybe he did know her and just didn't like what he saw. The other woman that she had seen him with had been so fit. Maybe that was the only kind of woman that Lieutenant Jacobs wanted. Maybe she wasn't his type, and she was just fooling herself. *Help me, Lord.*

God had taught her to stop being self-condemning and she didn't want to go backwards. She reminded herself what the Bible said she should be doing. *Casting down imaginations.*

God, I'm sorry if I misread this. You know I walked away when I thought he was already in a relationship. I just thought now that he seems alone again, maybe there was still a chance.

Callie had always believed Lieutenant Darrell Jacobs was the right person for the project, even if there could be nothing between them personally. *Lord, you know I prepared myself for that when I started researching him as a candidate.*

The life of Lieutenant Jacobs was very public because of the way he lost his hand. Also, he was a poster boy for the diversity and forward thinking of the department to allow someone who was handicapped to resume duties. But in all her research of the reporting on his life, she saw no indication that the beautiful blonde was still around.

Still, she had allowed for the possibility that maybe they married quietly, and Lieutenant Jacobs wanted to keep his family out of his public life…until she stumbled on the interview. *God, if this is another dead end for us, why did you let me find it? You know I wasn't trying to pry. I thought it was Your doing.*

The video of the interview played in her mind again. The reporter's teasing probe leading to Lieutenant Jacobs admitting he had never been married and there was no one special. Callie couldn't help it. It had brought the dream to life again. She thought maybe that was why no one right had ever come along. She had allowed herself to hope that maybe they had been saved for each other. But if he didn't even remember her…

She walked him down the well-lit hallway, passing doors on either side, explaining each department that the doors represented and how they related to what she had created for him. She opened her world to Lieutenant Jacobs.

The one thing she didn't explain was how much he had been the inspiration for the work she was doing. So much had been taken from him since the first time they met. She had prayed to be the one to give some of it back to him. She wanted to repay him even after she thought she would never be a part of his world. Was it wrong now to hope again?

Callie looked into the eyes as she had done years before. There were little wrinkles around them that had not been there back then. The twelve-year difference in their ages was perhaps more apparent. But Darrell's maturity suited her. Callie had never been in sync with her peers. In the depths, they were the same eyes. They both had changed but they were still the same people that God had brought together years earlier. She looked away and continued with her narrative on her project.

This meeting was her last hope. If it didn't work out, she wouldn't try again. She had been alone so long, hoping for someone that she could share her life with. But maybe it was all a dream and that was not what God had for her. Maybe there would never be anyone. If so, God was enough. But was it wrong to hope for a human touch like what she felt that night – someone that would hold her in the worst of times and just be strong? If Lieutenant Jacobs wasn't interested today, she would take it as God saying no, and she would move on, even if she had no idea where she would move on to.

Darrell liked the sound of Callie's voice. It was like a well-stirred southern tea, full of energy and sweetness. She identified the doors they were passing—electro engineering, mechanical engineering, synthetic polymers, hydraulic engineering.

She chattered and gesticulated down the hallway explaining things that Darrell could not really grasp involving the construction of various components of her "project," all the while holding his arm like he was escorting her to the ball. He liked it.

They arrived at the end of the hall at a door marked "Research and Development."

"Here we are," she said and let go of his arm.

Her card unlocked the door as before, and she swung it open for him. The room was spacious and occupied by several work areas composed of cabinets and countertops. Each countertop had shelves above it filled with various electronic and mechanical parts and tools. The cabinets and drawers under the countertops were labeled with other similarly related items.

Cardboard shipping containers were on top of and under many work areas. Some sat on the floor with packing material spilling out. Adjoining each work area was a computer center, most having multiple large monitors with keyboards, mice, printers and other peripherals that Darrell could not name. Amid the chaos, there were several people too intent on their work to notice their entry into the room.

"Hey, everybody," Callie announced. "Here is Lieutenant Jacobs."

Callie's statement had everyone's attention. The group became a flurry of hand wiping, unplugging, laying items down, saving their place on computer programs, and a general abandoning of the work that had engrossed them so they could move toward Darrell.

At the first workstation, a man approximately forty turned revealing a short spiky haircut and gentle Asian features. In his hands, he held what looked like a human arm. Where the arm should have been attached to a shoulder, there were electronic cables coming out that appeared to be connected to a computer.

The man gave a brief bow. "Finally, pleased to meet you." The man looked next to him at a mid-twenties male whose tall lanky expanse was hunched over something. The first man gave his tall, young co-worker a quick swat with the back of his hand.

The young man swung his head so that Darrell could first see the point of his nose sticking out past the neck length hair that looked like it needed combing. His head was down, looking into a smartphone, as it continued to rotate on his elongated neck. The man's large nose was twisted slightly to one side and accentuated his equally stretched-out face terminating in a spiky chin.

"Oh hey," he said, letting the rest of his long-limbed body follow the turn of his head. The young man rapidly thumb-typed on the phone's keyboard.

The arm that the Asian held waved at Darrell. The man holding the arm looked at the prosthetic in confusion then glanced over at the young man's faint smile that bent the opposite way of his nose. Looking back at Darrell, he gave his own wide grin.

"You two are real funny." Callie shook her head at them, smiling brightly. "This is Shin and Link."

She went on to point out and name the others that pressed in to shake his hand and say how glad they were to finally meet him. As his notoriety became apparent, Callie turned a self-conscious expression toward him. "I told everyone about how…suitable you would be for our project. They have been anxious to meet you."

The coworkers were quick to verify their support for having him participate. Callie pointed out that they needed to give Darrell a chance to see the scope of the project so he could decide if he wanted to be a part of it. When the conversation dwindled and people excused themselves back to their work, Callie steered Darrell toward a work area in one corner of the room.

While they were a little distance away, Callie gestured and said, "Ta Daaa. Meet the NIP."

On the table was another arm. It was composed of all black material. Mounted on a pedestal at what would be around the shoulder area, it looked like a more synthetic version of what the man named Shin had held. It bent at the elbow so that the forearm was approximately parallel with the table.

"N.I.P. stands for Neurological Interfaced Prosthetic, but it is really a whole lot more than that. I just thought the NIP name sounded cool."

Darrell raised his eyebrows. "What you just said sounds like plenty."

Callie's smile gave the impression she knew a secret. "That's just the beginning. And this is the law enforcement version, so it's customized to your needs."

"My needs?"

Callie averted her eyes to look at what she called the NIP. "I mean it's for law enforcement, of course, but…I needed a law enforcement officer to test the prototype and…well, yeah, it's for you."

Darrell swiveled his head to study the woman. "Why me?"

Callie seemed to be fixated on the NIP for a moment. She lowered her gaze and brought her eyes around to explore his. "Because you deserve it." She looked again at the arm on the pedestal. "You really deserve more. I listened to a speech you gave at one of the police academy graduations. You said that police work was a sacred calling that required a person to dedicate their life to it. You quoted from Romans 13:1, 'the powers that be are ordained of God.' I loved that. I want the NIP to be associated with a profession and a person of honor."

Darrell wanted to stop her. He was not the same person, and he didn't want the reminder. "That was a long time ago. I appreciate what you've done, but I don't deserve this."

At the comment, Callie's face softened as if her admiration for him deepened. "You're like Epaphroditius in Philippians. You deserve honor because you almost died for the work of Christ. You risked your life to help others."

The disparity of his self-image and Callie's words stabbed at Darrell. Listening to her, he wished it were true. He wanted to be what she said, even while he knew he wasn't. He wanted to snap out of it. To pull himself out of the depression, to rally and be happy for her sake. To reach for a life, again, beyond his work and his despair. Listening to Callie, having her near, made him wonder if he could go back. She made him want to. Maybe with her he could.

Darrell glanced at Callie's sweet smile. It wasn't that easy. He wanted it to be, and right then he almost felt it could be, but it wasn't fair to throw his burden on someone who believed he was worthy of honor when he knew he wasn't. He hated his mouth as he spoke. "I have no doubt what you've made is amazing, but I don't think I'm the right one to test it."

Callie's look didn't change.

She must still think he was being humble. He decided to fall back on what he always said when approached about a change to his handicap arrangement. "I'm really satisfied with my prosthetic. I have had a lot of input into it."

Callie kept her smile through his comment, nodding her head in understanding but clearly waiting for him to finish so that she could talk. "And I want you to have a lot of input into this one as well. I had hoped we could…work together to make it even better."

Callie straightened and renewed the glow of her face. "I know you're the right person. Please, just let me show you this. This is not some cosmetic arm. This is a piece of equipment–police equipment. It doesn't have to replace your prosthetic. You can use the NIP for on-duty and keep your old one for off hours. But I think you might change your mind once you try it." There was determination in her countenance.

Darrell was running out of arguments and out of resistance to the beautiful beseeching face. But it wasn't right to give her false hope. He was not what she needed. She deserved better. "I wish I could. It's just that I'm so busy right now and…and this is a whole arm, I only need a hand."

Callie stretched her slender fingers toward him, "You can have mine."

Darrell couldn't stop his smile that slipped out. She was so cute.

A thought seemed to flicker through Callie's mind. "I didn't mean…I meant…that was a joke. You need a hand, you can have my hand." She gestured with her palm. Giving up, she sighed. With a pleading expression, she reached out again. "Please let me show you how it works, and you'll understand. I know you're the right one."

Darrell felt his resolve slipping. It was as if Callie's words could make it so. He was almost ready to reach out and take hold of the touch that was offered.

"Callie." A voice behind Darrell made him jerk his head around. "The man has told you no. Now do not harass him." An olive-skinned man was standing off to the side of them. Darrell wasn't sure when he had arrived, but it seemed he had been there for a few moments and now chose to intervene.

The man spoke to Darrell as he held out his hand. He had an accent, but his English was clear and fluent. "Mr. Jacobs, I am Rajiomid Mishra. You may call me Raji, as that is easier for most westerners. No condescension intended. I apologize for Ms. Williams." He gave a scolding glance toward Callie as he shook Darrell's hand but then turned back to Darrell with a smile. "Please forgive her. I am afraid this project has come to mean a great deal to her, and since she has learned of your history, she completely connects you with it."

Callie jumped in. "He would be the best one. We talked about this. He already has a public platform and has proven his ability to adapt."

Raji looked at Callie with sympathy. "Perhaps. But if he does not wish to participate, that is his prerogative. We have others that will fit the project, perhaps even better – no offense intended, Mr. Jacobs."

"But he hasn't even heard what I have planned. Lieutenant Jacobs, please just listen to what I have to say." Callie seemed almost desperate.

"Callie." Raji bent his head purposely looking down at her with a scowl.

The woman was clearly caught off guard by the man's abruptness.

Raji softened. He put his hand on top of Callie's curls. Darrell detected a tenderness in his touch that seemed lost on Callie. He leaned his head in close to hers as he spoke. "Do not beg. It does not become you."

Callie's mouth came open. Nothing came out. She appeared embarrassed as she glanced at Darrell. The words came. "I didn't mean to…I'm sorry…I didn't want to lose you…for the project, I mean." She squeezed her eyes shut and shook her head in frustration.

Darrell fought the urge to move to the woman he'd just met and take her in his arms to comfort her. He wasn't sure what was going on between the man and Callie, but he didn't like it. He couldn't stand to see her in distress.

Raji put his hands on Callie's shoulders and was trying to steer her away. "It's all right, Callie. I understand. Try not to make a scene."

Callie glanced toward Darrell again. She gave Raji a confused glare.

The other man was turning her shoulders toward the door. "I want you to wait in my office. I want to talk to you."

Darrell resented Raji touching the young woman. *This feels so familiar.* He could tell Raji was not hurting her, still he wanted to grab the man, put him on the floor and tell him to keep his hands off her. *Keep calm. This is not your domain. You have no business telling the man that he can't sanction one of his employees.* He didn't want the man complaining to the department that he was interfering.

Callie was arguing with Raji. Darrell noticed that the man no longer had his hands on her – at least that was good. Finally, Raji told her. "Ms. Williams, if you want to continue with this project, you will go and wait in my office right now."

Darrell could tell that Callie was stunned. She narrowed her eyes at him. "Maybe I don't want to."

Raji quickly softened his voice. "Callie, you don't mean that. You care deeply for this work. I want you to continue. We will talk about it…in my office. He is not interested, and we have more suitable candidates. Let the man go."

Callie looked at Darrell who stood, speechless. *Maybe it's better this way.* Let her boss say no to the woman that he was unable to disappoint. Her disappointment now would be better than her disappointment when she found out he was not the man she thought he was. He wavered. Maybe there were gentler ways to let her down. He considered saying he wanted to hear Callie's ideas, but she turned and hurried out the door as her sleeve went to her eyes.

Darrell was angry—at Raji, at the situation, but mostly at himself. When Raji turned and began to make pleasantries with him, he was not in the mood. The man thanked him for his "forbearance" and apologized for what had happened. He assured Darrell that he would speak to Callie and that everything would be all right. Darrell didn't want to listen. He was afraid he might do something he'd regret, so he said he had to get going.

Raji received the information with a smile that seemed quite genuine. "Link," the man motioned for the tall kid to come over.

Raji seemed to inspect Darrell's face. Apparently, the odd emotion that he was feeling must have shown there.

"Do not worry about Callie, Mr. Jacobs. I will be able to make her understand. Genius such as hers commands a lot of maintenance. She moves from one thing to the next. Tomorrow it will be something new. I will channel her energy in a more suitable direction. This is for the best. ATS is not just about making prosthetics. It is about the next phase of human evolution where we merge with technology and become something different. Though not on the level that we are creating, there are other prosthetics that utilize biomechanical electronics, but I see you have never taken advantage of them. All of us have different paths. Callie's world is technology. It is what she does. And," he gestured to Darrell's hook, "it is not for everyone."

Darrell was silent; he feared what he might say.

"Mr. Jacobs is ready to leave." Raji turned to Link. "Could you see that he makes it to the door?" Raji's smile had progressed to satisfied jubilation. "Good luck with your future, in case we never meet again." He turned and left by the same door that Callie had used. The thought of Callie having to endure the man's condescension made Darrell seethe.

Darrell was considering going after Raji when Link motioned toward the door in the other direction. *Don't get involved. You won't be doing anyone any good.*

The kid took him back the way he had come. As they walked down the hallway, Darrell remembered Callie holding his arm, telling him about all the rooms that they passed. He had never met anyone like her.

The events inside the building seemed strange, surreal. He tried to assuage the awful feeling he had by telling himself that it would go away once he got home to some normality.

Normality. Darrell wondered why the normality of his life would be something that he would desire. Normality, for years now, had been depressing and meaningless. He went to work early, stayed late and went home to sleep. On his days off he did yard work, cleaned the house, watched TV - it was all meaningless.

Darrell continued to try and convince himself he was doing the right thing. *You can tell she is committed to her faith.* He had not heard someone quote the Bible so freely since he quit going to church. He couldn't get into that again. He couldn't be false. It was better he walked away before she was hurt any worse.

Link glanced back at Darrell who was falling behind his long stride.

Darrell guessed the kid to be seven feet tall.

The young man slowed. "So, you're dipping and not going to help Callie with the NIP?"

"It's better she finds someone else."

"That's hacked up, 'cause she was into you. She really wanted you to be the one...for her project, I mean." Link winked at Darrell, smiling under his thick, crooked, nose.

Darrell couldn't return the smile. "She must be very influential around here."

"Oh, yeah. She's prime online. Pretty DOS based but it fits her."

"Not sure I got that."

Link scrunched his brow then seemed to get the problem. "Sorry. You know. She's on point, right up there all the time...uh...knows what she's doing. But she's...kind of behind, I don't know...umm...old fashioned, conservative."

"Nothing wrong with that."

"No, not the way Cals does it. It's not me but it suits her."

"Has she always been like that?"

"Right from start up. She's solid-state hardware. Been running the same routines since I came here three years ago."

"Not the way Raji portrayed her."

"Yeah, well, he can be Coke on a keyboard sometimes. He's glitched because Cals keeps returning no results on his queries."

Darrell decided he didn't need any translation when it came to Raji. Link kept looking forward as he spoke. "Cals was a little different today though. Kinda overclocked."

They reached the end of the hallway and the exit door.

Link stepped out into the entrance with Darrell. Peggy looked up from her computer. When she saw it was Darrell, she engaged him with a smile. "So, you made it out. Will we be seeing a lot of you around here from now on?"

Link answered. "No, he's not interested."

"Oh," Peggy's smile disappeared. "Where's Callie?"

Link motioned his head toward the door. "Principal's office."

"Is she okay?"

Link's eyes went to Darrell and then back to the woman. He gave her a shrug and head shake at the same time. "I gotta go, though. If I don't get back to Shin, he might have to read the help file. Maybe we can think of a distraction to give Cals a break from the MaulerRaji." He considered Darrell with disappointment on his face. "Laters."

Link turned quickly for the door. Darrell heard the click. The young man pushed it open and ducked instinctively as he went through. Darrell watched as the door swung back slowly on the hydraulic closing device, closing on another chapter in the story he was writing for himself—a story that seemed to be locked in a place he didn't want to be, but he had no key to open it. Closing, closing, the door slid slowly into the frame and…stopped. Darrell's foot prevented the last inch of travel.

Darrell turned to Peggy. "I think I've changed my mind. Where is Mr. Mishra's office?"

With the same innocent look she had given Callie earlier, she said, "I have no idea how you could ever know that it is at the end of the hallway and around the corner on the right, third door. Other than maybe you saw his nameplate." Looking pleased, the woman picked up her cell phone off the desk. "I'll let Link know he doesn't have to set anything on fire."

Darrell swung the door open and called over his shoulder, "If someone reports an intruder, don't call the police. They're already here." He headed down the hallway.

The last interaction with Raji told him the man was set against him having anything to do with Callie's project. Darrell opened his old flip phone as he went. When someone answered he spoke quickly. "Hey, Julie. This is Darrell. Is the Chief in? Let me talk to him a minute."

Darrell saw Link standing just inside a doorway as he passed. The kid typed on his phone with one hand and used his other to direct Darrell further down the hall with a pointing finger.

Giving the kid a smile and nod, he answered as the Chief came on the line. "Hey, boss, I was sent over here to look into this new prosthetic arm. I think this has great potential. I just need your help with a little obstacle…" Just outside Raji's office, Darrell finished explaining what the Chief could do to help him. With the cell phone in one hand, he knocked with the other.

"I'm busy right now," came Raji's voice from inside.

Darrell turned the knob and pushed open the door.

Raji was seated sideways on a couch next to Callie with his back toward Darrell. Callie had a box of tissues on her lap. She stood up when she saw him, causing the box to fall to the floor. Her red eyes conveyed mortification and confusion.

Raji spun as Darrell walked into the room. "Mr. Jacobs, this is a private office. I must ask you to leave."

Darrell smiled at Callie - he was getting good at it. "Sorry to barge in like this, but there has been a big misunderstanding. You whisked Callie away before I really had a chance to think about all this. I didn't say I wouldn't help with the project. I was just trying to figure out all the logistics. I am sure if Ms. Williams and I sat down together, we could come up with a schedule that would work."

"I'm sorry," Raji thrust the words like a knife. "I think the best interest of the company is to make other arrangements for the pilot program. Now, please leave. You have upset everyone enough today."

"Mr. Mishra. I don't think I'm the only one that did the upsetting.

Didn't I see you with your hands on Ms. Williams in the room in there?"

Raji bristled and started to object, but Darrell talked over him. "I think what we need is to calm down before anyone gets the wrong idea about you sending Ms. Williams to your office. With all the workplace violence and harassment these days, you can see how someone could mistake something innocent. Just like the mistake about me not being enthusiastic about this project. I can't wait to be a part of it."

A cleansing wave of relief washed over Callie's face. She finger-pushed on her glasses and fixed her gaze on Darrell. A sigh came through her lips and pushed a smile out ahead of it.

"In fact," Darrell continued talking to Raji, "I have the Chief on the phone right now." Darrell began to talk into the cell phone. "Chief, I'm going to put Mr. Mishra on the phone. He is the main man over here at…uh…ATS."

Raji was putting his hand up as if to decline the phone, but Darrell ignored it, looked him in the eye, and hit the speaker phone. "I have been visiting with him about the project and telling him about how excited we are to be a part of it. I will let you talk to him. Go ahead Chief. Mr. Mishra can hear you."

The Chief's voice came over the phone. "Mr. Mishra, Lieutenant Jacobs has been telling me what a wonderful piece of equipment you have created for him. I want to tell you that the Department is grateful for your selecting us for your pilot program. I see this as a unique opportunity for the people of Colorado Springs to get to know the human side of Trans-Human Solutions – good for both of our organizations."

The Chief, likewise, gave Raji no room to interrupt. "I will be taking this to the next city council meeting and making sure that we can both take advantage of the positive public relations this will generate. I am sure the council will be getting out a letter to your board of directors letting them know how much the City appreciates your willingness to work with us."

Raji looked at Darrell, then Callie and then at the phone. "Well…yes." He took a deep breath and looked back at Darrell with a less enthusiastic smile than the one he had displayed when he thought Darrell was leaving. "We have certainly seen Mr. Jacobs' resourcefulness here today. I appreciate your kind words and the City's willingness to be a part of this. We definitely want this project to be viewed in a positive light and to do everything we can to make it a success—"

"With that in mind," Darrell inserted himself, "Miss Williams and I are going to go get started." Darrell walked to Raji's desk.

The other man started to object.

Darrell gave him an apologetic smile. "Sorry just needed to get your number. Chief, I will let you and Mr. Mishra discuss some of the details.

You can reach him at…" Darrell read the number off the phone on the desk.

Moving to Callie, Darrell offered his arm again. "If the offer still stands."

She wrapped her hand around his bicep, and he led her toward the door.

Raji drew in a breath like he might say something, but the Chief spoke again. "Lieutenant Jacobs, thanks for being willing to take this on. I know this community thinks a lot of you. Thanks for being willing to be in the spotlight again. The department is in your debt."

"My pleasure." He gazed at Callie as she looked up at him.

Ushering Callie out the door, Darrell spoke over his shoulder to Raji. "Thanks, Mr. Mishra, for allowing me to be a part of this. I will let you iron the particulars out with the chief. I wouldn't want anything to interrupt what Ms. Williams wants to show me."

The warm hands squeezed his arm. "Call me Callie."

Chapter 5

Callie took Darrell back to the black synthetic arm on the pedestal. She spent several minutes explaining the advanced materials, mechanical parts and artificial intelligent interface that she had designed into the construction of the arm.

She was enthusiastic and animated. Her gestures often resulted in a touch to Darrell's arm. He nodded encouragement as she spoke of the AI driving the synchronized combination of micronized pneumatics, hydraulics and servos. All the time he hoped for the next warm contact.

Much of the NIP's design Darrell did not understand. "So, you're a programmer?"

"No. Link's the programmer." Callie motioned toward the kid who was hovering around, typing on his phone.

"She can program." The young man raised his head at Callie. "But she does a lot more. She's the mainframe of ATS. She tells the cobbler elves in the other parts of the building what she wants, and they work on making it to her specifications. The NIP's her creation. I just give it a little smoke." Link exaggerated aiming his phone at the arm on the pedestal.

The hand swiveled at the wrist and came up with a playing card between its fingers. The fingers swept down and flipped the card spinning in Darrell's direction.

Darrell's right hand shot out and fixed the spinning card between his fingers. He held it up with a smirk and shook it at Link. "Careful, throwing things at a cop. We're trained to react."

Callie sashayed toward Darrell making a noise of approval. "Mmm, mmm, mmmm." She took the card and shook it at Link. "What do you think of those moves, Mr. Gamemaster?"

Link looked like he had opened a present. "A life-size avatar."

Callie frowned at the kid. "Let's not get ahead of ourselves. We can start training tomorrow."

Callie reacted to Darrell's puzzled expression. "You'll understand later." She shifted gears. "We have been working with this for years. It will take a while to understand how it all works, so we can just let that happen. I want to get into the features that will be helpful in your work." She sealed her commitment with a two-handed gesture, which looked like she was telling a pet to stay.

Darrell stayed. He enjoyed watching Callie. Her face glowed, and her eyes sparkled as she talked. It melted through some of the cynicism that had come to define Darrell's life.

Callie hurried to the next topic. "Now let me show you what it can do. You're going to like this."

Darrell doubted if he could ever be disappointed by the young woman that effervesced before him. He guessed she was no more than thirty, though it was hard to gauge her age. Often her face had the look of a ten-year-old showing him another shiny pebble she picked from the stream. When she explained the technical parts of her project, she acted as if she could be lecturing at Harvard. Yet there was no pretense or arrogance to her. Callie displayed her genius like a girl who had found something in the attic that she wanted to show him.

He had the day off. All that waited for him at home was yard work. He would pay the kid down the street to do it. He no longer cared about sleep, either. Like a good dog, Darrell stayed.

"So," Callie began, "I know that you only need a hand, but this is like the re-enforced sleeve that you wear with your hook. To get the full benefit from the equipment, you have to have the arm."

Up close, the NIP looked bulky. He didn't see how it was going to be practical. As gently as he could, Darrell told her, "I think it's a little big for me and it looks like it will be heavy."

"Just wait," Callie touched an area on the pedestal and the arm tipped and pivoted to an angle that was roughly that of an outstretched arm. The pedestal was attached around the exterior of the arm's base so that the opened shoulder of the arm was exposed.

Callie went to the end of the worktable and picked up an item. Finally, something that Darrell recognized – a ballistic vest similar to what he wore on duty. Callie slid it over her head and onto her shoulders. It made her look like she was wearing football pads.

"Where's your helmet?" he said as he smiled at the sight of her.

"Oh yeah," Callie said nonchalantly and headed back to the end of the table. She stopped and glanced back at him. "How did you know about that?"

"What? You mean I have to wear a helmet too?" He laughed. "I'm going to be quite the robo-cop."

"Wait," Callie said, holding her finger to her mouth as she pushed her full lips into a shushing motion that Darrell found attractive. "You won't have to wear the helmet. We will interface the NIP directly to the nerves in your arm. This is for me to demonstrate," Callie picked up a piece of headgear.

Darrell felt a little uneasy at the mention of "interfacing with his nerves." He felt a twinge of pain where his missing hand used to be. Pushing it aside, he focused on Callie pulling an item made of multilayered, interconnected plastic bands onto her head.

She wrinkled up her face as she wiggled the headpiece into her curls. Even after the headgear was in place, she held it in her hands while it vibrated and jerked. Projecting contacts moved inward, apparently digging through her hair to make some type of connection.

Callie fastened two clips onto her earlobes and took hold of the black box attached to the cable dangling down from the side of the headgear. She watched as a multitude of lights flashed red and green until they all finally settled on green. She gave a deep exhale and said "Okay."

Callie fastened the cables to a receptacle on the vest. With that completed, she walked to the pedestal and pushed her arm into the prosthetic. Darrell now saw that there was a circular collar on the shoulder of the vest that attached to the base of the arm. Callie rotated it, and Darrell heard it snap, apparently locking the two pieces together.

She looked his direction. "Now the headpiece doesn't work as well as a nerve interface, but this will give you an idea." Callie came away from the pedestal, lifting the arm effortlessly.

Darrell was amazed. "You must be a lot stronger than you look."

Callie moved the NIP into a pose like a body builder showing off her bicep. She quickly straightened up and laughed, waving Darrell off with her free arm. "It's the NIP. The pressure sensors and balanced driving mechanisms combined with the way the arm is connected puts the weight bearing into the shoulder and vest. So, you are really lifting the arm, and anything that it holds, with your body and legs."

She explained the NIP, as she moved it around between them. "The sensors all along the inside of the prosthesis make the arm react instantly to the movements of my arm inside it. It will probably feel lighter than wearing your hook. "Now let me see your hand." She reached for his real hand with the prosthesis. Darrell instinctively drew it back.

Callie smiled at him. "Lieutenant Jacobs, I would never hurt you." She widened her grin and added, "Besides, you're not scared of a girl, are you?" as she held the hand up and clicked mechanical fingers together like a crab claw.

Darrell eased his hand her direction with a suspicious gaze. Callie concentrated and moved the NIP in and took hold of his wrist. "The hand is composed of a complex joining of super-strong heat resistant polymers, and micro pneumatic and hydraulic cylinders covered with a tough elasticized skin. It could crush your hand, but it is pre-programmed to sense what it is grasping and apply the appropriate force."

"Thanks for telling me now that it's holding my wrist. What's the failure rate of your programing?"

"It releases by default. You're safe. I wouldn't risk your hand if you weren't."

Darrell pretended to be appalled. "I wouldn't risk my hand if I *was*."

Callie shook her head. "Hydrogel sensors all along the hand and fingers allow feedback concerning the pressure that the hand exerts. For instance, right now it knows it is holding onto a human, so the fail-safes allow enough pressure to hold you without hurting you. Try to get free."

Darrell tried to escape from the grip.

Callie struggled to stay balanced and giggled as he pulled her around, trying to get the mechanical fingers to release his wrist.

Darrell laughed along with her. When it was obvious the arm's grip was stronger than any human could exert, he stopped. "Okay, I'm convinced."

She released him, laughing. Callie proceeded to demonstrate grasping, lifting, and even crushing some items on a demonstration table nearby. The arm proved as capable as a human hand but with more strength. Darrell was impressed.

Callie stopped and scrunched up her face. "This headpiece squeezes my head to keep the electrodes in place on my scalp. Besides, like I said, this is not the best interface, so it takes a lot of concentration – yours will be a lot better. And, we'll give you more time with Bert." Callie took off the head gear and shook out her silky curls.

"Bert?" Darrell tried to remember. "Have I met him?"

Callie smiled slyly. "Oh, you will. You'll be spending a lot of time with him."

"Sounds like a big commitment. I hope he's a patient teacher."

Callie had a mischievous look. "I don't know if patient is the right word." Her brow furrowed. "But it is a big commitment. I know you're working on the murders that have been happening. I don't mind working evenings and Saturdays if you are too busy during the days. I'll bring the food." Callie's expression seemed to ask if the suggestion was appropriate.

"Yo, you better power up on that one."

Darrell spun his head to where Link was leaning against a table, still on his phone.

The young man looked up briefly at Darrell, but his fingers never stopped moving. He spoke as his eyes went back to the screen. "She can toast a pop tart like a boss."

Darrell raised his eyebrows at Callie while tipping his head toward

Link. "I think that means you're a good cook. So, based on that insider information, I think I'll agree to that arrangement. Your company and good food, too. How could a man say no?"

Callie gave a gracious head dip. "Why thank you, Lieutenant Jacobs."

"Why don't you call me Darrell."

Callie seemed pleased with the suggestion. "Okay, Darrell then."

62

Chapter 6

The man was huge, and his face showed nothing but anger. Callie tensed. She could tell things were about to get serious.

Darrell glanced her direction despite her earlier admonition to go about his routine like she wasn't even there. Maybe coming with him on this call was a bad idea.

Callie used her head to motion his attention back to the man. She had wanted to be merely an observer, watching how Darrell used the NIP to see if there were any design changes she could see from that perspective. Obviously, that had changed now. The man's anger seemed to be directed at her.

"Why you bring a…" the racial slur was shocking. "…to my house?" The man's bellow was meant for Darrell, but he was looking at Callie.

Darrell stepped between her and the man. "Watch your mouth. You don't talk to her like that." Darrell made a quick glance over his shoulder. His sorrowful eyes were giving her an apology when he had other things to worry about.

She felt the urge to run but tried to breathe steadily. She couldn't get caught up in her own fear. She was a part of this now and might need to help Darrell. *Focus on using the NIP.* Callie said nothing out loud for fear of distracting him from the very thing she knew he needed to do. During the basic NIP training, he had seemed ready, but maybe they had jumped into this too fast.

Callie watched as Darrell backed up and readied the new arm that was attached to the vest he wore.

The angry man grabbed the ax that he had embedded in a stump of wood behind him.

Callie saw Darrell's hand slap his waist where his gun should have been. They weren't supposed to need a gun. He gave a frustrated huff.

The hulking figure swung the axe, and Darrell moved the NIP to intercept it.

"Yes!" Callie's hands moved into fists in front of her at the success. The movement was swift and easy. Darrell's block put the force of the axe swing into the synthetic polymer exterior of the NIP where the arm was reinforced by micro shock absorbing hydraulics on the blocking surface of the outside forearm. Callie swelled as Darrell took command of the situation. The fear left.

It gave her the freedom to go into analysis. She was right. Watching all Darrell's videos had paid off. The reinforced surface was in exactly the part of the arm that he presented in a natural block. While able to survive some impact, the solar recharging units in the top of the arm, display and programming features located on the inside of the arm, and utility consoles on the bottom of the arm, were far more sensitive.

Darrell parried the blow down and away from him while he twisted the mechanical arm in, trapping the axe between the NIP and his body.

Callie was mesmerized by the flow in his moves.

Darrell performed a palm strike on the top of the ax to break the man's grip on the handle. He followed through for a two-handed jab with the axe handle to the man's stomach. The blow was ineffective.

Callie stiffened.

Darrell was making the arm movement, but the fingers of the NIP's hand fumbled and were not grabbing the ax. The result was a one-handed strike that only distracted the man for a moment. Darrell was frozen, staring at the hand as if willing it to move. The fingers flexed and reached toward the ax handle starting to form a grip.

"Look out." Callie watched helplessly as Darrell was nailed by a strike to his head coming from a huge ham fist.

Callie staggered backwards, watching Darrell hit the ground, sending dirt rising. He didn't move. Callie was paralyzed also, watching helplessly as the man picked up the ax. He stalked toward her with a maniacal expression.

Darrell finally started to regain some movement, but his body seemed sluggish.

"Darrell!" Callie turned and tripped. Her feet were tangled in some rope that she hadn't noticed before. Looking to Darrell, she watched him roll over, forcing himself to his feet. He staggered toward her struggling with the fingers on the NIP, trying to make them work.

The man raised the axe. "Where you going, little—."

In desperation, Darrell dived. Callie felt his weight come down on her, but he caught himself with both arms and softened the impact. His eyes looked defeated, remorseful. Over his shoulder, the axe was coming toward Darrell's back. It impacted with a sickening sound and Darrell winced. When his eyes opened, all they held was apology before his head fell against her chest.

The big man put his foot on Darrell and jerked the axe free. He raised the weapon toward Callie's head.

Callie watched numbly. Then everything was bright light.

"Stop it!" Darrell's voice was in her ear. "Stop it, Link."

The helmet he had pulled from her head dropped from his hand and he wrapped her in his arms, lifting her until she was sitting up on the white cushioned floor of the simulation chamber. As he held her, she felt their breaths come in unison, gasping for a calmer reality. Their panting slowed in harmony, and they gave each other tentative smiles.

"What are you doing?" Darrell was looking toward the observation window above him. "What was that all about?"

In the window, Link had his hands up as if fending off the assault. His voice came through a speaker high on the wall. "Game over, Darrellian fighter. You got chirped again. I don't write the script. That comes from you and the computer. I just plugged in the basic scenario."

"Why did you have me take Callie in where there was a racist killer? That was awful. She doesn't need to be in the middle of something like that."

Link shook his head and shrugged. "The characters were set to randomize."

Callie grabbed Darrell in a fresh squeeze. "It's okay. Link didn't know. There are people like that in the world. It's part of being black, so it has to be a part of real-world training. You stopped him from killing me. What more could you have done?" She pulled back and smiled. "Thanks for giving your life for me."

Darrell stood, bringing her up with him and pulling her foot out of the indent in the moving floor that had tripped her to simulate her getting caught in the rope. The floor reset to level. "That was too real. I would rather have you just watch from now on." He awkwardly pulled back like she might fall as he took his hands away. "I thought for sure that stupid machine was going to show...I couldn't have taken seeing that happen to you even as a simulation. I ripped off my helmet right before...Did you get...don't tell me. I don't want to know."

"You pulled my helmet off before it happened. You saved me." Callie almost said, *again.* "But I got stuck watching you ...I don't ever want to see that happen to you again either."

Darrell gave a sigh of irritation. "I didn't really save anyone. If this had been real...I couldn't get the fingers to work. I was doing fine before."

"It will come. BERT will get you there quickly."

"Well, I say BERT's a cad. What's that stand for again?"

Callie picked up her helmet. "Biofeedback Enhanced Reality Training. But like everything around here, it is more than the name implies."

Darrell snatched up his own BERT helmet. "See, he's too big for his BERT britches."

"This is all just to get you a jump start on getting the nerves in that arm operational again and to gather data for Shin to use in the operation. All the time you're in BERT your responses are being neuro-mapped. But you're learning too. It will all come together when you have the neuro interface implanted. You'll be surprised."

Darrell took a deep breath. "Okay. I guess we better get back to it then. I need to touch base with the team later and see how our murder investigation is progressing." He turned to the high window. "I'm ready, Link. But no more making Callie a part of the scenario." He turned back to her. "She's a…distraction."

Callie loved the look he gave her.

"Okay, Let's bust the grind on the simulations and swerve over to the basic exers again." Link's voice came over the speaker of Darrell's helmet.

After several more failures in BERT, Darrell was feeling frustrated. He was anxious to try something where he might make a better showing.

The kid continued. "The sims will give your skull jelly a jiggle so it'll get a hard lock on the exers and upload some new skills in your fingers. Then you can survive the next sim. The noggin knows man. The more reals it feels, the more skills it wills. You're not noodling the fingers fast enough under pressure. It's just been an age since your left hand turned up on the hardware installed list. But, no sweats, you'll be killin it 'fore long. We're early on the progress bar."

Darrell shook his head. *I think I understood part of that.* "Hey Link," Darrell watched the display change to the basic exercises screen as he talked. "Is there a training program for Link speak?"

"You're livin it live right now, Gundarrell – livin' it live."

Darrell was still shaking off the feeling from the scenario with Callie. Everything was a little too real inside the BERT world. Except the pain. It was experienced as minor electric shocks that barely registered but somehow made a big impact on the subconscious. But the scene with Callie had touched something much deeper. It left him uneasy, and he recognized it as an indicator of how important she had become to him in the brief time since they met.

He rotated his head and the sophisticated brain wave scanner that sat on it. As the new program loaded in BERT, the augmented reality visor on

Darrell's helmet came alive, and the white room around him formed into a control center with a strange keyboard in the middle.

Looking down at his stump, Darrell saw the NIP attached. He flexed the fingers even though he knew they weren't really there. The headset was sensing when he tried to use the nerves that used to be attached to his hand and transferring that information to BERT simulation. As Darrell moved the NIP around, he could tell himself all day long that it was really the wireless BERT sensor on his arm appearing to be the NIP, but he could never really convince his mind not to believe what it saw.

His stump was still tender from when Shin and Link had calibrated his nerves to BERT headpiece the day before. The needles Shin had used for the calibration were tiny acupuncture-type needles attached to sensors, but the nerves were delicate things to probe.

Shin was so humble that when Darrell learned he was a gifted neurosurgeon, it had been hard to comprehend. But Shin's hands were the hands of a master surgeon, steady and skilled. As the man had wielded the delicate needles, Darrell came to realize that Shin was as brilliant about the human nervous system as Link was with programming and Callie was with cybernetic design.

"Darrell," Callie's voice came over the speaker in his helmet, lifting his spirits the moment she said his name, "I've asked Link to concentrate more on your communication skills with the NIP. The simulations will then put you in stressful scenarios where you have to communicate with the NIP's computer to survive. You know, diffusing bombs with the virtual keyboard, that kind of thing. You have a strong background in martial arts, but you have never had to one hand type with your missing hand. Before you know it, BERT will have you typing faster with one hand than most people can with two. That way you'll be able to communicate with the AI computer in the NIP to do a lot more than just move the arm."

Darrell moved to the keyboard and examined it while he waited for Link to set up the next session. He was amazed that he wasn't tired. Time was running fast. He couldn't believe it was Wednesday already and yet he had advanced so far with the NIP that it was hard to imagine he had been at it for less than a week. Since he had begun the adventure on Friday, he felt like someone put his days in a blender. Things were blurring together so that it was hard to remember them separately.

He had signed forms, been measured for a custom-made NIP, had a thorough medical exam with blood work, spent a day with Shin and Link to calibrate and orient on BERT and was starting his second day of training.

When Callie said that, because of Raji, it might be best if they moved quickly on the project, he had told her it was probably best that way, and the Chief had agreed. His boss was probably thinking the new chapter in Darrell's story would be a positive spin to counter all the negative publicity police were receiving in the news lately, especially with the murders. Neither of them had envisioned how fast Callie's group could move.

Tomorrow, Shin and his team were going to spend hours mapping and surgically connecting the nerves in his stump to an interface that would attach inside the NIP. It was a lot to take in and think about.

Darrell told himself that he had made the commitment when he put his foot in the entry door and stopped it from closing. Even though he had not known the full extent of what he was getting into, he enjoyed the time he was spending with Callie. Like a warm ember, she was bringing the fire back to his blackened life.

Amid all the activity surrounding the NIP, he had several cell phone conversations with Shawn to keep up on the team's progress on investigating the murders. His only break since then had been on Sunday. Callie insisted on shutting down for the Lord's day.

"So where do you go to church?" she had asked him as they were leaving Saturday afternoon.

He realized he was going to have to come clean. "I'm not going to church."

Callie's expression was puzzlement before it changed to understanding. "The murders. I'm sorry, they must be occupying all your time. You must be working on them seven days a week."

That was actually true. Darrell gave her a half smile trying to determine how to explain his crisis of faith.

She continued. "I'm sorry. Here we are taking even more of your time. If we need to postpone this, we can. Don't worry about Raji. I will deal with him."

"No, it's not that."

Callie scrutinized him again. She reached a hand and laid that warming touch of hers on his arm. Her eyes said she was about to say something painful. She must be seeing what he couldn't say. "Darrell, if this isn't going to work right now for you—if you need to quit—we can. I understand. I shouldn't be asking so much of you at a time like this."

She didn't see at all. She was thinking of him, willing to sacrifice her dreams in consideration of him. He wanted to be honest with her, but looking into the pain she was feeling at the prospect of letting the project go made him unable to cause her more. He had to take the pain away from her. "No, I want to keep going. I want to be…I enjoyed…" He took her hand. "This is good for me. I don't want it to end."

An expression of elation filled her eyes to overflowing and she turned away to gather up her things giving a little sniff. She turned again, her face happy and bright. "So then I'll see you Monday." She had bobbed joyfully out the door leaving him with his lies.

Darrell was saved from more of the memory when the headset came alive with Link's voice. "Okay, Darrellquest, before we begin the basic exercises on the NIPian language, here's a little preparation scenario to get you in the mood."

There was a clank, and Darrell's right hand jerked upward. For a second, he knew it was caused from a powerful magnetic cable dropping from the ceiling and latching onto the metal of the harness on his arm, but looking up, Darrell saw his hand fastened to a pipe running overhead by a set of handcuffs. Everything became real. The only thing he had available to him was his NIP hand to operate the keyboard. Heat poured onto him as flames sprouted up around the room.

Darrell stayed in BERT the rest of the morning. The fire scenario had ended with the words "BERT simulation ended" and "failure resulting in fatality" flashing on the screen of the helmet Darrell wore.

Link switched him to the basic exercises. Starting with simple childlike games that involved a combination of one-handed typing and gestures, Darrell began to see patterns emerging. Then he would use what he learned in ever-more-complicated scenarios. The way BERT worked was unorthodox. It happened on a subliminal level. You didn't know you were acquiring skills until they were there.

The next time he faced the flaming room, the outcome was much different and produced a triumphant exclamation from Link. "Titanium deeds, Darrellwielder!" Link's voice said he was more than satisfied with Darrell's performance. "You have earned the ultimate positive reinforcement."

KENT WYATT

Chapter 7

Callie cleaned up what was left of the barbecued pork, potato salad, and baked beans she had brought for lunch.

"That was fantastic." Darrell patted his tummy as he pushed back from the break room table. He reached out and grabbed the last ham and cheese spinach puff as she started to move away with the plate.

She relished his satisfied look. "I don't know where you're going to put that."

"It'll just have to elbow its way in." Darrell popped the puff in his mouth.

Link did not look up from his phone, "Cals, you need to give my sister an experience round in your kitchen, so she can be a spoon ninja like you. When it's her night to cook, the dog dines out."

Callie held a plastic utensil in his direction. "You better stop being ugly about your sister, mister or I'll spatula slap you right now."

Link held his hands up in surrender.

Darrell moved his hook around before his eyes. "What's going to happen with my friend here after the operation? Am I going to be able to wear it with this new implant?"

Callie deposited the dishes in the sink. "Don't worry. I'll modify the sleeve and you can still wear it when you're feeling nostalgic. I have some polymer that will make the sleeve a lot stronger."

Darrell slid down in the chair feeling surprisingly contented. "I think I need a nap."

Callie moved in on him quickly, scooping up his arm. "Oh, no you don't. You come with me."

Callie led him to a large room, where she put on the headpiece and NIP. She saw Darrell notice the man shaped target wrapped in tinfoil. She hoped she was about to amaze him again.

"Callie, does your arm have a taser in it?" Darrell was fixated on the NIP.

Callie willed the prosthetic hand to form an "L" with the index finger and thumb. It reluctantly obeyed. She thrust the arm toward the target. The moment the arm went out, a compartment on the underside snapped open and a red laser dot appeared on the tin foil. In her mind, Callie made the gesture required to fire the Taser. Like pulling a confetti shooter party favor, there was a pop, small paper dots went flying, and the target quivered where two darts trailing copper wires had embedded in it. The distinctive arcing sound that was the hallmark of a taser on tinfoil crackled in the air. Sparks lit up on two locations on the target as the strong, pulsating electrical current traveled through the tinfoil between where the darts had stuck.

When the five second cycle was finished, Callie discarded the taser cartridge, freeing herself from the copper wires that connected her to the target. She pushed up her glasses and started explaining, "Okay, besides showing the taser, this is a good way to demonstrate what I was telling you before lunch. Since the only connection you have with the arm is through nerves that are normally used to control hand function, the NIP's computer speaks a form of sign language made out of unusual hand movements. You control the NIP's extra functions by thinking about making those motions. That way you don't have to relearn everything. The scenarios you're working on now in BERT are geared toward reminding you of the movements you have not used in a long time and learning new significance for those movements. For instance, since there is very little use for pushing your arm forward, flexing your wrist back, and making an "L" symbol – that movement opens the weapons console. You will be able to make it work a lot faster with the interface than I can using the headset. Since it is only my hand confined inside the arm, I can't connect with the NIP like you will be able to. I have to use the helmet. You will not have the handicap…of a hand."

Darrell observed her fondly. "Who else could make my disability an asset?"

Callie felt an internal warmth. "All the muscle memory hand gestures you are learning in BERT will really start coming together to form the NIP language. "

Darrell grinned. "Just by hand gestures, sounds a little unsafe. How do I keep from tasing friends and family by mistake?"

Callie gave him a look of mock vexation. She loved bantering with him. She was seeing that Darrell loved to tease, but he had been out of practice. That's what came of living alone too long. "It's not just a single gesture, it's the whole package. The taser doesn't arm if you simply make an 'L.' You have to thrust out your hand with the wrist flexed back at the same time. You don't do that to your friends, do you?"

Link was making the "L" sign on his forehead.

Callie sneered at him. "There's always an exception." She went back to her explanation. "Think of it like the shift key on a computer keyboard. Just hitting the shift doesn't do anything; you have to hit another key with it. To make it even safer, you can auto select non-targets with this button on the console. It then uses the image recognition algorithm to create a digital signature of the object that you select."

Callie pressed the button and raised the forearm of the NIP straight in the air, so the business end of the taser was pointing upward. A green dot coming from the bottom of the console appeared on Darrell's chest, and she pressed the button again. "There, now you're my friend, so the taser will not go off if you are in the line of fire."

Eyes on his phone, Link called out, "And don't make her un-friend you."

Darrell shook his head in amusement. Callie rolled her eyes.

"So, let me get this straight." Darrell showed Callie a raised eyebrow. "I'm learning this whole language of hand gestures for the NIP?"

Callie nodded.

Darrell eyed Link. "A language that Link created?"

Callie dipped her head in acknowledgement.

"I'm going to look kind of funny making all these hand motions all the time. And what if he messed up and one of them is really an insult? I don't want to go around getting slapped by people that speak sign language."

Darrell stood, smiling. Callie made a point of looking over her glasses at Darrell before she pushed them up.

Link was laughing. "Whoa!" He had both hands up forming a square like he was bracketing a movie scene. "Check this out. I'm trippin on this high-res image of the Darrellolater signing to some deaf babe and her going all virus alert and purging him from the system. Maybe I'll make that the next scenario."

Callie put her hands on her hips. "We don't need any babes in the scenarios. Darrell doesn't need any distractions."

"Just you," Darrell gave her a wink, "and we already agreed you're staying on the outside, where it's safe."

Just you. Callie cuddled the thought. *He's playing. Don't read too much into it.* She went back to her explanation. "You don't have to worry about the hand movements. You can shut the arm off and just do the movements in your head. Now don't think this is crude, but I figured I would make something good out of what people use as a nasty gesture. So, if you try to put up just the middle finger on the NIP's hand, instead of making that gesture the NIP goes into what I call cyber mode or Cmode for short. In your mind, you can use the gestures and the virtual keyboard to talk to the computer, but the NIP won't move – kinda like typing without a monitor hooked up. You just have to know you are hitting the right keys without feedback."

"It'll fry your circuits on the commence." Link made a face. "The first few cycles, you might want to close your eyes, so you don't freak."

"But," Callie finished her instruction, "you won't look weird or give away what you're doing or anything like that."

Darrell appeared to be picturing it. "So I can be talking with the NIP and no one will ever know?"

Callie nodded. "Communicating with the NIP's computer, virtually typing to text, send email, write a letter. It can clone remotes so you can invisibly operate a wireless instrument or appliance, all kinds of things."

"And this language that Link made is what I am learning in BERT?"

"Exactly." Callie was pleased with Darrell's comprehension.

"Good," Darrell smiled Link's direction. "I'm going to understand you yet."

Link quickly put his phone under his arm and slowly raised his long face toward Darrell to show an evil grin under his crooked nose as he wrung his hands together and spoke in a wicked voice. "Welcome to my world."

"Now that," Callie nodded toward Link, "is scary."

The young man's hands were a flurry of fingers over his cell phone and Callie felt the NIP move out of her control. It reached down and gave her leg a light pinch. Callie swatted the NIP's hand away and shook her finger at Link. "You better stop that, or I'll change the encryption key and lock you out, buster."

Link shrugged. "I'll get in."

"Not if I design a new chip to keep you out."

"I'll find a new hack."

Darrell walked over to Link. "Let me end this nerd battle." He reached for Link's cell phone.

Link snatched it out of his reach. Darrell's hook shot out, in and around, locking Link's other arm with Link's face toward the floor and the hook on the back of his neck.

Callie gasped before she saw the big smile on Darrell's face. He had Link fully restrained but wasn't hurting him.

Darrell leaned in. "Mind your manners. Gentlemen do not pinch ladies even with someone else's hand. We call that assault outside the cyber world."

Link grimaced. "Well, what do you call *this*?"

Darrell unwrapped the kid and gave him a good-natured squeeze around the shoulders. "Free education." Darrell offered his real hand. "I like ya. Don't want to see you get in any trouble."

Link grinned, stood and reached down to take Darrell's hand. "In the hacker world we'd call that a brute force take-over."

Callie couldn't help a soft giggle.

Link turned her way. "Sorry, Cals. I won't throw a bug your way if you don't send your muscle after me."

"Deal, Mr. Schimelpenig." Callie couldn't help enjoying the idea of Darrell being *her* muscle. She knew there were no commitments. But Darrell was still around.

Darrell looked up at the young man. "Schimelpenig, uh. So, is Link really your first name?"

Link looked at the ceiling, shook his head and sighed. "No. It's short for my nickname 'Uplink,' also a character from a video game I used to play a lot when I was little. Don't ask my real name."

Callie joined them. "Asterias Rubens," she whispered to Darrell behind her real hand. "It's a starfish. His mom is a marine biologist; has a thing for starfish. Sweet lady."

Link twisted his face in disapproval. "Thanks. Maybe I'll tell all *your* secrets."

"Don't have any."

"Oh really. Let me search the data base. How 'bout your daddy being a terrorist?"

Callie took a breath. "Sorry, I guess I deserved that one. But you should be proud of your name. It means you're really special to your parents. Not like anyone else." She swung the NIP up and dropped it heavily into Link's hands. "But what my daddy did isn't secret. It's pretty big news if you like ancient history. But I would like to be the one that tells people about it. It's not the same as being named after an aquatic creature. Besides, I like your name."

"Hey," Darrell grinned at the two. "My sister's a telemarketer and my name's Darrell – we all have skeletons."

Callie struggled with the stubborn headpiece and her embarrassment. Link knew she had come to terms with her daddy's death. He didn't mean anything. He just didn't have a sensitive bone in his body. If it was anyone besides Darrell… She kept tugging at the headpiece, but not having much success. As Link carried the NIP to a table off to the side, Darrell moved to help her. He carefully held the helmet while she let it wriggle out of her hair. She gave him a weak smile.

Darrell reached up and pushed back some stray curls from her face. "I was thinking. We have worked pretty hard. We all might be getting a little tired. Why don't we knock off and I can take you out to dinner to pay you back for that meal today?"

Callie had to run it through her mind a second time. "Dinner?" The thought seemed to take a little bit to slide into place. *He's asking me out to dinner.* "You're asking me out to dinner?"

Darrell reached out and gently took the helmet from her and handed it to Link as he returned.

The young man regarded it, then examined Callie and Darrell. Nodding his head with just a hint of a smile, he spun and headed back to the table.

Darrell was gazing at her. "Yeah, dinner. I'll pick you up. We'll go to a restaurant. Have a nice meal." He gestured like he was stating the obvious. "Not as good as yours, but you won't have to do the dishes."

Callie nodded. She didn't dare talk or she'd cry. She turned toward Link to mask her misty eyes. "Let's get this stuff cleaned up, Buster."

The way Callie turned away Darrell wondered if the dinner invitation was too soon. It had been spontaneous. The mention of her father seemed to bring her down, and nothing in him wanted Callie to be down. He hoped he hadn't made it worse.

Link, on the sidelines, appeared to be busy on his cell phone and oblivious to the interaction. A reggae ringtone sounded from Callie's pocket.

"I know that's you, Mr. Uplink, so you just let my song play and I'll read your message in a minute." Callie began to swing to the upbeat music.

The singer's lyrics bounced with the island rhythm. *"Dark and cold - the world for which I've cried. Don't let - the wet - darken me inside."*

Callie swayed with the music all the way to the table where she picked up items to put away. "I love this song, so I made it my ringtone."

"Like rain, the teardrops - block out what I see. But there is only one thing - that can color me."

Darrell followed Callie into the mood of the music. He joined her and Link in the cleanup as he listened.

"So, I tell my soul, oh soul, be happy anyway. Anyway it goes oh soul, be happy anyway. Walk by faith and not by sight, in your Savior's arms you'll be all right. Anyway it goes my soul, be happy anyway."

When he was with Callie, something stood guard against the inky blackness that wanted to claim him once again, and the world became nothing but her beautiful heart, singing to his soul, sending him the same message. A broad smile had infiltrated Darrell's demeanor and like ice cream in August, he melted. He believed he could be happy again.

They made short work of the straightening task under the inspiration of the music. Darrell guessed the dinner invitation was not ill planned after all. Abruptly the song ended, and Callie pulled out the phone to read Link's message as the kid walked out of the room with the NIP.

Darrell peeked over Callie's shoulder and read the text the kid had sent in response to Callie's hustle to clean up. **What's your hurry? You got a date?**

Chapter 8

Darrell stepped out the rear door of the ATS building into the employee lot where he had parked. He was pleasantly exhausted. Fall was just beginning, but the day was still warm. The fresh air was a pleasant relief from being inside participating in scenarios so much of the day. He felt good, better than good. Life had taken on a new excitement. He was looking forward to the evening with Callie.

The Callie that thinks you're a good Christian man.

Callie had told him that it was her night for Wednesday prayer meeting, but if they hurried, they could have an early dinner and she would have plenty of time. He had made excuses about being tired when she invited him to the service, but he had assured her he still wanted to have dinner with her. *Dinner but not church.* The dividing line between them was already forming, and Callie was innocently oblivious to it. He wasn't willing to cross over. But he was shamelessly pulling her across whether she knew it or not.

In his pocket, Darrell felt the business card that she had given him with her address written on it. *You took it without even saying a thing.* Guilt took his euphoria by the throat and threatened to choke it back into depression. He was toying with the idea of turning around and going back inside to straighten out Callie's misconception of him when movement caught his eye.

Across the street that ran behind the ATS facility was an open area. There it was again—something glinting on the hillside in the afternoon sun. There was a running or bicycle trail on the other side of the hill, but on top, where the glint came from, the slope was a bit rugged for either. Probably someone resting from a hike. Was the glint from a set of binoculars? That's what it reminded him of. He had seen it when he was in the narc unit. Pete would send him to check the surveillance positions for any giveaways like that. Maybe someone hadn't taught this guy. His mind hurried past the memory of Pete. There was another glint.

Darrell went to his car. He pretended to be on his phone. Callie came out and waved as she left. Darrell jumped in his car, waited a bit so she wouldn't know he was behind her, then followed her to be sure she was safe. He didn't want to scare her if it was nothing.

As he pulled out of the parking lot, he kept his eye on the ridge. When he had to turn away from the hill, he adjusted his rearview mirror to watch. A dark figure stood just before disappearing over the rise. Someone was hiding up there, scoping out the ATS lot. They left when he and Callie left. Whoever it was must be watching one of them.

There was no way to get up there or drive around in time to catch the person, especially since he wasn't sure. Maybe it was a bird watcher. It could have been a camera lens. But he had the feeling, the cop's sixth sense, and he knew better than to ignore it. Callie worked with defense contracts. Tomorrow was his surgery, and Callie and he would both be at the medical center instead of at ATS. If someone was surveilling them, he knew the watcher would be back. Maybe they could catch the person in the act.

Darrell followed Callie to the interstate and made sure that no one else was behind them. She headed south and he headed north to his house. As their vehicles went in opposite directions, Darrell had a feeling that he had not had in a long time. He felt the urge to pray that God would keep her safe.

Funny what comes back to you at the weirdest times. Well, God, if You still listen at all, keep an eye on her, for her own sake, even if I don't have any standing anymore.

He was almost going to ask forgiveness for still not telling her, but his internal prayer trailed off into emptiness.

Who are you trying to fool? is what whispered through his mind, and he had to wonder who was asking the question.

Chapter 9

Everywhere that Darrell went in "the Springs" (as the city was affectionately known), there were stories. In every neighborhood, he could recall events to which he had been dispatched: a disturbance in this house, a burglary in that. When he turned off Academy Boulevard onto East Fountain, Darrell began to remember rapes, robberies, gang shootings. The Crips warring against the Bloods, a lot of it happened here, back when he was working the streets. His mind drifted to his career in the Major Crimes Division. A man took his wife hostage in that place, talked for hours and then shot her and himself before the TEU (Tactical Enforcement Unit) could break in. Just northwest of there, a police officer was shot and killed when he tried to arrest a wanted man.

It was a rougher part of town. He imagined Callie growing up there. He could see her, kind and brilliant, trying to fit in, with a father who had apparently committed some type of terrorist act they had yet to discuss. What kind of bullying did she endure?

She kept her faith.

Darrell had entertained the idea of calling Callie and canceling, but he had not sunk that low yet. He was not worthy of her, but he decided that what he had to tell her was best said in person. He did not look forward to the evening any longer. She didn't deserve this.

He looked upward. *Why are You doing this to her?*

He wanted to say, "Why are You doing this to us," but he couldn't make himself part of the question. He knew the answer for himself. God had plenty of reason not to answer his prayers. But maybe he had plenty of reason not to pray. What had faith in God gotten him?

At about 4:30, Darrell pulled up in front of a small single story, brick-faced house. It was the nicest house in the neighborhood, not large, but neat and tidy. The property seemed to have spilled over into the lot next door where a large building had been added, much bigger than the house. It looked like a work area for Callie. She probably spent a lot of time there.

As he got out of the car, Darrell noticed video cameras on poles and on the house. One followed him as he moved. There were other cameras, probably ones that gave a panoramic view of the area. He realized that Callie had been hard at work making her property safe for her and her mother.

Callie hurried out. Her hair was neatly worked into a full black frame around her face with a few delicate curls gracing her forehead. She wore a full-length dress that had a pastel-colored floral design. It was modest, nothing revealing, but Callie graced it well. She had a lacy wrap around her shoulders and a large smile on her face. It dimmed some when she saw him.

"Darrell, are you okay?"

His inner turmoil must have crawled to the surface. He nodded and tried to look pleasant as he opened the door for her, instead of answering the question.

She seemed to resolve the issue herself. "I guess you had a pretty big day. I know we're pushing you hard and all of this is happening quickly. Shin says there is nothing to worry about tomorrow. You'll see. He is so good at what he does. I know it will all be fine or I wouldn't allow it." She fastened her seatbelt while he climbed in behind the wheel and did the same. Darrell headed to the restaurant they had agreed on.

The young woman let out a contented sigh and straightened herself up in the seat, putting her hands in her lap. "I'm looking forward to this. Thanks for asking me. I was hoping we would have some time to talk."

I wish I had a better topic. "I called ahead and ordered a table with some privacy." *In case there are tears.* It was in consideration of Callie. He hadn't considered it for himself. He was afraid he had emptied his tears long ago. He had lost so much in his life, and he was afraid he was going to lose again tonight.

Callie appeared impressed. "That was thoughtful. I researched a lot about you for the project. I read the article you wrote about communication being so important for a police officer, talking to people all the time and getting them to talk. When you said that a police officer could forget his gun and probably make it through the night but never his verbal skills, that just said so much. It is so important to communicate those things because all people know is what they see in movies – police are always just shooting, fighting, talking tough to people. You hardly ever see the communication side – negotiation, getting people to talk."

Callie smiled his way. "I think communication is one of the most important things in life. You talking to me, me talking to you, us both talking to God, God talking to us. The rest is just trimmings."

She gave him a sly look. "So, tell me a communication trick. What do I need to do to get the truth out of you?"

Darrell grinned. *You don't know that you're already doing it. But being honest tonight is going to cost me.* Tipping his head back, he strained to think. "A trick, huh?" It would be good to get his mind on something else. "Okay, one of the first things you have to know is there are all kinds of communication. Some people are better with words and others more fluent in body language and feelings. But a cop needs to know those things as well, at least in as much as it relates to his work. Sometimes people's bodies speak louder than their words."

Callie shifted in her seat. "I always figure I'm kind of an open book for most people to read. I mean, there are lots of things that my mind thinks that I have to stop it from thinking because I know that it is not what God wants me to be thinking. I hope my body isn't saying those things out loud, but I think everyone fights that battle. The Bible talks about the war we always have going on within us. We have to make sure we're listening to the right voice, I guess."

She faced him, again. "I think it helps to have someone that you can really trust to talk things out with. Someone that loves the Lord and wants to serve Him as much as you do. I mean I have my church family and they are great…but it's different than someone you want to share your life with."

Darrell risked a glance at her. It was a mistake. The sweet face brought a smile out of him he couldn't hold back. Callie met his gaze and glowed. He looked away. *Shows how much I know about body language.* He had sent a message he wasn't intending.

Callie continued. "It's hard to wait for God's timing. That's been the hard part all my life. Sometimes it takes a long time." She renewed her pleasant look toward him. "But when it happens, it makes all the waiting worthwhile, don't you think? We just have to stick with Him, and He brings things around in His time." Callie laughed at her own loftiness. "But do you ever get impatient and just have to ask Him, 'What's taking so long?'"

How do I answer that one? She spoke about God all the time. How could he tell her that he and the Creator did not speak at all anymore, that he stopped going to church on the day that Pete— How was he going to tell Callie that he wanted nothing to do with a God that let things like that— "Not for a long time now."

"Wow, really? I wish I could grow like that, enough to get past that impatience. You do seem really patient. Maybe you can help me because I really want to be like that. I know God made me the way I am, but sometimes I wish He had made me…not so…I don't know, my mind is always thinking of all these things, ideas, feelings, desires. It's like it just won't shut off and I can't be quiet…inside. You know, like it says in the Psalm, 'Be still and know that I am God.' I can never seem to be still. I feel like I'm missing something that other people can do and I can't."

"I think that most people would wish they could do half of what you can do."

"You really think so? I think most people just think I'm weird…normal people, I mean. In school, they all thought I was weird. Thinking back, I'm glad I was always in special classes, so I didn't have to hear all the things that my classmates said about me. What I did hear was enough. When I was able to graduate early and not have to go through high school, I was glad about that, too, but, you know, sometimes you just want to be normal, not a brainiac, which was one of the nicer things I heard. Boy, if it hadn't been for the Lord, I never would have gotten through it."

"People at your work seem to like you."

"Work is kinda like being in a special class. People like Link, well, that's easy because they're weird, too. When I was a little girl, I used to think that all I had to do was go to the special classes and eventually I would be like the other girls, like it was going to fix me or something. So I worked hard so I could go back with the other kids, but they just sent me to a more advanced class. Then I would work hard on that one.

"Eventually, I realized I wasn't going back, and finally I accepted my life like that. In that way, I guess I am lucky. I think it is hard for normal people to realize that. When I looked at Jesus, I saw that He didn't fit in either. People eventually killed Him because He was not what they wanted Him to be. But when I understood that God meant for Him to be like that and what it accomplished, well, for me, that helped me understand that God has a purpose for my life, even the weird parts."

Callie chatted about her life and her faith until they got to the restaurant. The meal was nice, and Darrell enjoyed listening to Callie, which weakened his resolve to break things off. If she was willing to take him as he was, perhaps...*Quit lying.* The words flashed in his mind like a blinding light. It angered him.

Why shouldn't we have each other? Who's to say we shouldn't? But he had to be honest about his own issue about God. He had to tell her that. *Callie is an accepting person. Maybe she can take me as I am.*

"So anyway," Callie was saying, "I was finishing up my Ph.D. in Electrical Engineering at UCCS when I met Raji. He needed someone to work on a flight simulator contract he had with the Air Force, so I worked on that on the side. It made his company a lot of money and new contracts, so when I graduated, he offered me this great salary, plus they were starting to work on what I was interested in—prosthetics. When I finished up with my degree, I went to work with ATS."

"How old were you?"

"21."

"Callie, you got your Ph.D. when you were 21 years old?"

"Yeah, I know, it sounds like a big deal, but it really wasn't. I just had to kind of go over stuff that I had been working on for years. They didn't have the funding for the equipment I needed to do what I wanted. It wasn't until I started working for ATS that I could really start advancing."

"So what's Raji all about?"

"Raji? He's a strange mix. He's a Hindu but he really doesn't believe it. It is just his family's religion. He came from India. Whenever I tell him about Jesus, he falls back on talking about reincarnation and how nothing really dies. He never addresses all the huge multitude of gods that Hinduism believes in. But, hey, I don't mind him arguing with me. At least he lets me talk about it. A lot of people can't do that at their work. Anyway, what Raji really believes in is evolution. Only it's not so much what he believes happened in the past as what he believes is going to happen in the future."

"Yes, he was saying something about that after we…after he sent you to his office."

"Not surprising. He preaches it at least as much as I preach Jesus. He thinks that technology is the key to the next phase of evolution – forget the fact that there is no evidence for a first phase. He says that we've reached the limits of human evolution and now we must become something different. He has this idea that humans are going to merge with machines and become something bigger than either."

Something about discussing Raji made Darrell uneasy about breaking things off with Callie and leaving her to deal with the man by herself. *See, I'm not just thinking of my own interests.*

"That's why the company is so hot on bionic-type prosthetics – he thinks it's the first stage of this evolutionary shift. For Raji, it really is not so much about helping people. That is just how he can get funding and test subjects to forward his research in artificial intelligence and trans-humans, as he calls them. He thinks someday the human consciousness is going to exist inside of synthetic bodies and be connected to every other consciousness in a vast collective computer-like network. It is a passion for him. I think he is trying to make it happen before he dies so he can upload himself and live forever. So I guess," Callie's face was mirthful, "reincarnation is not really cutting it for him. He is running from death like most people. I keep telling him that he can already be connected to something bigger than himself and live forever anytime he is ready to give his life to Jesus. But he would rather believe in his pseudo-scientific mysticism that has no intellectual promise and no historical data to support the concept."

"Does it ever scare you to be part of that?"

"I'm not a part of it. I'm part of helping people. This world is not what God intended it to be. It is always taking something away from people. I just want to give people back some of what God gave them originally."

"Judging from this prosthetic that you made, I would say you are giving a little more."

Callie frowned and shook her head.

"More than God?" Her laugh was dismissive. "No." She drew out the word. "What God gave you originally was a part of you and the life that you have. When it was connected to the rest of you, it was alive. It could heal, grow new cells, become stronger, more skillful, whatever your will and hard work determined…and God allowed. The mind/body package was a fantastic creation of God to put the human spirit into. It has allowed humans to survive what God knew our sin was going to make of this world."

Callie appeared thoughtful. "My prosthetic arm can't exist outside of technology, and we have just recently developed enough technology to make it possible. If we lost that technology this arm would quickly become useless through damage, corrosion, and a failing power supply. Yet man has been existing in this mind/body package for thousands of years without any of that technology. But on the other hand," she grinned, "pun intended, you should also remember that our bodies are nothing without our minds. We have been making extensions to our bodies so we could accomplish even more, right from the start. They have found gloves in Egyptian pyramids. That is why Raji is going to be disappointed in the end. His arrogance leads him to think he can make a better human when all we are really making is a fancier glove."

Callie tipped her head sideways, narrowed her eyes and gave him a slight smile. "You're playing with me. I can't believe a man of God like you would ever say that. You're just trying to get me going, aren't you?"

Darrell's slumping shoulders and preparatory inhalation must have been obvious to Callie because her face changed to fearful anticipation as she shoved up her glasses.

"Listen, Callie," Darrell hesitated. "that is something that I needed to talk to you about. I want to be honest with you, and I should have done it before now, but things have just been so wild."

"I know," Callie's forehead wrinkled with concern. "I'm so sorry. I didn't mean for it to be like this…I mean I hoped that you and I…but this has just been really crazy and…just give it a little bit of time to settle down. I know I get too excited, and I get pushy and…we can wait on the operation if you're not ready. Oh brother, what have I been doing to you? And I didn't mean to get into a big heavy conversation tonight and then jump on you. I didn't mean...I'm glad you're honest. It really opens up a lot of good discussion...but...ooooh, I talk too much."

Darrell reached his real hand across and put it over Callie's trembling fingers. "You don't talk too much."

Callie raised her glistening eyes like a flower opening. "You really think so?"

Darrell didn't want to go through with it. Something in him wanted to shoot himself in the foot before he caused this flower to wilt. But he had left her believing a lie long enough.

"This has nothing to do with your talking or the project or anything else going on. I just have to tell you something about myself because you have the wrong idea."

The Callie flower wilted. "I didn't mean to move so fast. I wasn't trying to drag you into anything. I know a decision as big as a relationship takes time and a lot of prayer. I know that a Godly man doesn't rush into something like that, and I wasn't expecting you to. I want to follow God on this, too. Of course, it's going to take a lot of prayer. I have been waiting for years. I can wait."

He looked away from the eyes that searched him. "There are some things that time can't change."

In his peripheral, he saw her head sink.

She pulled her hands away. "I was so sure God told me that you were alone, that you needed someone. Did I get it all wrong? It was so strong. Oh, Darrell, if I have compromised you in any way with someone you are already seeing, I'm so sorry. Please just tell me and I will leave right now. I can get a ride." Callie had begun picking up her purse, retrieving a tissue, wiping her eyes, looking to make sure she had everything and scooting her chair out to get up.

"Callie, please stop." Darrell took one of her hands again. "Just listen to me for a minute. It is not any of those things. There's no one else. In fact, I...like you very much...I think more than that...It is very sudden, but I guess it can happen that way and be all right. Back when I was still following God, I would have said that it should be a matter of prayer. Now, I don't know what to do. All I know is I would give anything in this world to be able to be with you. I have felt better in these last few days with you than I have for a long time. I didn't think it was possible to get that back. And I am willing to work around anything that...might be a conflict."

Callie looked at him like he had confessed to murder. She sank onto her chair. "You said, 'When I was still following God.' You said it like you're not anymore. What are you talking about?"

Like air from a balloon, Darrell let out his breath, but the pressure was still there. He felt like a condemned man that just passed up his last chance at a pardon. When he was with her…there was something, a connection perhaps that went deeper than anything he had ever known before. He was too old for infatuation, definitely too hardened. If he still spoke in such terms, he would have called the connection spiritual. Now it was life to him, the condemned, but he had to confess.

Whatever it was – Callie was special. He couldn't lie to her. He still had that much honor in him, and her presence brought it out. "I'm sorry. I should have told you sooner. The things that you read about me, the things that I wrote. They are not me anymore. Yes, I used to follow God. When I was young, my parents raised me as a Christian, but I never really got into it. Then… some friends got me going to a Bible study at their house. Christian things started making a lot more sense. It was really starting to click. I could see it. When I was in the hospital after the shooting, a doctor said something to me. He said that my hand was just a little part of me. That got me thinking about what I was and who I was. I determined to turn my attitude around and beat the depression that was setting in. A chaplain came and talked to me, and the pastor from the church my parents used to attend when they were still alive. It just seemed like over and over God was talking to me, telling me, through various people that He was not finished with me yet. People talked to me about how He must have something special planned for my life. Back then it all made sense. I prayed with the pastor. Then I really became committed. I went to church and still kept going to the Bible study. I even did some speaking about *my testimony*," Darrell made quotes in the air, "talking about the shooting and how God helped me through."

Darrell didn't know where to go next. He worried that his words might somehow erode Callie's faith if that was possible. *If that was possible*…he knew firsthand that it was. If anything could do it, it was lost love. "Some things happened, and it all ended for me. Now I would just rather not have anything to do with the whole Christian thing."

"The whole Christian thing?" Callie repeated staring at the tablecloth in front of her.

Darrell continued. "But you were right. I am alone and I do need someone. There is no one else."

Callie remained unmoved. "This is worse. You're not with God, and I could never leave *Him*."

"I'm not asking you to. I thought if you wanted to try…"

"Try what? It's not about what I want to do. It's a matter of what I should do. Life is full of wants that God says no to and part of 'the whole Christian thing' is about saying no to wants when they get in the way of saying yes to God."

"So, God never wants you to be happy?" Darrell felt the same old pang. The guilt he didn't need.

"Darrell, I don't know what you thought you had, but it wasn't a relationship with God, or you wouldn't even be asking questions like this."

"Listen, nobody worked harder at it than I did. I was in church whenever I could be. I believed it all. I went on missions' trips, gave my time and money just like I was supposed to do. And I was happy with that life. If anyone did the leaving, it was God." A woman from another table glanced over, and Darrell realized he had raised his voice.

"Darrell, would you please take me home?" Callie whispered—her face expressionless.

Chapter 10

Before starting the car, Darrell sat quietly for a moment. He had to say something. "Callie, I'm sorry. I didn't mean to hurt you. That's why I didn't bring this up right away. I guess I knew this would never work for you…no matter how much I might want it to."

Callie appeared mesmerized by the dashboard. Her normally pretty mouth looked lifeless, like the smile had died. "I never gave you a chance to tell me. I just went on and on making a fool of myself because I was so sure God told me you were the one."

"Maybe I am, and God just likes to take things away from people." As soon as the words were out of his mouth, Darrell regretted saying them. "I'm sorry. This isn't fair to you. You are the best thing that has come into my life. I don't mean to hurt you."

With a slight movement of her head, she glanced his direction then looked back at her lap. "What happened to you?"

"What else. A girl. You really want to hear about the other woman and what your God is capable of?"

The resentfulness in Darrell was coming out, and he was disgusted at the way he was talking to Callie, but he couldn't stop himself. It seemed to have the opposite effect on her than what he expected. Her face seemed to soften and some of the life came back.

"I know what He's capable of." She straightened in her seat as if in preparation. "But I do want to hear what happened."

"Okay. I'll give you the condensed version. That will be long enough." Darrell ran his fingers through his hair. Sitting for a moment, he considered where, or if, he should begin. He decided he needed to give a little background. "When I was in the drug unit, I had a supervisor named Pete. He was a great guy and became a good friend, the best of friends. Before I was shot, Pete introduced me to a woman that had just started with the police department and who was coming to the Bible study that Pete and his wife hosted. Pete taught some classes at the academy, and he met her there. He went on and on about what a fantastic girl she was. She was beautiful, she was smart – tops in her class, easy to be around and talk to about anything. Her name was Jodi, and I should meet her. So Pete and his wife got us together on some double dates, and she was everything that he said she was. We started dating regularly. She got me to go to Pete's Bible study. I got her into Jujitsu, and she ended up being pretty good. It was just one more thing that we could do together. There was a group of us that used to go running together, Pete and I and a couple of the other guys from the unit, and Jodi started going with us. She fit right in. She was just like one of the guys. We would laugh and joke. Everywhere I went, I was the envy of every man around because Jodi was what they all dreamed of having – the perfect lover and playmate."

Callie took in a tight breath. "You must have been very happy."

"I was. Life was very easy – just like it was supposed to be. Then the shooting happened. That devastated me, and I was sinking into depression. Like I said, a lot of people really started talking to me about God, and it motivated me to move on. But Pete and Jodi also helped me get through it. I would wake up and there they would be.

"I thought God had really blessed me, and I started realizing how close I came to dying. I decided I better live my life differently. Jodi was really active in the church, singing on the worship team and organizing mission trips. She was great with the teenagers – every girl wanted to be just like her, and every teen guy was in love with her.

"The women of the church had a harder time accepting her. I think the married ones didn't want her around their husbands and the single ones couldn't compete. At the time, I thought that was Jodi's only fault. She just got along better with guys than she did with women, and she generated a lot of jealousy."

"I can imagine." Callie's had a wounded countenance.

"Just like that. She does it even when she's not around. Plus, we started getting a lot of guilt thrown on us about living together."

"You were living with her?"

"Yeah. Like I said, just like that. Anyway, I did ask her to marry me. She said we should give it a little more time. I also noticed that she started being less romantically inclined. She started letting herself go around the house. She was a perfectionist about fixing up if she went out, but at home, she seemed to go out of her way to look less attractive. Maybe it was my imagination, but she seemed to stiffen when I touched her with my stump.

"Other things changed too. It started being all about her career. She started putting in a lot of hours at the PD. For a while, she worked in recruiting. You can imagine how well she did. She was all over the website. They tailored a uniform to fit her just right, and she and a department body builder named Andre were plastered on billboards and mall kiosks. Applications were up and people started asking her to autograph a poster, a magazine ad. Her picture was everywhere. I started feeling a little of what the church ladies felt.

"Then things changed again. She told me that she wanted to be able to spend more time with me, and she wanted to see if she could get on the Vice/Narcotics team. Since we were not married, she was able to talk them into letting her come on the team even though I was already working there. I didn't know how it was going to work. She was such a celebrity she could never work undercover. But I was wrong. She just put on a black wig and heavy makeup, and no one ever recognized her. With how she dressed, for those kinds of assignments, I suspect that the dopers and dealers were never looking at her face.

"Because of our relationship, they put us on separate details. We saw less of each other. When we were all out to eat one day, Pete was making Jodi blush by telling me how they had to quit putting her on the prostitution stings because it wasn't fair to the johns and how the prosecutor was worried about claims of entrapment. He slapped me on the back and told me I was a lucky guy. By that time, I was starting to figure, *lucky*, maybe not so much.

"One day, Jodi got back from a three-day training she had been on and she was upset, but I had no idea why. The next day, while I was working, she moved out – everything. She wouldn't answer my calls. I was one of the last to hear that she and Pete had an affair at that training. Pete himself came and told me. He told me how sorry he was and asked my forgiveness. Pete explained that the next morning, he knew it was wrong, and he told Jodi that it was a mistake and they had to tell me. I guess that is why she moved out, to avoid the drama. Maybe Pete should have been as kind to himself as he was to the poor entrapped johns down on Nevada Avenue.

"I could only wonder how many times she had been in bed with men less honorable than Pete. Pete confessed to his wife, but she wasn't as forgiving as I was. She left with the kids. Three months later, Pete shot himself with his own duty weapon. He did it at the back entrance of the coroner's office. I guess he wanted to make it easy for everyone. Jodi got a job in California, and I'm sure she's a big hit out there." Darrell stopped talking and looked out the window, watching people coming out of the restaurant.

They sat in silence until Callie broke it. "You were rocky soil."

"What?"

"The story that Jesus told about the sower…he sowed his seed. Some fell on rocky soil. You received the word with joy, believed for a while, but had no root, and when trials came…" Callie pushed herself up in her seat and faced him. "Darrell, I'm sorry. There is nothing else I can say except you can't blame God."

"He's guilty by default. If I know someone is going to murder someone, I have a duty to stop it, if I can. And I am sure you'll agree that He can."

"Then why don't you?"

"Don't I what?"

"Stop the murderers – Lock them up, kill them."

"I don't have that kind of power. I don't know who is going to kill someone. All I can do is guess. God knows everything, right?"

"Well let's take something else. You know who the dope dealers are, don't you? So lock them up."

"I told you, I don't have that kind of power."

"Why not? You lock someone up after a trial. If you got enough police together, deputize some citizens, build some more prisons, you could do it."

"Not legally, without that trial."

"Okay, so we aren't talking physical ability, we're talking legal authority. Well, then who makes the laws?"

"Okay, I see where you're going with this, but…"

"Now wait a minute, before we go any further, I want to make sure you do know where I'm going. Do we agree then that even though we have the knowledge and physical ability, we limit ourselves for some reason?"

"I know you're talking about free will – we limit ourselves because we are a free society. And, in the same way, God has given us free will, so He limits Himself for the sake of our free will."

Callie was smiling again. "See, what was so hard about that?"

With Callie's sweet smile beaming up at him, Darrell found it hard to be upset even after dredging up all the dark memories. There was a joy in her that was contagious. He smiled back. "What if I'm a Calvinist and don't believe in free will?"

The smile did not break from her face. "Then you really have no argument, because as a Calvinist you believe that God has perfectly planned and ordained everything from before the beginning of time. So no matter how bad it looks to us, it is what is best and how can we with finite knowledge argue with Omnipotence? Actually, both those views are probably correct, but we as humans can't comprehend how that can be possible. We have to trust Him."

"It's not that easy, Callie."

"Yes, it is. You're confusing being upset at God with having an intellectual argument against what He does. You just need to have a long talk with Him and get this all ironed out."

"Some things don't iron out so easily."

"Well, they sure don't if you don't pick up the iron. But anyway, you better take me home. If I hurry, I can still make it to Wednesday night service. You're welcome to come with me."

"I don't think I'm ready for that."

"Okay. Thanks for saying 'not ready,' instead of 'not ever.' Get some rest then, because we have a big day tomorrow. Shin wants us there bright and early."

Darrell was astounded. "I thought you said it wasn't going to work out."

Callie tipped her head, pressed her lips together and sighed. "Now you're confusing our relationship with my project. Besides, maybe you're not as far gone as you think you are. All you need is to put down some roots."

Darrell sniffed a laugh. "That sounds like a proposal."

Callie cocked her head and gave him a stern gaze. "It is, but it's not coming from me."

On the ride to her house, Callie tried to encourage Darrell about the operation and the training ahead. She forced herself to be upbeat. The pain Darrell had inside needed that. She had to keep him out of depression. God had finally brought him into her life for a reason, of that she was sure.

Practice what you preach, she told herself. *Give God room to work and keep your heart out of the way.*

Darrell dropped her off, and she walked to her front door, by herself, trying not to think about how it felt to hold his arm. She paused on her porch, watching him drive away. Out of the corner of her eye, she saw her mother looking out the window, also watching.

Her mother had been napping when she left. Now Callie was going to have to face the firestorm that Mama was going to unleash on her because a white man had dropped her off. She could almost hear her mother now— "Calnisha Ruth Williams, have you done lost your mind?"

Callie hoped she wouldn't be forced to reveal that Darrell was also a police officer. Her mother had been glued to CNN lately. People were rioting in Ferguson, Missouri because a young black man had been shot by a white officer. White police had become the favorite target of her wrath.

Callie didn't need any more stress. She thought her life was finally changing and the promise she had longed for was finally coming true. She had waited so long – praying, fasting, longing. To have it snatched away from her after just a taste seemed cruel. She had some ironing to do with her Savior as well.

It was prayer service tonight. She could find a corner – a little time with just her and God. She needed to understand maybe a little part of what He was doing – just so she could survive until morning – one day at a time. After praying, she could be around her church family and worship the Lord with them. She would try hard to thank Him for this just as much as she had thanked Him for a dinner date in her office earlier. God knew what He was doing even with her broken heart.

Chapter 11

Darrell recognized the smell – disinfectant, clean cotton, freshly opened medical instruments. It connected in his memory with the scent of blood and gunpowder. It was the aroma of pain.

The sounds of the IV machine, the periodic hum of the blood pressure cuff as it tightened on his arm mingled with the recall of gunshots and explosion. There was something just out of reach of his memory that was playing with his stomach, making him uneasy.

Over the years, there had been times when he could almost remember parts of the event that his brain had buried. Now, back in a medical bed, his subconscious apparently recalled that day. But like a kidnapper keeping his victim locked away, his mind kept the memory prisoner in the backstreet hideout of his lower-level consciousness. Darrell could only hear the captive's muffled screams in the tiny bit of sweat forming on his upper lip and the faint churning of his belly.

"Is this the first time you've been in the hospital since the shooting?" Callie stood near the bed as the nurse prepped it for moving down the hall to the operating room.

"The first time as an inpatient, yeah." She was reading him too well.

"I'm sorry. This won't be incredibly painful. It's just tedious, but they don't have to put you out. Does that make it better or worse?"

"I guess we'll find out. I'm okay."

"Shin won't let me go in with you, but I'll be right out here the whole time."

"Hey, at least you're adding something. I lost something in the last operation and never got it back."

Callie's smile showed concern.

"But there's this girl I know," Darrell put on a look of confidence, "that's trying to change all that, and it's awful nice of her."

Her smile broadened. "Just a temporary replacement until God gives you a whole new body. You just make sure you don't miss that day, okay?"

"Still not saying 'not ever.'"

After bringing in the heavy metal case that held the NIP and dropping it off with Shin, Callie stationed herself in the waiting room. They had decided that the arm would serve as the best protective sleeve for Darrell while he healed. There could be no better protection than the high-tech polymer with which the NIP was made. Since Darrell's stump would "float" inside the NIP, it would be putting less pressure on the healing appendage than conventional sleeves. Plus, it allowed Darrell to get accustomed to the arm immediately.

Callie smoothed the pretty dress she was wearing. She had wondered if it was the right thing, considering the situation. She didn't want to give Darrell false encouragement. She had stood in front of the mirror in the predawn, wrestling with her own motivations. But after praying, what came to her was that it was something that she would have worn anyway since she wasn't working in the lab that day. She was overthinking things.

Sitting in the post-op waiting room, she prayed. She pulled the long sweater that she had worn against the cool morning temperature around her. Because of the lengthy nerve mapping involved, Shin had them arrive just as the sun was coming up. But Callie realized there might be other reasons she felt chilled. The operation was lengthy but not dangerous. Still, she hadn't liked how white Darrell had looked. Maybe she was pushing him toward places he was not ready to go. "Please, Lord," she whispered, "help me not be making a mistake. Forgive me if I am, and please protect Darrell."

Reggae music came from Callie's cell phone. She pulled it out to check the text message. It was from Raji: **We need to talk. Meet me at Famous Flavors Diner.**

Callie heaved a sigh and texted back: **Can't. Need to be sure surgery goes OK.**

After a moment the reply came. **Must insist. You want to hear this. Very important.**

"Oooh." She let the hand holding the phone drop into her lap as she stared at nothing, thinking. *What could he want?* Well, she was hungry. *Better to eat now while the surgery is just starting.* She wanted to be there for sure when it ended.

Ok, be there in a minute.

Perhaps something came up. Now she was getting curious. What could it be that she would want to hear?

Chapter 12

In a different room, though with many of the same smells and sounds, Darrell awoke. His body was tired, but the apprehension was gone. He felt rested, a little sore in his left arm but other than that he was good. The heavy dose of painkillers that Shin had given him when the operation was done had put him out, hard. He wondered how long he had been asleep. The light from the window said it was evening.

Darrell felt disoriented. He forced his mind to remember the last few days timeline to get some mental footing. It would be Thursday night, almost a week had gone by since he met Callie last Friday. It seemed like more and less. His mind had been learning on accelerated BERT time, absorbing weeks' worth of information in a couple of days, but being with Callie had made the time fly. The thought brought back the pain of their dinner conversation.

Darrell tried to move his stump and realized he was wearing the prosthetic. It shocked him. He didn't remember them putting it on. Flexing the new arm, he felt some pain but marveled at the movement. The feeling and sight of the fingers when he wiggled them gave him a strange sensation. He was conscious of moving them, but they still felt alien. Even the training in BERT had not prepared him. He felt a twitch in his chest. Shaking it off he looked around the room for Callie and found Shawn instead, sitting in the chair by the wall, working on his cell phone.

When he saw Darrell move, he stood up and came to the bed. "That looks weird. I finally got used to the hook and now you have fingers. You need to make up your mind if you're going to be a pirate or not – maybe an eyepatch. But right now, we have things to discuss."

Darrell pushed aside the odd feeling. He raised his arms toward the ceiling in a long reaching stretch. "I'm fine, thanks for asking."

Shawn smirked. "Those niceties are for mere mortals, not bionic supermen like yourself."

"I'm not too super yet. So, what's up?"

Grabbing the chair from across the room, Shawn sat beside the bed. "Our killer seems to be on vacation. We have been working on trying to catch up with him before he gets bored."

"And?"

"Here's where we're at. Some of this you already know." Shawn flipped back in his yellow pad. "Not a lot of prints on the enhancement box. What few there were, belong to the family. I've got Christie trying to interview the install people, but, as you know, she had trouble getting information from the company."

Christie had been on the major crimes team for about three years. She was a smooth interviewer, and Darrell felt confident she would work well as the point with a difficult company.

Shawn continued. "It's local, established a couple of years ago, but it's really expanding. She searched the web and I guess they are advertising a lot in some other major hubs around the nation— New York, Chicago, Cleveland, St. Louis and Los Angeles, positioning themselves to grow nationwide, I suspect. Christie has only been able to talk to the main people on the telephone. They travel a lot, setting up the new locations. She said a manager from the company asked her a lot of questions about why she wanted to interview the installation techs, but I guess I would too if I were him. They wouldn't let her talk to the people at their offices because they said they did not want the company's name associated with the investigation, and she would need to work through their attorney."

"That's not very friendly."

"No, but Christie threw your name around a lot and said you were a mean guy and would make her serve a subpoena on them if she couldn't get the information."

"I'm sure they were really impressed."

Shawn shrugged. "Well, actually they seemed to be. You do have a bit of a reputation. They checked their schedules and gave Christie a different installers name for each of our victims. There's no one person we can point to as having been involved in all of them. It's possible this is just a coincidence. I'm sure they must be doing a lot of these installs around town."

Darrell wrinkled his brow, but before he could object, Shawn held up his hand. "I told her to track them down anyway. If nothing else, maybe one of them saw something when he was at one of the houses that might help. I think she has talked to all but two of them and nothing remarkable yet."

Darrell nodded his approval. "How is Carlos coming on the alarm company?"

"The Deepclad Security company was a lot more agreeable. They called in the employees that installed the alarm and let him talk to them right there. Three people worked on our victim's house, the salesman and two installers. They are all bonded and have pretty clean backgrounds. The salesman had a DUI, I think. The installers have nothing to do with the code, and they didn't know anything helpful. The way the code works is the salesman helps them set up an initial code, so he would know that one. The homeowner has the ability to change that code, but Carlos checked and found out the code had never been changed from the one the salesman set up."

"So, he knew the code?"

"Yes, but he was supposedly out of town at a conference for the company on the day of the murders. Carlos is trying to verify that."

"How did he seem to Carlos?"

"Carlos said he seemed fine – appropriately shocked about the murders, helpful and not too nervous."

The news did not dissuade Darrell. "Still, he is the only one with the code, and no one could get in without it. That's a pretty good suspect."

"There may be another person who knew it. The alarm company has the woman's brother listed as a responsible person related to the alarm. That means, if the owners are out of town and an alarm goes off, that person can be contacted and should know the code. That brother is in Taos, New Mexico, making arrangements for their parents to come up for the funeral. They retired down there. He has agreed to come in to talk when he gets back."

"Nothing is ever easy." Darrell shook his head in frustration.

"That's not true. Wasting time, that's easy." Shawn gave a double eyebrow raise for emphasis.

"Umm, no kidding. But I really think we are on the right track here somewhere. There is some connection. We just have to dig it out."

As Darrell finished his statement, Link followed his crooked grin through the door. "How you do'n, Darrellonger?"

"I'm okay. The ole stump hurts a little but not as bad as I expected." His entrance gave Darrell somewhere to direct a question that had been on his mind since he awoke. "Link, where's Callie?"

Link looked around the room in confusion, then back at Darrell and shrugged. "I'm clicked. I thought she'd be here in permanent 'waiting on input loop' until your eyes opened. Raji's been a popup and had me bit clicking on BERT proj for some reason, so I just got here. She wasn't at ATS." Link's fingers flew across the keys on his phone. "There. I sent her a PI." Link rolled his tongue around his cheek, made a popping sound with his mouth and began explaining before he was asked. "A party invitation or a private invitation but it has a double meaning like a private "I" for investigator because they find people. It will set off an alarm on her phone, so she knows we are looking for her."

"Yeah, well I don't mean to be a whiner, but she promised me she was going to be here every minute to fetch and carry and all I have are you two ugly mugs. By the way, Link, meet Shawn. He's a sergeant in the detective bureau and keeps me straight."

Shawn was staring at Link like he was still processing what the kid said.

"Connect up, fellow ugly mug." Link slapped his hand into Shawn's. "Any main of the Darrellarol is good on my contact list."

Darrell frowned. "Link, this isn't like Callie, is it?"

"No way." Link turned his attention back to Darrell. "I can't believe she's not here. The RajiRat hasn't been around either. I got a text from him saying he needed me to be ready for a project demo next week. I've been in batch mode all afternoon trying to get that ready, but I haven't heard from him since. Maybe he's got her breaking bits, too. She might be at her fortress of solitude. She uses her home lab for quiet work."

"I don't think she would put up with not being here. I'm calling her - forget this text stuff. Let me see your phone."

Shaking his head, Link pointed, "Darrellgon you are such a technotard. You have a phone right there on your arm, remember. Power up, dude."

Link smirked at the look on Darrell's face. "Put the hand into silent mode – remember how."

"I do, but it's not a gesture I use regularly. I am always afraid the hand is really going to do it, and I'm going to be offending someone." Darrell willed the NIP to display the middle finger, but nothing happened. He tried to move the hand and it did not respond – so far so good. The arm's computer should still be interpreting the movements he was thinking.

Link's face gave him encouragement. "Now relax and link up. Even though you didn't get as much time in BERT as I wanted, you still should be able to download from the old gray drive." Link tapped his temple. "Don't try to over flex the skull jelly. Let it do its thing. Just ride the circuit."

Darrell had learned that was also the best way to understand what Link was saying. If he concentrated on the words, it was senseless. However, when he relaxed and responded to what it felt like the words were telling him, it seemed to work. The old gray drive just knew.

"If you have to, turn on the screen on the inside of your arm. It will display the steps you are taking so you can tell your invisible movements are being interpreted correctly. But you'll be really prime when you can do it without looking."

When he gazed at the inside of the arm, the screen was barely discernable from the other dark color of the arm. Only the more glossy, reflective quality of the surface revealed where the display was located.

In his mind, Darrell made the combination of keystrokes and gestures to turn on the display. The hand didn't move but the computer responded, and the screen lit up. His efforts faltered for a second until he yielded to Link's advice and relaxed and let it happen. The BERT training took over. He gave Link a see-what-I-did glance. The kid looked down from just below the ceiling and moved his head up and down in silent encouragement while Shawn craned his neck to watch.

The screen displayed Darrell's contact list, and he moved through it until it got to Callie's entry. Pleased with his progress, Darrell made the gesture that told the computer to place the call.

The screen blanked and went red – not the response Darrell anticipated. Dark black letters flashed on the red background – "Self-Destruct in" and a running digital clock appeared below the words, steadily counting down from 10 seconds…9…8…7….

"Link!" Darrell cried out in startled desperation. The long thin face looked back at him in a questioning manner and Darrell speechlessly thrust the screen toward him.

In panic-induced slow motion, Darrell perceived the crooked side of Link's mouth raise first, then the other, in a wide grin. "Gotcha ya, Darrelleen." He used his own phone to cancel the fake screen on Darrell's.

Before he could stop himself, Darrell's real hand slapped the smile away. It was all he could do to make it a slap and not a slug. "Don't do that stuff!"

Darrell had pulled the blow at the last, so the strike was slight, but the shock registered on Link's face, which was frozen, mouth open and slightly to the side where the hit had sent it. For a moment, he blinked his eyes. "Whoa, sorry man. Didn't know you were going to send me a hard copy."

Shawn was leaned back in his chair in a breathless laugh.

With an eye glance sideways at Shawn, Darrell shook his head in good-natured disgust then, nodding, said, "Good one, kid."

Link's smile returned but faded slightly when Darrell added, "Do it again and I'll take this arm off and beat you with it."

Unexpectedly, Callie's voice said, "It's me!" Not since training had Darrell heard the perky recording that she had assigned as her ring tone on the arm's phone.

Darrell smiled. "There she is now. She must have known we were talking about her."

"It's me," the phone rang again.

In the cyber world, Darrell made the invisible gesture that answered it with the speaker phone. "Hey, I thought you were going to be right by my side when I woke up." His tone was lighthearted.

Callie's voice broke in, over the arm's speaker. She spoke rapidly, "Darrell, I don't know what these guys want but they are telling me to talk to you. I think they are..." He then heard sounds of Callie's muffled attempts at continuing becoming more distant and then it sounded like the call was dropped. There were a few clicks, and a male voice came on. "Now y'all know I got yo' woman and that I'm serious and you bedda be listen'n."

Chapter 13

The words and their meaning seeped through Darrell's ears directly to his heart. Something about Callie's voice and the man's tone told him instantly that this was not a joke. Like two hands around his neck, Darrell's thoughts were grabbed by twin realizations - the man was dangerous, and he had the person that mattered most to him. It produced sudden panic. "What's going on. What do you want?"

"Good, I got yo' attention."

Darrell shoved the fear to the back. He was listening intently. He estimated that the man was in his twenties.

"Jus' cuz she black, don't think I won't hurt her. Gunna depend on you."

"Listen." Darrell needed his mind focused. "I don't know anything about Callie's projects. And I'm sure she doesn't have them in her head." Darrell hoped Callie could also hear him and would get the hint to play dumb no matter what she knew. "You are going to have to get her files, and for that, you are going to need her help." Darrell needed to be thinking as much as listening. He could search for clues in every subtle background noise after the conversation was over if he could…He silently locked eyes with Link and mouthed the words "record this."

It took a second for Link to process what he was asking but then his fingers began to fly over his phone.

Darrell addressed the caller. "Whatever she is working on that you want, you'll need a lot more information. So, it won't do you any good if you hurt her."

"Hey man, shut up," the voice used profanity along with the command. "Y'all got no idea what you' talkin' about. Yo' the only one that can help with what I need. So if you wanna keep yo' little friend alive jus' keep ya mouth shut and listen. I've called to solve the murders y'all been investigate'n."

Darrell's mind did the equivalent of a power brake – mental wheels locked, tires smoking. "What?"

"I called to confess. What so hard 'bout that?"

"You don't need Callie to do that."

"I think I do."

"Why?"

"Cause I want you to do sum'pin and I wanna make shor' you do it. You gonna do what I tell you or I'm gonna do sum'pin real bad to this girl! Y'all go ahead, imagine how a body be die'n real slow. Now, I promise ya, I can imagine sum'pin worse. I got lots'a 'perience. But it up to you if that happen o not. Ya listen'n?"

Darrell noticed Link was working frantically on his phone. Surely the kid could figure out a way to record the conversation. He seemed to be able to do everything else on that thing. Darrell needed to keep the man talking so Link had time to at least get something. "What do you want?"

"Now you ask'n the right questions." The voice paused. Darrell heard a paper shuffle. "I want you to call a press conference, and yo' gonna tell 'em that if rich white people wanna stop die'n us black folks gotta stop die'n first. That's why I killed all those whiteys—for the black folks you pigs be kill'n on the streets." (The voice interlaced profanity throughout the tirade.) "I kill'em. Right in their rich houses. Eye fo' eye, pig. For every black life you done took, I kill me a white one. An' they ain't the last. We gotta score to settle and it ain't gonna stop 'til we even. You kill more, I kill more. Tomorrow, yo' gonna call the news and tell them that. First thin' in the morning,"

"My department will never let me do that."

"You ain't gonna ask nobody. You call the news on yo' own. You meet 'em someplace away from the other cops so nobody gonna know 'til the word's out. You don't let noth'n stop ya. You know I got this woman, and you know what I can do."

"I know what you can do, but I believe you're capable of doing something good also. Let Callie go. She's a good person, she's not white, she's not a cop, there's no reason to do anything to her. It's going to look horrible if you hurt her."

"You talkin' and not listnin'. Do I need to go in an look horrible right now…while you talkin'…or you gonna shut up?"

"I'm listening."

"I'm gonna send ya a text with what I wantcha say. You get the news together and ya read it. That's all ya need a do. Once I see it on the news, I'll call you and tell you where to find yo' woman." The tone of the man's voice seemed to be winding down the call.

Darrell looked at Link. "You realize once I do this, my department's going to fire me or suspend me. I won't be able to make any more statements for you."

"That's your problem."

"How do I know I can trust you after that…that you'll let the woman go?"

"You better do it right, cop. Watch your phone for my text."

KENT WYATT

Chapter 14

Darrell tried to continue the call, but it was obvious by the sound of the phone that the man had disconnected. After he had called out to the voice a couple of times just to be sure, Darrell activated the disconnect on his phone and checked the screen to be sure that no one on the phone could hear him. He whirled on Link and said, "Tell me you were able to record some of that."

Link gave him a who-do-you-think-you-are-talking-to scowl. "Of course."

"How much?"

"All of it. The NIP has a continuous loop audio/visual recorder that automatically backs up five minutes when you tell it to save. But it's an irrelevant elephant."

Darrell snapped his impatience at Link. "A what?"

"Irrelevant elephant – it sounds like a big deal but it's probably not important."

Darrell let his fear go on Link. "You want to talk *of course,* well, of course it's important. That recording is our only hope of gaining a clue as to where they have Callie."

Darrell turned his attention to his sergeant. "Shawn, call the cell phone company and have them ping the phone and get us a location. They can probably only give you a mile or so radius or the closest tower, so I'll listen to Link's recording and see if I can hear anything in the background that might be able to narrow it down. We've got to hurry in case they are going to move. I didn't like all the clicks after Callie talked. They might not be in the same location."

Shawn took out his phone and stepped down the hallway to get a better reception.

Link spoke up, addressing Darrell. "You're burning a Hasty Wasty. You don't have to do all that. I got a pin in it."

Darrell continued venting on the kid. "Link, we don't have time for this, speak English. Every second going by is Callie slipping away from us!"

"I know!" Link yelled. "I'm into Cals, too. She's the only solid thing I know. She's like a mother and sister to me all networked together. That's why I am telling you calling the cell masters is a waste of time because you're not slowing down and listening! I already know where she is - at least pretty close anyway."

Anger became elation, bypassing the sheepishness Darrell might have otherwise felt. "Really? Did you have GPS tracking on Callie's phone or something?"

"Again, *of course,* but that's another irrel..." Link focused. "That's not going to do us any good either. He shut it off and even..." Link's eyes fluttered in concentration as he spoke carefully. "...erased the tracking app so I couldn't turn it back on. Whoever he is, he's a guru...I mean...never mind. He also blocked the cell tower info so I couldn't see what tower he was hitting. But I knew what tower my phone was using, on this side, so I knew his phone had to be talking to that tower also. I did a mimic signal through your phone and made his...Callie's phone, think it was the tower talking to it, so it let me in. While he was talking to you, I was talking to Cals's phone. Because he thought he had me blocked at the tower, he must believe his own hashtags and gotten brain swollen because, once I got in, I was able to turn the Wi-Fi back on. Most cell phones are continuously searching for Wi-Fi signals to connect to, so even if they aren't connecting with them, they ping on them and get the site information."

Darrell interjected. "Link, all I really care about right now is where is Callie?"

"Sorry." Link bowed his head and shook his disheveled hair as if scolding himself. "Her phone is pinging on the Wi-Fi of an extended stay hotel out on Newport Road near the airport."

Darrell grabbed the kid by the arms without thinking. "Link, you're a gift from God."

Link smiled, pointing at the prosthetic that gripped his bicep. Darrell removed it and gave his own thin smile as he wiggled the fingers. "Good. I'm going to need those."

The NIP signaled the arrival of a text. Darrell checked it on the NIP screen. It was a more official sounding notice of the man's intent. Darrell read it through in case it contained any obvious clues.

Shawn came back into the room. "Darrell, there's someone that wants to talk to you," A man dressed in casual jeans and a light jacket followed him. The evening was not that cool. Darrell suspected the jacket concealed a duty weapon.

"Special Agent Spencer Brock, FBI," the man said as he offered his ID and a handshake. "Lieutenant Jacobs, right? I was hoping I could talk to you for a minute."

Darrell returned the handshake. "Agent Brock, you either have terrible timing or it's excellent. We're just leaving, and I don't have that minute to spare. However, we are involved with something that's right up your alley if you want to come with us. A girl has been kidnapped and –"

"We know about Ms. Williams."

Darrell was stunned. "How could you possibly know that?"

The agent appeared to expect the question. "Your name and Ms. Williams' have come up in the monitoring of some other persons of interest this morning. We believed there was some concern so we came down from Denver earlier but couldn't find Ms. Williams. Your captain informed us about the medical procedure you were undergoing. The intercept did indicate some threat toward Ms. Williams, so when we couldn't locate her, we obtained a court order to monitor her phone. Unfortunately, that did intrude on the conversation you just had. I apologize for that, but as you said, perhaps the timing is perfect. We want to offer our help. My partner just informed me we were able to get a track on Ms. Williams phone, with a 90% confidence level on the northwest side of town. We've got agents heading in that direction right now to secure the area, and we will have our SWAT team here within the next two hours."

Link expressed his doubts through the face he made. "Sorry man but your elephant won't even swim."

The agent stared at Link. "Excuse me?"

Darrell made a verbal insertion while he smiled Link into silence. "That's just his way of saying…what you're telling us is really important but…we need to hurry. Where was this exact location? Because we thought the call was coming from somewhere else."

"Really?" Darrell did not like the undertone that came with Brock's word. "Where are you getting that information?"

Darrell was calculating. "We have our own computer expert." He didn't look at Link. "It's a source I trust."

Brock's smile faded. "The Bureau has been working these kinds of cases for over seventy-five years, Lieutenant. I understand that Colorado Springs is a progressive department, but I am fairly confident in the FBI's expertise in these circumstances. We work directly with the cell phone companies."

"What was the location that your ping showed?"

The agent scrutinized Darrell. "In the conversation, the man asked you to make a press release. You told me you were in a hurry. What were you planning to do?"

"Something similar to what you are planning, I suspect."

"Okay. So you weren't planning on making a press release because that certainly wouldn't be in the best interest of your department, public safety, or your investigation. "

Darrell had always worked well with federal officers, but he thought Brock might be an exception. "I'm aware of that."

"Did you know this man that called you?"

"No. I don't believe so."

"I understand from people at Ms. Williams's work that you just recently became involved with the project Ms. Williams was working on."

"That's true."

"Never met Ms. Williams before?"

"No, I don't believe so."

Brock fixed his eyes on Darrell for a moment. "You'd know if you had met her before, wouldn't you?"

"Yes…I'm sure I would."

"Did you have dinner with Ms. Williams last night?"

Darrell took a breath. "Yes." He was certain that agent Brock already knew the answer.

"Was that a professional meeting or social?"

Darrell felt his jaw tightening. "Social. Ms. Williams and I developed a rapport rather quickly. But there were some obstacles, and we discussed the situation, and it was mutually decided that a relationship would not be a good idea at this time."

Link's head turned in Darrell's direction, but Darrell did not attempt to get a look at his expression.

Agent Brock was concentrating on Darrell. "Did that make you angry?"

Darrell lowered his head and took another long breath. "Agent Brock, I appreciate you investigating Ms. Williams's disappearance. I understand there are many questions you will have for me, but right now, I think it's more important that we locate Callie than to get bogged down with this questioning."

Brock raised his head when Darrell used Callie's first name. "I'm sorry this is frustrating you. We have other people that are handling that part of the investigation. Forgive me if I'm speaking out of turn, but you need to step back from this. Ms. Williams seems to be more to you than just a kidnap victim, and things like that can lead to mistakes."

"Or it can lead to a proper respect for the danger to an innocent woman." Darrell was sorry he said it.

"I don't appreciate that, Lieutenant. We have the highest concern for Ms. Williams's safety. We're already coordinating with your department, and they have accepted our assistance. I certainly am sorry for what you're going through. But you need to let us handle this to keep you from facing any conflict of interest. At this point, all we know is your name was mentioned in the same communication as a threatening message concerning Ms. Williams, and now she's missing. You have to admit, that was a rather strange call you just got. I believe you are aware that Ms. Williams is a contributor to defense contracts. We are facing national security issues as well as the danger to Ms. Williams. Objectivity and precision are going to be a must if we hope to resolve this situation successfully."

Darrell tried hard to hide the anger Brock's statement provoked. "What do you want me to do?"

"Just rest. You just went through an operation. Also, since your name was mentioned in the intel that we have, it would be safer if you did not leave here. As a matter of fact, my partner and I have been told to stay here as a precaution."

Darrell did not even care what they might suspect him of. All he wanted was to get Brock out of the room. His involvement had become a liability. "Okay, well I guess this is where I'll be then. But you will let me know when Callie is safe, won't you?"

Brock's relief at avoiding a further confrontation was apparent. "Absolutely. I do have a few more questions for you, while I'm here."

Darrell put on an exhausted, sleepy expression. "I'm sorry, Agent Brock, it's going to have to wait. I'm not feeling well after that operation, and I'm still a little under the influence of the anesthesia. I'm afraid I'd fall asleep on you and not give very reliable information. Perhaps in the morning."

Brock put down the note pad he had taken out. "I see. As you mentioned, a woman's life is at stake. You seemed eager to be a part of this a little bit ago."

"Yeah, I think I was a little over eager. I think the suddenness of all this is hitting me. I am feeling a little sick. Forgive me if I have to bow out until I come out from under this a little more. I'll rest and give you a call."

The agent's dark eyes inspected Darrell's face. "Well then, I'll get out of your hair and let you rest up." Brock gave a final smile. After another happy-to-meet-you handshake for everyone except Darrell, he walked away. Shawn saw him to the door and closed it once he was down the hall.

Chapter 15

"What's up with the difference in location?" Darrell questioned Link when the agent was gone. "Who's right?"

Link shrugged, "I'm going with the only one here guru enough to talk to Cals's phone instead of calling the cell masters. The Brocklehead didn't seem too wired on the techno. He just had the cell masters ping the phone. This hacker's inline enough to keep me out…almost." Link grinned and raised his eyebrows. "It wouldn't be hard for him to hack the cell code and spice the location info. Did you audio in what Brock said? The ping hit was on the other side of town from the Wi-Fi. One of those has got to be digited. If you can hack one, why not hack both? I'm processing that they had an out-of-memory moment on hiding the Wi-Fi and that location's real. They underestimated me. Happens a lot."

"Makes sense to me. I think. What you mean is that they faked the ping to the cell phone company but forgot about the Wi-Fi. So, we still have the upper hand. Let's get moving."

"Wait a minute," Shawn said, mouth open, shaking his head. "We can't go do this alone, and Brock is right—you certainly shouldn't be trying to hit the streets right after an operation."

Darrell was getting his jeans out of the closet and pulling them on. "We don't have time to wait. You heard how long it is going to take them to get a team in here. Besides I don't want Brock to go anywhere near the other location. He doesn't take it seriously enough. We're twenty minutes away from the Newport area, and we're going to get there in ten."

Shawn continued his complaint, glancing up at the tall kid. "Link, now that you have a connection, can't you follow where they go?"

"Sure, the phone still thinks I'm the tower. I can get us as close as the nearest Wi-Fi. The hotel's signal is really weak, so I am guessing they're not in the hotel, but they're close by."

Darrell made a frustrated sound. "More complications. We need to get there quick."

Shawn followed Darrell, his hands out in a pleading gesture. "Let Link keep tracking them, and I'll call the Chief. We can get some guys there and make sure nothing happens until our TEU team can get staged."

Darrell gave Shawn an exasperated look. "We have no guarantee that they will keep her alive that long. They also might move her and leave her phone behind. You heard what Brock said. The Bureau is taking over. The Chief is a good man, but he would have to err on the side of caution. I'll need to give him more than I have right now in order for him to help. Besides I can't wait on the decision-making machine. The Feds are already heading to the other location, and I'm starting to get the feeling that's exactly what our kidnappers want them to do."

Turning to Link, Darrell held forth the shirt in his hand. "What am I supposed to wear? The arm won't fit in my shirt sleeve."

"Oh, here. Callie had some shirts made with Velcro and no sleeve on that side." Link pulled a duffle bag from the bottom of the closet and slid it to Darrell.

Without even thinking, Darrell jammed the fingers of the arm down to hold the edge of the bag against the floor, as he would have done with his hook. He winced in pain with the impact. Tears came to his eyes, but he shook it off and jerked the zipper open with his real hand.

Link shook his head. "Darrell, remember, you've got fingers on your hardware list again." The kid wiggled his own.

Darrell grabbed what looked to be a black T-shirt and kick-slid the bag back at Link. "I'll put it on in the elevator."

Shawn scowled as he made his way to the door. "Okay, you're the boss. But I don't like it, and I doubt if the staff is going to like it either, so just remember whose idea it was if something goes wrong."

Darrell stopped so suddenly Link almost ran into the back of him. "We can't go. Brock will be watching. He everything but told me that I was on house arrest. If I leave here, he'll be on the phone, and I'll be getting a call from the Chief before I'm ready."

"So, what's our program?" There was desperation in Link's voice. "You said they might kill Cals."

Darrell didn't answer. He was forming an idea. After a moment, he looked at Shawn. "You're right. There is no way I should be leaving this hospital right after an operation."

Chapter 16

Callie twisted in vain against the duct tape that bound her wrists and ankles. It was cutting off her circulation, causing her hands to throb with each rapid beat of her heart. Since she had been grabbed and thrown in the van outside the restaurant where she had gone to meet Raji, she had been roughly handled, right up to the point when they tossed her into the room where she now lay. No one had wasted time hurting her unnecessarily. They had just shown her no more consideration than they showed the stacks of old tarps that shared her makeshift cell.

She had known terror before. She had been younger and more susceptible to fear, but what happened to her then felt more understandable in a way—like animals attacking her, acting on instinct with little thought to what they were doing.

She discerned the difference in her current situation. These men had purpose, and they were committed to whatever plan they had, a plan that involved her, and she had no doubt they would do to her whatever would serve that end. She had to distract her mind from thinking about what end that might be.

She had always listened when the government people came in and gave security briefings at ATS. She knew that because her team worked on military contracts, there was some danger. They had mentioned the possibility of kidnappings and urged them to be alert and report suspicious activity.

Why hadn't she stopped to think how strange it was for Raji to want to meet her at a restaurant? He would have called her to his office. How could she have been so stupid? Callie clenched her facial muscles in agony at the memory. She had too many distractions, too much on her mind.

She admonished herself to focus and decide what she needed to do next. The FBI had given all ATS employees a self-defense course. The female agent that taught the women stressed looking for opportunities to disable the bad guys and escape. The agent spoke of how such people would not be merciful. She had made it clear that the government could not concede to any demands made by kidnappers. They would do everything they could to rescue her, but in the end, survival was up to her if she ever found herself in such a situation.

But Callie had felt the strength of the men who had grabbed her. Her leg ached, reminding her of the consequences of her attempts at fighting back. The only affect her kick had on the huge dark-skinned man, black freckles covering his cheeks, was a quick reaction. He had not seemed particularly angry when he kicked her back. But the blow had sent a clear message that they would hurt her if necessary. The only advice from the security training that seemed applicable was to remain calm and think. Her initial panic had subsided into basic fear, so at least she was thinking again, even if her mind was racing.

She couldn't understand who the people were and what they wanted. The man that demanded the code to her cell phone as they drove out of the parking lot of the restaurant seemed to be the leader. He scared her the most. His manner conveyed an evil she had not known before. She had given the code because she knew there was no compromising information on it, and she believed the freckled man would cut off her finger, just as the leader told him to do.

The scary man had not spent long with her phone and then put it in his pocket. She guessed that he disabled the tracking program. He did not seem interested in anything else that might be on it. They said nothing else to her directly and asked her no questions. The tape they had slapped over her mouth the moment they had snatched her up had been removed briefly when they told her to speak to her "lover, Jacobs."

Why had they said that? What did they mean when they said she needed to convince him to cooperate with them and everything would be all right? They must have seen her with Darrell on their *date* and assumed it was something more. They must have been watching them.

In the dark of the room, Callie tried to think of anything that she could do. Sudden and clear, one word came to her – *pray*. The fear had been overwhelming her thoughts. She knew the word had not come from her own mind. *Lord, forgive me for not thinking of You first. Thank You that I am still alive.*

As she lay on her left side, arms bound behind her back, she had no way to stop the tears as they began to leak out the corners of her eyes. She blinked as drops ran from her right eye into her left. Callie tried her best to wipe her cheeks on the shoulders of her sweater, but she feared she might knock off her glasses. She didn't know why she had been allowed to keep them. She thought the freckled man was going to take them, but then he seemed to change his mind. So that was the next thing for which she thanked God.

Then emotion invaded her thoughts again. She rolled onto her back, looking up to heaven. *Why is this happening?* The cry from her heart came out as a muffled whimper that reminded her that the tape over her mouth prevented her from crying aloud. She sobbed until the tears were gone. At some point, she had rolled back onto her side because her nose was also dripping with the tears and making it hard to breathe with her mouth covered. She breathed in quickly several times to replenish her oxygen. Then she took a long slow cleansing breath. *I'm sorry,* she began again, *for not being stronger. I don't know what's going on.*

An idea rolled around in her mind for a moment before it came out in her prayer. *But You do.* She remembered the Psalm: "When I am afraid, I will put my trust in You." *There is nothing about what's happening that You do not control. I don't know why You are allowing it to happen…but I know You can help me. Please get me out of this.*

Another thought came from somewhere outside of her—*Darrell is coming.* He had saved her before. The thought brought hope alive.

Immediately doubts tried to overwhelm the idea. How was he coming? How would he even know where she was? She began to calculate the situation. If the man had disabled the tracking program on her phone, which she was sure he had, how could anyone find her, let alone help her? Ever since that day they first met (which Darrell obviously did not remember), Darrell had always held a higher place in her mind than anyone else, but now in the dark, she had to face the truth of the situation. *Darrell is just a man.*

Darrell. Callie felt a little deceptive for not telling him that she knew about the other woman. She couldn't tell him about that without telling him about them meeting before and the circumstances. She just didn't think he was ready for that. It would seem like she was trying to…maybe it would never be important.

She remembered the first time she had seen the woman with Darrell. Callie had made her way through the crowd, finally confident enough to talk to him…her hero. She even remembered what she had worn. She had compromised a little on her modest style of dress, just to look her best for him. If God wanted them to be together, perhaps He would allow her that little leeway, she thought. She had thought a lot of things back then. She had thought that since Darrell had lost his hand, perhaps he would need someone…someone like her. While she was still some distance away, she saw them. The woman soaking in the limelight on Darrell's arm looked like a model from a fitness magazine. Darrell wouldn't need Callie.

Callie had seen "the other woman" as Darrell called her. It led Callie to walk away and not look back. Lieutenant Jacobs was lost to her. He belonged to another. It rocked her faith—in Darrell, in herself, in God. She had taken her father's death better than that day.

For a while, she thought maybe the other woman was God's punishment because of her compromise. She had come to know the Lord better than that since then. But at the time, she was angry.

What had Mrs. Fairchild told her? "Sometimes God lets our hurt become anger, so it will be loud enough for those outside of Heaven to hear." Mrs. Fairchild had heard that cry, and God had used the saintly old woman to help her through. Yes, God used "just people" all the time.

Mrs. Fairchild had also taught her that nothing on earth was worth compromising something Heavenly—not even someone special like Darrell.

Callie took another deep breath. The darkness of the room concealed the softness that crept into her eyes from all but One. *You even turned my anger at You into something good. You can get me through this. But, Lord, if Darrell is coming, please protect him. He's angry and lost just like I was. Have mercy on him just like You did on me. Please keep him safe. You know how much I can take, but Father, I am begging You. I would rather You just let me die than to make me have to go through Darrell's death.*

Callie let her praying change to listening. After a while, it turned to something else.

Arash was sure he heard something as he walked down the hall. He listened, turning a black freckled cheek toward the room where he had thrown the woman. He eased to the door and focused. After a moment, he identified the sound. Even with her mouth taped, she was humming a tune. It was upbeat and lively. After a moment, Arash recognized it as the song that the Arrow had come across as he was going through the woman's cell phone. He remembered the English words to the music the woman hummed with her mouth taped and hands bound, and it astounded him. *Anyway it goes, my soul, be happy anyway.*

Chapter 17

Darrell peered around the pillar of a covered entrance on the east side of the medical building. He flexed and wiggled the fingers on his new arm, grimacing occasionally from a twinge of pain. He made the movements behind the cover of the duffle bag that he had on his left side. He had placed the strap over his head, so the bag was pulled up high to conceal most of the NIP. It was dark, and in low lighting, a person would probably attribute the bulkiness of the arm to loose clothing. Link had shown him how to put the arm's lasers into standby mode so they would not be seen in the dark.

As he exercised his ability to control his new cybernetic appendage, his focus was on the far south end of the parking lot. He had no view of the back parking lot where he and Shawn had left their unmarked cars, but that was not what he was interested in. He had his attention on the dark SUV that was parked not far from the only vehicle exit out of the parking area of the facility. They were watching all right.

Darrell noted that the dark vehicle was backed into the stall so anyone inside would have a forward view of the building and most of the parking lot. Thankfully, they had ignored Link when he left in his vehicle.

Darrell could hear Link breathing in the earpiece over the open cell phone line they were maintaining. He could tell by the speed and depth of the kid's breaths that he was nervous. Darrell stopped his flexing, put the arm into Cmode and sent Link a text: **Still no sign of anyone behind you?**

After a moment, he heard Link's breath pause as he was obviously listening to the text to speech conversion of Darrell's message.

"Not so far." The kid's response came through the Bluetooth headset in Darrell's ear just as if Darrell had spoken to him directly. "I did just what you told me and turned onto Acacia Drive and drove slow to see if anyone turned with me. I took all the turns you told me to take, and I don't see anyone behind me. I am just turning onto Cragwood now."

Okay, stay down the street from the cul-de-sac until I get up there. Cragwood dead ends right behind the medical complex so you'll stick out like a sore thumb to anyone in the parking lot if you drive to

the end.

Darrell was counting on most of the FBI resources heading to where Brock had pinged the cell phone, leaving only Brock and his partner to watch the med complex. Good surveillance took a lot of people, Darrell knew. When there were too many things happening at once and not enough people to cover it all, the possibility of mistakes became greater. Darrell was hoping to trigger such a mistake in a few minutes.

While he waited, his mind ran through question after question: Who had taken Callie and for what real purpose? What connection did they have with the series of seemingly random murders? Callie's kidnapping and the bizarre demands the man had made would also take that investigation in a whole different direction. *What have we stumbled onto?*

But all of those concerns were not for the moment. Right now, he had to focus on Callie and how to get her back. *If it's not too late already* – he pushed the thought from his mind.

He knew what correct police procedure would be in such a circumstance. But Darrell was convinced that the man he had heard on the other end of the line had no intention of ever releasing Callie. A man like that would kill Callie sooner or later.

Link's ability to pinpoint Callie's location so quickly had presented a rare opportunity that he feared would be lost in preparation for doing things the correct way. He knew his supervisors could never support what he was planning, and he wouldn't blame them. In the light of officer safety and tactics, he couldn't support it either. Which was why Darrell was not going to ask permission for what he was going to do. It was Callie's life in jeopardy, and he wasn't going to miss the only chance to save her.

Darrell's thoughts were interrupted as Shawn's car came around the side of the building.

Okay, Shawn is in sight now and getting ready to leave the lot, he informed Link.

Shawn was driving quickly, just as they had discussed. Passing by just one row over from the SUV, he was making it look like he was on a mission. Darrell could picture what was going on inside the surveillance vehicle. Brock would be wondering where Shawn could be going in such a hurry. Shawn's vehicle sped toward the outlet onto Union Blvd. They would be scrambling to make a decision. Should they follow him or keep watching the surgery center? Darrell was counting on them doing do the same thing he would do.

As Shawn's car turned out onto the street and headed south, the SUV began to roll forward without headlights – it was working. It moved slowly toward the exit, timing it so that they came out onto Union just after Shawn vanished around the corner. The SUV's headlights came on, and a moment later they also rounded the corner and were gone.

They took the bait. Now it would be up to Shawn to lead them on a lengthy drive around town.

"Great! Just like you said." Link's voice betrayed his excitement.

So far so good. But Darrell knew he had very little time. If he were in Brock's place, he knew what he would be doing right now. He would be bringing up another unit from somewhere to replace him and make sure Darrell did not leave also. He had bought himself a narrow window of time. But he knew he could not leave yet because Brock had his number, and he would also call…The arm's incoming call beep went off in his ear with such perfect timing that it gave him a start. He quickly stepped back inside the Surgery Center so there would be no wind or traffic noise. He spoke to Link over the phone instead of using the text feature. No one was around and he did not want to take the time to type. "Okay, he's calling. Pray our little magic trick works. We need him to think it is more important to follow Shawn than to come back to the lot." The phone beeped again. He carefully went through the steps that Link had shown him to start the playback of the recording they had made in the hospital room. Another beep. Over the NIP's speaker came the sounds of IV machine and monitors. Darrell let the phone beep one more time then put Link on hold and answered it in his best drugged sleepy voice. "Yeah?"

"Darrell. This is Spencer Brock. Where is Shawn going?"

"What?" Darrell forced his voice to sound confused.

"Shawn just left the clinic in a hurry. Where is he going? Is everything okay?"

"Listen, I'm sorry," Darrell put a little sound of irritation in his voice. "I fell asleep. I didn't know he left. The doctor gave me extra medication so I could sleep. Maybe Shawn got called home or something." Just for effect, he added, "Have you heard anything about Callie?"

"No, nothing yet." Brock seemed to be buying it. "Could I get Shawn's phone number from you?"

Darrell paused for just a moment to continue the effect of not thinking clearly then he recited the number to Brock. The agent gave him a quick courtesy "thank you" and got off the phone. Darrell disconnected the call and brought Link back online as he hurried to the door. He quickly scanned the parking lot and the street. He looked for movement and new vehicles, with or without headlights. It looked clear, but he had no idea from where they might be bringing another surveillance unit. He hurried out the door and headed north across the parking lot.

"I'm leaving the hospital now and should be up on top in a few minutes."

"Okay." An undercurrent of exhilaration laced Link's voice.

The medical complex had been cut into a hillside with a residential cul-de-sac on another tier above it. Link was supposed to meet him there. The builders had created a high stone wall behind the complex that was probably intended to prevent erosion and add to the aesthetics of the parking lot. Climbing that would be difficult at the least and very suspicious. Darrell headed toward the sidewalk that came down the hill, following the road, and met the parking lot. Starting where it was level with the parking lot, the sidewalk was bordered on one side by a see-through metal fence to keep pedestrians from falling over the drop off that increased as the sidewalk followed the incline and on the other by a three-foot concrete barrier to protect them from the traffic coming down the off ramp.

As he skirted around the metal fencing, he used the opportunity to again scan the area. There were a few vehicles moving on the street. Any one of them could be the next surveillance team. He kept his head down to conceal his face, but none seemed to have any interest in him or the complex. At least he was out on the sidewalk where he would be hard to distinguish from any other pedestrian. He pulled the duffle up higher to conceal the NIP.

Darrell was halfway up the rise of sidewalk that was taking him to the higher cul-de-sac. He set a brisk pace, wanting to sprint, but he knew that would draw even more attention to himself. If any of the vehicles coming down the off ramp was another surveillance unit, his only chance was for them to think he was a college student heading to the UCCS dorms at the top of the hill.

He was sure they would have sent a new unit as soon as the other one left to follow Shawn. That had been almost ten minutes ago. He figured it would take no longer than twenty to thirty minutes for the other vehicle to get there. Even less if they were…Darrell saw a flash of light across the asphalt at the far end of the parking lot. The light raced quickly up onto the grassy slope and lit up the retaining wall behind the complex. He knew instantly that it was the lights from a vehicle coming into the entrance of the surgery center. At that hour it couldn't be anyone but the new unit.

Chapter 18

Darrell could not see the vehicle because the building was between him and the source of the headlights. The lights shifted and were gone. In a second, they reappeared reflecting off the asphalt on the northeast side of the building. Darrell could just make out the crunching of tires as they encountered small pebbles on hard asphalt– the vehicle was still moving through the lot. They must be coming up the other side of the building instead of taking the position the other unit had maintained. Darrell began to hurry up the sloping walkway as he tried to think what the people in the vehicle might be up to. Then he realized… "Link," Darrell kept his voice low. "They're here, they're checking the parking lot."

"Rodents!" came the reply in his earpiece. "What's our program sequence?"

"Just be ready. I'm about halfway up the ramp. Definitely don't come to the end of Cragwood. They'll see you. I'll have to walk down to your location once I get up there. If I stay on the other side of the cul-de-sac, they shouldn't see me from down in the parking lot."

"Okay."

The long, thin building was circled by parking spaces on all sides. The car was on the long side, but they would soon come around the building and head down the thin side toward the back lot. When that happened, they would be facing directly toward where Darrell was walking. He would be elevated above the lot, but these people were suspicious already. They were searching, probably with orders to make sure Darrell didn't leave the building. At this distance, he would be right in their line of sight. Occasional headlights from the traffic coming off Austin Bluffs illuminated him. The moment the vehicle came around the building, he would be on display. Darrell ran.

"Darrell, what's going on?" Link apparently heard him puffing into the phone.

Darrell had no breath or time to spare for the conversation. The sidewalk curved around the parking lot as it rose up the hill. If he could make it a little farther, the angle of the medical complex combined with the way the sidewalk curved would give him a few more seconds of cover. He glanced back. The nose of the car pushed out from around the building. Sprinting, he put the complex between him and the vehicle again.

Periodic glances on the run showed the car's lights washing across the area of retaining wall where he had just been, travelling his way but maintaining the same speed. The car was now on the thin side of the complex and Darrell knew it would not have far to go before it had a full view of the back lot and of him. He was running out of cover and running out of wind from the uphill sprint.

The surgery and medication had taken the fire out of Darrell. The landscape made a dizzy dance in his head. He felt like vomiting. Stumbling, Darrell grabbed the fence beside him to keep from falling. A feverish heat on his face told him he was in danger of passing out. "Please God. I need to get to Callie."

"Darrell, you all right?" The impulsive whisper must have reached Link whose voice was combined with engine noise like he was driving.

Through blurring eyes, Darrell watched as the glow of headlights grew brighter at the corner of the building. The front of the surveillance car came into view.

Darrell pushed off the fence, grabbed onto the concrete barrier and rolled over it onto the narrow two-lane roadway, pulling the duffle with him. Headlights immediately blinded him as he hit the pavement. Tires squealed and he was buffeted by the wind of a vehicle as it passed within a few feet. Tiny bits of gravel pelted him as his heart took a pause to evaluate if there was any reason to keep beating.

The car didn't stop. Darrell prayed the driver wasn't on a cell phone to 911 about a crazy guy that jumped onto the roadway. The barrier sat right on the edge of the street, leaving no space for him to get out of traffic. Resting against the concrete divider, Darrell let the dizziness subside. He had no choice but to stay in the roadway. If he moved the surveillance car might see him.

"Darrell, key in some input. What's going on? I'm freaking up here. I'm coming to get you." Link's car revved in the background of the call.

Pulling the Bluetooth from his ear, Darrell strained to follow the crunching sound of the surveillance vehicle's tires in the parking lot below. They either did not hear the squealing or had passed it off as a reckless driver.

Darrell couldn't risk a verbal conversation with Link. Concentrating on the NIP, he sent a Cmode message. **Don't move, they're in the parking lot just below the cul-de-sac. They'll see you.**

Darrell had to get going again. The dizziness and nausea returned as he bent over. How was he going to help Callie if he kept getting sick? Every minute was time running out for her. Crouching low behind the barrier, he moved up the off ramp.

As he collected himself for the next push forward, he heard one of the men below call out, "I'm sure it's his car and the engine's cold. Have Brock call to make sure he's still in the building."

So they had made it to his car. Darrell was reluctant to risk movement. If the man was outside his vehicle, he might hear it.

A car came down the off ramp in the far lane. Taking advantage of the noise, Darrell advanced about 15 feet then he froze again. He waited, listening. Nothing. He'd have to risk it. Fighting the nausea, he pressed forward, keeping each movement as quiet as he could.

Headlights blinded him. Squeezing his eyes shut, he pulled himself against the barrier. This time the vehicle laid on its horn as it raced by.

It was over, he was sure of that. There was no way the men had not heard the horn. He might be able to make a break for it and get Link to pick him up, but the men would certainly know it was him. Getting in a pursuit with the FBI would do no good. Even if he could lose them, just getting away was useless. They had to believe he was still at the complex for his plan to work.

"God, please! I just need a little help for Callie's sake." Darrell plotted what to do. He would call Carlos and wake him up. While he stalled the men, Carlos could get on the phone and put a team together to try to rescue Callie. Link could show them where Callie's phone had called from and hope she was still with it when they got there. He knew the whole thing was going to take forever, if Carlos would even do it. He had no idea how he and Shawn were going to stall that long but that was the only thing left to do.

He disconnected the phone with Link so he could call Carlos. When he put the earpiece back in, it was dead. He must have turned it off somehow when he pulled it out. He had never used Bluetooth before the crash course Link had given him. In the dim light, he tried to get the device going as seconds clicked by.

Headlights were in his eyes again as another car came barreling off the street above. He pulled back against the barrier, but the car was not turning. It was heading for him as if it knew he was there and was going to smear him along the concrete divider. It was too late for him to do anything but turn away from the lights.

The car braked to a stop. Darrell glanced toward the heat coming off the engine. The vehicle rocked from movement inside, and the passenger door came open, almost hitting him. It took a second for Darrell to perceive Link's wide-eyed face staring at him.

The kid pulled his long frame from the car, easily stepped over the barrier, and addressed the men below. "Sorry, didn't want to get out on the other side and have someone hit me. Hey, have you guys seen a dog running around here?"

The door of the car was wide open. Darrell took the hint and, staying low behind the barrier, crawled toward the opening.

"No," one of the men responded to Link's question. "But a car was honking at something up there. It might have been trying to get across the road."

Darrell pushed the duffle bag inside and was just getting ready to slide onto the floorboard when a loud ringing came from the NIP. With the Bluetooth off, the default ringtone was coming over the speaker again. Brock was calling and he didn't dare answer it. He fumbled the finger manipulations to silence the phone. It rang again. He knew the sound was carrying down to the men below. Link had stiffened.

It rang one more time before Darrell got it silenced. Link broke his shocked pose and pulled his own phone from his pocket and made a show like he pushed a button on it. He called out to the men, "That's my sister. It's her dog and I'm not answering that until I find him. Thanks for your help."

Darrell had used the moment to pour himself onto the passenger floor.

Link slammed the door and ran around to the driver's side yelling to the men, "No one's coming, so I'll risk it." He jumped in and sped off down the road.

Darrell would have laughed if he had any humor left. "Where did you come from?"

"It didn't sound like you were going to make it to the cul-de-sac. So I backtracked and went up the hill to where I could get on Austin Bluffs and make it down to you."

"Good job. Great thinking on the dog thing."

"Hey, that's real world. We are always looking for my sister's glitched up mutt." The kid grinned at Darrell. "Was that FBI Brockbuster calling again?"

Darrell examined the screen on the inside arm of the NIP. "Yeah."

"What are you going to do?"

"Find a quiet spot and pull over. By now, Shawn should have given them the speech we planned. They have nothing on Shawn to hold him, so they have to take his word. Now we just have to convince Brock I am still at the surgery center."

Once they were in a deserted parking lot, Darrell had Link kill the engine and he started the recording of the hospital sounds again. He called

Brock who picked up on the first ring. "Darrell, is everything okay?" His mock sympathy was thinly disguised. "Why didn't you answer the phone?"

"Sorry, the doctor was in here. I'm not doing well. I'm sick. They think I'm having a rejection of the new implant they put in." Darrell turned the interrogation back on Brock, hoping to break his momentum, "Were you calling about Callie?"

"Well…no. It's too soon to know anything yet."

Darrell went on before the man could say more. "Did you get ahold of Shawn?"

Brock hesitated for a second. "Yes."

"What did he say?"

"He said he was just tired and wanted to get home quickly."

"Oh, good. At least nothing else is wrong." Darrell needed to end the call and get moving. "Look, I need to let you go. I'm not feeling well. The doctor is going to keep monitoring me tonight. It's probably the stress of everything that's going on. He said if I can get some rest, things will probably be all right. They just gave me some meds to get me to sleep so I'm not sure I will hear the phone. Keep trying if you have something on Callie. I want to know when she's all right."

"Okay…uh…forgive me. I'll let you go." Brock ended the call.

Darrell threw open his door. "Link switch places with me. We've got to get there fast."

Chapter 19

The men were talking loud enough for Callie to hear them, but they were speaking in a foreign language. She had no idea what they were talking about. Math and science were her thing, languages weren't. All she could tell was that they were excited about something. She could also hear a television. She wondered if they were watching some type of televised prize fight or sporting event. The tone, volume, and cadence of their activities seemed to transcend language. Whatever was going on seemed to have brought on a celebration.

The cheering went on for a few minutes, then a voice spoke over the noise. Callie shivered. It sounded like the man that had demanded her cell phone code. It was hard to distinguish individual voices because of the accents, but her fear knew.

The man spoke for a while, and then there was more cheering. Eventually, there was the sound of the voices dispersing, and the work noises resumed.

Callie decided they were loading trucks. She heard the large overhead doors opening and noises that reminded her of when she had to stop beside a semi-truck at an intersection – loud deep engine noise, squeaking and hissing of air brakes, and thunking of large transmission gears. Men called to each other, and she heard things being carried, pushed or dragged. It went on for a while. Then she heard the truck leave. Next the doors would close.

She had heard it happen twice, so she surmised that they had loaded two trucks and were working on a third. Each time a truck left, it seemed she heard fewer voices than before. She guessed that people were leaving on the trucks.

Callie sat with her back against the wall. She had spent over half an hour praying and singing to the Lord. The praise songs helped her grab onto something familiar and firm. She had continued until she felt the impression to get up and see what she could do.

The only time the lights came on was when Freckles entered the room to check on Callie. In between, her eyes became accustomed to the dark, and she was able to see some of her surroundings from the light coming around the door.

She had wriggled her way to the wall and finally got into a sitting position. From there, she had been able to slide up the wall and stand. She even hopped around a little. The hopping was noisy, and she feared it might bring Freckles to investigate.

The room was empty except for several piles of old tarps. Despite the dirty feel of the rugged canvas material, she made one of the two-foot-high piles her perch to give her aching body a little relief from the hard floor.

Freckles had peeked in on her just before the celebration. When he saw that she had sat up, he didn't seem to care. Walking to her, he pushed her head down bending her forward at the waist so that he could check to see that her hands were still taped together behind her back. The maneuver had pushed her head against her knees, forcing her legs out straight and putting her face almost to the floor. It had given her an idea. Callie had always been flexible. She had tried to slip her hands to her front, but she was not built for doing that. The new idea, though, it might work.

So far, Freckles had not checked on her while the loading was going on. She should have a good deal of unobserved time to try her new strategy. Callie pulled the heels of her shoes against the floor until she got one shoe off and then the other. With her toes, she pulled off her socks. Then she spread her knees apart and bent forward at the waist until her face was to her feet. Callie raked the pretty painted toenail of her big toe across her cheek until it caught on the edge of the tape that covered her mouth. The moisture from her tears had helped loosen the adhesive. She hooked and rubbed the tape until she finally had about an inch of one corner loose from her face, then leaned back and rested for a moment.

She leaned forward again. This time she got her big toe under the sticky side of the tape and her second toe on the other side and squeezed and curled her toes in as tight a grip on the tape as she could get. She eased at the adhesive. She pulled another three inches from her face when her grip slipped. Callie sat back in frustration.

After a short break, she bent forward again. This time, with the longer piece of tape sticking out, she got a better grip with her toes. She brought her other foot across and reinforced the hold she had. Jerking her head up quickly, she tore the tape from her cheeks.

"Praise God," she breathed out.

Callie took a moment to just enjoy breathing fully. For the sheer pleasure of being able to do it, she opened her mouth wide like she was doing facial toning exercises. *Just because a girl has been kidnapped and bound with duct tape doesn't mean she can let her appearance go.* Callie indulged in a whispered giggle.

She stopped. Was she losing it? *You don't know how much time you have; don't waste it.*

If Freckles came back, she wondered what he would do to her if her mouth was un-taped. She decided not to think about it.

Bending at the waist again, she chewed at the tape that was around her ankles. She had managed to bite chunks off the edge of the tape and pull loose some strands when she had to sit up to catch her breath.

Everyone was apparently out at one of the trucks. With the area quiet, she could hear the television better. It was not a prize fight; it was the news. Callie could hear a reporter talking about the rioting that was going on somewhere.

She had already decided that the group that had her were terrorists. No wonder they were celebrating. There had been so many police shootings lately that had resulted in riots. The United States tearing itself apart was great sport for its enemies.

Callie wondered what type of terror the group planned on unleashing on her country's own soil. She did not know if they were loading guns, explosives, chemicals, or all of it. Whatever they had planned, with the amount they were moving out of the building, it must be something big.

She stared down at the frayed edge she had pulled loose on the gray band encircling her ankles. If she did get her feet free, what would she have accomplished? She didn't know, but she decided she had nothing better to do.

KENT WYATT

Chapter 20

"We can delete key all but that one," Link had been using the internet to research the seven or so buildings in the industrial area around the motel as the possible hideout for the kidnappers.

Darrell followed Link's pointing finger which indicated a dark building just northeast of them.

Link scowled at the large, single level edifice that might have been offices and a small manufacturing complex. "Looks like it's been reformatted. There's a 'for sale' sign out front."

"Or someone's devilishly clever," Darrell declared, having a revelation. "Buy the building and leave the 'for sale' sign. You know how long it takes realtors to come and get their signs, especially a big one like that. Perfect cover—everyone thinks it's still vacant. Check out the privacy fence out back. It looks newer than the rest of the grounds. That would definitely hide a lot of suspicious activity."

Sliding and tapping on his phone, Link huffed a sigh. "Cals's phone is off. I don't know if it's still in the area or not." The kid took a glance around then pointed to the parking lot's back exit. "Cruise by the building, and I'll see if the wife's home."

Darrell wrinkled his brow, turned and gave Link a reprimanding look.

The kid threw his hands out, shrugged and shook his head. "The Wi-Fi. I'm gonna check the Wi-Fi signal."

Darrell pulled onto the road as if he was just another hotel guest taking a back way into town.

As their car drove past the building, Link gave a satisfied exclamation. "Yo, wife's gone. Our mystery building is as far as the hotel's signal reaches. That's gotta be where Cals's phone called from."

"Okay, I'll circle back around to Vapor Trail. We can park the car over there, and I can come in from the back."

Darrell killed his lights as he came onto Vapor Trail and was soon easing the car to a stop. There were trees blocking any view from the building. He turned to address Link. "I need you to stay with the car. Is there any way you can get video from the NIP so you can see what I'm doing?"

Link grinned and held up his phone which displayed a similar view of his crooked smile. He tapped the shoulder of the arm in several places as he spoke. "You've got a whole array of cameras on the front, back, and the outside of both shoulders, even one in the hand so the view won't get blocked when you fire the Taser. I'll be the Mario cam over your shoulder—cell phone data linked wherever you go. Say the word and I'll post a panoramic video on your favorite social media." Link apparently read the look on Darrell's face and put his hands up in defense. "Just an icon on the desktop—not saying I'm clicking it."

Pulling out a laptop from his bag and a computer tablet, Link soon had each screen filled with multiple views running from all the cameras. "The Darrell cam is online. You do the rush down, and I'll be your backup—let you know if some creeper is ganking from the rear."

Darrell's eyes rolled in contemplation of the statement. He gave up and pointed his finger at Link. "Do that." His other hand pulled the Smith & Wesson M&P handgun from a holster in his waistband.

Link's eyes widened. "Yo dude. This is get'n live, isn't it?"

"*Real* live." Darrell shook the gun slightly as he held it barrel up between them. "But this isn't much if they have assault rifles."

The humor had drained from Link's face. "You keep talking like this is going to be a multi-player game. There was only one antag on the phone. What part of the help file did I miss."

Darrell patted the two M&P magazines in his pocket, taking inventory while he spoke. "I don't have enough time or information to work it all out right now, but Callie said *these guys* and someone was taking Callie away before that man started talking to me. That is at least one, probably more like two, other people. And I don't think any of those people hacked Callie's phone. In my mind that says: one caller, two thugs, one hacker. And all those clicks before the man came on – like the phone was being transferred. Maybe they're in more than one location."

Link nodded like the reasoning was opening up a new perspective.

"Then there's the big question, why is the FBI involved? Brock said, *Persons of interest*. I think we are dealing with some type of organization. And that might mean some serious weaponry. Any machine guns hidden in the NIP that you haven't told me about?"

Link laughed nervously. "Sorry, dude, it's not a boomstick. That only comes in the advanced level model."

"So *now* you tell me I got the economy version." Darrell stretched the NIP and grimaced when pain needled his stump. "I'm going to need that backup even more."

Examining Darrell, Link pulled up one side of a smile. "You look like you could use some serious health points. You're not going to exit out on me, are you? 'Cause I'm out of mana."

"Not if I can help it. I'm not gonna lie; I'm not doing so hot. But I'm not going to sit around in that recovery room while Callie might be doing worse. Let's just hope the rest of our plan works. You have Shawn's number ready, right?"

Link nodded. He noticed the kid's Adam's apple convulse in a swallow. Darrell expressed the only thing that made sense. "You know what Callie would tell us to do if she were here?"

"Yeah, she'd be telling us to pray."

"I guess that wasn't too hard to figure out, was it?" Darrell glanced heavenward. "God, please help us save Your girl."

Link looked up also. "Backup copy to that."

"Okay." Darrell took a deep breath.

He pulled the earpiece out of his pocket and looked at it. "I will be keeping this real quiet on the approach because I need to hear, and this earpiece cuts out part of the sound. I'm also worried it's going to fall out."

"Hold on. I can do some tech boosting." Link reached over and opened a compartment on the top of the NIP's shoulder. "The arm has high-definition sound enhancing software." He pulled out a set of wired earbuds.

Darrell inserted them and was pleased that he could put in the left bud with the prosthetic hand. The buds had holders that wrapped around his ears and held them securely.

"You won't lose these as easy, and…" Link tapped on his computer keyboard for a bit.

The earbuds came to life with amazing clarity.

"Let me know if you need me to turn up the volume."

"No, that's perfect." Darrell was suddenly aware of a diesel engine sound coming from the direction of the target building. "Okay, I need to get going." He slapped Link on the shoulder and gave it a squeeze. Then he was off.

Darrell hurried away from the car, into the darkness. He didn't know what the engine sound might mean, but he had wasted enough time. He found he could run easily with the arm as it moved perfectly with the motion of his stump. He was thankful that the terrain was flat and that so far, he wasn't getting sick.

Sitting in the car, Link's eyes darted from screen to screen as he followed Darrell's movement. He set one forward view and one rear to low light so the area stood out in stark black and white contrast. Every shadow tightened his nerves until it revealed itself as something other than an enemy.

Link was glad that he wasn't left out, but knots of tension were building in his neck. Chess popped up in the margin of his thoughts. His search parameters were looking for something to fill the parts of his multi-layered mind that weren't occupied with the screens. He wanted to drive out the imaginary visions of Darrell exploding into red mist and "game over" flashing across the screen. But he rejected the idea of calling up an app for fear it would distract him at a crucial moment. *There are no one-ups in real life. You only get one chance.*

It was a new sensation. He never feared distraction. His brain could work out machine code bugs while he roleplayed on one device and chatted on another. Pressure was never a factor before.

He tried to slow his breathing. A bead of sweat threatened to enter his eye and he swiped it away quickly so it wouldn't hinder his view of the screens. Poising over the device controls again, he noticed his hand shaking.

He couldn't do it. Darrell needed someone else. Someone with more nerve. Another cop who knew how to handle the…but the situations app menu only had one entry and it was Link. Besides, who else could manage this many screens, keep up with this level of data coming in? Humility didn't get in the way of Link's realization of the unique skill set he possessed.

Link heard Callie's voice in his head, something she always told him. "God made you the way you are for a reason. You better start talking to Him and find out what you're here for."

Okay, so talking to God was something he could do with the idle part of his mind. He knew people liked to close their eyes when they prayed but that wasn't an option, so he opened a chat box in his head. *God, I'm looking to link up here. LOL. I don't know if You're real or not, but Callie believes in You and she's pretty solid state. If You're irl—that means In Real Life, but I guess You know that—I could use some hit points right now.*

Link thought about the little he knew about God. *Callie says You like to run your programs in the background.* Callie spoke about it having to do with faith, commitment, motives, and people having a real choice. It had sounded interesting at the time, but he hadn't thought of it much since then. If God could hear his prayers, He must be able to hear his thoughts too.

Link's mind got a buzz out of recreating language from the mashup of tech talk, gamer slang and reworked vocabulary that floated in his head. Just talking wasn't enough to occupy the distinctive firing of his neurons. The idea of God communicating on an even higher level caused a rare feeling of intimidation and stimulation—like Darrell putting him in the arm lock—easy and unexpected but with a gracious feel.

Maybe I should have connected all those times Callie gave me a God tech tip. Hope You're not tilted over my lack of "faith and commitment." But I'm online now and Callie says You're always ready to reboot.

Link took a slow breath, then another. *We both know I don't have the experience points for this game. I don't know why I'm here, but Darrell and Callie need me not to hack this up.*

Link sighed. The normal way of communication wasn't enough. His language skills seemed inadequate. Something inside him breathed out his plea in a communication protocol he shared with only one other being. Like plugging into a high speed hardwire, years of disconnectedness were overcome with forgiveness, and something uploaded.

This is just another first-person shooter game. The message came like he had always known the voice.

Link visualized Darrell as part of the black ops roleplay on his gaming computer.

You got this. Trust me and keep the Uplink open.

Focusing on the screens, Link began to play the game.

Chapter 21

Callie decided the tape tasted like chewing on a cheap purse, flat and plasticky. She spat the last piece onto the floor and then flexed her leg muscles. Only a few strands ran between the tops of her ankles. As she worked them back and forth, the strands broke apart. She crossed her legs and pulled one up and one down, rotating so she could peel the tape off the backs of her ankles. She closed her eyes as the tape pulled off bits of skin. Rip! Her legs were apart.

Callie was frozen for a moment, teeth clenched. Wiggling her legs, she tried to shake off the pain. She bent in half to blow on her red, raw ankles. In a quiet tone she whined, "I don't think this beauty treatment is working." She shook her feet again. "Ooh, that stings worse than a soldering burn."

Okay, Callie, no time to enjoy your wonderful new experiences. She braced her liberated feet against the floor and slid herself up the wall to a standing position. Her legs were stiff from inactivity, but it felt good to stand normally. She hobbled quickly to the door. The sounds of truck loading had stopped. Heavy boots were coming down the hall and then she heard the jingling of keys.

Darrell had to stop, hands on his knees, as a wave of nausea overcame him. The line of trees that ran from his location to the north side of the target building was perfect concealment. He rested a moment then moved up, hidden in the trees, until he was just north of the privacy fence behind the building. As he got closer, he could hear voices. He wondered if Link could…

Link got a message from Darrell. **Can you filter out the engine noise so I can hear the voices?**

Link isolated the various sounds and dropped the volume on the diesel engine. The voices were clearer, but they were speaking in a foreign language. Link wondered if they had the right place. He tried to use software to translate the audio, but there was still too much sound clutter.

Darrell concentrated on the voices. They sounded Middle Eastern, nothing he could understand. The conversation sounded rushed, and he heard one that seemed to be directing the others. Darrell was listening intently when, without warning, light illuminated the building and foliage in front of him.

Everything in Link's forward view monitors was a blur. There was a thud in the earpiece and the same monitors were suddenly dark. Link panicked. "Darrell! What happened! You okay!" There was no answer. He looked at the other monitors and tried to make sense of them. Small points of light penetrated foliage. Like one of those strange perspective puzzles, the view Link was seeing finally shifted in his mind and made sense. Like when he was a kid, lying on his back on a camping trip, he was looking at starlight through the trees. But it was Darrell's rear monitors that were showing the view. Comprehension came to Link. Darrell was on the ground, face down.

Arash worked the key into the lock on the door to the room where the woman was held. Though he had been ordered to check her frequently, he justified stretching it out as long as possible by telling himself he needed to get the equipment loaded and on the road.

Arash had determined not to spend too much time around the woman. During the process of restraining her, he had held her, and it had affected him. She was certainly desirable. Even stained and dirty, her face was pretty, and her disheveled hair only added to her casual charm. But there was something else.

The woman's face conveyed hurt and fear but no hatred. When their eyes met, something had pierced him, as if the woman had some power inside her that passed between them. It had moved inside and brought thoughts he seemed unable to control. He found himself considering how she must feel, how badly it had hurt when he kicked her, what fear his threats produced. They were questions that had no place in his mission.

Arash tried to ignore her and had treated her with deliberate indifference to try to rid himself of the distraction. But she intrigued him with her fearless humming of happy tunes. It made him regret what he would have to do to her in the end.

He had entertained the idea of asking the Arrow if he could have her instead, to at least spare her life and perhaps... But he knew that was impossible, and it would not solve his dilemma. So he had decided to check on her as he was ordered but not spend much time doing it and to think of her as little as possible.

He opened the door and switched on the lights. The girl lay curled facing away from him. He could clearly see that her hands were still taped behind her back. She stirred only slightly when he turned on the light. He switched them off again. *Let her sleep.* Then he quickly moved back to the work at hand and tried his best to put her out of his mind.

Callie waited until she heard the man move away. She stretched her legs which she had curled up to hide them behind her body so he could not see where only tatters of the tape now hung.

"Thank you, Lord," she whispered. She had been silently begging God to make him go away, and that had happened. He had not checked on her as he had been doing. He just left. She knew it was a miracle.

Chapter 22

"Darrell! You online, Dude?" Link could still hear breathing but there was no other verbal response. Then a text message paraded across the screen on his phone.

"I'm okay. Turn the sound back to normal. You tuned out the diesel noise so well I didn't hear that truck coming onto the lot until I saw the headlights hit the building. I dropped because the gate started opening and I was afraid I was going to be exposed. Can you see if the coast is clear before I move?"

Though obscured by branches here and there, all Link's monitors displayed a surrounding view again. "Whoa Darrelldown, you scared the ram out of me."

With the panic gone, Link realized he could still see one view toward the fence, from the shoulder's side camera. Through sticks and grass blades, he could see that the gate stood open, and a truck emerged. Another semi waited outside ready to pull in. It must have been the lights of the waiting semi, as it turned in from the street, that had illuminated the building.

"Looks like you're clear now. I don't see anything to suggest they saw you." Link watched as the camera swung back and forth while Darrell low-crawled to a thicker part of the brush and then rose to a crouching position.

Darrell's whispered voice came through Link's headset. "Sorry about the scare, had to drop quick..." The statement trailed off as if something had caught his attention.

Link zeroed in on a shape illuminated by the waiting truck's headlights. He recognized the image from the military games he played. "AcuDarrell, you were righteous about the assault rifles. The guy at the gate has an AK-47."

Link heard Darrell suck in a preparatory gulp of air. The view from the Darrell cams showed him leaving the brush where he was concealed.

"Have to move quick." Darrell spoke it as a rapid exhalation.

The view on the monitors rushed across the open space toward the trucks. The image stabilization feature of the cameras allowed Link to see the exiting truck block the view of the man at the gate as it moved out wide to get around the other semi. The motion of the camera from each of Darrell's footfalls added to the jerking image of the semi, which gained minor amounts of speed with each shift of a gear. The view raced right up to the semi-trailer and underneath it. Then everything spun.

Link stared in disbelief as he held his breath. There were punctuated groans of pain along with the creaking and grating of metal and the overwhelming bellow of the diesel monsters. His fingers felt numb, and he realized he had a tight hold on the dashboard of the car. This was like no game he had ever played.

Now that Callie was free to move around the room without the risk of noise and injury, she let her engineer analytics kick in. Fear took a back seat.

Callie needed something to cut the tape from her hands. All that shared her makeshift cell were thick canvas tarps. Taking a seat on the nearest pile, she leaned backwards so she could use her bound hands to examine the tarp's construction. The surface had an oily finish to repel water. Callie winced at the sting it caused on abused skin. *Ignore it. Freckles could be back any moment. He's not going to wait for you to be a wimp.*

Evenly spaced along the edges of the tarp were metal grommets to attach ropes or bungie straps. She began to finger the round metal holes. They had sharp edges that might work on the tape, but they were tight against the tarp. She picked at one, trying to pull it out from the canvas to expose the edge.

Callie's fingernail broke. "Okay, I've had it with this spa. I want my money back."

Next idea, Callie. Folding the tarp over, she used one grommet to pull at the edge of another. Spending painful minutes of messing with the grommets yielded nothing, and Callie flopped her body on the canvas. The tears were trying to come again.

If I'm going to cry, it's going to be for the right reason, and to the right person. Letting the tears become part of her petition to the Lord she begged for the strength to get up and keep trying.

Darrell had seen the AK-47 held at the side of the guard who was standing at the gate, scanning the area. He had no doubt these were the people who had kidnapped Callie. He also saw a rapidly unfolding opportunity. The open gate was his way in, and with the possibility of Callie being inside, he wasn't going to miss it.

Adrenaline slowed everything down, and his opportunity had presented itself like a curtain rising on the act of a play already in progress. The noise, light, darkness…one driver pulled out…the other waited…the guard watched…*they're all blinded by headlights.*

The exiting truck moved between Darrell and the man at the gate. *There…move now…* the trucks were going to pass side by side. Darrell rushed across the field…*low, below their mirrors…*he rolled under the first trailer.

It hurt every time the NIP hit the ground. It hurt more when Darrell used the arm to grab onto some of the metal under the belly of the trailer, but he didn't let go.

When the trailers were side by side, Darrell dropped and rolled toward the next trailer. He was almost out from under the moving semi when the rubber of a rolling tire grabbed at the sole of his shoe. Darrell felt his foot being pulled toward the ground where the tire was waiting to crush it. Throwing everything into his roll, Darrell jerked his shoe out, leaving a chunk of the rubber sole behind.

He continued rolling until he saw the metal underbelly of the waiting trailer above him. The air brakes released with a woosh and the semi lurched. The thick twin I-beams that comprised the supporting framework under the trailer began moving above him.

Darrell flipped around, peering toward the gate from under the shadow of the trailer to see the guard. The face the headlights illuminated seemed unaware of Darrell. *If he spots me, I'm dead.*

Darrell centered himself under the trailer and scrambled to pull himself up into the network of parts above him. He wrapped both arms around the metal cross member of the supports designed to hold up the front of the trailer when the tractor wasn't attached. Hunched over, he kicked his legs upward trying to get his body wedged in the framework. It wasn't working. He was wearing out.

Darrell tried to give himself a boost by pushing up with the NIP. Lightning pain shot through the end of his stump as he put the weight of his body into the prosthetic. The torment flashed through his arm and into his neck. Darrell's legs dropped back to the ground in his agony, and he was barely able to hang on with his real arm. Nausea threatened to overcome him.

Chapter 23

Callie rose. *God is keeping you going for a reason. Try something else.*

Darkness obscured the corners of the room where the small amount of light coming in around the door was too feeble to overcome it. Callie confronted the dark. *Maybe there's a nail sticking out of the wall somewhere.*

Moving to the wall, Callie twisted her upper body to feel along it with her fingers. It must have been a meeting room at one time because there was a decorative molding that ran along each wall at just about the height of her waist.

Coming to a joint where the two pieces of molding had been joined together, Callie felt the lower corner of one protruding. Not much, but maybe... The corner wasn't sharp, but it had a point. She turned and put the tape that entrapped her wrists against the pointed end and rubbed it up and down.

After a minute or so, Callie jerked her wrists away and shook them up and down, gritting her teeth at the heat on her enflamed wrists. The movement made it worse. "Ooww." She gave a Thumper rabbit tap of her foot. "Don't think of the pain. Think of something else."

She examined her progress. The only difference she felt was the fiery sensation moving up her lower arm. Perhaps the heat would eventually burn through the tape—if she could take it that long.

Callie returned to working the surface of the tape rapidly over the pointed molding. *Think of something else. What would Darrell be doing?* Did he care enough to come after her? Was there any way he could find her? She alternated between flexing her aching shoulders and then doing partial knee bends to generate the brisk movement required. *What if he does find me?* Anxiety passed through Callie. *Why did I say anything on that call? Please, Lord, help him.*

The top of the tape slid off the molding and caught on the edge just as she pushed with her legs. The force lifted the molding, tore it from the wall, and it broke with a loud "crack!"

"Veto that!" Link shouted aloud when he watched Darrell fall again. He could hear him gasping and moaning. The view showed that he was sometimes moving with the truck but other times he was letting it drag him. He had his right arm draped over a metal support.

He's not using the NIP. Link checked the diagnostic indicators. The prosthetic was working.

He remembered the look of pain on Darrell's face when he had used the NIP to hold the duffle bag down. Even though the floating feature of the arm limited the pressure, Darrell's freshly attached nerves were just too raw for the severity of impact they were receiving.

The truck was easing forward and swinging out to make it into the gate which was getting closer all the time. As soon as the truck headlights passed the gate guard, his eyes would quickly adjust and, in seconds, Darrell would be visible to him and his AK.

Maybe Darrell can hit escape on the whole thing and make it back to the trees. Link shook his head at his own idea. Even if Darrell got out from under the truck and ran, Link knew he wouldn't make it. Link tried to shake the image of Darrell being torn to pieces by automatic weapons fire. The poor guy was barely able to walk, let alone run.

In the rear camera view, the sharp contrast of the night vision lit up the rear axles of the truck. The big, tandem tires were ready to crush Darrell should he fall in front of them.

Link's hand was shaking, ready to pull off the headphones and look away if…Maybe he should call the other cop. What was his name? Link shook his head in frustration. He never forgot things like that. Was he being a coward? Should he leave the car and run to help Darrell? *You'd be late for the party, and you don't know the dance steps.*

Link arched his shoulders against the shudder that went through him. Which would be better, to be shot or crushed? *God, please don't let me just sit here like the joystick's unplugged.* The only movement on the monitors was the bouncing of the truck. "Wiggle the mouse, Darrell. Don't quit." He wanted to reach into the monitor and force Darrell to…

Link grabbed his phone. That was it. *Thanks, God.* He punched and slid his fingers in a frenzy as he stared at the view of the tires behind Darrell and the space between them that was packed with metal and air hoses. He shouted, "You're button mashing ain't making it, Darrellduck. You need some coyote time so here's a new option box." He worked the screen on his phone as he talked. "Let go."

Callie's whole body clinched. The sound seemed to hang in the room even after the broken wood clattered to a standstill on the floor.

Holding her breath, Callie listened for running footfalls down the hallway or the jingling keys that would signal her doom. Instead, she heard only the television and the distant sound of work and engine noise.

Callie slid her foot through the dust on the floor, searching for the piece of molding. Her house remodeling projects had taught her what happened when wood broke.

Her toes found the board. Kneeling with her back to it, she examined the wood with her fingers. "Lord, You know what I need. Please just let it be…" She felt the end, jagged and sharp. Some broken points were like short little ice picks, but she knew those would be too flimsy. However, at one edge of the break was a thick corner that tapered to a point.

With her taped hands Callie couldn't hold the board in any way that would be effective. She covered her mental canvas with the art of her ideas, painting new thoughts over the ones that wouldn't work. One image defied her efforts to disregard it. *Oh, that's simple.*

Darrell blinked his eyes and tried to focus. He felt like he was spinning and had to swallow bile that rose in his throat. Not since the night of the shooting had he felt such pain. He clung to an iron railing that was pulling him along.

Memories floated in with the pain and pushed out everything else. His mind found a connection—something he had been trying to remember.

Darrell watched a man walking up the street as he sat completely still in a car. Then he was out of the car…chasing the man down the street…an overcoat flapping like a goose trying to take off.

The man was on the ground. He smiled at Darrell. It was the face he had remembered, and it triggered a wave of fear. Darrell turned to run, and he heard explosions behind him… couldn't use his hand…then pain…like the pain in the prosthetic that he held limp at his side, too afraid to move it.

What was the steel he was hugging tightly with his good arm? He didn't want to…

"Let go." He could hear someone saying, "New input, Darrell. Listen to the little voice in your ear. Let go and lay on the ground."

The voice had to be crazy. He didn't want to be on the ground. He wanted to be up. He had to get up or the man would see him. The man with the... Things came back into focus.

Darrell was under a semi. His legs were dragging in the dirt, and he struggled to get them under him so he could push himself up. He needed to be up where he could hide from the man who was guarding the gate with the AK47. It was no use. His legs couldn't get enough strength to propel themselves upward, let alone wedge him there until he passed the man.

The only other choice Darrell had was to pull his gun and shoot the man. But even if he could shoot straight enough to take out the gate keeper, there were the men in the trucks and there had to be others. The noise would alert them. The war would be on, and he would be outgunned and in no condition to fight. He would die and he would fail Callie.

"Let go, Darrell. I'll do the driving." It was Link speaking into his ear.

Whatever Link had in mind appeared to be the only option. Darrell released his grip. He went to his knees and put out his real hand, trying to catch himself. "Oouf." The ground pushed his ribs against his lungs and the air left him.

"Keep your head down."

Keep my head down? Darrell didn't think he could raise his head. Lying down was what his body wanted to do...just lie there and escape the pain. He was too exhausted to even care about the truck tires rolling heavily on either side of him and the presence of something passing close above his head.

"And Darrell," there was reluctance in Link's voice, "I'm sorry, but this is probably going to up your agony meter."

Still holding the board, Callie eased her legs under her and stood. Dragging the board to the corner of the room, she braced the good end of the molding in the corner, where it wouldn't move and got the point against the tape on her wrists. She didn't want the stick to jab her in the back, so she bent forward and pushed backward.

The tape gave way with a tearing sound, sending Callie stumbling sideways. She managed to grab the stick so it wouldn't hit the floor.

Steady again, Callie tried to pull free from the strip of tape that remained. Even taking her pain level to the verge of tears couldn't snap it. She looked to Heaven and gave a quiet, sarcastic laugh. *Duct tape—the pinnacle of man's achievement. Forget gun control. This is the stuff they need to keep out of the wrong hands.*

With a frustrated huff, Callie glanced around for inspiration. The door captured her attention. She hurried across the room. As she had estimated, the board reached to the top of the door frame.

Wedging the flat end of the board against the lip of the frame, Callie maneuvered the broken end until it was pushing down against what was left of the tape. She had to bend her knees to get the board onto the last strip of tape, which was perfect. She simply stood up and split the tape the rest of the way.

The tip of the board tapped the floor hard as it fell and again clattered loudly to rest. Callie listened. Still, no one came. She pulled the rest of the tape free from her red irritated wrists.

Link watched the monitor until the hardware between the first set of rear trailer tires was right above the NIP. He pressed the button on his phone that initiated the auto grab feature of the NIP. The prosthetic swung up quickly and grabbed onto a metal support, raising Darrell's shoulders, and locking a grip in place.

As Link had predicted, Darrell groaned.

"Sorry, man. Trust me, I'm emo for you. Don't do a hard shut down on me when this is over, okay? Right now, you need to put a mute on it 'cause here comes the dude."

The NIP held onto the metal in a bicep-curl type grip and lifted Darrell's upper body. The shoulder cameras were almost upright. The image of the gate guard advanced from monitor to monitor. He disappeared behind rolling rubber as the trailer moved by the man with Darrell safely hidden between the rear tires. The lights that lit the yard made the shadows under the rear of the truck even darker as Darrell slid unseen into the stronghold of the enemy.

Callie calculated while she blew on her wrists. Getting loose seemed like the easy part. Now she faced something foreign to her experience. *First state the problem.* They were going to come back for her. They had no reason to let her live. They were going to— *Don't focus on that. Focus on the problem. Get to the core.* They were going to come for her. *Problem stated—move on. Identify options based on resources, evaluate the alternatives, implement the best decision.*

She couldn't out fight them…well maybe if she had a weapon. *Get real Callie, a sharp stick isn't going to cut it, and even if they were careless enough to let you get a gun, could you use it? Irrelevant—not a choice available. Stick to the moment.* Resources—a sharp stick and canvas tarps.

What would the men do to her? What was the best defense if they tried to shoot her compared to strangulation? Callie shook her head. Also, irrelevant. Something was wrong with her thinking. Part of the process was missing. Engineering was art to her. It was fun. *Yeah, because you didn't have to worry about dying.* She needed the freedom to be creative.

Options—fight, run, hide, all the above, some of the above, none of the... It wasn't working. Fear was winning.

Resources—a sharp stick and canvas tarps…and God.

An internal voice spoke over her thoughts. *Give me a minute.*

"I don't have a minute to spare." The words tumbled from her lips and matched the caliginous atmosphere of the room.

Callie lowered her head. She hobbled to the tarps and dropped onto the nearest pile. Looking up, she whispered, "Be still and know."

Callie took the minute. She thanked the Lord that she was alive and that her hands and feet were loose. *Lord, I need Your peace in the middle of all this. That is the true miracle, isn't it? It's not as big of deal for You to change our circumstances. The real trick is changing us.* Her breathing slowed and she let the idea sink in that nothing was out of God's control.

The strength of Callie's brain was that problem solving was like art. Data, theories, and calculations were like the paint and palette of her mind.

In the studio of Callie's thoughts, she approached the easel which held the problem. The assets she had available circled it like blobs of color. She pictured her freedom and safety like a rough sketch she hoped to produce out of the medium she had to work with.

How could a sharp stick and tarps help her escape the armed terrorists who would be coming for her. Ideas came like brush strokes where she grabbed color and applied it, seeing what she could make. She couldn't out fight them, or out run them…unless she had a head start.

A bright image decorated the empty page as Callie mixed the tints and hues, searching for the effect she envisioned. When the composition didn't fit, she painted over it and tried a new approach. A head start wasn't enough.

Callie needed more options. What else did she have available—a stick, tarps, and…a dark room. *Be creative, Callie. Think of something wild.* The men would come. She couldn't stop that. All she could control was what they found when they came. She lifted the fabric of her dress and fingered it, thinking of the problem in a different way. *If I could turn invisible—that would be wild.*

Callie envisioned Freckles in the hallway, using his keys on the lock. In her mind she saw him open the door and look in. She walked to the entrance, put her back to the door and scanned the room. Putting the finishing touches on her art, Callie formed her plan. She cringed mentally at some of the things it would require but if it worked…*I get a head start and then turn invisible—just like magic.* Looking at the ceiling, she smiled. "Thank You."

Time to make this work. Callie still held the thin wood molding. Pinning about two feet of the board to the floor with her foot, she lifted the other end until it snapped. She dropped the long half and snatched up the shorter stick. *Not the best tool but at least it won't conduct enough current to electrocute me.*

Turning to the switch beside the door, Callie flipped on the lights. She blinked. *Whoa, that's bright.* She couldn't let it be that bright when they came to get her.

Callie used the sharp edge of the broken molding to gouge into the drywall at the base of the switch cover. She dug under the plastic plate until she could break it, giving her access to the wiring inside. *Thank you, Lord that I took electrical engineering instead of sociology.*

Callie wedged the point of the stick behind one of the wires attached to the switch. As was standard, the electrician had left an ample amount of extra wire in the box. She worked the wire out to where she could get a grip on the plastic insulation. Using her stick and her fingers, she bent the wire back and forth until it broke, and the room went dark again.

Letting her eyes adjust, Callie hardened her resolve to move to the next phase of her plan. *Father, it's up to You to keep them out of here long enough for me to get ready.* She had to get rolling, literally. After that, would come the part she really didn't like.

Chapter 24

It had been far too long since he had checked on the woman, but Arash suspected that she would be right where he left her, sleeping. *She must be exhausted to be able to sleep through her fear.* The thought was unwelcome. *What do you care about what she is feeling?* She was an infidel woman. She deserved no consideration.

But the thought held its ground. Arash tried to force it out by going over the exit plan. They still needed to get the cars loaded and the studio packed up. They had been pushing hard and everyone was tired. They needed to have the entire operation on the move before the Arrow detonated the explosives at Jamal's location.

How many would the explosion kill? *That is not worth wasting thoughts on either.* Arash felt uneasy. He was not superstitious, but it was as if his contact with the woman had opened a sore inside him that festered with thoughts of life and death…and compassion.

He imagined the bombs they had planted detonating, consuming close to a dozen of the Great Satan's FBI agents—men with guns, moving quickly, in para-military formations, ready to neutralize a target. *But they will be the ones neutralized.* Why did it give him no pleasure?

Arash thought about Jamal. He had befriended the gang member, converted him to Islam, and groomed him to die a glorious death for Allah. There was no reason to feel sorry for him. He had nothing in this life to be proud of or to look forward to. Death in the name of jihad guaranteed him a paradise of pleasures. For Arash the man was a tool in their plan, that was all.

Jamal's stereotypical street accent had been perfect for their purposes. The FBI would associate it with Jamal's racial culture, that was key. The man would use his voice to lure the SWAT team further into the center of the storage lot where there would be no chance of their escape. When the dust settled, they would leak the audio of Jamal's phone call with the police lieutenant. Natural bigotry would do the rest. There was plenty of bitterness on both sides of the racial tension in the United States to fulfill their purposes.

I wonder if Jamal is scared? There it was, pity, trying to creep in again. He would not have considered that before. It was the effect of the woman. What had she done to him?

Callie placed her hands under the last roll of tarps that lay on the floor like a giant burrito. She grimaced as the grimy waterproofing on the thick canvas burned into her raw wrists. Putting everything into her legs she lifted one end of the tarp roll.

Struggling to get the roll to stand up against the wall, Callie was overwhelmed with their odor. The tarps smelled of old, dirty oil, not the fresh machine oil she used in her workshop.

When she had the roll in place, Callie leaned beside it and panted. The heavy rolling and lifting was more exercise than she had done in a while. She was glad that the truck loading seemed to be taking longer than before. *God, please keep them busy.*

Surveying the room, Callie was satisfied with how things appeared in the blackness. Her eyes were adjusted, but anyone who entered would be coming from the bright hallway. She was also thankful for the darkness because it made it easier to do the next part. Callie removed her long sweater and pulled her dress off over her head.

The truck pulled across the lot, and the loud hiss of the air brakes sent a shiver through Darrell. He was fully alert again, and Link returned the NIP's control to him.

As the driver's door opened, he loosened his grip and lowered to the ground. *Pulling with the arm doesn't hurt as bad. I need to remember not to push with it.*

The area between the truck's rear wheels was dark, but Darrell rolled over and pulled himself tight against the inside of the driver's side tires to maximize his cover.

The driver got out and walked to one side and then the other at the rear of the semi-trailer, disengaging locks. He returned to the driver's side, and Darrell heard the sound of fast-moving hydraulics. A new shadow appeared and lengthened quickly. The rear gate of the truck was coming down, concealing Darrell even more. When the door stopped, it was resting on the ground, forming a ramp with I-beam type reinforcement that was as heavy as the railing of the truck frame.

Through the gap between the rear tire and the ramp, Darrell saw an overhead door open in the back of the building, and a police car roll out. It headed for the ramp. Darrell could make out a blue "Denver Police" badge on the door.

The knowledge that the long years of preparation would soon be over should have been enough for Arash, but tonight had not gone well. Some of his uneasy feelings were probably caused by all the little problems that always seemed to surface. He berated himself. *You've been too long away from real battle, too long in this foreign country doing hidden work, mingling with the Americans.* He had come to see them as regular people – smiling at him, offering him pleasantries or even assistance sometimes.

You're losing your stomach for blood. It was better dealing with the drug dealers and prostitutes they used to accomplish what they needed. It was easy to loathe them.

Even more, Arash loathed this change his country had taken. He hated hiding in the shadows, working for years on promises of one grand victory, never seeing the small ones.

Especially disheartening was the success of the Iraqis and others around the Middle East. *Our enemies are humiliating us—acting like real men, fighting real battles in the name of Allah.*

Everything had become a lie for Arash, and he was tired of lies. He was tired of being told to have patience, tired of living in a land that also had no stomach for war. It was hard to still believe what the Arrow preached about the payoff for the years of tedious manipulation.

He did not share the Arrow's triumphant feeling over the reaction to the incidents in the other states. It was a poor harvest for the seeds they had planted. There should have been a more violent response, and it should have lasted longer. They needed to see a significant death toll if the plan was to work.

The Arrow had assured him when they generated their own events, in conjunction with triggering the devices they were planting in Denver, they would see such results. In his patronizing way, the leader had explained that after several days of devastation in the centrally located city, they would activate the devices in the other areas, and the chain reaction would begin. Arash knew the plan. He didn't need it explained again.

Did he still believe in the plan? *You need to focus on your work and stop these thoughts.*

The component manufacturing portion of the operation and the studio were shipped out. Once the cars were on the trucks, they could pack up the few tools and items they had left, sanitize the building of anything that might connect them to it, and leave without a trace while law enforcement concerned themselves with the explosion across town.

The city had been a curse to them since the beginning. He could not understand why the Arrow had insisted on staying all these years.

Now there was the woman. Kidnapping someone connected to the police detective seemed like insanity to Arash. How could it not invite more inquiry when they needed less. More and more he wondered about the leader's mental stability. But no one dared question the Arrow's obsessions. The leader was still angry that they had not killed the American policeman years ago when he forced them to destroy their first site in the city and sacrifice one of their best programmers.

It was useless to question the Arrow. It would only produce more doubt in him about Arash's loyalty. It was also sure to earn him another lecture on the careful craft of social engineering. He was in no mood to endure the Arrow's condescension as he explained that it was the combination of layer upon layer of induced thought patterns that would bring the desired results. Subconscious and real-world stimuli acting on a carefully chosen subject could overcome the deepest social programming. He had heard it for years and he did not want to hear it tonight.

Besides they had no time. The new vehicles the Arrow saw on the wireless cameras they had planted in the area around the storage lot where Jamal was hiding had to be the FBI SWAT team arriving sooner than expected. The leader was giddy with the excitement of soon being able to detonate the explosives.

Arash wished the Arrow had listened to him and put the woman with Jamal to be killed in the explosion. But the leader did not want the woman's body found too quickly. He wanted the search for her to continue as long as possible. Now it fell on Arash to deal with her.

The mental echo of the tune the woman hummed kept coming to Arash. His stomach felt hard inside, and the feeling radiated out into a dull ache in his shoulders, back, and upper arms. His breathing was shallow with occasional deep inhalations that came out in uncomfortable sighs. The Arrow wanted it to be a knife, for the effect it would create when her body was found. *Why a knife?* Arash did not want to have to touch her.

Since Darrell was hidden for the moment, Link took the time to make the call. Surely the guard with an assault rifle would be enough to convince them. If Darrell was right and the other site was a trap, they were running out of time.

Shawn answered on the first ring, "You got anything for me?"

Link hurried with the explanation. "Something is definitely booting up. There are semi-trucks doing an input/output loop and a dude guarding the gate with an AK-47. Now they just loaded a police car onto one of the trucks."

"Police car…one of our cars?"

"I don't know. It looks a little different, but I've been too busy watching Darrell's back to enhance the video."

"Video? Where's Darrell?"

"He's inside, under the truck that they are loading the cars onto."

"What! I thought the idea was that you were going to check out the place and try to find out for sure if Callie was there. How did he get inside under a truck?"

"A random set of circumstances met Darrelldogood?" Link didn't like the awkward sound of his own voice.

"I should have known he would try to do this on his own. Okay. I'm at home because I didn't know where else to go. They followed me from the hospital, just like we thought, and are outside. Not a very trusting fellow, this Brock. Can you send me that video?"

"I'm emo you have to ask."

"I'm disappointed it's not in my inbox already. Send it in something I can forward on. I will call the Chief. I know how he feels about Darrell, so I doubt if he went along with this investigation willingly. I will see if I can get you some backup without getting arrested on federal obstruction charges. I know at least two FBI agents that will be on their way to help shortly."

Callie crouched in the darkness, shivering. She pulled her sweater further over her bare legs. Holding the piece of rope she found in one of the tarps, she began to call out to God in her mind. *Please let this work.*

Blind their eyes, Lord. Make them see me where I am not, and not see me where I am. I have to believe you got me this far for a reason. I still think Darrell is coming.

Was it crazy to believe that? The feeling persisted despite all the odds against it. But she had been disappointed before.

Darrell was not the man she thought he was. He had lost his faith to adversity, unable to stand the fire. Now he had built an idol in his mind of what God was like, not so he could worship it but so he could hate it. *Forgive him, Father. If he really is coming for me, please keep him safe. He needs rescuing more than I do. Please, win him back. Soften his heart so he can see himself for what he is and You for what You are.*

Callie had to check her feelings. She had to keep her compassion for Darrell contained within the area of Christian love. The same she would have for any lost soul. God made it clear in Scripture that, as a believer, she could not be connected, or "yoked" together as the Bible called it, with someone who had not given his life to the Lord.

She wiped her eyes on her sweater. *Lord, You're going to have to help me with that one. You know where my heart wants to go.* She tried to quiet her mind as God was teaching her, but Darrell kept popping back into her thoughts. She considered things she might say to him, ways she might change his mind.

Callie sighed. She had to let God have Darrell. He was the only one that could really reach him. Again, she had the impression that Darrell was on his way. *Even if Darrell and I can never be together, please do not let him die without You, especially if he's trying to save me.*

There were footfalls in the hallway. Callie froze. Then came the jingling of keys. It was time.

Chapter 25

"I called Shawn," came Link's voice in Darrell's ear. "He was not happy that you're in there, but he is trying to get us some help. So just stay hidden and hang on."

Probably not an option, Darrell texted through the arm. **They just loaded two Denver PD cars on this truck. They are putting on some smaller items, but I'm afraid they'll be moving this truck soon. Looks like everyone is in a hurry in here. These cars must be fakes that they are going to use during whatever attack they are planning. That is probably what Brock got wind of. It has got to be something big to consider using fake police cars.**

"What are you going to do if they move the truck?"

All I know is what I'm not going to do. I'm not leaving here without Callie.

Arash took hold of the doorknob. He had the knife concealed in the back of his pants so the woman would not panic when she saw it. Since she was bound, it would be easy to make it quick and accurate and go back to his work. When it came time to load her in the SUV, she would be dead and no longer a problem to him.

Arash's hand quivered as he turned the key in the lock. He had killed women and even children while fighting the Kurds. *You can do this.* He rested his hand on the knob without turning it. *But should I?*

The woman was an American, second only to a Jew in deserving of death. He tried to bring up the hate he had been taught since his birth. He could not find the feelings. They were replaced by the thoughts of the woman's humming in the middle of what had to be a nightmare for her.

This is what the fight for Islam demanded. Being faithful was killing a young woman, bound in duct tape, that he was convinced would have done nothing but good to him had they met on the street. It no longer felt right. *From where are these feelings coming?* It must be a devil whispering into his heart.

Arash's father had been a Cleric and had him studying the texts since his youth. He was not a novice believer. He knew what the holy writings said about jihad. He had always despised the Muslims that called themselves moderate. There was no such thing. To follow Islam was to burn with hatred against those who did not bow to Allah. But now his own fire had been quenched.

If Arash wasn't going to kill the woman, what would he do? *Get in an SUV and leave?* His eyes strayed toward the direction of the exit. Could he alter his situation and still not change what he was?

Like shedding a dead skin, Arash realized he was not that person anymore. It was a compelling powerful transformation. Whatever had moved inside of him since his contact with the woman had opened his eyes.

Leaving the woman in the hands of the Arrow was no different than killing her himself. Somehow, he knew that his future was dependent on what he chose to do about the human being that waited on the other side of the door. Someone was definitely whispering to him, but he was no longer sure who the devil was.

Arash dropped to his knees outside the door and placed his face to the floor. With his heart opened to his Creator he groaned aloud, "Please, show me what is right. Please tell me what I must do…"

"Arash! What are you doing?"

Arash stood quickly to face the Arrow who stood in the hallway staring at him. "Praying." Arash was surprised at the conviction in his own voice.

The other man looked at him with a suspicious expression. "There is no call to prayer at this hour. We have no time. Have you taken care of the woman?"

Arash did not know what to say. What came out was, "I was just going in."

"And over this, you need to pray?" there was a hint of contempt in the Arrow's voice as he came forward quickly and grabbed the doorknob. He pushed the door open and moved into the room. Arash followed, in fear of what the Arrow would do to the woman and not knowing what he, himself, would do about it.

The leader stopped about six feet into the room. "Turn on the lights!"

Arash ran his hand along the wall by the door until he encountered something that felt wrong. "The switch is damaged."

"She must have done it. You idiot, have you let her get free? Where is she?" The Arrow searched the dark room until his eyes found his objective. Arash traced his gaze. In the corner, out of the light, was the dim image of the colored print of the woman's dress.

The Arrow rushed forward in anger. "You harlot! You'll regret..."

Arash moved after him, trying to decide what to do. He almost ran into the leader's back, when the other man stopped abruptly and stared.

Arash jerked at what he saw. The woman was upright, leaning against the wall in the corner, but her head was gone. The neckline of her dress ended in empty darkness. *Did someone already...*

Anguish, beyond his control, washed over him. It lasted only an instant before reason came back. How could she be standing?

As Arash's eyes became accustomed to the dark it became clear that the dress was draped over a rolled-up tarp that was standing in the corner. A noise behind them caused both men to turn. The door slammed shut followed by a "whump" sound, plunging the room into deeper darkness. Arash felt the Arrow move and bump into his shoulder.

The smaller man shoved Arash out of the way with a noise of disgust. "She was hiding behind the door and now she's gotten out."

Arash trailed after the man as he moved warily in the dark toward the door. The other man grunted as he struck something. A sliver of light formed as the door came partially open. The Arrow was pulling at the knob but rolls of tarps were on the floor in front of the door and the leader struggled to move them.

The woman must have had several tarp rolls standing upright behind the entrance so that they fell in a domino stack against the door when it closed. Arash marveled at the ingenuity of the woman. This time, he was only half surprised at the regret he felt knowing that she would run right into the arms of the men outside.

The Arrow forced the door open enough to slide through. Arash grabbed the door with a powerful arm and with far less effort, jerked it open wider and joined the other man who was glancing around the hallway. The girl was gone. They both pounded down the hall toward the exit to the fenced yard.

166

Chapter 26

The plodding coming down the semi's ramp was the leaden tread of men who had finished a grueling task. The driver came around to the same area where he had operated the controls of the rear ramp. The sound of the hydraulics accompanied the rapidly widening space between the ramp and the ground.

Still under the truck, Darrell aimed his M&P pistol toward the gap that was forming. If someone saw him, he would shoot, but he wanted to wait until he got inside the building. His strategy was simple. Stay hidden until he had a chance to slip inside the building. Once inside, he would enter and start taking out every hostile he encountered in his search for Callie. He hoped he could avoid shooting and hold the surprise factor long enough to find her and barricade them somewhere that he could hold off the remaining kidnappers until help arrived.

To load the cars, the truck driver had parked near the middle of the lot. The easiest way for him to leave was to turn toward the building. The maneuver would swing the truck toward the rear door of the structure, and Darrell would hang on underneath and let it drag him along, providing cover to get close to the entrance.

Darrell decided it didn't matter why the group kidnapped Callie—if they were getting ready to move, they might be finished with her. His desperation outweighed his anger at God. *Give me time to get to her.* Since it appeared that the loading was winding down, they might decide to…*Please, don't let them kill her.*

He had seen six men so far – seven counting the truck driver. The big man had gone back inside. One man stood guard at the gate, now closed except for a small gap he was using to watch the road. The other four had been doing the moving and now they walked back toward where they had leaned their assault rifles against the wall.

The sound of a door slamming against the side of the building ended Darrell's threat inventory. The big man and another average sized man burst into the yard. The ramp stopped moving.

There was something familiar about the smaller man. As Darrell tried to place him, the man began yelling. He was obviously the boss because everyone stiffened at his voice. No translation was needed. Darrell knew something major had occurred. The foreign words the men in the yard were using combined with accompanying head shakes did not satisfy the man's heated inquiry.

The leader barked at the guard at the gate. The guard pushed the gate open and disappeared outside the fence. Snapping a command at another of the men, the leader gestured after the guard. The underling grabbed one of the rifles from the wall and also headed out the gate.

Looking toward the truck, the leader gave another order. Darrell tensed, his gun ready. The driver ran to the cab of the truck. In the dark of his concealed location, Darrell rolled his head to watch him climb in. The door slammed on the building. The others had gone inside. When the driver's legs crawled out again the butt of an assault rifle dropped into Darrell's view.

The man stood for a moment as if he did not know what to do. The rifle butt lifted out of sight, and Darrell heard the sling being pulled over the man's shoulder. The legs moved to the rear of the truck, and the ramp started closing again.

Whatever just happened had changed the pace. It might also increase the threat to Callie. Time for a new plan.

Under the cover of the loud hydraulics, Darrell rolled out on the opposite side of the truck. He moved to the front as the man secured the latch on the driver's side rear trailer door. Crouching as he slipped around the truck, Darrell followed the man's legs as they moved to latch the other side.

Darrell was at the opposite side of the trailer when the legs turned to face the building and the AK rattled with the transition to the man's hands. Thrusting out the black synthetic arm like a cop stopping traffic with his fingers forming the letter *L,* Darrell stepped around the corner of the truck and centered the red dot on the man's back. The Taser popped.

"Whoa, Dead Eye Darrell!" Link was yelling. The camera in the NIP's hand showed the man hit the ground all stiff and quivering. Darrell was on the man before the five second cycle could finish. Link watched for the computer to switch back to the shoulder camera once the hand was lowered, as it was programmed to do, but Darrell moved quicker than it could process the image. Link saw the back of the man's head zoom in, filling the monitor, and then the view was obstructed, and the man's groaning became muffled. Link was shocked when the view switched back. The black mechanical hand drove the man's head into the dirt and Darrell was pummeling the side of his neck with his fist like a hammer.

The enemy was limp as Darrell dragged him behind the cover of the semi tires.

Link broke his stunned silence. "You okay, Darrell? That was one intense rush down there. You aren't losing it on me, are you?"

"Trust me," Darrell's voice came to Link over the speaker, "it's not as easy to knock someone out as the movies make it look. I don't want this guy back in the game while I'm taking on the others. We're not playing nice now, so prepare yourself for worse than that before it's over."

Darrell searched the exterior storage compartments on the truck and found some rope and duct tape to tie and gag the man. He finished by rolling him on his side and binding him against the tires with quick knots.

Link followed the view as Darrell grabbed the AK from the ground.

"Maybe this will help even the odds." Darrell checked the magazine and made sure there was a round in the chamber. The images on the monitor pulled Link along for the ride as Darrell ran for the building. The protection of the truck receded in the rear cameras. Link found himself wishing for a joystick to slow everything down, as the forward view showed the door to the building rushing to meet him.

KENT WYATT

Chapter 27

Shawn finished up his conversation with the Chief. The FBI had opened an investigation, according to the Chief, concerning Darrell's name being associated with some suspicious communications they had intercepted from a known hate group. Because of Darrell's reputation, Shawn had been able to convince the Chief to help with the current situation.

The Chief told Shawn he would call the commander of the police department's TEU team. They were assisting the FBI at the other location, but he would see if they could get them to the Newport scene in time. He said he would also warn the FBI team that they might be walking into a trap since the terrorists seemed to be at another location. The Chief seemed convinced by the video Shawn sent him, but he was still concerned about how long it might take to get help to Darrell.

Shawn walked out the front door to his car. Turning to the SUV that Brock and his partner were in, he gave a quick wave, jumped in the driver's seat of his own car and took off down the street. He wheeled his vehicle toward Darrell's location with the SUV in hot pursuit.

Just above the roll of tarps that held Callie's dress, there was movement. A ceiling tile raised, slid to the side, and Callie reached down to retrieve her garment. "Come on." She tugged on the fabric that was pinned to the wall by the tarps. "Don't rip." The cloth slipped free, forcing her to regain her balance on the wide I-beam where she perched in the ceiling.

Callie sighed with relief as she pulled the flower print material into her hideaway. It smelled like the tarps, but it was undamaged. The dress was filthy but so was she, so with a careful mixture of balance and contortions, she wriggled back into the soiled garment and put on her sweater. Re-covering the ceiling tile with insulation, she breathed, "Thank You," to her Heavenly Father.

Callie tried to brush the grime from her skinned knees then noticed her hands. *There just as dirty, that's not going to help much. Who knew climbing a tarp roll would be such an ordeal.* The dirty oil that was ground into the wounds made them miserable. *It got you into the ceiling and away from them, so stop complaining.* All she wanted was a bath…without anyone wanting to kill her outside the bathroom door. *Sorry, Lord. Thank you, again.* There was no way the scheme would have worked without Him.

When the men had walked into the room, she had feared that Freckles was going to stay by the entrance, and he would have been able to tell that no one really went out the door. She had been holding her breath as she watched him through where she left the ceiling tile cracked. It was a miracle he didn't hear her let out her air when he finally followed the other man into the room. Then she nearly panicked when she couldn't get the tarps to fall on the first tug. How the two men didn't figure it out—with her in the ceiling jerking on the rope until the stick that held the tarps upright behind the door finally came loose—was a miracle.

The sound of boots coming back down the hallway reminded Callie that she didn't want to waste the time the ruse had provider her. She needed to decide her next move.

From the direction of the entrance to the room, Callie could hear doors banging in the hallway. A glow came from that direction as light leaked into the ceiling space around the fixtures being switched on to search the rooms.

So far, her trick had them searching every other room, but it wouldn't take long for them to start looking deeper. She knew she shouldn't have risked getting her dress, but if she was rescued or captured—either way she wanted to be clothed.

Callie headed away from the sounds and the faint illumination, feeling her way along the I-beam, moving into the deeper darkness. Every few feet, she had to crawl through one of the roof braces that rested on the I-beams. The braces were constructed of metal tubing welded together at angles that made navigating the ceiling awkward. *This architect has it out for me.*

Callies foot slipped. She saved herself with a grab onto a piece of angled metal. She allowed the thrill that had rushed through her subside before moving again. *Girl, maybe you should have minored in gymnastics because the last thing you need is to fall through the ceiling.*

Callie had been near the back wall of the room in which she was held when she started crawling the I-beam, so she knew she must be over a different room now. A dark shape was in front of her. A muscle tensing spasm went through her until she saw it was a heating duct that blocked her path.

She would have to crawl over it or monkey climb on a roof brace to the next I beam and try to go around. She peered through the dusty darkness. The duct work continued out of her visual range.

Callie put her leg over the rectangular metal tube meant to carry heat and air. She hesitated putting her foot down for fear she would miss the I-beam. Her bottom dropped onto the duct. The metal pushed inward with a metallic pop. Callie sat motionless, listening. There was no change in the indistinct sound of the men's movements—no indication they heard. Putting her hands on the edges of the square duct, she eased herself off the metal, lessening the noise. Then she found the I-beam on the other side with her foot and dropped onto it.

The noise of the searching sounded closer. A fixture off to her right lit up. Her attic escape must have taken her above a room down a different hallway than where she had been confined. She speculated that her pursuers had made it to that hallway. *Where do I go from here, God? They'll be watching the exits.* She needed a place to hide.

Her hands felt gritty from sweat and the dust that coated everything. As she brushed them off, she had a disconcerting thought. *I've been leaving tracks.* All it would take is one person to look in the attic and her trail in the dust would lead right to her. There would be no hiding.

Father, if You've got a rescue planned, any time now would be good. It was either that or something to make them abandon the search. Callie's jaw shuddered with the acceptance that there were other possible outcomes she didn't want to think about. God had still not taken death from the world. People died, and sometimes they were killed. She confronted Heaven with her gaze. *Please don't let me be another loss in Darrell's life.*

Arash watched the men around him searching for the girl with blood lust in their eyes. Everyone wanted to be the one that found her, courting the favor of Allah and the leader. Not long ago he knew he would have had that same look. He knew these men. He had trained them, fought with them, called them brothers. But now they no longer seemed human to him.

Arash needed to find the woman first. He hurried along the hallway not knowing where he should start, but he had to look like part of the activity. *Where would she go?* Without realizing the steps to get there, he found himself standing at the entrance to the room which had been her prison. *You last saw her inside.* It was an unconscious thought, but it made sense.

Shoving the tarps further into the room, he made entry. Arash used the flashlight on his cell phone to examine the damaged light switch. *Effective sabotage.*

He aimed the light around the room and stopped on the rolled-up tarps that had fooled them earlier. Something wasn't…It wasn't there.

Arash hurried to the tarp roll and ran his hand over the rough surface. *She had returned for it.* A piece of insulation clung to his fingers when he pulled his hand away. He studied it. His eyes lifted to the ceiling tiles above him. *So clever.* But it would not be long before someone else figured it out.

Now what? He dared not try to go up after her. She would not trust him, and she might panic, expose herself sooner. He could not call to her for fear of being heard.

The sounds of the searching men reminded him that they would not rest until they found the woman. *What will you do when that happens?*

You're a dead man already. Another spontaneous thought, but Arash knew it was true. When they came back from the yard, the Arrow had glanced at him. It was brief but Arash had seen the mixture of silent rage and paranoia before. Allowing the girl to escape was the last inexcusable act.

The lingering death sentence occupied the smaller portion of Arash's thoughts. What to do about the woman was his greater concern. *Why is she so important?* He felt like the eyes of God were upon him, waiting for his decision, conveying the impression that there were greater things to fear than death.

Behind Callie, there was the sound of a ceiling tile lifting. She flattened herself on the I-beam as a spear of light slashed into the attic gloom. The glow of a flashlight beam traveled across the ceiling. Her area lit up as the circle of light skimmed the top of another duct about six feet to her left. The beam was passing directly over her, but there was no outcry. The duct to her right hid her from the source of the light.

The flashlight moved away and left the ceiling. Callie's stomach clinched. Were they examining the I-beam?

The man with the light called excitedly to someone else. Even though she couldn't understand him, Callie knew. *He's found my tracks.* Every part of her wanted to move, to flee before they had her…every part but the one that engaged her muscles. That part was listening to something besides her fear. *Be still.*

The announcement from the man caused a clamor of shouts and rapid conversation through the building. Callie heard a ceiling tile pop up and plop into the insulation, behind and to her left. Another beam of light probed through the attic. The reflected illumination allowed her to see her surroundings. *Thank God the heating ducts are hiding me from both of these guys. Don't even breathe.*

The first light vanished. In a few minutes, the room lights came on just on the other side of the heat duct to Callie's right. The second searcher's light was still slicing through the dark of the attic, stopping frequently to examine potential hiding places more closely.

Callie prayed. *You hid me once, Lord. Please don't let them see me.*

In the room where the lights had come on, something grated across the floor. Scrambling and thumping noises followed, and another ceiling tile flipped just on the other side of the duct work from her. She was close enough to hear the insulation being shoved aside. She saw the circle of light, dancing on the ceiling, as the latest man shimmied into the attic. The beam came over the top of the duct work and moved across the area just to her left. *He's so close.* Again, no shout. The searcher would have to crawl further into the attic to see over the duct that shielded her. Instead, he pulled out of the ceiling.

Voices grew louder as a door was opened just below Callie. The insulation around her came alive with glowing light. The foreign conversation below her stopped as about three feet in front of her the insulation began to rise.

KENT WYATT

Chapter 28

Darrell's fear for Callie drove him forward, but he had to temper his rapid advance into the building with caution. *No mistakes, not now.* Callie's life depended on him.

He turned the knob on an interior door. It bumped against something. The something moved and spoke to him, the man on the other side of the door apparently mistaking him for one of the other men returning.

Darrell gave a grunt and set his rifle against the wall just inside the entrance as he casually opened the door. The man continued to address him right up to the minute when they faced each other. Darrell grabbed the man's rifle, spun his hands to put the leverage to his advantage, and jerked the weapon downward, cleanly out of the man's hands. The confusion on the other's face gave way to wide-eyed astonishment, which Darrell wiped away with the butt of the rifle.

Arash's stomach had tightened when he heard Shahin yell that there were handprints in the attic. The younger man had the scent. Arash hurried toward his voice.

Even though the Arrow had interrupted Arash's earlier prayer, something inside him still cried to God. As he caught up with Shahin, a new wrestling match was going on in his heart.

To not kill the girl was one thing, but the only way Arash could see to save her would be for him to kill all these men, his brothers. The conflict was forefront in his mind as he hurried to keep up with Shahin who was hustling into the next room, rambling about the prints leading that way.

While Shahin used the point of his AK-47 to poke at the ceiling tiles, the struggle inside Arash reached a climax. The woman's faith led her to sing joyful songs in the face of horror. His faith led him to watch silently as men around him hunted an innocent, helpless person.

Sudden clarity flowed into Arash. He felt like he had stepped out of a fog that he had been walking in all his life. He had no time to mold it into anything structured.

Shahin slung the weapon over his back and started toward a desk on the wall. He put one foot on the desk and prepared to give a jump.

Arash placed his hand on the man's shoulder. "My brother, let me, I am taller."

Shahin brushed away Arash's offer. "It is not a problem. I can crawl up."

Arash did not remove his huge hand. "Please do not deny me this opportunity. It is I that this worthless woman has made a fool of. I owe her."

Shahin smiled weakly. Arash knew the younger man was seeing his opportunity slipping away, but he bowed to Arash's size and authority and stepped down from the desk.

Arash hefted himself up. He had to bend below the ceiling because of his height. Pushing up the ceiling tile, he shoved the insulation out of the way as he went. Once he had an opening, he reached his hand out for Shahin's flashlight. The man hesitated but handed it over.

As he raised up into the attic, Arash saw two other flashlights probing into the shadows. One of them turned toward the sound of Arash pushing into the tight space. The man's light blinded him. Arash chastised his underling good naturedly, and the beam went elsewhere.

Switching on Shahin's flashlight, Arash saw large, dark, tear-reddened eyes staring at him. The girl was flattened against an I-beam that ran next to a large, galvanized heating duct.

Arash did not allow his light beam to linger but moved it back and forth as if he had seen nothing. He turned a complete 360 using the light to examine the area. He pointed it at all the dark areas just as the others were doing but, in its glow, he examined how well the girl was concealed. She was in a perfect position between two heating ducts that separately branched around her. Arash estimated that the room he was in was the only one from which she could be seen if she stayed down.

Arash called to the other men. "She is not here. Do you see her over there?" When the men said they did not, he told them, "Keep searching, she must be over there somewhere. When you find her, bring her to me. The honor will be yours, but I will be the one that makes sure she never defies a man again."

Arash pulled out of the ceiling and spoke more quietly to Shahin. "You were right; the dust tracks keep moving that direction." Arash indicated the next room as he climbed down. He looked kindly at the young man as he handed back his light. "I am sorry, Shahin. You are a good man, and it was wrong of me to seek my own personal satisfaction. Go and look without me. You were the first one to think of looking in the dust. You should be the one to find her. Go quickly before someone else takes the prize from you."

Shahin smiled broadly and turned to hurry out of the room but stopped. The Arrow blocked the doorway.

Link was unsure how it happened. One second, the man was standing in front of Darrell holding an AK and the next he was on the ground and Darrell had the gun. The blur of movements in between had been too much for Link to follow.

Link's heart was pounding. He wanted Darrell to stop so Link's nerves could rest, but he knew that couldn't happen. Even under pressure, smart-alecky remarks popped in and out of Link's mind, but he was afraid to say anything for fear he would cause Darrell to miss something. He watched the cameras for any sign of an enemy, dreading seeing one for fear it would be too late to warn Darrell. Deep breaths. He began to purposely inhale to relieve the anxiety.

Darrell was down another hall and at another door.

Link suspended his breathing for a moment.

Darrell peeked in but it was out of the view of Link's cameras. Apparently, nothing was there because Darrell was opening the door.

No pause feature on this game, Link thought as he sucked in another breath.

"How gracious of you, Arash." The Arrow moved into the room holding an AK. His face displayed a sinister displeasure. "Where is your weapon?" His eyes searched the room while he spoke as if he was giving a lesson. "Even though we are moving, it is careless not to have it nearby. You have been making a lot of mistakes lately." He continued into the room and around Shahin who turned like a cat watching a dog that was circling him. The men had all seen the leader's anger come out of nowhere. He raised the weapon barrel up with one hand and placed the other hand on the younger man's shoulder while he continued to address Arash. "It concerns me, these mistakes."

Arash shifted his stance, prepared. Perhaps the leader saw it because he shifted his other hand back to the rifle and moved away from Arash, closer to the middle of the room. He was about twenty feet away, the gun was still pointed up. Arash was quick for his size, but he did not underestimate the Arrow. They had trained together. Even though the man was not a warrior, he could still drop the barrel and direct a full-auto barrage at him, and at that distance, he would not even have to aim.

The leader stopped. Glancing back and forth between the two men, he abandoned his calm demeanor.

"I want you to comprehend this! We need to leave! If the girl is up there," he shouted, his eyes glued on Arash, "then she can die there!"

The assault rifle blazed into the ceiling. Along with the thundering of the rifle and the sound of shredding ceiling tile, there were metallic pings and a cry of pain. Arash dashed toward the leader as the other man swiveled the rifle down and in his direction.

"What was that?" Link's voice was in Darrell's ear just when he needed to listen. He jerked the synthetic hand off the gun and slashed it across the camera's view in a silencing gesture as he peaked around a doorframe, following the sound. Men came pouring out of doorways along a hall just ahead. Darrell instinctively flexed his knees and almost opened fire, but the men were all running the other direction, toward the shooting, and didn't notice him.

Darrell hesitated, processing what happened. He moved quickly to the first room figuring it must be empty now. It was. In the sudden flow of bodies, he thought he had seen four men come out, head down the hall, through the door, and around the corner. The shooting must not have been planned since it startled them.

Darrell dashed from room to room checking only long enough to be sure no one was there to shoot him in the back. He begged, *Not Callie, God. Please.* Whispering, he fired instructions at Link. "I need to find Callie now! I'll be moving fast and focusing all my attention ahead. You to concentrate on everything behind me."

Chapter 29

Arash lay, teeth clenched. He had been shot before. This was worse. He panted involuntarily. Movement around him crawled, but his thoughts raced. His leg had crumpled immediately, so a bullet must have shattered his hip. His hand was trying to hold in the sticky heat that ebbed from the wound just below his waist. He had seen such wounds before. There would be no rising from it. What should he do with his last moments? Had his defense of the woman already condemned his soul?

Arash blinked to focus into the dark hole that had been ripped in the ceiling. The woman had to be there still. If she had been killed, she would have fallen into the room. Was she also wounded, clinging to the I-beam, thinking the same thoughts? No. She would not have his doubts. A calm entered Arash. He had done the right thing. He had tried to save her, but in his heart, he felt like she had saved him.

Where were the others? Arash had heard Shahin cry out in pain when the shooting started. He rolled his eyes, searching for the other man. Shahin was there, hand covering his cheek, blood dripping around it. One of the bullets must have bounced back and nicked him. Shahin's eyes were locked on the weapon the Arrow was now pointing at him.

Sound in the doorway sent Arash's eyes that direction. The other men filled the frame, each with an AK at ready, trying to make sense of the scene. The Arrow's wild look melted. He eased his rifle to a relaxed position and called out, "Brothers, please lower your weapons. There has been a tragedy, but everything is over now."

"What's going on?" The man who spoke locked gaze with Arash and started toward him.

The leader raised his arm between them. "Be careful. He attacked me."

Arash did not bother to defend himself, didn't know if he could. Soon it would not matter.

"I have had to do something that breaks my heart. For some time, I have perceived that Arash was no longer loyal. I could not believe it because we have been together so long. This was the only way to find out.

When I threatened the infidel woman, he turned on me, but Allah has prevailed."

The Arrow laid his rifle on the floor and approached Shahin with a look of compassion. "I am sorry, my friend. I never meant to hurt you. I know you are faithful to Allah. For a moment, I did not know who was my friend and who was not. Arash and I have been together so long, I could not believe this if I had not seen it."

The leader looked at the men who had relaxed their guns but still appeared in shock, staring at where Arash lay.

The leader brought their attention to himself. "Someone get bandages for our brother. He has been injured accidentally." When no one moved the leader gave the order directly to the nearest man, who jumped as if he had been slapped, slung his rifle, and hurried off.

"Now all of you, listen. We are in the land of the enemy. I know there are many temptations. I thought Arash was stronger, but apparently I was wrong, and he was seduced. If one person gives in to these temptations, it weakens us all. Allah has purified us. We are strong again. This is a confirmation that the plan is from him, and we will all share in his glory. But we must hurry. Forget the search for the girl. We will abandon that part of the plan. Everything is loaded, and it is more important that we leave immediately for the new location. All we have left to do in this city can be accomplished from our alternate site, which has not been compromised. We will burn this place and the girl with it."

Arash looked at the ceiling again. The woman needed to get out. The tiles blurred. The leaders voice came as if from a tunnel.

Two of the men still standing at the door moved further into the room.

Arash followed the movement, and his focus came back. The Arrow reached out to Shahin. The younger man flinched, but the leader gently touched the blood-covered hand that Shahin held against his cheek. When the Arrow removed his touch, he displayed Shahin's blood that had transferred to his fingers.

"When one of us bleeds, we all bleed. This is a sting from Allah to wake us. We are at war. The weapon we have armed is more powerful than all the bullets and bombs that our military has stockpiled, and if we succeed, then the enemy will bring destruction on themselves without us spilling more Persian blood." He paused, then continued. "But first we must care for this loyal one." The leader looked to the doorway and shouted, "Where are those bandages?"

As if in answer, the lone man still in the doorway came stumbling in, hit so hard from behind that his rifle skittered across the floor as he went sprawling onto his belly.

Behind the cover of the doorframe, Darrell pointed his AK directly at the two men who still held their rifles. "I hope you speak English because you're about to die if you don't let those guns fall."

Both weapons hit the floor.

"I want everyone's hands straight up, now!" Darrell put enough menace in his voice that the entire group complied. The man he had kicked from behind got to his feet without the aid of his hands, which he kept raised through the process.

Darrell took a second to evaluate the situation. Five men stood with their hands high. One had a rifle slung across his body and a blood-stained face. Darrell eyed the rifle. *The way he has it across him will take as long to unsling as to pick it up if I have him put it down. Better not give him a chance to touch it.* One of the other men had a mustache and the other a full beard. Darrell didn't like the look the bearded man gave him. *Keep an eye on that one.* There was a man on the floor doing some serious bleeding. At the far end of the room was a closed door that he would see come open if any attack was coming from there. "Where's the woman?"

The leader, the man that Darrell recognized, addressed him in English, pleading, "Please, we have had an accident here, and these men need medical attention. One may be dying. Let me go for a first aid kit, and we can explain this while I am treating him."

"I think I met someone you sent to do that already. He won't be coming back. Funny you didn't mention him." Darrell tossed a first aid kit he had dangling on his support hand to the man he had kicked and motioned with his head toward the bleeding man, "Use a thick bandage and get some direct pressure on that man's wound."

The man went to the bleeder and soon had his hand pressed against his hip causing the wounded man to groan feebly.

Darrell stayed just outside the doorway where he continued to use the door frame for cover in case anyone in the room tried anything. Looking directly at the leader, Darrell kept his focus wide so his peripheral vision could catch any movement from the others. "You're the only one here I know. We met a long time ago, and if you remember me, then you'll understand why I would really love a reason to shoot you. But every one of you can pick up your wounded, walk out that door, get in that truck outside and leave, providing the girl you kidnapped is alive and you give her to me right now."

The leader spoke before anyone else could respond. "You have made a grave mistake. I am not sure who you think I am, but there is no girl here. Just because we are Middle Eastern does not mean…"

"He's lying, Darrell." Callie's voice came from somewhere high, making the leader jump.

"Callie! Where are you?"

"In the ceiling. I didn't want to distract you earlier, but that guy is lying. He just tried to make Swiss cheese out of me, but he hit a metal beam instead."

The leader inserted himself again. "All right. Forgive me for lying, but I was scared. You have the girl, now let us leave as you promised."

Darrell narrowed his eyes at the man. "That offer expired while you were lying to me."

Link's voice exploded in his ear. "They're coming up the hall to your left!"

Darrell jerked his head and saw two other men just as they saw him. One of them raised his rifle, and Darrell leaped into the room as bullets tore up the door frame. "Callie, get out of here!"

At the same time the leader yelled something and fled toward the door at the other end of the room from Darrell.

Darrell stuck his rifle out the opening from where the immediate assault was coming and blazed a volley. There was an outcry of pain from one of the men down the hall. Darrell drew back, and another round of bullets gnawed at the wood of the framework.

In the room, Mustache and Beard rushed Darrell while the one that was tending to the bleeder dove for the rifles on the floor. Things that were happening in a blur were like slow motion to Darrell.

Darrell took the greatest threat first. His AK tore up the man going for the guns before the others were on him. Mustache reached Darrell first and grabbed his AK with both hands. Darrell went backward, allowing the man to push him, which created distance between Beard. The first man was fooled by Darrell yielding and drove forward. Suddenly Darrell pivoted to the side, let his prosthetic shoulder make a painful hit to the inside of the doorframe, and used Mustache's momentum to toss him into the hallway, twisting the rifle out of his grip. Darrell heard the sound of full auto fire in the hallway as he delivered a side kick to Beard's knee, jamming his lead leg. Mustache groaned, and Darrell heard him drop to the floor with a thud. Beard grimaced from Darrell's kick. Darrell continued the swing of the rifle, slamming the barrel of the AK into the side of Beard's head. The blow sent Beard stumbling to the right, dazed but still on his feet.

"Look out!" Link yelled in Darrell's ear.

Across the room, in the seconds that the entire encounter took, the man with the bloody face had unslung his rifle and was trying to get a shot around Beard, who was staggering from Darrell's hit. Beard went sideways. Bloody Face saw his chance and fired.

The shoulder of the NIP jerked violently backward, but Darrell was able to dash to Beard's right. Beard came to his senses and threw up his arms, trying to shield his head. Bloody Face's rounds sent wallboard pieces flying where it impacted beside the door, but none hit Beard.

Bringing up his AK, Darrell targeted Bloody Face who was doing the same to Darrell. Beard shoved Darrell, sending him stumbling forward and forcing Bloody Face to re-aim. Keeping his AK pointed at Bloody Face, Darrell tried to land on his forearms, to spread out the impact. Clenching his teeth against the torturous wave of pain, Darrell pulled the trigger. Bloody Face's bullets spattered on the tile floor next to Darrell but ended abruptly when Darrell's rounds found their target, and the man crumpled to the floor.

Darrell's world spun. The adrenaline that had carried him through since he heard the first gunshots was finally overcome by nausea and the stabbing pain in his stump. He tried to use his real arm to rise despite the agony, but a crushing weight hit his back. A powerful arm locked around his neck and immediately cut off his wind. Another hand grabbed the NIP at the wrist and attempted to push it to the floor sending more pain.

Instinctively Darrell turned his Adam's apple into the bend of the elbow, trying to gain some space to breathe, but the lights were going out. The NIP dropped to the floor. In his fading thoughts, Darrell could tell he had lost control of it. Blackness closed over his mind.

Chapter 30

"No way!" Link shouted at his electronics. The images from the arm were gone. He had seen the man across the room fire at Darrell and then everything went blank. The programs were open and running, but they produced empty, black boxes on all his devices. Link was using the Wi-Fi hotspot on his cell phone to receive the feed. He checked the phone. It was working, but he wasn't receiving the NIP's signal. *Something must have killed it at its source.* Link cringed at his own word choice.

The input void left him with one scene filling his thoughts. Link had never witnessed someone die before. In hideous replay, the image of the man going for the guns and Darrell's bullets striking him was banging against Link's brain, playing over and over in his mind causing an almost physical pain in some unidentified part of him. He struggled to keep it from extending to the obvious thought that the same thing had happened to Darrell.

Callie had listened when Darrell told her to get out of there. She scurried, on all fours, down the I-Beam, diving through the roof braces, putting as much distance between her and the room as possible, remembering the fear she had felt when the rounds came ripping up through the ceiling around her. The air was still full of the long-dead dust that had been brought to life by the same bullets that she thought were going to kill her. She choked it down with each gasp of air.

But Darrell had come. When she heard him enter the room, taking charge of everyone below, it had made her heart leap. He was there, willing to give everything for her - always her hero. She had cast her praise to the Lord and thought the nightmare would soon be over. Then everything was automatic weapon fire and commotion.

Callie stopped. She must be several rooms away by now. All was quiet. The gunfire had ended, and there was a stillness that did not feel natural.

She heard glass breaking somewhere behind her accompanied by the sound of sudden combustion. A few minutes later, from the other direction, she heard the same sound. Callie knew the sound—she had heard gasoline ignite before. The noise was repeated two more times in other areas. She started crawling again until she heard a different sound, one that produced a jolt of dread.

Ripping away a large chunk of insulation, Callie lifted a tile. Smoke immediately stung her eyes. She fanned it away and saw what she feared. The wall on the opposite side of the room was on fire. She quickly dropped the tile but she knew that the smoke would soon be invading the attic and would be far worse than the dust. The acrid smell from the little that had come up when she opened the tile was already biting her lungs.

Where was Darrell? She had not heard him since things had gone wrong in the room. How could she have left him?

Grabbing a roof brace, she got herself headed back the way she had come, then hesitated. What if Darrell was making his way toward the exit and expecting her to do the same? No. If he was able, he would be looking for her, calling for her if he could. He would not leave her, and she was not going to leave him.

Callie backtracked down the I-beam and through the braces. It was easier because the attic was growing brighter. She paused again. There was a flickering glow playing on the underside of the roof. She peeked above some of the heating ducts. Flames invaded the attic through sections of the ceiling that had already been destroyed at the far end of the building. The licking fingers of the blaze below were obscured by billows of smoke that were heading her direction. She took off again, ignoring the cry of her tortured knees as they pounded the metal and the ache of her shoulders as she plunged through the roof bracing.

Callie got to the room where she had left Darrell. She peered through the hole in the ceiling, examining the room through the destroyed tile. Poking her head through the hole, she saw a man lying in a puddle of blood, then another. There were several bodies in the room, and she feared they were all dead. There was a desk under the same tile Freckles had peeked his head through earlier. She lifted the tile and dropped onto the desk.

Tears began to trickle down Callie's cheeks. She scanned the room but did not look at the bodies any longer than she had to. The horror of it was only tempered by the fact that Darrell was not among them. She whispered her thanks to God as she slid to the floor. She was hurrying out of the room when she heard a groan from behind her. She eased toward the man making the noise. The blood under his right hip had gathered in a pool. His face was hideously pale but there was something that she recognized.

"Freckles," she breathed after a couple of moments. The man opened his eyes and gazed at her as if taking time to focus.

"Still alive," he said hoarsely in English. "Good. I feared they would have killed you and this would have been for nothing."

Callie did not know what he was talking about. "Can you move?" she asked him.

He shook his head and grimaced.

"You're too big for me to lift, but I'll try to get out and get help."

"You need to hurry. They intend to burn the place."

"It's already on fire."

"Then I pray I die soon. I have seen men burn." The man was going to say more but stopped himself.

Callie wanted to ask him why they had kidnapped her, what it was all about. But she knew there was something that God would want her to do first.

"Are you ready to die?" she asked, drawing a little closer, but still wary.

The man regarded her through droopy eyes. "Is anyone? I thought I was until I met you."

Callie was confused again. She did not have much time, though, so she didn't hesitate. "You need to ask God to forgive your sins. You need to trust in Jesus. He is the only way you can be right with God before you die."

"Is such trust what made you hum your tune?"

"What?"

"It does not matter. Mohammad, Jesus, I have neither now."

"You can have Jesus."

Arash looked at her, then his eyes drifted away in thought. "Jesus must be something more than what I thought because if it had been you here and I there, I would not be wasting my time talking to a dying enemy."

"He is more. You didn't know it, but He performed a miracle just tonight. I prayed that your eyes would be blinded, and you didn't see me when you looked in the attic. You looked right at me but didn't see me."

The corner of Arash's mouth turned up. "Jesus did not blind my eyes. That happened a long time ago. If anything, He opened them. That is what saved you. I saw you but said nothing."

"You saw me?" The significance of it rushed into Callie's mind. "Is that why you got shot? Trying to stop them from shooting me?"

Arash looked at Callie as if examining a piece of art. "A greater miracle than the one for which you prayed, I am thinking."

"It was an act of faith." Callie's face flashed with a sudden inspiration. "I have something to tell you. When Jesus was dying, there was a man there on another cross. He was a criminal and admitted that he was getting what he deserved, but he asked Jesus to remember him when He got to Heaven." Callie had to wipe away tears as she continued. "Jesus told the criminal that he would be with Him in Heaven that very day. All he had to do was ask. And that is all you need to do. If you do that now and mean it, none of what you did in the past matters."

The man closed his eyes. Callie thought he was gone, but then he spoke with his eyes still closed. "I would have Jesus do this for me if He is willing."

Callie wiped her wet eyes. The tears had washed the dust and smoke from them.

Arash opened his eyes again. "Go. It is all right. I will lay here until I fall asleep. I believe I might sing a song."

She reached and touched his shoulder. "Try to stay alive. I want to know you better."

"I believe some day you will. Now please, go so what I have done will mean something."

As Callie stepped away, she noticed that smoke was pooling around a smoke detector on the ceiling near the door. *They must have disconnected the alarms.* The gray billows flowed over the top of the door jamb and spilled into the upper part of the hall. Callie ran toward the exit. She had to step around another body. There was no sign the man had been shot. A look of surprise seemed to be fixed in his lifeless eyes. His mouth was wide open, and his hand was at his throat, where there were deep red indentations. In the hall was another man that had been shot. Callie had to jump to avoid stepping in the red puddle around him.

She decided that it was too late to worry about noise, so she ran down the corridor, jumping over another dead man, calling Darrell's name. She turned the corner and saw him. Halfway down the next expanse, Darrell was dragging himself along the hall using the NIP. Laser beams were shining out from the NIP, into the smoky atmosphere of the hallway. He must have been injured because his head was down on the floor and his body limp except for the arm that was moving him forward by alternating back and forth in the way that it pushed. As she ran to him, the NIP raised in a strange, twisted manner. Callie slid to a stop when she saw the prosthetic thrust out and the Weapons console open. "Darrell, it's me. It's Callie."

A synthetic voice came over the speaker of the arm, "Stop. Do not approach or you will be fired upon." Callie tried to move to the side of the hall, but the arm followed her like a cobra ready to spit. The prosthetic was the only part of Darrell that was moving.

She realized what was going on and called out to the arm. "ATS Prosthetic, Jacobs, Darrell, voice input computer access, user ID Williams, Calneshia, password 04A1000tngs2sing, disable Rescue and Defense Mode."

The arm did not move. She tried again, carefully enunciating each word and number. No response.

Like an unearthly sentinel, the arm stood guard. It was protecting Darrell just as she had programmed it. But it should not be protecting him from her. Darrell was unconscious (she prayed) and the arm had gone into ARMED Status (Automated Rescue Mode with Enabled Defense). It was a feature of the prosthetic that she had kept secret, programmed on a special chip she designed and installed in the shop at her house. She had known there would be controversy over that ability of the NIP, so she chose not to advertise it. Police work was a dangerous job, and she desired to make it safer. She wanted Darrell safe.

And that was exactly what the NIP was doing. The device's smoke and heat sensors had detected the fire danger, and it was trying to get Darrell out of the building and protect him while he was incapacitated. But now it was keeping her from helping him. He could be dying, and for some reason, it perceived her as a threat when it should be recognizing her as a friend.

"Facial recognition refresh," she called out again to the arm. "Recognize: Williams, Calneshia."

Callie moved so that she could look directly into the camera array on the shoulder of the NIP, and she immediately saw the problem. There was a gaping hole in the synthetic material just under where the camera array was mounted. The exterior was thick enough in that area, that apparently it deflected a bullet leaving a chunk broken out of the material. The curve of the synthetic shoulder had forced the round up and into the camera section, which also held the input microphones. That section of the arm was gone, apparently ripped off with the exiting bullet. Callie mentally derided herself for putting all the sound and video processing hardware in the shoulder. Even the camera in the hand was routed through that processor, so the arm's computer was essentially deaf and blind. Operating only off its lasers, heat, vibration, and other sensors, it was viewing any approaching mass as a threat. Callie's mind began doing inventory. Its Wi-Fi connection would also be gone, so remote deactivation was out, even if she *could* find a computer or a smartphone.

While examining the arm, Callie inadvertently moved closer. Ow! She jumped back and grabbed her chest.

"Stay back. Do not make me hurt you." The voice warned. Callie sucked in a fearful breath. "The CO_2."

Chapter 31

Pulling the front of her dress out away from her body, Callie could see a small round burn mark in the material. Rubbing her chest, she looked at the NIP's weapons console. The Taser had been fired, its cartridge expended. But Callie had named it a *weapons* console because it had two. Callie stared at the small hole next to the Taser. It was the firing port for the second component that she had not discussed with others – a sealed CO_2 (carbon dioxide) laser tube focused through special lenses. Unlike the other lasers in the NIP, it could generate heat that exceeded most cutting torches. The laser had pulsed just long enough to make a painful but superficial burn to her skin. It was a warning shot. She knew if she got any closer to Darrell, a more powerful pulse could reach her internal organs. Callie backed away from Darrell. Soon, the arm resumed dragging him down the hallway.

Callie became aware of the progress of the other danger that was threatening them. Her eyes were stinging and the tickle in her lungs made her cough. The smoke was visibly swirling in the air of the hallway. The highest concentration was coming from behind her. That was why the NIP was moving the other direction. And it was moving rapidly, striking the floor hard as it planted the gripping surface of its hand on the floor and pushed, first one direction and then the other, to keep Darrell moving in a straight line. The men had set fires all over the building. The NIP's computer had no way of knowing that it was going to encounter fire in that direction as well, and regardless of the speed it was going, the one-arm mode of travel was not fast enough. They needed to get out *now*.

She began to search for a way to disable the laser. She fanned the smoke away from her face. Since smoke was detrimental to lasers, she knew the problem would solve itself when the smoke became thick enough to reflect the beam and reduce its power. But the laser was not the only thing that was susceptible to the smoke, and she feared they would be dead before it got that thick. Perhaps she could reflect it long enough to get to the manual fingerprint shut off. She ran into a bathroom, but with no tools, she was not strong enough to tear one of the mirrors off the wall. Searching around the room for something to break the mirror with, she grabbed the toilet tank lid. She reared back to shatter the mirror but halted. Even with its reflective ability, the mirror would still heat up and be difficult, if not impossible, to hold. But the white toilet lid, made of thick ceramic, would protect her longer. Holding her heavy shield with both hands, she ran back to the hall.

The NIP had moved too close to the left side wall and was sliding Darrell along it. Its sensing lasers had less power to penetrate the smoke, which had thickened, taking away more of the NIP's ability to navigate. Before it could get the correct angle to move forward, the arm had to push itself off the wall, which had dramatically slowed its progress.

Callie took a few seconds to think through her strategy. She knew since the computer could only see her as a laser-measured blob, it would be aiming for center mass. She also realized the faster she moved, the less time the laser had to concentrate its energy on one spot. She closed in on Darrell until the NIP detected her and snapped up like a snake. Callie crouched and ducked her head so she could keep as much of her behind the lid as possible. She ran toward Darrell. She felt a burn across her arm as her movement exposed her skin. With clenched teeth, she adjusted the lid toward that side and drove on. The lid was heavy for her, but her adrenaline was giving her extra strength. With her head down, the first thing she saw were Darrell's legs. Callie dropped to her knees and pushed the lid toward where she knew the arm would be.

Since its laser was not effective, the NIP grabbed the side of the lid and began to squeeze.

Callie felt that the arm was weak. The laser had drained its power. She held the lid with one hand and reached to the armpit area and felt around until she found the fingerprint reader. The panel slid aside with the recognition of her biometrics, and she quickly pressed her fingerprint against the shutdown button. The NIP slowly eased itself to the floor as it powered down.

Just as he had seen Darrell do when they were scouting out the building, Link turned off his headlights as he came around the curve just south of the target building. He let the car ease to the curb by a tree that was growing next to the street. He decided he could not stand waiting any longer, but he was still not sure what he was going to do.

As he contemplated his next move, a semi and an SUV came hustling around the building and turned north. Link watched the taillights until they turned left and drove out of sight. Darrell had said it looked like they were loading up to leave. That must have been them. But was it all of them? Link decided to drive up to see. He figured if anyone started shooting, he'd be better off in his car.

As he approached the building, his eyes darted around, searching, expecting a bullet to come through the windshield, his foot ready to stomp on the gas. Behind the front entry doors, fire blazed in some type of foyer. No wonder they left. But where were Darrell and Callie?

He hustled the car to the back. There was an SUV still sitting inside the fence. Link drove into the back fenced area and aimed his lights into the SUV from as far away as he could. It looked empty. He saw smoke coming from the gap at the top of the large overhead door. If Darrell and Callie were in there, they were in big trouble. The place was burning on all sides.

Link jumped out and ran to a walk-in door next to the large overhead that was closed. He opened the door and smoke poured out sending him spinning away, coughing, squeezing his eyes shut from the sting. Looking through the windows in the overhead door, Link saw a blaze glowing across the room, through the smoke. The dark fumes flowed toward the door Link had just opened, which was the only outlet. Link strained to see through the haze, which was lessened as smoke poured out. The other end of the large bay was not as congested. The walls there had not been touched by the fire, but there were no doors in that section of the wall.

Link knew he had to do something. He had played video games all his life, aways taking risks, maneuvering his characters to do wild things. Now was the time for a real-life move. Something rad.

Chapter 32

Callie checked Darrell. *Breathing. Thank you, Lord.* She grabbed hold of his legs and began to drag him, thankful for the tile floor that made the task easier. She slid him into the bathroom from where she had taken the toilet lid and shut the door. She could smell the smoke, but there was none visible in the room.

She soaked several paper towels in a sink and put them over her mouth. She ran into the hall, smoke burning her eyes. Trying to stay low, she went to the room where she had left Freckles, she could barely make it inside. Smoke poured from the holes in the overhead tiles and covered the ceiling.

She ran to Freckles. Dropping the paper towels, she grabbed him by the legs and pulled. She was only able to make it halfway to the door before she had to retreat to the hall for a breath. She returned and pulled Freckles out of the room. There was no way to avoid the blood. Half-coagulated clumps clung to his back as she maneuvered him out of the way of the door and closed it to contain the smoke.

Bent over, hacking, Callie paused then moved to the man's face. It was ashen. She bent her ear to his cheek – nothing. Feeling for a pulse, Callie sobbed when her fingers felt nothing but empty flesh. She examined his freckled face. He had kicked her, bound her, and terrified her, but Callie loved him. She knew the love did not come from herself. The look on his face seemed peaceful. She wondered if he had been singing. "This day you shall be with Him in Paradise."

Callie rose and hurried to the other end of the hall, hoping for a way out. "Father, help me stay calm." A coughing binge stopped her in the hall, bent over. She tried to crouch and run but she was soon hacking again. Trying it once more, she made it to the end of the hall. She had to get on her hands and knees to get out of the smoke. The door ahead of her must be the only thing between her and a major fire. She could feel the heat. Smoke oozed steadily around the top of the door frame. She dared not open it to look, but it would probably not be long before the fire burned through. "Please, Lord. Darrell's not ready." She went to the floor on her forearms, head between them. "He was trying, God. You promised not to let him slip out of Your fingers. Don't let him slip away from You. Please, don't let me lose…I mean…" She shook her head with internal agony. "God, You know what I mean."

Callie rose, pulling out the neck of her dress to wipe her eyes on the cleaner fabric inside. She turned back, looking in all the rooms along the way—no windows, no other doors. Crouching, running, coughing, she passed the bathroom where she had left Darrell and continued toward the other end of the building. The smoke drove her lower, and the heat got worse. The men had deliberately set fire to the only two routes out of that area of the building.

Callie crumpled against the wall. "Please, please." She sobbed out her plea. "I don't know why, Lord. Why? If we're going to die, You have to help me. I'm scared."

Coughing and weeping, Callie headed for the bathroom on her hands and knees. She didn't want to die without Darrell. She didn't want to watch him die either, but she would try to wake him up and try one last time to reach his heart. She prayed as she scrambled down the hallway. "Please, if we can't live, would You let me be able to talk with him before it happens? Help him give his life to You."

A vibrating rumble snapped Callie from her prayer. *No, Lord, please.* The walls shook. Her eyes darted to the ceiling. *The building must be coming down.* Her lip trembled at the thought of being buried in burning rubble. There was the cracking and thumping of breaking lumber falling to the floor on the other side of the wall next to her.

Callie wanted to stand and run, but thick smoke above demanded she keep crawling. She passed the door to the room from where all the noise was coming. From the other side of the door, another sound came that made her shudder. Someone was coughing. One of the men must still be in the building and only the door separated them. In the other room, someone struggled, moving things out of the way, advancing toward the door she left behind.

She moved as fast as her crawling allowed. The door behind her creaked open. She continued to crawl, hoping the smoke would keep her hidden. The coughing came into the hallway. She could almost feel a rifle pointing at her back.

"Cals!" a voice called from behind her, between coughs.

She turned and looked up at the towering figure. "Link?"

The young man gagged as he fanned his hand at the thick atmosphere that was pouring from the hallway into the room like water down a drain.

"Get down so you can breathe," Callie motioned with her hand.

The young man dropped through the smoke like a jet breaking

through cloud cover.

As Link took in enough air to speak, Callie's anger outran her fear. "You're here, too?" *God, what are You doing? It isn't better if more people die with me.*

As he crouched like a spider on the floor, Link's crooked grin seemed out of place in such a situation. "I drove…cough…their SUV…cough…through the wall." He shook his finger toward the open door through which the smoke was being exchanged for fresher air. "Definitely rad."

The dispatcher's voice blared through Shawn's radio. "Ida Ten, I copy your request for fire and EMS, 1500 block of Newport Road."

Shawn screamed into the parking lot with Brock's SUV following. He slowed as his lights illuminated Link's vehicle and a group of people huddled nearby.

Callie had Darrell's head in her lap, and Link crouched beside them, coughing. Darrell wasn't moving. Jumping out, Shawn rushed to them. Relief washed out some of the anxiety when Darrell rolled his head around to look at him.

Callie's face was a mix of concern and frustration. "Darrell's going to tell you…" She had to stop and cough. "…he's fine and just needs rest, but he needs to be checked out by an ambulance."

"That sounds like him." Shawn squatted and patted Darrell's shoulder. "At least I know you're well enough to still cause trouble, but that doesn't take much for you."

Darrell managed a nod and half smile.

Turning to Callie, who was coughing again, Shawn gave his best reassuring expression. "Don't worry, ambulance is on the way."

Shawn noticed Brock coming their way with a phone to his ear. He put it away as he walked up and surveyed the group. His face displayed shock, and it took him a moment to speak. "I'm not sure what's going on, but your chief convinced our SWAT commander to pull our team out of the storage lot just as they were about to move in on the man that called you on the phone." He was facing Darrell. "The barricaded suspect we were negotiating with sure sounded like the same guy."

Shawn started to explain, but Brock stopped him with an upraised hand. "I just got word, one of the rental units was packed with explosives. The whole place blew up right after they got out. We've got a few injuries from flying debris, but everyone except the suspect made it out alive." Brock scanned the group. "It sounds like I have the bunch of you to thank." He narrowed his attention to Callie, "I'm guessing this is Ms. Williams."

Chapter 33

Darrell stroked Callie's curls as she quivered, deep in dark dreams, her head on the side of his hospital mattress where she had finally succumbed to slumber. It was the only time he touched her. When awake, Callie resisted any intimacy between them. He knew that she was being honorable to God.

It should have been one more reason for him to be angry at the Almighty's dealings in his life. Yet somehow, he was not. The familiar anger seemed to be missing, eclipsed by the miracle that Callie was alive.

The only time that Callie had left him was to work on the prosthetic. Darrell flexed the NIP in front of his face. She and Link had reconnected the feed from the camera in the hand so that it went directly to the computer instead of having all audio-visual go through the shoulder. It would be much harder for incidental damage to disable all video now.

Incidental damage. Darrell remembered how Callie numbly repeated the term when one of the other engineers had used it over a cell phone conference call. He adored how her concern made him feel but disliked seeing it unnerve her to the point that she obsessed with making the changes to the NIP. Darrell felt there was something Callie wasn't ready to talk about, like the burn on her left arm that she proclaimed as "nothing" without further explanation.

A mixed feeling of pleasant melancholy came over Darrell. His mind drifted away as he recalled what happened when Callie had brought out her latest addition. To Darrell it had looked like a vehicle key fob. "What's that?"

"A biometrically locked wireless remote so I can still control the arm if other means of communication get knocked out again."

Darrell gave an impressed expression. "Great. Now you can always find me in a parking lot."

Callie smirked. "I should have put in a remote 'strangle the smart aleck' feature."

The NIP grabbed Darrell around the throat, and he cried out in gagging wheezes. "Hey, cut it out. I can't breathe."

In wide-eyed panic, Callie fumbled with the remote until Darrell dropped the arm, laughing.

Callie grabbed the box of hospital tissues and began beating him with them. "Oh. You're as bad as Link."

Darrell let her have her revenge for a few whacks, then he wrapped the NIP around her waist and pulled her in close.

Callie took in a breath. "What are you doing?"

Darrell admired her eyes at close range. "It's not me. It's the NIP. Must be defense programing—bringing your opponent in close makes strikes less effective."

Callie sighed as she turned her head away with a slight smile. She took her time pulling out of the embrace. "Yeah, seems pretty disarming, so maybe we should avoid moves like that."

In the reverie, Darrell remembered how the look on Callie's face thrilled him, but he felt like he had violated her trust. He had told her, "I'm sorry. That wasn't right of me. I got carried away." It had been Darrell's turn to look away in shame.

When he had turned back, Callie examined him with a sad expression and asked, "How's your ironing coming?"

Darrell inspected his lap. After a moment he engaged her sad eyes again. "I don't ever want to lie to you."

"I appreciate that." She gathered up her things. "I need to go."

Even in the memory, Darrell squeezed his eyes shut at the pain of what he had done. "Forgive me."

Callie had stopped at the door without turning around. "I'll be back."

At his relieved sigh, she had added, "Forgiveness is a good place to start in any troubled relationship." Leaving it at that, she had walked out.

Darrell let the ache of the memory fade by studying Callie's sleeping face. He had prayed she would come back, and she had. The word prayer seemed to fit more of his inner conversation lately.

Callie jerked in her sleep.

He stroked her head again, then paused, wondering if he was wrong to do so. She shivered, and he rubbed his hand through her hair. It was not for him. It was for her. She would do the same. The nightmares were coming less often as their brains processed the violent events they had endured.

Callie's torment was worse for Darrell than his own. The kidnapping had forced his heart to confess. He loved her. It had given him small glimpses of the agony that losing her would be—worse than losing his hand. He found himself being thankful.

In the empty hours of convalescence, an odd summation of fate had been knocking around in the kitchen of his consciousness. What it cooked up was the realization that if he had not lost his hand, he probably would not have met Callie.

He paused his hair-stroking-therapy-for-bad-dreams and flexed the NIP, scrutinizing the synthetic exterior. Then he let his eyes trace the smooth skin of Callie's face. "I'd give my right arm for her, too."

As soon as he said it, a gentle thought floated in and stuck like a post-it note. *I want more than that.* It was firm, unyielding – the final word. And yet, to Darrell, it felt less like a demand and more like an invitation. But still, he wrestled.

"It's amazing how quickly you can heal when you're not running, jumping and being shot at." Callie, Link, Shawn, and Agent Brock watched as Darrell pounded the fist of the prosthetic into the mattress he was laying on.

Each face conveyed various levels of emotion.

"They've given me my release papers. A week is enough. Time to get back to work."

"That's why Brock and I are here." Shawn sat his nylon bag on the windowsill and began fishing in it. "We need to discuss our next move."

Brock turned to Callie and Link. "I wish I could have you two in the conversation, but my supervisors are adamant about the classified nature of this case. Please forgive me."

Callie gathered her items. "We need to get back to ATS anyway. Raji messaged us a long list of assignments for this new government project of his." She fixed her attention on Darrell. "I'll need to check up on you, um, frequently, to see how the NIP is working in your regular routine. I want to keep tabs on your progress and make sure you're doing all right…with the prosthetic."

Darrell warmed at the thought. "That's good. I know you need feedback to see how the NIP performs. Call anytime, or…stop by if you want to."

Callie smiled. "I will. Thanks for sending Christie and the others to look after me. Christie's been great. Mama hasn't made one complaint about having a white cop in the house. She also said when you were well, she wanted you to come by so she could thank you for saving my life."

Darrell gave a little head shake. "I must have gotten the best end of that story. Seems like there was plenty of saving going around on everyone's part, but I will look forward to meeting her."

Brock glanced between them. "Callie, I'm a little envious of Darrell because I won't have much excuse to connect with you again. Remember, if you or Link ever want a job at the Bureau, I know we can put your skills to work. I'm sure it would be a pay cut, but you would be serving your country." His raised eyebrows conveyed the humor he intended.

Callie shook Brock's hand. "I'll have to think about that but right now, I have things I need to do where I am."

Brock's eyes made a brief move in Darrell's direction then engaged Callie again. "I understand. But I'll be talking to the brass about getting in on BERT training if the government buys into it."

Brock turned slightly to include Darrell in his next statement. "I also want to apologize again for what you went through. It's not every day the bureau gets manipulated like that. It is particularly embarrassing for me personally. I'm sorry I was more of an obstacle than a help." Brock hung his head. "I'm glad you two have been gracious enough to give me another chance at working with you to find these clowns."

Darrell waved him off. "You've apologized enough. Callie's safe and that's all I care about. Whoever these guys are, they did a good job of making me look like a suspect. I probably would have done the same thing you did. I don't think any of us will take anything for granted again on this case."

Once Callie and Link were gone, Darrell began the conversation. "We need to get back to the murder investigation." He gave a grateful look toward Shawn who stood, notebook in hand. "I appreciate you and the team putting so much time into trying to find Callie's kidnappers while I was out of the game, but I think we need to pick up where we left off before this began."

Brock seemed both surprised and relieved as he spoke to Darrell. "I was also going to suggest that the trail had gone cold here in the Springs. I'm glad we're seeing the same things. For now, I think you and your team have done all you can. We are going to be concentrating our efforts in Denver. We have assessed the top terrorist targets and are actively searching for the phony Denver police cars."

"And you're sure that Raji was not involved?" Darrell threw off the sheet and held the back of his hospital gown closed as he got up.

"Positive. We have been able to establish that the text messages that Callie received did not come from his phone. The people we are dealing with are experts. This wasn't a simple spoofing like a telemarketer. They were able to make the message look like part of a continued text string from Raji that was already on Callie's phone. No wonder she believed it was him."

Darrell nodded, "Just making sure. I didn't think Raji would have been involved. If he was behind it, he wouldn't have used his own phone to text Callie the messages that lured her to the kidnapping site. He's not stupid about technology. Besides, I don't think he would ever put Callie in danger. She is the goose that laid the golden egg for him, and I am sure that he has feelings for her. He might like to get rid of me, but not Callie."

Brock gave a small chuckle at the comment. "Plus, he has been in meetings with government agencies practically night and day about them possibly using BERT. He has some high-ranking officials for an alibi. His background is clean, also. We haven't found anything in his past or present to suggest terrorist leanings – just the opposite. He comes from a non-religious family who actually left India because of the religious violence."

Darrell nodded. "Callie told me something about him worshiping technology."

"Probably true. And I think the profile that we are looking for are people that know technology but are using it to wage a religious or ideological war. Our linguists tell me the voices on Link's video of you rescuing Callie are speaking Iranian. We're still chasing all the leads the video gave us, but so far none have yielded anything to locate them."

As Brock and Shawn spoke, Darrell pulled his clothes from the closet.

Brock went on with his assessment. "It's too bad we couldn't get a helicopter up in time to find them when they left the Springs. Our best lead is the phony Denver PD cars. They must be somewhere around Denver. Our search of what was left of the site where they held Callie suggests they moved an extensive operation. I don't think they left anything behind here in your city, and I don't think they're coming back. There's no reason you can't get back to your own work. You know I'll keep you fully informed about the kidnapping investigation."

"Actually," Darrell stepped into the bathroom to dress, leaving the door partially open so they could hear him, "I think that if we solve the murders, we'll solve the kidnapping."

There was quiet outside the bathroom. Darrell pulled his pants on while still wearing his hospital gown and then gladly stripped off the only form of clothing he had worn for the last week.

Brock broke the silence. "Okay, let's hear why you're thinking they're connected. I thought we all agreed that the guy posing as Callie's kidnapper was also lying about being your killer."

Darrell stepped out of the bathroom and grabbed the gym bag that Callie had provided. He pulled out one of the special Velcro shirts and glanced at the other men. "Why did they kidnap Callie?"

"To use her to bait the SWAT team into the trap," Brock said it like it was obvious.

Darrell pulled on the shirt and fastened the Velcro around the NIP. "But why Callie? Why not some easier target? Anyone would have worked. Why would they risk going after Callie when they knew we were connected? Surely, they realized they would only cause me to do everything I could to find her. I would pull in the whole investigation team to get her back." Darrell took one of the chairs to put on his shoes.

Shawn was smiling. "Sounds like these guys have you all figured out for the brief time you've known each other. I don't think I know you that well."

"What it sounds like is that you already have the answer to the question." Brock smiled but wrinkled his brow.

Darrell paused, planted both feet on the floor, one sock on and one sock off, and looked at the others to emphasize his pronouncement. "The question is the answer. They not only knew that's what I would do, they were counting on it." He resumed with the next sock.

Brock leaned forward in his chair. "So why would they want you to do that?"

"That may not be the right question to ask."

Shawn turned to Brock with an amused look. "Okay Watson, do you ask, or do I?"

Brock caught the drift. "Go ahead if it will make him happy."

Shawn turned back to Darrell. "What *is* the right question to ask?"

Darrell smirked, "Humor me my theatrics. It's not what they wanted us to do, it's what they didn't want us to do."

Brock pointed his finger like he got it. "Keep investigating the murders."

Shawn was nodding as well. "We must have been getting close."

"And," Darrell jerked on his shoes, "when we think realistically about how long such a ploy would keep us off the murder investigation, it tells us two other things about their plans."

Brock sat back and exhaled. "We don't have much time."

Shawn tipped his head toward Darrell. "And?"

"And," Darrell took a long breath, "they took a big risk with this. So, why does a fighter expose himself like that?" He opened his hands toward the other men. "To get an opening for a better shot. Whatever they have planned is big enough for them to risk it all to make it happen. And they are not worried about the consequences after that. They intend it to be a knockout."

Shawn gave an eyebrow raise and slight grin. "Or a death blow."

Chapter 34

After grabbing fast food, Brock followed Shawn and Darrell to their office. Shawn spread out the large binders that represented the murder investigation file on Darrell's desk.

"You know," Shawn tipped his head back, flexed his shoulders and directed a comment to Darrell, "this case was tough enough before. If you're right, now we have even less time to solve it and more at stake."

Darrell considered the mass of information spread out before them. "It's not all bad." He looked up as he said it. "Now we know that the answer is here; all we have to do is find it." Poising his hands over the desk in an all-inclusive gesture, he spoke to the binders, "Okay, what do we have?"

Shawn massaged the back of his neck. "Four dead families, each killed in a locked house with no signs of forced entry. All stabbed with a knife obtained in the house which was always left in the last victim. Lots of blood transferred between victims, yet the only handprints or shoe prints are those of the victims."

Darrell gave a frustrated exhale. "Every one of these looks like a domestic murder/suicide scene."

Brock stared at the files on the desk as well. "So the only thing that made you think they were connected was the close time frame and the similarities?"

"Exactly." Darrell leafed through the first binder. "That is why we have been behind from the beginning. If we had started putting this together before the third murder scene, we would have been down these roads long ago. When the second one came in, we were suspicious because of the bizarre coincidence, but then we got another one and we knew something was going on."

"Okay," Shawn pulled out a pad and started jotting notes as he talked. "Let's look at the list of suspects that we left off with – other family members, which the lack of connection between the families, not to mention our current theory, seems to rule out. The alarm salesman – he had the code to the security system on the last scene… but there were no security systems in the others so that kind of breaks that connection."

"Unless he had been in all the houses trying to sell them a system recently," Brock suggested.

"We were looking into that." Darrell let his mind revisit the idea. "He has an alibi that we were in the process of verifying."

"Maybe that's what they didn't want you to keep working on."

Shawn continued with his list. "Then there are the cable enhancement employees." Shawn put his hand down suddenly on the pad and looked up with mock fear on his face. "But please don't tell me it's them. I had an appointment for them to install my system today and now if they are on the run to Denver, I might never get to see 'Final Death' in 4D."

Brock's face showed his confusion.

Darrell shook his head. "Shawn doesn't think real murder and carnage is enough, so he watches all that slash trash. Now he wants it to be even more real than reality."

Shawn shrugged his shoulders with a grin. "Charles Manson, Ted Bundy, Jeffrey Dahmer…amateurs."

Brock sniffed in a chuckle. "Maybe you should be investigating closer to home. Where was he on the night in question?"

"Watching something worse on television," Shawn quickly countered. "And I have the pay-per-view bill to prove it."

Brock let his smile dwindle. "Okay, so if we think the ones that kidnapped Callie are behind this, all we are really looking for in this list is who got them into the houses. But here is another question we have to answer regardless of who that person is. Everything we have on this group says they are terrorists. So, what's in it for them?"

Darrell shrugged his shoulders. "To terrorize."

Shawn shook his head. "Yeah, but think what we're saying. Radical Muslims are sneaking into homes and killing one family at a time? They usually look for opportunities to maximize the body count."

"Maybe they're trying a new way to terrorize." Darrell leaned against the desk. "Think about it. No one would know if they were safe. In the heart of the United States, they can kill normal everyday people right in their homes. What could be more horrible to the average American? We live oblivious to the terror that some of the world experiences daily. Even mass shootings always seem like something that happens somewhere else to someone else. To touch us in our own homes would be a game changer."

Brock showed skepticism. "But how on earth could a terrorist group hope to continue to operate, over and over, right in the middle of urban neighborhoods? It wouldn't take long before they were caught or ran into a homeowner with a gun and there would be a shootout. How are they not leaving more evidence? Terrorist groups are not known for their light touch. There are a dozen reasons why this doesn't make sense."

"Most of those reasons are still true even if it isn't terrorists." Darrell was thinking as he spoke. "None of this gets any harder for a sophisticated group of terrorists that are well-trained."

Darrell paused, head cocked to the side, staring at the ground. Brock was saying something, but the words didn't register. A new thought was running around in his mind. He raised his head and looked at the two men.

Shawn had his hand up, signaling for Brock to wait.

Darrell appreciated how well his partner knew him. "And maybe if we look at it a different way it starts to make more sense."

Shawn cocked his head toward Darrell. "Now what are you thinking?"

"I'm not sure I want to tell you about this next theory." He gave them a sheepish look.

"Oh, why stop now? If we're going nuts, let's do it right." Shawn's grin let Darrell know he was with him all the way to the funny farm.

"What if the killer was already in the home?"

Shawn gestured toward his pad. "You still think it is these cable guys or the alarm installers. They install the system and leave someone hiding in the home?"

"I thought about that, but that still does not answer a lot of questions. No, what I'm thinking is worse than that. Maybe we have had the killer right in our hands on every scene. Maybe he was right there in the house with us."

Brock joined in. "Whoa, are you trying to say that he waits until the police arrive and then slips out under the noses of a dozen cops, or," Brock drew out that word like his mind was getting around a new idea, "are you thinking that this guy *is* a cop?"

"No, thought of that, too. That only gets him out of the house. There is only one theory that accounts for the fact that the killer can commit such a violent crime and not leave any evidence behind. Remember what we thought about the first murder scene? Everything looked like it was a domestic murder/suicide. That is what we would be thinking about every one of these scenes if we had any one of them separately. It is only because we have more than one of them that looks the same that makes us abandon that line of reasoning. What if our first thought was right? What if every one of these scenes has a separate killer right in the home? This sounds crazy, but it fits the evidence. Maybe that is where we went wrong. We were trying too hard to find one killer. Take the last scene we worked. Imagine that we were looking at it by itself. Who would you have said was the killer?"

"The husband." Shawn was starting to track with Darrell. "You think the husband killed his family and then killed himself, like a suicide stabber instead of a bomber? Wow." Shawn was shaking his head again. "How would you get anyone to do that to their family, and for that matter, themselves?"

"I don't know, but you and I both know people do it all the time without a cause. If you convince someone of a cause, it gets even easier. But there is something else. Maybe this wasn't really their family. Remember the bios on the victims? In all of them at least one of the spouses had been married before. All of them had gotten remarried within the last five years."

Brock put it into words. "Sleeper Cells." He paced away from the desk then came back with an odd expression. "The CIA spooks have been feeding us intel about radical Muslims coming into the country and setting up lives here as sleeper cells, waiting to be activated to commit terrorist acts on US soil."

Darrell pushed off the desk and sat in a chair. "You recruit suicide terrorists and then send them out to find a family to absorb themselves into. Get a lonely divorcee on the rebound and then just assume a life and wait until you are activated. All it would take is a phone call."

Shawn shook his head in disbelief. "How do you brainwash a guy enough to stab himself?" He seemed to regain his sense of humor. "The good news is I might still have a relaxing evening with murder and mayhem on the menu."

"I wouldn't say that too loud," Darrell put an ominous tone in his voice. "Think about it... no one in this country really knows who they can trust. How many more are out there? If this is true, what do we do? If we warn people, what do we tell them—'If you've been married in the last five years your spouse might be a killer, don't trust them.'"

"I knew it," Shawn said, "That's about how long I've been married. I never like the vicious way my wife cuts up vegetables. I always get the feeling I might be next."

Darrell couldn't appreciate the humor. "Just think if everybody really had to start thinking like that."

Shawn didn't let up. "If I ever go missing, look in the soup."

Brock sighed, looking at the desk. "Nobody's going to buy this unless we have more. The only reason I'm not laughing is because of Callie's kidnapping. It gives us a terrorist connection we can't explain any other way." He gestured toward the binders. "This is top priority. Let me get these cases to a profiler. Maybe we can find a common denominator, something that links the victims and possible killers. If these are sleepers, there must be someplace where they are all trained or recruited. I'm going to make some phone calls and get this started. How can I get copies of these files?"

"Wait a minute," Shawn interjected. "How do the Denver PD cars fit into all this?"

Darrell shrugged. "I don't know. But it suggests that Denver is where the next sleepers are going to be activated."

"I'll get some agents to start coordinating with the PD up there and prep them, but first I'm going to have to sell this as a real possibility to my bosses. For now, we will run off the assumption that Denver is the next target. Maybe somehow we can get ahead of it."

Chapter 35

After they finalized their plans, Brock and Shawn left. Darrell stayed to leave instructions on copying the files for Brock. He took some time to get his office back in order after his long absence. The phone rang. *Shawn or Brock must have thought of something else.* Darrell cradled the receiver against his ear. "Lieutenant Jacobs."

"Then it is true. You are still alive." Darrell recognized the voice as it continued. "Don't bother trying to track me this time. It won't be possible. Out-thinking law enforcement is usually not a challenge, so I was not really trying last time. I am not sure who helped you, no doubt one of Calneshia's co-workers. But trust me when I say that now, you have my full attention."

"You're the last person I would have expected to hear from." Darrell pressed the record button on his phone but feared the man wasn't merely boasting about being untraceable.

"That is why I am calling. I wanted you to fully understand what you have started. I don't take lightly when someone challenges me. Not that what you have done will really mean anything in the end, but you came right to my door, so you can expect me to return the favor. You'll be hearing from me soon. Furthermore, I am dedicating all the rest of my acts of terrorism to you. Your country will have you to thank."

Darrell wanted to explode, but he didn't want to challenge the man. "Who am I going to have to apologize to?"

"You'll know when it happens, and no apology will be sufficient for what you have brought on your own people."

"Something tells me your plans would have progressed with or without me."

"Well, perhaps. Then let's just say that your interference has helped me refine my focus for my next act. When it comes to you, Darrell, I plan on keeping things close to home."

Fear rushed upon Darrell like a mugger out of an alley. He had not talked to Callie since he left the hospital. *Who's on her security detail tonight? Carlos.* He froze the NIP's movements and composed a text to the detective. **Received a credible threat. Be extra sharp. Have the on-duty patrol units cruise the area.**

He had never really thought the terrorists would come back to the Springs. Now he just wanted to call and make sure Callie was all right. But he knew he needed to find out what the man had to say, and he also wanted to do what he could to diffuse the feelings the terrorist might have for revenge. "You got plenty close last time. It was you that made me do what I did when you kidnapped Ms. Williams. You've hurt me plenty. Why don't we just leave it at that?" He had taught it many times in hostage negotiation. *Never act like you don't take the threat seriously. You run the risk of forcing the bad guy to prove what he can and will do.* "You don't want me in your business, and I don't want you in mine. Let's both just walk away. You've left the Springs, so we have nothing to do with each other anymore. The only conflict we've ever had was from me doing my job."

The man's voice held an unnerving calm, like seething anger had turned to deadly decision. "Yes, I guess we're both just doing our jobs. Let me share a little about mine with you. Your country is not safe anymore, Darrell. My job is to see that your own sins betray you. Your thirst for pleasure will bring judgment on you right where you live, and I am honored that it is my hand Allah has chosen to strike the blow. And Darrell, you can expect this one to hurt more."

The call ended. Darrell was on another call within seconds. "Carlos, do you have Callie in sight?"

"Christie's with her. Hang on a sec." Darrell could hear Carlos talking on a radio, confirming with Christie that Callie was all right. "Yeah, Boss. Christie says everything is okay. Her and Callie are just having girl time. You sound worried. What is this credible threat?"

"Don't tell Callie this. I don't want to scare her anymore. But I got a call from the kidnapper, and he made threats to hit me close to home."

"You're kidding me. This guy's nuts. We won't let it happen, Boss. You know how these guys are. They make a lot more threats than they ever follow through with. But we'll take it real serious. You rest easy."

"I want to come over and help, but right now I think Callie would be able to tell something was wrong, and she's been scared enough."

"That's okay, Boss. We got it."

"Be careful."

"Always."

Darrell knew he could trust Carlos and the others. He also did not want Callie around if the terrorists decided to come after him personally. *I hope they do.*

Chapter 36

As Shawn drove home, he cranked up the heavy metal music to drown out the thoughts that came with silence. The guttural lyrics gave voice to something inside him that he hid beneath the jokes.

Weight of the World
Deep in my vein
Knife in my gut
Blood like rain
Where is the hope
They promised in vain

As he entered his home, his wife Sandy gave him a kiss then pulled back and examined him. "I sent the kids to their dad's. I figured you'd be tired. Everything okay?"

Shawn tried to brighten his face. "Sure. We just had to postpone saving the world until tomorrow, and you know how I hate waiting."

Sandy smiled and shook her head. "How's Darrell doing?"

"Relatively unscathed as far as I can tell. They released him back to work. He seems to be healed, and his new arm is repaired. He was back on the job today, making more work for us. I think the issue between him and Callie is bothering him the most."

"Callie sounds really great. I can't wait to meet her. I hope they can work it out."

"Yeah, she is definitely unique. She certainly turned Darrell around. He was actually smiling for a while there. But I don't think she'll ever back down from her beliefs."

"Would you want her to? Maybe that's why she's so unique."

Shawn stretched his neck and rotated his shoulders. "Too heavy of subjects for me. They're going to have to figure it out themselves."

"Oh, I almost forgot. There's something in the living room that's going to make you smile."

"Woohoo, finally." Shawn headed that way but turned back. "The install guys weren't Middle Eastern, were they?"

"Not at all. They seemed like a couple of nerdy college dropouts.

Why?"

"Sorry, private work joke."

"Whatever. Don't be bringing up things and making me curious when you can't talk about it. Anyway, it's installed but you've got to set it up. Are you going to watch something gross?"

"Of course. It's supposed to come with a free pay-per-view showing of Final Death. I haven't watched it yet. I have been saving it for the maiden voyage of the 'future of entertainment'."

Sandy waved him off. "Go relax then and I'll read my book."

Shawn shook his head at her. "No guts, no gory."

"All right, go rot your brain, and I'll order a pizza that you can bite into while you're watching all that guts and gory. All red and gooey, should go well together." Sandy wrinkled up her face at her own joke.

At home, Darrell stood by the NIP pedestal that Callie had set up in his bedroom while he was in the hospital. He had loaned her his keys, and now she was everywhere in his home. She had filled his refrigerator with her delicious cooking. The house sparkled with her touch. He thought of her moving around in his home, cooking, washing his dishes, straightening up around the place…like she belonged there.

He pushed the NIP into its storage pedestal, released it from the vest he wore and pulled his stump out. He was thankful to get out of the vest. Even though the ballistic fabric was the latest, lightweight material, it was still body armor, and he was glad to get into the soft cotton T-shirt. It felt good to be comfortable. But Darrell kept his gun, just in case.

As he pulled down the shirt, he instinctively tried to use both hands to do it. He swiped the air near the end of the shirt before he realized that his left hand had nothing with which to grab. He stared at the flesh-colored synthetic connector on the end of his stump. The NIP was becoming a part of him, but it caused a strange set of feelings. He thought about wiggling his fingers, which seconds ago would have produced movement in the hand's digits. Now there was nothing to move. Like the phantom feelings he had when he first lost his hand, it was a quandary that his mind had difficulty resolving—like living two lives.

On the dresser lay Darrell's hook, modified to fit his new stump attachment. He picked it up and carried it into the living room with him.

Carlos sat in his car in front of Callie's house. He stretched and yawned then grabbed his cell phone. "How you doing in the back, Rich?"

His partner sounded bored. "Everything's quiet back here. Callie sure has a nice back yard."

"Yeah, whole place is top notch. Hey, you interested in pizza?"

"Sure. Get me sausage and onion."

"Okay, as long as you stay away from me after that. I'll see what the girls want."

Carlos dialed and leaned forward, looking at Callie's house as he rang Christie's phone.

"What do you want? Us girls are busy."

"Hey, you guys interested in a pizza if I buy?"

"No way, Callie's cooking for us. And she's been making pies, nervous energy she calls it."

"She doesn't have to keep doing that."

There was a pause on the other end. "She says, 'Didn't your mama ever tell you not to argue with a lady?'"

"Oookay," Carlos sat back. "If she's gonna bring my mama into it, I guess she gets to feed us. Besides, that keeps Rich away from the sausage and onions."

"She says you can come and get it in a few minutes. I'll pass what's left out the front door. If you're good, there might be a little pie left."

"Okay, but I'm gonna make a round right now and check everything. With Callie's cooking, I probably won't be able to walk after that. And before you get too happy with the baked goods in there, you just remember we're only here to protect Callie. Anything could happen to a pie thief."

After a brief learning curve, Shawn sat in front of the TV with everything enhanced. In a few minutes, however, the terror on the screen had lost his attention. The turmoil inside him was raging despite his happy-go-lucky exterior. He mulled over a thought that kept nagging. He didn't like it, but it wouldn't go away. *You know what you have to do.*

Chapter 37

Darrell hadn't made it far after he left the bedroom. With his hook in his lap, he sat in his easy chair, listening to the quiet. It was the first time in days he had been away from Callie, except to sleep. His house felt empty. So did life. He wanted to call just to hear her voice. But what would they talk about? He didn't want to scare her. Neither of them were up to reliving the events of the weeks before, and they had exhausted the subject of the NIP. There was no future to discuss, no other plans to make.

He pounded his good fist into the arm of the chair while he clenched his teeth and squeezed his eyes shut. What was it that kept him from just telling Callie that he was going to start going to church again? It wouldn't be that hard to jump right back into that life again. How much of it had been for show? He knew it would not be enough—not for Callie, not for God.

I want more than that. It was still sticking to his mental bulletin board.

Carlos hiked to the end of the block and cut around the alley. He got on the radio. "Hey Rich, don't shoot me. I'm coming up behind you."

"That depends on if you're bringing the pizza or not." Rich made the threat sound routine.

"Better than that, Callie's cooking. Be ready in a few minutes."

"Well then, step forward, lowly messenger. Since you bring such tidings, you may live."

Darrell's Christian life before had been like living with and without the NIP. He had kept it separate from his "real" life. There was church and there was home. There was church and there was work. There was God and there was his other life.

Clenching the harness attached to his hook, he felt the nylon. It seemed so long since he had worn it. He pulled the soft sock cover on his stump and then slid the plastic sleeve over it. One handed, he drew the harness over his head and behind him and attached it around his other arm. Pushing and pulling the prosthetic in and out he watched the hook open and close. It felt familiar, but he missed the fingers. Again, the mental confusion lurked around the edges of his mind. The conflict went beyond the parts of him that he could see. "Okay, God, what do you want?" What had Callie said? He needed to pick up the iron.

Across town, Link's sister came into the house. She had a small beagle in her arms.

Link looked up. He had a game running on the computer, Facebook on his tablet, and a chat session going on his phone. He was taking it easy that night, not taxing his brain too much. "Was that malware mutt networking with the neighborhood again?"

His sister ignored the question. "Link, did you know there are cops watching our house?"

"Oh, yeah. Forgot to put you on the share list for that fact. They think those terrorists might come back in town. Better keep that data-deficient hound in the house, or they'll give you a ticket."

"Well, haw. I just talked to them, and they don't give dog tickets. That's Animal Control. The one out front's kinda cute. I'm going to make some spaghetti and see if he wants to come in and eat with us."

"A.A.B.T.C.O.D.," he spelled at her.

"I'm not listening. Besides, I don't even know what that means."

"Above And Beyond The Call Of Duty."

Darrell got up and walked to the bookcase. There was his Bible, where he'd left it years ago. He pulled it from the shelf, returned to his chair, and thumbed to the concordance.

"You took my hand. What was that all about?" Darrell asked the air in the room. He remembered a Scripture and after a little searching, he found Matthew 5:30.

And if thy right hand offend thee, cut it off, and cast it from thee: for it is profitable for thee that one of thy members should perish, and not that thy whole body should be cast into hell.

"Thanks," Darrell said. "That doesn't give me much hope for the rest of my body."

The word "body" seemed to stand out on the page. He looked it up in the concordance and found the Scriptures that pertained to the body. There were a lot of references. He decided to concentrate on the New Testament and started reading. Among other things, he read about taking no thought for the body because God would take care of him. He moved through references about Jesus giving His body for him. There was the prophecy Jesus gave about raising up the temple in three days, and He was really talking about the temple of His body. He read how Jesus' body was laid in a tomb, but three days later it was not found there. Darrell took note that the Apostle Paul wrote to the Roman Christians that their "old man" was crucified so that the body of sin might be destroyed. Later in the same chapter he admonished them that they should not let sin reign in their mortal bodies. It made him think of Jodi and he remembered how Callie had reacted when she found out they had been living together.

"I guess I didn't really let You in that part of my life, did I?" Darrell began to realize that he had been blaming God for everything that occurred during that time – wondering why God would let that happen. After all, he met Jodi at a Bible study. The nagging thought that was becoming clearer was that he had no one to blame but himself. "I guess halfway wasn't good enough." The weight of the thought rested on his mind. "You know You expect a lot, don't You?"

As if in answer, he also found in Romans, chapter seven, a conversation comparing life to marriage. We used to be married to sin, and the only way to get out of the marriage was to become dead to the law by the body of Christ. The next part had always given Darrell a lot of trouble because of all the talk of wanting to do the right thing and not being able to, and not wanting to do the wrong thing and doing it. He could certainly relate. He found himself crying out with Paul, **O wretched man that I am! Who shall deliver me from the body of this death?**

Carlos moaned. "I'm dying."

Rich watched him suffering in the car seat beside him, no sympathy on his face. "You shouldn't have had the second piece of pie."

"I know. Don't remind me."

"Well, you'll have to die by yourself. I need to get back to my backyard post. I think the boss's terrorist is just blowing smoke, but he's done some pretty insane stuff already."

Carlos remained in his reclined position but gave a wave of dismissal.

Rich got out and headed off into the dark, leaving Carlos alone with his overstuffed stomach.

Shawn rejected the idea. He could not go through with it. It was unthinkable.

It's time.

Life was never what it seemed. In his mind, he pondered how little life and death really meant. All the people around him had the dream of something more than a miserable existence - it was a trick that they played on themselves to avoid the truth. It was all a lie they were living.

It is better not to prolong the inevitable.

What was he thinking? How could he even…

It is what you have been called to do.

He thought of the act of it, how it was supposed to be done. His head began to hurt.

Fortunately, the body theme carried Darrell into the next chapter of Romans, and he liked the start, that there is not any condemnation. But again, it was confusing.

"You know You're making this really hard. What do You really want?"

Darrell went back to the body verses. They told him that the body was dead because of sin, but the spirit was alive. Then they got down to it and explained that if he lived for his body he would die, but if through the Spirit he killed the deeds of the body, he would live. If there was one thing working homicide had taught him—either you were dead or you weren't. He had to die to himself and let Christ live in him – every part of him.

It seemed to Darrell that his mind understood what he was reading so much better than it ever had before. He smiled as he voiced his thoughts. "It's just like they teach in officer safety class. You can't wait for the other guy to shoot first. Reaction is always slower than action. If I let my opponent get the first shot, he wins. I can't just wait around for some temptation to come along and then figure out how to beat it. I have to act first and commit every part of my life to You. Then it's not about sinning or not sinning anymore. It's about living my life every day for You, no matter what happens."

As if mirroring his heart, once he got past the sin issue, the chapter became more uplifting. It talked about God adopting him, and that he was a joint heir with Christ, and that all the problems of this life were nothing compared to the glories of the life to come. The body theme kept him in chapter eight as it talked about how the adoption someday would include the redemption of the body.

He went on reading to the end of the chapter. It had always been one of his favorite parts of Scripture. He loved reading how all things worked to his good. But now he could finally believe it. The horror of all the past did not go away, but God had turned it around in his heart and in his reality. Darrell could see it. He could see how nothing could separate him from the love of God.

Inside his mind, a voice seemed to be saying, *"Just because you lost your hand, it doesn't mean I stopped loving you. Jodi betrayed you and Pete died, but I never stopped loving you. Sin took its toll. You played at the Christian life and just gave me the scraps you had left after you had lived for yourself, but I was always loving and waiting."*

Darrell finished the thought aloud. "For a relationship deeper than my circumstances."

Tears tracked down Darrell's face. He felt what Romans spoke of earlier in the chapter—groanings that could not be uttered. He saw how completely and hopelessly he had failed his Creator but how none of that mattered now.

"I'm sorry." Darrell's heart opened. "Take it all God. I've already proven I can't do anything without You." Darrell had picked up the iron, now God was doing the ironing.

He had no concept of how long he sat. The tears stopped. He felt clean, years of bitterness and unforgiveness washed away. He sensed that he had learned what God was trying to teach him. Finally, all he felt was a strange calm, a calm that at the same time was filled with anticipation. "What now, Lord?" He felt almost giddy. "Is there some kind of test?"

For almost an hour Shawn wrestled with himself—and lost. He finally took notice of the horror show that was playing on the screen. He had seen it all before. He was mentally prepared. It was something that he could do.

It is what you were meant for.

Shawn got up and went into the kitchen. Sandy was reading in her chair by the window. She looked up and gave him a smile. Since they had married over four years ago, he had come to love the way the light from the window fell on her hair. But he knew that was all over now. He opened the drawer and selected the largest knife he could find.

Chapter 38

For a while, prayers came out of Darrell as sighs and unspoken gratitude. He closed his eyes. He opened them. He looked upward. He looked inward. Through it all he came to know his Father.

Darrell's phone rang, startling him out of his internal conversation. At first, he started to put the arm into Cmode, and then he realized that he was wearing his hook. He dug in his pocket and found the old cell phone that he had not used in weeks and flipped it open. "Hello." There was silence for a moment on the other end. Just as Darrell was about to repeat his hello, he heard Shawn's voice.

"Hey, Darrell. Hope I'm not disturbing you."

Darrell was politely dishonest when he responded, "Of course not. What's going on?"

"Well, I got that new TV enhancement, and I was wondering if you wanted to come over and check it out with me. It's pretty amazing."

"That's all right, Shawn. I will see it sometime, but I think I'm pretty tired tonight and I have something that I need to do." *I want to call Callie. Boy, do we have something to talk about now.*

Again silence. Then Shawn spoke. "Well, I really wanted to talk to you about the case. I think I have figured out a way we can wrap this up a lot faster."

"How's that?"

"I really think I need to talk to you in person. It's important. I want to see what you think about my idea before I present it. I want to call Brock first thing in the morning, but I want to get your take on it first."

"Okay. I'll stop by for just a minute."

It might be a good excuse to get out. Maybe he could go by Callie's house afterward. His thoughts of the terrorists were eclipsed by the news he had to share. He could call her from outside her house and see if she wanted to go for coffee, a nice public place. The crew could hang around outside.

"Great," Shawn's voice interrupted Darrell's thoughts. "It won't take long."

I hope not. The thought of seeing Callie had taken over. He wanted to tell her what he had gotten "ironed out." Why hadn't he just told Shawn that he would see him tomorrow? But something in his voice hadn't sounded right. *I'll make it quick and then call her when I'm ready to leave Shawn's place. She'll want a little time to get ready before I get there.*

Once in the car, Darrell began to rehearse his upcoming conversation with Shawn. He wanted to make it quick. He tried to speculate what his partner might have come up with. He ran his own theory through his thoughts.

There was one thing that Shawn had said that made sense to Darrell. It was one thing to blow yourself up or shoot yourself. All that took was to pull the trigger and in theory, you would never know what hit you, so to speak. But to stab yourself, well that took a level of commitment that few people could talk themselves into. The other thing that did not work in his theory was the inefficiency of it. Once the killer had dispatched the ones in the family he had infiltrated, why not go to the neighbor's house? It would be easy. The neighbors would invite him right in. If the goal was to kill, why not keep going until something stopped them?

The answer jumped into Darrell's mind, crystal clear. The killers were from the home but whoever planned it wanted it to look like someone outside the home had done it. It had to be a stabbing because it would be too easy to determine, through gunshot forensics, that a wound was self-inflicted, too easy to reconstruct from the place the gun fell and the high-velocity blood splatter. And the killer had to restrict himself to one family because they wanted the killer to appear to be one of the victims. But why?

Darrell began to rerun the conversation with the terrorist leader, in his mind. Maybe it was true that America's own sin would betray her, but what did that have to do with the killings? What else had he said - something about our "thirst for pleasure." Darrell tried to view the conversation in relation to the case. It did not seem to fit completely with what had happened. What strange things to say if they did not relate somehow. Perhaps the man's arrogance had led him to give some unintended clues.

Before he knew it, Darrell was at Shawn's house. He pulled up in front and turned off the engine. The house was too dark for how early it was. He got out and headed to the front door.

"Help me!" The horrible scream made Darrell jump and instinctively reach for his gun. Before he drew it, he realized that it was the TV he had heard. *Boy, the new sound is impressive.* That must be where everyone was, watching TV. Darrell rang the doorbell.

Instead of answering the door, Shawn called out, "Come in!" His voice emanated from somewhere in the interior of the house. "Be out in just a minute."

Darrell made his way into the living room. The television was playing, but no one was around it. It gave him an uneasy feeling. There was something about the whole situation that did not feel right. On the couch was a plate of pizza that did not appear to have been touched.

"I'm sorry," Shawn called out again. "I've got something I have to finish up, so go ahead and sit down. Check out that enhanced screen I told you about."

Darrell was perturbed that Shawn was still harping on the TV enhancement. The show on the screen had switched to a quieter scene. A low, sinister music was playing as a young woman moved through a darkened room. Darrell could hear water running elsewhere in Shawn's house.

He went ahead and sat down to wait. He immediately noticed the difference in the screen and the sound. Things did seem to jump right out at him, but the sound was a big portion of the package. There was such detail in it. In daily life, there was so much background noise that most people tuned it out, but those sounds were a big part of the perception of reality. Shawn's new system included those noises. He almost thought he could hear the subtle sound of voices, like someone talking down the block while you were in your house - too indistinct to understand it, but there it was, none the less.

It caused Darrell to think about the case. It also had something subtle in the background. The more he thought about it, the more he was convinced there was something there. Perhaps they were onto something more in the original investigation.

More characters had entered the scene on the movie and were interacting. The language was filthy. Not something that he would have paid much attention to before. Darrell thought to himself, half joking, "Okay, Lord, is this the test?" Something leaped into his mind. *Your own sin betrays you.*

The girl on the screen was barely dressed, something he *would* have taken notice of before. Now he was ashamed for watching it. He got up and moved to the side of the TV where the images were out of his view. But he could still hear the filthy language. A hopeless feeling pushed its way in like a big man crowding into the seat next to him. He was failing the test. What was the point in even fighting? He had only been kidding himself to think that he would ever fit into a life with Callie. Why did he even care who killed those people? They were probably the lucky ones. The pain of life was over for them. He became more upset the longer Shawn took. Was it hopeless? Was this what he really was?

Inside Darrell, there was a flicker, a spark that began to grow.

"Father, forgive me," he said under his breath. "I never want to be without You again. You're big enough to cover my failures, but I have died to this, and I am going to let You live. One little victory at a time."

He marched over to the television, reached behind it and pulled the plug on a power strip. Instantly the feelings began to subside. Having the TV off was like taking a shower. He felt cleaner.

Darrell stood, letting relief wash over him when out of the corner of his eye he saw something that made him jerk his head around. It was Shawn. He was standing in a doorway across the room. The couch was between them. "Who gave you permission to shut off my television?" Darrell thought Shawn looked like he had just gotten out of a real shower. His hair was wet, and there were beads of water still on his arms. Darrell looked him over without saying anything.

As he met Darrell's gaze, Shawn's face sagged. "That's all right. I don't need it anymore."

But to Darrell, it was not all right. Everything about Shawn was "not right." This was the man that had kept things light when Darrell had been too serious. Now he looked despondent. Darrell glanced around. "Where's Sandy?"

"She's out," Shawn came farther into the room.

Darrell could see that Shawn had his right hand behind his leg. Adrenaline poured into Darrell. He began to process volumes of thoughts in milliseconds. He would never have considered needing his gun in Shawn's house, but suddenly, even with it, he felt vulnerable.

You know Shawn. He's always joking. He's probably got some prank behind his leg. You're not going to need your gun.

There was no way he could draw his pistol fast enough if Shawn was concealing a weapon in his hand. Shawn had the advantage of youth and size.

What was he thinking? *This is Shawn. You're letting the last few days get to you.*

Shawn could be on him before he could get his gun out, and then he would have his only hand occupied.

Good grief, Darrell – this is Shawn. You're thinking paranoid. They had worked side by side for years. *It's Shawn.* This was not a man he could shoot. Not a man he would have to shoot. *The conversation with that terrorist has you acting crazy.*

Shawn was moving around the couch, still hiding his hand behind his leg. Darrell's hand involuntarily began to slide toward where his weapon was holstered.

But it's Shawn. He's always had your back. You love this man. Darrell's memory vomited a statement out in front of him. *You can expect this one to hurt worse.* A chill raced up his back and shook his shoulders. *Trust your instincts.*

Darrell looked into Shawn's eyes. There was something missing, but it was still Shawn. *You can't shoot Shawn.* He let his hand drop away from his gun. Darrell abruptly moved forward with a big smile on his face and held out his right hand. "How you do'n tonight, buddy?"

Shawn stopped and regarded the extended hand for a second. Suddenly he brought a huge butcher knife from behind his leg. He dashed forward bringing the knife up for an overhead strike. Darrell was ready. He had closed part of the distance with his feigned handshake and leaped forward before Shawn was completely prepared. He brought his prosthetic up and caught the knife blade right at its hilt between the "V" of the open hook. Letting Shawn's momentum continue downward, Darrell forced the ends of the hook into the back of Shawn's hand and knuckles. The leverage and the pain broke Shawn's grip. Darrell brought his right hand across and grabbed Shawn just above the elbow. A strong pull jerked Shawn one way and sent the knife flying the other.

Shawn went stumbling forward and to the left while Darrell spun around his right side. He tried to grab Shawn in a submission hold, but Shawn was already countering. He ducked and spun out of the hold, windmilling his arms to clear Darrell off him.

Shawn snatched a lamp off an end table and swung it at Darrell. Darrell used the hard plastic of his prosthetic sleeve to block it, and the lamp snapped. Darrell grabbed the back of Shawn's neck with his hook. The gouging pain forced Shawn forward, but with a wild swing, he hit Darrell on the side of the head with what was left of the lamp. Dazed for a moment, Darrell lost the advantage. It gave Shawn enough time to duck out of the hook hold on his neck and drive forward into Darrell. Wrapping Darrell in a strong bear hug around his waist, he took him to the ground.

As he went down, Darrell wrapped his legs around Shawn's waist and hooked one foot with the other, jiu-jitsu style. Shawn came down on his knees, and Darrell's leg lock forced him back so he could not get a hit at Darrell's face. Darrell immediately shot the curved portion of his hook into Shawn's ribs. Shawn grimaced but seemed unnaturally driven. He responded by grabbing the hook, where it attached to the sleeve, with his right hand. Darrell was an expert at escaping a grab to the hook. He twisted his hook up and over Shawn's wrist. The pain and leverage released the grip. Shawn recovered quickly and grabbed the hook itself. Before he could get a good grip, Darrell twisted the hook out between Shawn's fingers and leveraged his way loose again. Darrell had his right hand up, guarding his face but didn't use it to strike. He wanted Shawn to focus on the hook. He brought it across and hooked it behind Shawn's neck again.

Shawn panicked and grabbed the hook with both hands and drove it to the floor on Darrell's left side. He was snatching at the harness, trying to detach it.

It was the reaction that Darrell had been waiting for. He hooked his right leg over Shawn's head and made his move with his right hand. With a swift maneuver, Darrell brought Shawn's arm into his chest and dropped backward extending it into an arm bar hold. Shawn struggled briefly but groaned as any movement brought pain.

So complete was the lock up with his legs that Darrell could release his right hand and fish his phone out of his pocket. He called 911. He could tell that the dispatcher did not know whether to believe him or not when he explained the situation. But once the patrol cars were on the way, he told Shawn, "Just relax, buddy. We're going to get you some help." The other man wiggled in a futile escape effort, and Darrell tightened his leg grip, causing Shawn to moan.

As Darrell waited, restraining his partner and friend, everything focused in his mind. So many questions answered. It was unbelievable, but it all made sense.

The officers came in warily and stood with incredulous looks for a moment. "Shawn's wife, Sandy," Darrell's desperate tone snapped them out of it. "I think he may have done something to her. Look around. See if you can find her." A couple of officers came to help Darrell, and the others spread out in a search of the house.

Shawn muttered, "It doesn't matter anyway. We're all going to die. Why put her through the pain? Why should any of us go through the pain?"

Darrell advised them to cuff Shawn's right hand, which was free, extending helplessly away from Darrell.

Someone called from the kitchen. "She's in here. She's alive but in bad shape."

An officer applied a cuff. Darrell heard someone telling the ambulance that it was safe to come in. Once a couple of officers had Shawn secured, Darrell swung his leg back over and released the lock. The officers finished the cuffing and picked Shawn up, moving him to the door.

Fred Mooney, a sergeant, gave Darrell his hand. "Your head's bleeding," Fred pointed to where the lamp had connected. Darrell ignored the statement. He looked at Shawn. His partner just continued to stare at him as they took him out. He was rambling, "Why did you stop me? It's just going to keep hurting. There's only one way to end it. You shouldn't have stopped me."

Darrell walked directly to the TV console. "You got a glove?" He pulled on the latex glove that the sergeant offered and eased the television enhancement box off its stand. He used his hook to pull the cables loose from the back.

Fred was watching with a stunned look as the ambulance crew entered and hustled the gurney through to the kitchen. "What happened to Shawn?" He turned to Darrell with a look of sad confusion.

Darrell held up the box. "This did, I think."

Fred's confusion continued as he gazed at the innocent looking electronic component. "What's that?"

Darrell considered the black plastic case. "If I'm right, it represents our thirst for pleasure."

232

Chapter 39

Callie connected with Darrell's sad eyes as he lugged himself out of Shawn's hospital room. He patted the shoulder of the officer who was guarding the door and came toward her. She did not wait but hurried forward and enclosed him in her arms.

He returned the embrace. His face pressed into her hair and his words were warm and soft on her ear. "They've put him into an induced coma, hoping his brain will repair itself."

She squeezed her sympathy into him. "I'm sorry."

There was a tremble in his inhale. "I thought I was going to have to shoot him. How could he do that to Sandy?"

"I'm thankful it sounds like she's going to survive."

Darrell nodded against her head and pulled her tighter. "How could anything make someone do that?"

"The mind is a powerful thing. If we let it go the wrong places, it will eventually pull us there with it. We did a lot of research on all this when Link and I started working on BERT. I think we might be able to use BERT to reverse the effects on Shawn. With God's help, there's hope. I'll get all my church to start praying. I won't mention the cause of his illness."

"I guess you heard then. They want to keep the information about the MEamp quiet."

Callie detected something in his voice. "You don't sound like you agree."

"I'm not sure the factory recall story is enough. Even with the money offered to anyone who turns in one of the boxes, how are they going to know they got them all when they don't know how many were out there in the first place? I understand the fear of panic, but what these things cause is worse than panic."

Callie drew back and tipped her face up toward Darrell's. She needed to know where he was emotionally before she told him about her conversation with Brock. There had been no time for them to talk since the incident with Shawn. Was he ready to move past the grief and hear her plan?

The pain stayed in Darrell's eyes, but the corners of his mouth turned up as he looked at her.

Callie wanted to fall against him again and hold him, comforting him with loving support. He had just lost his friend to something close to death. But being in Darrell's arms caused another stirring inside. She heard her own words. *The mind is a powerful thing.* She could easily lie to herself, fooling her mind into believing another embrace was all innocent emotional support while she absorbed the love she wanted so desperately. But there was nothing innocent about a lie, and God could never bless it if both their hearts were not committed to Him first. She couldn't let it continue. Giving his arms an affirming clasp, she pulled away. It was like tearing a piece out of herself.

Darrell's smile grew.

The sight was unnerving. Didn't he feel the same pain? Callie probed his features. Was the smile sarcastic? The thought entered her that perhaps the hurt she had caused him had made his heart as hard toward her as it was toward God. She spoke before her inner feeling leaked to the surface. "Some of the secrecy is because of me." Callie walked toward an empty waiting area a short distance away.

Darrell followed. He scrunched his brow, but the smile continued. "Why's it because of you?"

"I told Brock about a plan I have." Callie tried to sound professional, but she was unsettled. Had Darrell's love for her died so easily? She was ashamed that it should feel worse for Darrell to not love her than for him to not love God. She continued so he wouldn't sense her torment. "When Link and I dissected the MEamp that you gave me, we found that it receives information as well as sending it. Anything that comes through the cable or satellite the MEamp is hooked to is recorded and sent back to the MEamp source. That includes internet traffic. I believe they use it to build a profile on the people using it."

Darrell's troubling smile was replaced by a curious scrutiny. Still there was no sign that her pulling away had bothered him as it would have before. Something had changed. An uneasiness took over her mind. Maybe God was intervening. Maybe it was His way of answering her dilemma. When this was all over, perhaps Darrell would just walk away.

Callie couldn't think about it right now. Besides, she needed to tell Darrell about her idea. Only God knew how much time they had. "We are hoping we can use an active MEamp to track the signal back to its source. If we can catch who's doing this and stop the broadcasts, then the boxes will be harmless. We have a meeting at the FBI office in Denver tomorrow to discuss it. Brock wanted me to see if you are up to being a part of it. If you don't want to, I understand. Link and I can work with Brock and his team if you just want to step away from all this. I know a lot has happened—not much of it good."

Darrell's smile returned. The idea apparently pleased him. "I have something to tell you."

Callie didn't want it to end like this. She couldn't take it right now. She needed to be sharp in order to help Brock. Too much was at stake. "Can it wait? I don't think I'm up to much more conversation right now, and you have been through a lot. I'll let Brock know you need to be here for Shawn and Sandy." *There. That should be an easy way out for him.*

Darrell frowned. "What's wrong?"

"I just have a lot to pray about before tomorrow."

"Maybe we could pray together."

Callie didn't know what to make of the statement. Was he mocking her?

"I did what you suggested. I got things ironed out with God. It really wasn't that hard in the end. I prayed and read the Bible, and He showed me a part of myself that I didn't want to see but needed to see more than anything. I was blaming Him because I didn't want to face my own failures. I gave it all to Him, and He cleaned me out." Darrell moved closer. "You were right. What I had before wasn't a real relationship with God. I know that because now I know what a real one is, and there is no comparison. I'll never be the same. I could never live without Him again."

Callie stared. She feared speaking. The words seemed like a dream, and she was afraid to disturb it. But there was Darrell standing in front of her professing something that changed everything. She knew her Heavenly Father well enough to know He gave good things, but for this to happen at this time was more than she could have hoped for. More than she deserved.

Darrell grabbed some tissues off a waiting room table. He used one to dab tears from her cheeks. His touch was gentle, caring.

Callie examined his face. He was right. It was really there—the joy of the Lord. She grabbed him and held tight for all the right reasons.

Chapter 40

The Denver FBI office was an impressive structure with its multicolored mirrored windows reflecting the morning sun. It was surrounded by a compound that conveyed both the concept of immaculate groundskeeping and high security.

Once Callie, Link, and Darrell had navigated the check-in process under the escort of Agent Brock, they were shown into a conference room. Darrell pulled out a chair for Callie and took the seat to her left. Link plopped on the other side of her.

Across the table, Brock indicated the man beside him. "This is Agent Carlton of the Department of Homeland Security." The man's broad chest and thick arms filled his suit. He had a wide, stern face with a complexion darker than Callie's.

Brock introduced everyone and began. "I have briefed Agent Carlton on your backgrounds. The Bureau has been struggling to get a lead on the phony Denver PD cars that Darrell videoed. No luck so far, but we still believe the cars are an indicator that the next target is in Denver. The best theory we have about what Failak is planning is that he is going to trigger the MEamps to start a rash of domestic murders in homes around Denver to tie up resources so they can attack whatever target they have planned. The cars must be for infiltrating the target. Perhaps they are going to pack the cars themselves with explosives. There are a lot of important places you could go with a police car."

Darrell decided to wait on sharing what he and Callie had discussed the night before.

Brock picked up a stack of papers bound like a college thesis. "Callie has an idea that I think has merit. Since the search for the cars and our intelligence hasn't yielded anything, we have been given the green light from both our agencies to try Callie's strategy." He gave the papers a shake for emphasis. "Our people reviewed your report on the MEamp and were very impressed. I'll tell you, there are some heavyweight words in here: binaural beats, flickering ganzfelds, hypnagogia, and brainwave entrainment and synchronization."

Link raised one hand as he continued tapping and swiping with the other. "She had to use the sausage interfaces for those." He wiggled his fingers. "You should see what the Shakespeare chip was going with."

Brock and Carlton made brief eye contact with each other as if to make sure they weren't losing it.

Darrell put his hand on the table in front of the men. "It's like learning a romance language. Don't think about it too much. Just go with the feeling."

Callie gave an embarrassed shrug. "I couldn't use the speech-to-text. It translated those words as 'buying Carl's beats and flicking can welds to a hip Godzilla.'"

The Agent's faces didn't change until Brock shook his head. "Callie you may have to dumb this down a little for us."

Link gave his reassurance without looking up. "Don't worry. Callie doesn't talk like me. It'll be dumb enough for you guys."

Callie swatted him.

Link gawked at her and shrugged. "What?"

Darrell intervened. "Callie just go ahead." With half-closed eyes he gave a don't-worry-about-it wave at the agents. "It'll get easier."

Callie took Darrell's advice. "Link and I did a lot of research into these topics when we started BERT project. There was some experimentation with this back in the sixties and seventies, but it never really went anywhere. Back then they decided the influence it exerted on people was not significant enough to be useful or dangerous. It was determined a person could not be made to do something that was against his or her natural inclination."

Brock appeared speculative. "I guess the invention of the high-definition televisions and digital sound has changed all that. Now it can make killers out of ordinary people."

Callie scrunched her face. "Not exactly ordinary people. It appears they look for individuals already predisposed to certain patterns of thought as indicated by their media choices. I won't go into everything I learned in my research, except to say that there has been manipulation going on in our entertainment industry for decades. People are watching some scary things, and you don't have to dig very deep to find it. Failak and his team are taking advantage of some of the negative ways our own music, movies, and television shows have been eroding our society for years. You are what you consume."

"Not something that brings pleasant thoughts," Darrell shook his head in disgust. "But I think we need to fill you in on the new developments because we need to move quickly with Callie's plan. First, tell me what you know about who we are up against."

Agent Carlton cleared his throat and had everyone's attention. "The video of the terrorists you encountered confirmed what we already suspected. The leader of the group is a man named Failak." The agent pulled a photo from a file on the table in front of him and laid it before the group.

Darrell took in a deep breath as he reached toward the picture.

Callie gasped. "That's him."

Picking up the photo, Darrell blew out the breath and sat back in his chair. "My old friend." He felt no friendship. "We keep meeting. It's good to have a name to go with the face. Tell me about him."

"The DHS has been doing its best to track him, but we're afraid he has been able to slip in and out of the country largely undetected. We have suspected he's been living in the US for years, off and on."

Darrell handed Carlton the picture.

The big man turned it for everyone to see. "The intel we have on him has mainly come from his faint computer footprint. The internet buzz in the Muslim world sometimes refers to him as the 'Arrow of Allah.' His name means a type of arrow. We suspect that he was the behind-the-scenes organizer of most of the Iranian cyber-attacks over the years. He has been associated with such groups as SOBH Cyber Jihad and Parastoo. We have been tracking him for some time as a major player in attacks such as the intrusion into the computer system of the Bowman Avenue Dam in Rye, New York, in 2013 and the 2014 infiltration of the Navy Marine Corps Intranet, just to name a couple. Though others were charged in some of the crimes, we found signs of Failak working behind the scenes. He likes to shield himself behind individuals that he grooms and manipulates to do his dirty work."

Carlton put the picture back in the file. "We know some about his past, but, overall, he's a well-kept Iranian secret. We know that he is the son of an Iranian software engineer, named Alireza Hamadani, who was rumored to have created some of the first computer viruses. Hamadani was highly connected with the Ayatollah Khomeini government after the 1979 revolution. He was killed in 1988 when a US Navy warship accidentally shot down the civilian airliner he was on."

Agent Carlton's description triggered Darrell's memory. "The USS Vincennes."

Carlton gave an impressed nod. "That's the one."

Darrell considered that God had been preparing him. "I remember seeing that on the news and later I had to write a high school paper about it. It was a strange tragedy."

Carlton went back to his briefing. "Failak was under sixteen at the time and already a computer genius himself. Besides being a jihadist, the rumor is that he blames the US for his father's death. I guess he is doing everything he can to destroy us."

Darrell pondered on the possibility that a darker supernatural power had been working in the terrorist's life. "Bitterness is an ugly thing," Darrell felt Callie's hand find his under the table.

Carlton's head bobbed in agreement. "In Failak's case, it's very ugly."

Brock turned his attention to Darrell. "So, tell us about what you came up with last night."

Leaning forward, Darrell started. "I did some thinking because things weren't adding up." He put his palm up like it held the problem. "Okay. I'm a terrorist. I want to spread fear in people, demoralize them. How does the serial killer angle play into that? It's been bothering me. A terrorist doesn't want to hide behind a story like that. He wants the credit."

Brock made a similar gesture toward Darrell. "Well, he did take the credit…on the phone call you got."

"Finally, after he tried to make us think the killings were domestic murder suicides, then a serial killer, then a racially-motivated crime. Three attempts to make these killings look like something else and then they finally act like it was a terrorist plot all along. If they wanted to terrorize people, why wouldn't they take the credit immediately? Scare everyone and make them suspect each other?"

"Maybe they wanted to get a few under their belt before they started bragging." Brock grinned to soften the sick humor.

"You're not far off." Darrell shifted his position in the chair as he continued to address the agent. "Colorado Springs was an experiment. Or maybe I should say, a rehearsal. They wanted to see if the MEamps could cause certain individuals to kill in a real-world environment, but they didn't want the MEamps discovered. So they caused the killing to be done in a way that would make it look like a domestic suicide. When the killings continued, it started looking like we had a serial killer, and that was all right with the terrorists, too. But when we started asking questions around the MEamp office, that was too close. So they kidnapped Callie and tried to make it look like a racially motivated serial killer. It was like a magic show, all illusion and misdirection. That's why I called it a rehearsal. But the magician broke the first rule of magic—never show the same trick twice to the same audience."

Darrell glanced around at his own audience. "All of us were right about a lot of things, but we just didn't see how it all fit. But Failak kept trying to fool us, kept showing us all his tactics. We got to look in his magic trunk and see all the props."

Brock was smiling and nodding. "I'm guessing this makes sense, and you're going to tell me something that I need to know."

"Yeah," Darrell grinned. "I know the trick he's going to do next." Leaning forward he put out his fist. "Look what he's got to work with." Darrell held up a finger. "We have the MEamps," another finger, "we have the Denver PD cars," and another "and we have the gang member that tried to blow up your SWAT team—they didn't find him overnight."

Abandoning the finger display, Darrell decided to be more direct. "I don't think there is a site Failak plans on hitting in Denver. I think Denver *is* the site. But I don't think he plans on stopping there. I'm pretty sure Failak has aspirations of bringing down the whole country."

Brock furrowed his brow. "Not to belittle these deaths, but I don't think the country is going to fall apart over a series of domestic homicides in Denver."

Darrell gave Brock a look of agreement. "I think the MEamps in Denver are programed for a different purpose. I think Failak means to start a race war."

Brock spent a moment in thought before he spoke. "Fill in the blanks here for me."

"Christie, one of my detectives, said the management of the MEamp company were all out of town because they had been expanding into a lot of areas including New York, Chicago, Cleveland, St. Louis and Los Angeles. I think Failak's group has been influencing the racial tension we are seeing in those areas."

Agent Carlton's face registered a revelation. "That matches up with things that we were following. Some of the same internet voices were active in the instigation of problems in some of the most violent confrontations regardless of where they occurred. We also found videos of surveillance footage that captured people involved in inciting some of the crowds. No matter what part of the country it was in, we kept seeing some of the same faces."

The agent made a disgusted sound. "I get tired'a hearing all this garbage. I know there is plenty of racism in the country. Where I grew up in Georgia, a black man had to be careful going out after dark. I had a bunch of crackers with shotguns gonna kill me one night. But a white cop saved my life. It's why I got into law enforcement. I've met some bigots on the job, and some of them have tried to stand in my way. But worse than that were the ones that acted like I was never gonna be able to make it without their help."

Callie gave a supportive motion of her hand toward Carlton. "Don't you hate that. It's like you're Charlie Brown's Christmas tree." Callie's voice took on a squeaky pathetic sound, and she rocked her head back and forth as she spoke. "Poor ugly scraggly little thing, let me wrap a blanket around you and put you in this warm corner 'cause nobody's ever going to want you. God taught me no matter what kind of face that comes out of, it's the devil talking."

Carlton boomed a baritone laugh and pointed at Callie. "She knows what I'm talkin' about."

Darrell used his hand to cover his chuckling.

Keeping his wide grin, Carlton moved his finger to indicate Darrell. "And your man there is laughing at you."

Callie snapped her gaze to Darrell. She gave a cute cock of her head and grinned. "Well, *my man* can just laugh."

Darrell felt heat move to his face. *Her man.* It must be obvious how he and Callie felt about each other. He wondered if the embarrassment showed in his smile. It had been a while since anything had produced the feeling. It charged his senses.

Callie lowered her gaze and looked away, but Darrell could see a trace of a smile. Looking up again, she addressed the group. "It all relates to what we found in BERT research. I read an article about a guy that used what's called 'social engineering' to get some people to commit a robbery even though they didn't start out with the idea. Over a period of time, the social engineer learned the subtle motivations of certain target individuals. He used that knowledge to build suggestions in their minds associated with sounds, words, colors, all kinds of subconscious mechanisms and then triggered them under just the right circumstances until they finally decided to commit the crime. In the end, the people thought it was their own idea."

Darrell took advantage of Callie's lead-in. "I think Failak and his group are manipulating people all over the country to socially engineer racial violence. It looks like the next part of their plan is to use the MEamps to weaponize people with racial hatred, get them to start acting on that hate. Like Callie said, it's a short walk to violence for a lot of people. They just need a nudge and a reason."

Callie joined in again. "I know it's possible because it happened to my daddy without having a MEamp involved." She transferred her gaze and found her memories on the ceiling. "He hated white people. In his mind, he lumped every white person with all the bigots he ever met, and he turned into a bigot himself. That's when some radical Muslims got a hold of him. Their brand of Islam gave him religious permission for his prejudice. His hate festered until the terrorists convinced him to blow up a whole bus full of white Christians and himself along with them." Callie glanced around the table. "When people hate it's possible to push them to do horrible things."

Darrell squeezed Callie's hand and addressed Brock. "That gang member who tried to blow up your SWAT team, I think they planned on using him up in Denver, only they decided to deploy him early to get us off the MEamp scent. But they still have the Denver police cars. If they can dress up a couple of Caucasian thugs to look like cops, put them in a cop car, and send them into the black neighborhoods to rough up the citizens—more fuel on the fire. Pretty soon the National Guard comes in and more people die. A few days of that and Denver is on fire. Then, on to the next city. If the terrorists could get us fighting ourselves, it would take a lot of pressure off what they are doing in the Middle East and elsewhere. Maybe even take the United States out of the picture completely."

"Surely, they will call this off." Carlton wrinkled his brow. "They have to know that we are onto them since you and Callie escaped, and the phony recall of the MEamps should tell them we are onto the boxes as well. How do they think they'll get away with it?"

Darrell shook his head. "Failak's defining feature seems to be arrogance, and he thinks this will be the death blow…as a friend put it. Also, Callie did another examination on the MEamp box last night, and she found something that you need to hear."

The statement put Brock's attention on Callie. "Something that changes the plan?"

Callie shook her head. "Mostly just accelerates it. After Darrell told Link and me what he just told you, we took another look at the boxes. The MEamps are programmed to download the data they collect each week. Obviously, Failak was smart enough not to put any link to his physical location in the boxes. The MEamp's programing contains a schedule for when it is to listen for an IP address to know where to send the data. If I were trying to prevent someone from tracking me, I would have the data routed through a series of servers across the globe before it is sent to my actual location. So Link and I have created a tracking program to follow the download all the way to the source. Once it arrives at its final destination and Failak starts crunching the info, a program hidden in the data will send a signal back, giving me his location."

Callie grimaced as she pushed up her glasses. "I know it's a programming feature, but this part's kind of freaky. Once someone hooks up a MEamp, it establishes its presence in that location. I found a couple of ways that it does this, but I might not have found them all. If it is disconnected or moved, it will not receive the signal telling it where to send its data. If the box doesn't communicate when it is supposed to, the programmer, obviously this guy Failak, knows that it might have been compromised."

Darrell added an explanation. "That is why we believe Failak could be thinking he has everything covered. He knows what boxes are still in play."

Callie nodded. "For our plan to work we had to find a MEamp box that was still in service and belonged to someone that Failak would be interested in—someone who was racially motivated toward violence. But it has to be a box that we could gain access to in its original location."

Callie reached over to pat the long back slouching next to her. "Link found a person we believe will be the perfect candidate to use for the bait. He is a young man that has already been talking racial violence online and viewing all the right kinds of things on the internet and movie channels. He lives with his mother who talks on social media about being disturbed about what her son is into. There is every indicator that she will cooperate with us. Link was able to find through the mother's social media account that the young man will be away from home today."

Callie took a breath. "And we need to do it today. After two this afternoon, there are no further downloads scheduled. Right after that last download there is an upload scheduled. It's my guess we have discovered Failak's timeline."

Callie glanced around to be sure everyone was following her. "Right after this download, I think he intends to start transmitting the mind-altering signal to all the boxes that are verified to be in their original locations. We have to hurry, so I can swap out the data on the box with a version that has my program attached before it is time to send. I should get a signal back fairly quickly telling us where you guys need to go to collect Mr. Failak. But not long after I receive the IP address for Failak's location, the MEamp will start transmitting the signal that sets his attack in motion. You won't have much time to find him and stop the broadcast."

Darrell loved listening to Callie's mind work. This time, however, he wished she had come to a different conclusion. He inhaled to share his own deduction, and it wasn't much better. "Having Callie's timeline in mind, I'm sure Failak will also make his move with the phony cop cars this afternoon. I suggest we saturate the area with undercover units and see if we can catch the fakes when they roll in. Link has created a program to monitor all the internet cameras in the area with image-processing software that is programmed to look for police cars."

Brock surveyed the participants. "You're right. This definitely accelerates things. Carlton and I will start putting the plan together on our end. Darrell, if you and Callie can handle tracking Failak through this MEamp, I would like to keep Link to help set up this hunt for the PD cars. Let us know when you find his location, and I'll send you the calvary."

Darrell leaned back to look past Callie at their young friend. "Remember, they don't speak Link. Go easy on them."

Slumped down in his chair, Link sent Darrell a sideways gaze. "Initiating translation program now." He looked across the table. "I need to set the parameters. You guys speak English, right?"

Carlton's face said he was unimpressed. "Denver is a big city. How did you find this perfect candidate?"

Link made a quick glance from his cell phone. "I did a society party search for anyone gone deep aggro on the color issue who also recently got a hardware upgrade called a MEamp. Linked 'em up and it gave me a grocery list of this dude's home docks. His speed dial listed his maternal unit, so I looked at her fence and saw she would probably not be a fan of his latest data stream."

Brock and Carlton both looked at Link with blank faces.

"Oops, Sorry. The translation app wasn't quite loaded yet."

Darrell held up his hand. "Allow me, gentlemen. He said that he searched the social media sites on the internet for anyone with violent racial tendencies who lately acquired a MEamp. When he combined the two it gave him a list of addresses in the area. One looked good, and he found the guy's mom on his contact list. Her posts gave him the rest of the picture."

After a second, Brock responded. "How did you do that kind of search on social media?"

Without taking his eyes off his phone, Link responded. "Once you get past the gatekeepers and disable all that friend request nonsense, you can search about anything."

Darrell looked down at the table and shook his head. When he looked up, he noticed Brock and Carlton were still scrutinizing Link. Brock had his mouth opened slightly.

The silence in the room caused Link to look up. He examined each face, his fingers still poised over his phone. "Do I need a lawyer?"

Chapter 41

Callie knocked on the door of the apartment at the address that Link had given them. Darrell hung back a little to be less intimidating. A small black woman answered. She looked to be about thirty-five and had the lean look of one accustomed to hard work. Callie introduced herself and then Darrell displayed his badge and police ID.

Her eyes went wide. Leaning her head back, she heaved a sorrowful sigh. "Oh no. What's that boy done now?"

Darrell sat on the couch in the living room of the woman who had identified herself as Nandi and listened to Callie explain the situation to her. Callie had rapport, so he let her do most of the talking.

The room's furniture faced a large flat screen television. A gaming console sat on the floor before it and beside that was the MEamp. Cables slithered across the carpet like umbilical cords pumping electronic poison into the dark monster. The television was off, but to Darrell it still looked sinister.

Nandi summed up what Darrell and Callie had been explaining. "So, you want to use my MEamp to catch some crooks? Is that what I'm getting from you?"

"Yes, ma'am." Callie used a respectful tone.

"I should have known it was no good when my Antonne came home telling me how some man was handing out free coupons down at the park for this TV thing. I don't like it. Makes everything look too real. Gives me a bad feeling every time I watch it. But I can't tell that boy nothing anymore. He got so big for his skin that he don't listen to me. I just go in the other room when it's on. I'm glad he's out of town on a school trip. You do whatever you want with that thing. I'll be glad to be rid of it."

They had about an hour and a half before the MEamp transmitted. Darrell was worried they were cutting it close, but in less than thirty minutes Callie had everything ready to go. "There," she declared. "The trap is baited. Now we wait for the vermin to come looking for the cheese."

Nandi was frowning. "I don't want to be labeled. Are you sure this ain't gonna be hooked up with my name?"

Callie gave Nandi's arm a squeeze. "These are really bad people. We need to stop them so they can't hurt you or anyone else. This will help us do it."

Nandi smiled. "It's kind of exciting, ain't it?" Her smiled faded. "I just don't want my boy in the middle of it."

"We don't want anything to happen to him either. But from what he's been posting, he already had his mind set in that direction. This might get him out of it. Besides, these people are terrorists, and they want to start a war right here in Denver. If we don't stop them, we are all going to be right in the middle of it."

Shaking her head, Nandi looked fretful. "Those Arabs are the scariest people on the planet. We should'a wiped 'em out a long time ago."

Callie gave her a bright smile. "Oh, I know some Middle Eastern people I could introduce you to that would change your mind. Scary people come in every color. They can even be family members. Even though the devil likes *us* to use stereotypes, I've noticed he's an equal opportunity employer himself." She finished her statement with a wink at Nandi.

Nandi was nodding, "You're right. I wasn't think'n. I wish you could talk to Antonne. He's been listening to all that black and white stuff down at the park. Thugs, looking for a good excuse to go out and beat people up and steal stuff, if you ask me."

Darrell sat off to the side while Callie and Nandi talked, and the time passed quickly. Without warning, the synthetic voice of Callie's computer spoke. It repeated, "You've got a bite," over and over until Callie hurried to it and silenced the alarm. She examined the monitor. "The box is sending the data." Callie began to type on the laptop, busying herself with the technical activity of following the signal to its source.

Darrell got on the phone to Link and told him what was going on.

"I'm processing in batch mode, Darrellman. Got my cape on and ready to do good deeds," he said. "The Brockbacker has me wholly connected. I've got a van full of pixilation and digital eyes on everything. I'll be looking for the baddest pretending to be the finest." Darrell heard Brock in the background but couldn't tell what he said. Link came back on. "Okay, and the Brockthesaurus says we will also be looking for *civil unrest.*" Link announced the last part with an exaggerated official tone.

"Good, you do that," Darrell told him. "And stay safe."

With Callie in the other room, Darrell addressed Nandi. "Thanks for helping us. You have my gratitude along with all of law enforcement. You might be saving a lot of people."

Nandi grinned and looked at the floor. "I ain't really doin nothin'."

Darrell spent some time assuring the woman how much her cooperation meant. As they chit chatted, Darrell snuck looks at Callie who sat and gazed deep into the computer as if she might see Failak there. She moved the cursor and tapped the keys periodically, twirling a stray curl of her hair.

Darrell watched her until she let out an elated, "There you are," while grabbing the pad and pen that she had beside her. She scribbled on the sheet, tore off the page, walked over, and handed it to Darrell. "He's running off an IP address that comes back to a cable provider, naturally." She turned back to the screen and looked up the address she had given him on a map program. "And he's not far away. Up by the railroad tracks close to the end of Downing Street. But if you're right and he has it wired to explode, then he will probably be operating it remotely using some type of mobile hotspot. In that case, he could be anywhere."

"That's why we have to get him to come back home. So, it's time for me to make a house call." Darrell could see the fearful look on Callie's face. "Don't worry. We won't get close to the building. I'm going to see how that new toy you gave me works. I plan to do a little surgical application of ballistics." He could see that his assurances helped a little, but Callie still looked worried. He reached out and gave her arm a squeeze, then turned for the door.

Callie grabbed him from behind in a hug. With her head pressed against the back of his shoulder, she told him, "Don't get hurt." She quickly let go and stepped back.

Darrell turned and gave her a smile. "What? Do you think I'm reckless?"

"After what Link told me about that night you came and got me–yes."

"That was different." Darrell made a gesture as if his statement explained everything. "I had a lady I was trying to find."

"Well, just remember," Callie's face pleaded, "now you have one to come back to."

"Yes, ma'am," Darrell responded and walked out, still smiling. If it was in the will of God, and he hoped it was, he was definitely coming back.

Chapter 42

Link could tell something was wrong with the man he was watching on one of the webcams he was monitoring. His black shirt and black basketball shorts made his white skin stand out even more. He didn't look like a basketball player. He was tall with broad shoulders but had a belly to match. He glanced around, searching, like an animal looking for prey. Link pointed him out to Brock. "Pixel in on that guy."

Brock came over. "Where's that at?"

Link quickly referred to the corner of the screen where the display showed the location of the camera. "Sixteenth Street Mall at Arapahoe."

They both watched in disbelief as the man ran across the street to where a pretty young lady was sitting in a chair at a sidewalk café. Her scarlet skirt looked expensive, as did the white top that contrasted with her dark skin. She had her back to the man and was talking on her cell phone and never saw him coming. The man grabbed the legs on the chair and jerked it out from under the woman, sending her sprawling onto the pavement. She crawled under a table as the man tried to beat her with the chair. Brock was already on the open line they had with Denver Police as Link watched people nearby rush to stop the attacker.

Darrell gave the commands to the NIP to sync with the Precision Guided Firearm that Callie had provided. Using technology similar to what fighter jets used to lock onto a target, the rifle incorporated a laser rangefinder, a high-resolution color imaging system and a computer running an image processing algorithm – all integrated into a sighting scope mounted on top of the weapon.

Callie had explained that the NIP used some of the same technology, and she had shown Darrell how to integrate the prosthetic with the rifle. She had designed the electronic components for the weapon, and with

Brock's help, she had obtained permission from Raji to borrow the gun from the ATS lab. He suspected that no mention was made to Raji of Darrell being the one using it.

"Why don't you just cut the power?" Deek Bauby, from the FBI's sniper team, was watching as Darrell set up the high-tech weapon.

Darrell pointed in the direction of the building and tipped his head as if sighting with his finger at a large gray box behind the building. "They've got a generator, and Callie was sure the equipment inside would be running off uninterrupted power supplies."

Deek was silent for a few moments then said, "Sure you want to try it this far away?"

Darrell nodded while he kept working. "The whole place has cameras with audio. Wherever Failak is, he's watching and listening. But at this distance, the audio shouldn't be able to pick up the sound with this silencer. The wire should drop so fast past the lens of that backyard camera that no one will notice. We can't give Failak any reason to think it's a trap. We're going to use his own surveillance to make him think it's a problem with his equipment or software. We have to have the right bait to catch the right rat."

Deek's head was tilted back, and his eyes narrowed as he watched Darrell verify that everything was ready. "If this thing is so great, why did Brock think you needed me?" He had grudgingly obeyed Brock's order to let Darrell make the shot because of the NIPs superior hold and its ability to integrate with the rifle's software.

"Because he knows that pulling the trigger is only part of being a good sniper. I wouldn't have been able to get us set up in this location like you have."

Deek snorted. "You know if you make this, I'm going to have to start looking for another job."

"Don't worry about it. These things cost over $20,000 apiece. I doubt if even federal law enforcement will be seeing them anytime soon. And when they do, I'm sure you'll be the first to get one."

Another snort.

Deek had managed to find a structure high enough with a direct line of sight to the building, which Callie's efforts had identified. In Darrell's sights was the large co-ax cable running into the building and beyond that was an empty lot. His aim-point would put any stray rounds harmlessly into the dirt. He painted the cable with the sighting systems laser and pressed a button near the trigger of the weapon, locking it in.

"Good tag," Deek announced as he examined the image in his smartphone, which had been connected to the rifle through Wi-Fi. "So now that thing takes the shot for you?" Deek's voice sounded dubious.

Darrell let out the breath he had been holding. "Pretty much, I guess. I pull the trigger but it doesn't fire right away, is what I'm told. The arm and rifle work together, and when everything is lined up just right, then it fires."

"Sounds spooky. Not like real shooting."

"We'll see." Darrell inhaled again.

The black cable stood in contrast with the lighter-colored ground behind it, another benefit of the lot as a backdrop. Even though the movies made hitting a thin cable child's play to the marksmanship of the show's hero, Darrell knew the impossibility of such a shot at that distance. But Callie said it would work. He prayed she was right.

As Darrell moved his finger to the trigger of the PGF, his phone rang, announcing that it was Brock. Without moving he answered it with the NIP. "You know, you're interrupting my shot."

"Darrell, it's started." Brock's voice sounded rattled. "Failak is working hard toward that death blow you were talking about. We can't keep up with the number of people we're seeing attacking others all over this part of the city. We're trying to concentrate on accounting for all the DPD units. It may be harder than we thought. I never expected it to be this bad. Denver already has all its officers going to calls, and they're bringing in all their off-duty officers. I'm just afraid that a cop's going to have to shoot one of these crazies and get people turning on the police. If mobs start forming—"

"Okay, okay. Let me try to get this thing disabled, and maybe we can at least keep any more from being affected." Darrell disconnected the phone, concentrated on the shot, and pulled the trigger. Nothing happened. That was disconcerting at first, but the arm kept moving the crosshairs to the dot on the cable. The rifle jumped, and Darrell heard the silenced report, but it surprised him when it went off. If he had not felt the weapon cycle, he would have thought it was someone else firing.

"Ah," Deek exclaimed. "You zinged it but no cut. That is unbelievable you hit it at all. I am *so* replaced."

Through the lens of the scope, Darrell could see the cable bouncing up and down from the partial hit. He waited for it to settle down and then turned the laser on it again to get a fresh lock. Through the scope, he could see insulation and wire sticking out from where he hit it the first time. Darrell made sure the laser was on what was left of the cable in that same spot and pressed the lock button. He sighted in and squeezed the trigger. 'Wait for it,' he told himself as the NIP moved the sight to meet the lock mark and, Thwack!

"Whoa! Clean break." Deek took off his FBI cap and swatted Darrell with it. "I want one. Think your friend can score me one of those? I don't have $20,000."

The cable was gone from Darrell's sights. "You never know. Once we get through this maybe she can make you an official field tester or something." He panned down to where half the broken line hung from the side of the building. "Okay, Failak, my old friend, come on down. I still owe you one," he whispered into the stock of the rifle.

Chapter 43

"So, what's Antonne wanting to do with his life?" Callie probed lightly, praying Nandi wouldn't feel invaded.

Nandi shook her head and gave a sigh. "I don't know. That boy's gonna worry me to death. He wanna be a big man, but he don't work hard 'nuff in school. Then there's always someone on the street that's got a quick way to make it. I keep telling him, get an education and stay away from them hoods he be hang'n with."

After a lingering silence, Callie spoke. "I'll be praying for him."

"Girl, I wish you would. He's a smart boy. He can make sump'n of himself if he just try. I'm always tell'n 'im, you gotta work hard cause it's harder for a black man. I know it's been hard on me, tryin' to get a job. I walk into the job office, and they wanna give me a mop. Right away they start showin' me all the motel jobs. I been cleaning up after nasty white people most of my life. But working hard is what got me my job as night auditor at the hotel where I used to clean."

Callie nodded in understanding. "I did a lot of cleaning jobs in college. God blessed me with an academic scholarship that paid for my tuition, but I was too young for anyone to pay me to work in the field I was studying. My first couple of years I cleaned to pay for my gas to travel across town to get to school and to help my mom. She's been sick a lot."

Nandi looked off into the corner in thought. She had a haunted expression when she turned back. "I should have gone to school instead of getting hooked up with Antonne's dad. Maybe I could be an accountant or somethin'. I like that part of the job I do. When the ledger doesn't add up right, I get excited. I know that sounds funny, but it's like a mystery I have to solve. Like this big caper you all involved with. It's like that for me with numbers. If I would'a been like you and not gotten tied down with a man until after I had my college, maybe I would be staying at that motel instead of checking people into it."

Callie ached for the woman. "Do you feel like God is nudging you toward being an accountant?"

Nandi made a scoffing sound. "I wish I knew what God wants me to do. I can barely keep this roof over our heads. I got no money or time to go back to school. I just wanna make sure Antonne doesn't get stuck like I am. He needs to go to college so he can compete with all them white folks."

Callie shifted in her chair. "Education isn't the only path to knowledge or success. As humans we like to limit things— 'this is the only way it will work, this is where your life is, this is what you are.' Don't let someone else put you in a box that God didn't put you in. I know when you're black, that's all some people see." Callie leaned in with an encouraging look. "But God knew what he was doing when he made every one of us. He doesn't want it to be a competition or a war or anything like that. It gets complicated. I've seen it work both ways in my life."

Uncomfortable memories tried to accuse Callie of her own failures. She knew where they were coming from. *Okay, devil. You wanna talk about that, let's talk about it.* She knew the Lord could take the enemy's lies and use them for good, if she was honest. "There was one time my company had me scheduled to be the keynote speaker on cybernetic research in prosthetics at the American Orthotic and Prosthetic Annual National Assembly. It was taking place at a hotel in another city, so I got to the hotel the night before. When I arrived, I saw my own picture on a poster they had in the lobby. I have to confess it made me a little prideful."

Nandi gave Callie an encouraging touch on her arm. "You *should* be proud, girl. That's a big deal."

Callie gave a half laugh, recalling the incident. "The next morning, before I got in my nice clothes, I went down to see where I needed to haul the things I was using for my demonstrations and how things were going to work. There was this really stylish white woman giving directions to all these wait staff who were hustling, trying to get the conference rooms set up. I thought she would be a good one to ask.

"I told her I was there for the conference and wanted to find out where I needed to set up. She looked unhappy and told me to follow her. She took me through the kitchen and started talking about how I was supposed to be there at 5:30. We went into a storeroom, and she looked through some clothes on a rack. When she turned around, she handed me a waitress uniform and told me to change in the bathroom and if I hurried and got to work, she wouldn't report me."

Nandi's face was fuming. "And you was the main speaker? I hope you told her off. Just 'cause you're a black woman, people think you're a slave."

"I did tell her off. I told her who I was and said just because I was black didn't give her the right to assume I was the hired help."

"Good for you. I hope you got that racist white witch fired and sued that whole hotel."

Callie shook her head. "The woman turned whiter than she was already. She started crying and begging my forgiveness. But I wasn't listening. I told her I worked hard for my degree. That I deserved respect. I told her I wanted to talk to her supervisor."

Nandi nodded aggressively. "It's what she deserved. Just 'cause she was white, she thought she was better than you. If I ran this country, I'd make every privileged white woman be scrubbing a floor somewhere. What did you do, girl?"

"I was going to walk out and find her boss, but this pretty Latino girl came running in and got between us. She started begging me. She was talking fast in broken English and Spanish, saying, 'Please, Señora. Don't tell. Don't tell. She good boss. She a good Christian lady. She no bad person.' The white woman stood there crying while this little girl was almost on her knees pleading with me."

Nandi had lost some of her hard look. "What happened?"

"That's when God broke me. I looked at the uniform in my hand. The girl was wearing the same thing. Everything opened up in my mind at that moment. It was all about my pride. I realized that I was insulted to be asked to wear something that this little girl was grateful for. I wondered when I got so much above someone who worked hard cleaning for a living. The girl was thankful for a boss that was willing to give a second chance to a woman that showed up late for her first day on the job, regardless of what color she was."

Nandi said nothing. Her face seemed deep in thought.

"God spoke to me, clear as anything. In my mind I heard the Scripture from Matthew 23:12. "For those who exalt themselves will be humbled, and those who humble themselves will be exalted.""

Nandi wrinkled her brow. "Just 'cause you got a little prideful doesn't mean that what she did was right. That woman was a racist. It's wrong."

"I don't know anymore. Maybe we both assumed too much. I stopped even caring about whether she was or wasn't. I do know what God was dealing with me about. I tried to tell them it was all right, that I wasn't going to say anything, but I was so embarrassed I just wanted out of there. I never saw the woman again. I'm sure she avoided me. I don't know if she could even function after the way she acted when I accused her. I kept thinking how the girl said she was a good Christian lady. I had to wonder if looking for racists had gotten more important than looking for my Christian brothers and sisters. All I know is God used that woman to teach me something."

Nandi's face was still troubled. "Why would God be usin' some white racist to teach you somethin'? White people got no idea what it's like to be treated like that. They're the ones that need to be learnin' somethin'. More comes out of stuff like that. I don't mean nothin' at Darrell. He seems nice and all, but I'm always scared for my boy. Cops be always wantin' to shoot black kids just 'cause they're black."

Callie gave the woman a soft look. "I know you're scared for Antonne but all the cops I know are good people. They wouldn't hurt him unless they were scared themselves."

"Well, there's bad ones. Look at what happened back east. Those boys got shot and the riots and all. Those cops shot those black boys for no reason."

The statements troubled Callie, but she kept a kind expression. "I wasn't there, and I try not to get caught up in all the media hype. That stuff is really all about what sells. I know one thing, there's bad black people, too. From what you said earlier, it sounds like Antonne's in more danger from the so-called friends he's hanging out with. If we can get through tonight, maybe Darrell would be willing to talk to him."

Nandi wiped away tears. "I think it's gonna take more than talk. I don't know what I'm gonna do. I'm workin' all the time. I can't keep an eye on him like he needs. He needs a man around, but his daddy run out on us right after Antonne was born. Why men always be doin' that?"

Callie took Nandi's hand. "I don't know either. I guess it's fear and sin. They're scared of being stuck with less than what they want. They don't understand that family is something you make and not something you acquire."

Nandi nodded at Callie. "Darrell said you was real smart."

"He did?"

"Yeah," Nandi took back her hand to wipe her eyes again. She straightened herself up in her chair. "We was talkin' when you was bein' the computer geek." Nandi grinned. "You got somethin' goin' with him, don't you? If you don't mind me sayin' it. I see the way he be lookin' at you."

Callie tried to conceal how much the statement thrilled her. "Maybe."

"How long you known him?"

Callie sat back and looked at the floor. "Since I was eighteen years old."

"Oh girl, that's so sweet. Was he like your high school sweetheart?"

Callie did not know how to answer the question. How could she explain the years of entangled complications that were her and Darrell? "Well, it's not quite that simple."

Nandi put her hand over her mouth and shook her head. "Oh, that was dumb. That can't be right 'cause he's a bit older than you. How long you been together, though?"

Pausing for a moment, Callie considered the right response. "We're not…really. I mean we both want to be, I think, but things weren't right before. God had to work a lot of things out in both of us. And now that we're ready…" She glanced toward the window. "Everything's gone crazy." Looking back at Nandi, Callie gave a tired smile. "But if we can make it through this, I think it might happen."

"Check it out, girl. You been waitin' on God all these years?" Nandi shook her head in disbelief. "You must really love him."

Callie wondered who Nandi meant. "Darrell or God?"

Nandi was thoughtful for a moment. "Both, I guess." She turned away and studied the sky out the window. "I should'a made more time for God. Maybe if I had taken Antonne to church more, he might'a found friends that weren't criminals. I should'a done better by him."

Callie elbowed Nandi playfully. "Antonne or God?"

Shaking her head in amusement, Nandi realized what she'd said. "Both, I guess." She leaned back in her chair and stared at the ceiling. "I think God's talking to me, too." Leaning toward Callie, Nandi seemed resolved. "I have begged God to change my boy, but I think I need to be prayin' He'll change me first. Can we pray together for him and for your Darrell?"

The idea settled in Callie's mind like a warm biscuit on an empty stomach. *My Darrell.* She put her arm around Nandi, and they prayed like warriors.

"The byte box just caught a car going by Welton and Twenty-seventh," Link called out.

Brock flipped pages on his pad, where he had been logging the Denver PD activity. "Hold on. The what?"

"Sorry," Link said, "the *computer.*"

Brock referred to the map and compared it with the police calls. "That should be a unit running to a disturbance call just north of there."

"I've got another one at Market and 20th."

"They've got a pedestrian hit and run there. A black guy in a car ran down three white teens that were on the sidewalk."

"Whoa, what was that?" Link was scrolling back to a monitor view that had displayed for a few seconds and moved on to the next. "Do you have anything at...uh...Colfax and Broadway? 'Cause there's two cops beating a man at the bus stop in front of...uh, what is that...it's...United Nations Park."

Again, Brock referred to his pad his eyes running down the list. Dropping the pad on the counter, he grabbed the phone to the Denver police dispatcher that had been helping him off and on. "Suz, what have you got at Broadway and Colfax?" He listened. "Well, you better get someone there. I think we just found one of our fake units." He turned a worried face to Link. "Nobody's called out there."

"Well, not only are they there, but they're gathering quite a crowd."

Brock gave the information over the FBI radio then answered Link. "I'll bet."

One of the units responded, reporting that traffic was backed up making it hard to get there.

"That's one of the busiest intersections in the city—perfect place to make a show. Let's hope we can catch them before they start a riot."

"Too late." Link's eyes were fixated on the monitor before him. A crowd had gathered in the street. He could see people throwing up their hands, and they appeared to be yelling. The two white men in uniform hurried back to the police car as some of the members of the crowd advanced on them. A young black man ran around the police car. To Link, it looked like he was moving to help the man who had been beaten. One of the men in police uniform was already in the driver's seat. The other stood by the passenger side with the door open. As the would-be rescuer went around the rear of the police car, Link saw the standing officer raise his arms, apparently holding a gun. The officer's hands jumped several times, and the young man stumbled and then collapsed onto the sidewalk. The shooter jumped in the car, and they sped away, leaving behind the injured men and an enraged crowd.

Darrell and Deek watched the black van as it slowly rolled down the street, Deek with binoculars and Darrell with the rifle scope. They had no plan and no help. When Brock told them he was pulling the four undercover units that they had surrounding the area where the building was located, Darrell had objected until Brock told him about the shooting and promised to have them return as soon as he could.

Now Deek and Darrell were on their own. He had no doubt the van was there to resolve the problem at the building, and he was counting on Failak being in it. But now he was also concerned that Failak would be in the van, and they would not have enough resources to catch him.

"Okay," Deek said, "the van's pulling into the front of our building. Looks like this is definitely your boy. How you wanna play this?"

"Minute," Darrell said, looking through the scope intently watching to see who got out. The door on the side of the van slid open. The scope's display was excellent. The face that was embedded in Darrell's memory began a sweep of the area. Darrell avoided the urge to pull back as Failak looked right at him at one point. The distance and the gray tarp that Deek had rigged to look like another one of the gray air conditioning units that shared the rooftop with them would make it impossible for Failak to see them. "That's him," Darrell verified.

If Deek felt the same compulsion to duck, he did not show it. "Looks like there are two people in the front, one driver and a passenger. Unknown if there are any more in the back. We're already outnumbered with what we can see. We don't have many options except to hope some of those other guys get clear and get back up here in time before they leave." Deek's voice became background noise to Darrell's thoughts. After a few moments, Darrell came back to see Deek examining him.

"What's on your mind?"

Darrell shifted his grip on the rifle and held it toward Deek. "You wanted to try this, here it is."

Deek took the weapon with a bemused look on his face

Darrell outlined his thoughts. "Here is how I see it. These men have killed numerous times. If they get away, they will almost certainly kill again. I am going to try to make an arrest, but if it doesn't work, are we on the same page that we cannot let them leave?"

Deek considered that for a few seconds. "That's not the way we usually do things. I take the shot, but I have to have a supervisor give me the green light first."

"This isn't a usual situation. These are terrorists that are in the process of tearing this city apart, and your supervisor is busy with that part of this issue. This part is up to us." Darrell eyed Deek for a moment then started easing his way backward on the roof. "I know you'll make the right decision when the time comes. I am going to try to give them a chance to live, but if something happens to me, disable the van first and then stop anyone that tries to run."

"I thought you said this guy likes to rig the building to explode. How are you going to keep from getting yourself blown up?"

"I've got a plan, but there are a few unknowns that might foul it up. I just wanted to make sure we're clear on plan B."

Deek's single nod and facial expression said he didn't like the sound of the whole thing but had no argument under the circumstances.

Darrell continued. "So from this position, we have a view of the front, the back, and the west side and the cameras monitoring those areas. Your job is going to be to blind them at the right time and to cover me while I make my move. I've got to hurry, so I'll explain the rest of the plan over the headsets while working my way over to the building. And," Darrell gave Deek a thin smile, "if you get a chance to keep them from killing me, I'd appreciate that too."

Chapter 44

Deek lay on the roof liking the feel of the rifle. The wide view in the scope was great. He estimated that Darrell should be getting close. "They're still inside," Deek spoke into his headset.

"Good." Darrell panted in Deek's earpiece, obviously running. "They should be figuring out that the problem with the transmission is outside, so we need to control what they do from now on. I am going to be in position in a minute. Go ahead and take out the cameras on the front and rear of the building and make sure they don't come out that back door."

Deek leveled the rifle sights on the front camera. Even silenced the rifle report was loud. He was glad he was a long distance away. The weapon jumped, and pieces of the camera flew across the lot. He pivoted the barrel to the rear camera with the same result.

"Okay, cameras are out of commission. I'll knock and see if anyone's home." Deek opened up with a volley of rounds that struck the rear door at an angle and either penetrated the metal skin and embedded in the door or ricocheted off into the empty lot. He hoped that from inside it would sound like someone hitting the back door with a hammer. He waited to see what would happen.

The front door of the building came open.

"Okay," Deek started a running account for Darrell's benefit. "One man came out the front door. Now the man is out of the van. They both have AKs. The one from the building is telling the other one what's going on. Uh oh, they're splitting up. One is going around the other side, so I won't be able to see him. The one on this side is moving down the side of the building. They'll be at the back soon so you better move." Deek panned the rifle, but there was no sight of Darrell. He didn't like the fact he couldn't see the man who was on the other side of the building, but they would have to take that risk. He kept narrating. "He's got his AK at the ready pointed at the back of the building. He's halfway down the building. You don't have much time."

He saw Darrell spring from his hiding place at a sprint.

Deek turned his attention back to the man he could see. "He's moving faster now. He'll be around the corner any second."

Through the scope he could see that Darrell made it to the new hiding place and was just climbing inside as the man rounded the building's corner and the second man appeared from the other side as well. "Both men are in the back yard now," he informed Darrell. "They're looking around. They spotted the bullet holes in the door and the camera. Now one's pointing at the cut cable." Looking at the men standing there holding their AK's, Deek let a thin smile play over his face. "I know we talked about me putting some rounds at their feet to send them back to the front, but since I have this fancy rifle…" His voice trailed off. Then he said, "I came up with a better idea to kind of even up the odds a little."

Thwack! The stock on the AK47 that one of the men was holding exploded, and the rifle flew out of the man's grip. He grabbed his hand in obvious pain, then began shaking it like it was stinging.

"Ooh, I love this rifle." Deek hummed. "Hope you didn't get a splinter, there, buddy. Hey, Darrell, you just go ahead and play with the terrorists as long as you want and don't hurry back for this gun. And, by the way, I think they finally figured out that I'm up here shooting at them. They are both heading back to the front of the building. My buddy, splinter hand, is going inside and his partner is jumping in the driver seat of the van. I've got him covered, through the windshield, just in case. Look out. Here comes the other one out the door with Mr. Failak himself. They are definitely making a getaway. Naughty, naughty," Deek said as if scolding a bad puppy.

Twack! Twack! Two rounds from Deek's new toy hit the ground directly behind the men as they hustled to the van. "Uh oh," the expert sniper said mockingly. "Missed. You boys better run before I get you in my sights again." Deek kept his finger off the trigger as the other man ran around to the passenger side, and Failak jumped through the side door, which was still sliding shut as the van tore out of the lot.

"Oops, guess they got away." As he said it, Deek was up and heading for the ladder to get off the roof with his new baby cradled in his arms.

Behind him, a series of earth-shattering concussions went off and rattled everything around.

"Whoa!" The exclamation burst from Deek's lips as he whirled around. Smoke and debris, some still falling from the sky, was all that was left of the building. He stared in disbelief for a minute realizing that nothing in or around the building could have survived. "That wasn't supposed to happen."

There was a thundering boom.

Callie and Nandi jerked. Out of instinctive fear, Callie glanced to the living room where the MEamp still sat on the floor receiving its evil instructions. She feared if she turned it off she might give them away. Would Failak send someone after them if he knew Antonne's machine was the one that betrayed him? Besides, she didn't want to touch the dark box that represented all that was going wrong. *As long as we don't turn on the TV, it can't affect us.*

Both women moved to the small balcony of Nandi's fourth-floor apartment. As Nandi slid open the door, the sound of sirens came to them from multiple directions. Callie was tempted to call Darrell, but she didn't want to jeopardize what he was doing or put him in danger.

"You worried about him, ain't ya?"

Callie looked at the woman, who had apparently followed her gaze to the north, and nodded a weak, moist-eyed smile.

There was smoke rising from several areas, including where she knew Darrell had gone.

Callie called Link. "What is going on? Is Darrell okay?"

"No input," Link clicked keys. "We heard from him when they were at the IP site but we've been key whacking since then. This town's gone doomscape."

"What are the police doing?"

"High-speed *networking* that's *not working*. It's a system crash. They can't keep up. We need to reboot this city."

Callie heard someone talking in the background. Link was acknowledging what the person was saying. "Hey, Cals, sorry. I got'a stream 'cause Brock doesn't want us to miss anything, and this is a lot of screens even for me to watch."

"Okay," she told him. "Call me if you hear anything about Darrell."

"I'll try."

Callie headed to Nandi's kitchen and sat at the table.

The other woman followed. She sat in the chair across from Callie, rocking back and forth. "I heard what your friend said. If the police can't help, what we gonna to do?"

Callie delayed her answer as she searched the internet. "Remember when you said you wish you had gone to church more?"

"Yeah."

"How would you like a chance to reconnect? I have a whole lot of church numbers here. Would you be willing to help me start calling them?"

"What you think'n girl?"

Callie took a deep breath and let it out. "Even if the police can't handle this, I know God can. But I know He likes to work through people. Have you ever heard of a prayer chain?"

Nandi gave a tentative nod.

Callie sent the woman a serious look. "I want to start the biggest prayer chain you've ever seen."

"Okay. I'll get my phone and somethin' to write down numbers."

Callie nodded without looking up. She was engrossed in the church search, the plan she was forming in her mind, and her worry for Darrell.

Nandi moved toward the living room. "I'm going to see if there's anything on the news."

Chapter 45

The van flew through the streets. Failak sat in the swivel chair in the back of the van. He faced forward watching the road. To his right, opposite the side door, was a bank of computers and monitors. Behind him was a bench seat. Behind that bench seat, Darrell crouched, concealed. Most of the plan had worked.

Pounding the back door on the building with rounds had gotten Failak's men to come out the front and move to the back, giving Darrell the time he needed. He was able to leave his hiding place across the street and make it inside the van while they were at the back of the building. God had answered his prayers by providing a perfect place to hide behind the rear seat. The whole thing had been a risk, but it beat confronting them in a building they might blow up.

The part of the plan that had not gone so well had been getting them at gunpoint before they could blow up the building. Darrell had wanted to let the van get far enough away before revealing himself, just in case. Deek must have played the deadly sniper role so well they thought they needed the blast as cover. The explosion had shaken the van so badly they were lucky it didn't damage it.

Now that stopping them from detonating the building was no longer an option, he decided to see if they would lead them to the rest of the group. With the NIP in Cmode, he sent texts to Deek and Link telling them what was going on. Link responded that he had tapped into the GPS in the NIP and put up a map with a little devil symbol moving in a real-time indication of their position.

Darrell texted back. **A devil, huh? Thanks. I'm in this van, too, you know.**

They made their way downtown and pulled to a stop. Failak and his men got out so Darrell risked taking a peek. They were in an alley. Through the windshield, Darrell watched the terrorists walk between a building and a semi-trailer and out of his sight. The semi-trailer had a clean, new paint job and soda logo, but the underside looked like the same trailer he had hidden under in Colorado Springs. He guessed the two phony police cars were inside. No wonder no one could find them.

Hunkering down, Darrell sent the information to Link, who told him Brock was coordinating his men in that direction. His anxiety had reached an uncomfortable level, by the time Link sent him the message that the SWAT team was in place and ready to move in. **Remind them not to shoot at the black van,** Darrell texted back.

In the back of the van, Darrell kept his pistol at the ready, but he knew better than to try to enter the gun fight. The team that was engaging the terrorists was a highly-coordinated tactical unit that trained together and knew each other. Being in plain clothes and from another agency, he would be a liability and probably get shot.

Fast moving footsteps went by. The SWAT team was moving in, passing up the van because they knew Darrell was inside. He crouched in silence for several minutes.

Boom! A flash-bang distraction device rattled the area. There was a cacophony of gunshots up and down the alley. Voices shouted what sounded like exclamations and commands in a foreign language. A pause. More shooting and shouting. Another moment of silence, then a massive volley of gunfire erupted.

Darrell heard the driver door on the van come open. The vehicle rocked with the motion of someone leaping inside, then the engine revved. Momentum pushed Darrell forward as the van careened down the alley in reverse. It slid to a partial stop, lurched forward, and took off again.

Stealing a look over the seat, Darrell recognized the back of Failak's head. He ducked back into his hiding place. The leader was letting his men cover his getaway.

Darrell lay on the floor and slid forward under the seat to the computer area of the van. Pointing his M&P, he stood so Failak could see him and spoke to the man. "I know I've said this before, but don't move."

Failak's whole body shook as he jerked his head around to see who it was. The van swerved up onto the curb and headed toward a newspaper dispenser and decorative park bench mounted on the sidewalk.

Bad move, Darrell. "Watch the road!"

Failak snapped his head forward and slammed on the brake, causing the tires to screech. The terrorist hit the steering wheel as Darrell came staggering to the front. The dispenser and then the bench vanished under the sliding van with an awful crunch. A grating sound reverberated through the van until the vehicle came to a halt at an odd angle. Darrell slammed into the back of the passenger seat, spun around, and ended up between the seat and the passenger door, scrambling to pull himself up.

Failak recovered and slapped his hand on the empty passenger seat. In panic his gaze fixed on something on the floorboard.

From his odd angle, Darrell saw the pistol Failak was looking at and turned his own M&P handgun toward the man.

Lunging, Failak grabbed Darrell's weapon with both hands, turning the barrel away from himself.

Twisting the gun back and forth, Darrell gouged the metal sight into Failak's palms and snatched the gun back. He brought the NIP over the seat, trying to get a hold on the man.

Failak pushed back, out of range of the prosthetic. He pivoted, jerked the door open, and took off running.

Darrell grabbed the headrest with the NIP and jerked himself out of his wedged position. Placing both hands on the seat backs, he launched his feet over the center console, across the driver's seat, and out the open door. He holstered his handgun as he took off.

Seeing Failak running ahead of him flooded Darrell's mind with images of a man running, his coat flapping like a goose. For a moment his brain was in two places, the images were so real. Darrell blinked, and the flapping-goose coat was gone. *What was that?*

Failak cut between two businesses. He had a good lead.

He's too dangerous to let get away. This might be my only chance to stop him from killing again. Pounding to a stop, Darrell drew his gun. He leveled the sights on Failak's back and brought the NIP hand up for support.

Like the phantom pains he felt in the past, a stab went through the prosthetic hand where there should be no pain. His sights dropped. *Was the NIP malfunctioning?* Darrell gritted his teeth, ignored the pain, and brought the sights back on target.

Failak rounded a corner and was out of sight.

Darrell sprinted again, slamming his gun back into the holster. The pain shot out of the prosthetic hand, into his synthetic wrist. *That can't be the NIP.* It had to be his own nervous system. *Did something get damaged?* He balled his fist and ran harder, giving his hand a shake as he rounded the next corner.

Failak was ahead, still running.

Stopping, Darrell drew his gun and forced the NIP up through the pain. He saw everything in high speed—his real hand holding the gun, black mechanical fingers trying to add support. But there were two images again. Superimposed over the NIP were mangled fingers dangling. Darrell dropped the NIP and held the gun one handed, sighted and started to squeeze the trigger.

Failak made the next corner.

Gun holstered, Darrell poured everything into his sprint. The pain tumbled up through the arm of the NIP. More memories came with it—gunshots, an explosion…Pete. He remembered it all. His mind had found what it had lost. *There's no way you're going to catch him now.* The pain poked at the end of his stump. *One of the most dangerous men in the world, and you let him get away. You're not a good cop.*

No! It doesn't matter what I am. God, I need your help.

The pain pulled back from his stump, then his arm, his wrist, hand, and tingled out the end of the synthetic fingers until it was gone. He quickened his pace and turned the corner.

Failak stood a short distance away.

Hand on his gun, Darrell halted. Failak was staring down the street at a crowd. Some of them were engaged in smashing the windows of a business while the others yelled and cheered. A gunshot would bring them after him.

Before the group could spot the two men, Darrell rushed forward, grabbing Failak's shirt with the NIP. He jerked him, causing the man to back-pedal around the corner where Darrell threw his back hard against the wall and pinned him there with the NIP to his throat.

Failak brought his hands up and tried to clear the NIP off him with a double palm strike. It lifted Darrell a bit as the force transferred into his stump and vest, but the arm still pinned the other man to the wall. Failak tried a strike to the inner elbow of the NIP but winced when he hit the poly-synthetics, which did not give. He abandoned the NIP and tried a roundhouse punch at Darrell's face with his right fist. Bending the NIP at the elbow, Darrell brought it up to cover his head causing Failak to connect with hard plastic again.

Shooting the NIP over the top of Failak's striking arm, Darrell rotated the NIP around, trapped the arm in the bend of the NIP's elbow, and twisted the terrorist backwards, putting pressure on the man's shoulder.

Failak grimaced and cursed Darrell.

"Quiet," Darrell whispered. The hold had the man immobilized with the NIP doing the work.

Failak panted for a moment then sneered. "Yes, all I have to do is yell and your own American brothers will come and kill you."

"Kill *us*, you mean, don't you? I noticed you weren't rushing to embrace that group." Darrell pushed Failak to the brick wall and twisted his arm behind him so he could pat him down.

Finding no weapon, he spun the man and grabbed his right wrist with the NIP. "Let's go." Darrell gave the prosthetic the command to lock the fingers in a handcuff grip and pulled him in the opposite direction of the crowd.

After about half a block, Failak leaped backwards and yanked down on the NIP trying to free himself. Darrell used the momentum to close the gap Failak had created between them. Twisting the NIP up and back, he brought Failak's arm over the man's own shoulder. With a strike to the terrorist's elbow, he flipped him backwards. Darrell dropped in a crouch, landing Failak's spine against the hard asphalt. The air gushed out of the terrorist's lungs in an unpleasant sound.

Darrell had him by the throat. "Listen good. You try something again and I'm going to break some bones and leave you to the mess you've created. I'll do what I can to get us both out of this alive because I'm a professional, but understand, you're not my first priority." Darrell gave Failak a moment to catch his breath, then lifted him to his feet and hauled the man after him.

While they fled, he called Link on the NIP's phone. He didn't like Failak hearing what they said, but he couldn't afford the distraction of texting.

The young man answered with, "Whoa, FlashDarrell, you're moving too fast and making me wanna take another look at my lunch. I was watching the NIP cam view of the dash and trash you did on your new bestie. I think you need to move up a level or two on bad guys. Not many experience points in that round."

"I'm glad you think so, but we could use a lift out of here. You saw that crowd back there. I don't think it's a good idea for us to hang out downtown."

"Okay, yeah. Righteous, programming on that." Link sounded like he was checking something. "The SWAT team is in a standoff with part of the terrorists that were in the building. All the other capes are in the middle of the mayhem. We're going to do a rescue run your direction in the surveillance van, but a lot of the streets are blocked, and Brock is trying to avoid any meet and greets, since he is the only one with a gun."

Darrell dragged Failak along as he talked. Around another corner, he stopped. At the far end of the block, two men carrying sticks saw them and began to move their way.

Darrell hurried to put distance between them. He made his way back to the van to see if it was possible to get it off the bench and use it to leave the area. As he came across the empty lot and out between the buildings, he saw the van on fire.

The three people that appeared to be responsible were moving in a pack down the street. Darrell remembered Failak's gun that was on the floorboard. None of group seemed to have the weapon. He hoped it was on fire and not tucked in the pocket of one of the arsonists.

Darrell spun to move away from the gang. He rounded another corner, and two groups of people, one white and the other black, were spread out down the block in combat with whatever weapons they had been able to lay their hands on. Darrell hurried on while he spoke to Link. "We're surrounded by affected people fighting each other. We could sure use a way out."

"Processing the input, but system resources are limited. Can you find someplace to park until we can get to you?"

Darrell heard gunfire. "Watch yourselves. I hear shots to the north."

"Might as well archive that one. The cops just yawn at those reports now." Link's voice didn't sound as nonchalant as his words. "The only good news is the count's gone down. I think people are running out of ammo. Most of the gunfire calls coming in now are people saying they had to defend themselves. The cops say, 'That's nice' and move on.

"You really know how to spread the cheer. Be careful, anyway. Not to be selfish, but you're the only ones that know where we're at. I will see if we can find a safe place to hole up. Where are you now?"

Darrell kept moving, searching for any place that looked secure. He did not want to get himself cornered. He ducked into another alley.

"Link, which way should we head? Can you check your monitors and see if there are any areas with less fighting?"

No answer.

"Link?" Darrell stopped. He heard faint static on the line. Then the phone made the tone indicating a dropped call.

He tried to call back. After one ring he heard, "I'm sorry, all circuits are busy now." He tried a text. **Link?** There was no response.

Chapter 46

Darrell needed to get back online with Link, or they were in even bigger trouble. He pulled Failak into a narrow alley, stopping about halfway down. Turning the NIP so he could see the screen, he held Failak's arm at an awkward angle which resulted in a string of complaints that Darrell ignored. He searched for Wi-Fi signals in the vicinity. There were a few but all indicated that they were password protected.

Something flashed by Darrell's face. Crash! Ceramics shattered at his feet, spattering him with broken pieces. Jerking his gaze upward, revealed two dark faces looking down from the roof above. They had just dropped another flower pot bomb. Darrell shoved Failak back. The pot crashed where they had been standing. He tugged his prisoner into a run.

Their attackers began to wildly launch projectiles. A brick hit Darrell's back, but the ballistic vest absorbed the blow. He heard Failak yelp and guessed something had connected, but neither man slowed. In seconds, they reached the end of the alley and put the corner of the other building between them and the roof-top assassins. Darrell ducked into the first doorway, pulling Failak in with him. **Link?** Darrell tried another text.

Failak rubbed his shoulder. "You are going to get us killed. You're putting us both in danger by keeping us locked together."

Link? *Please, God. Let it be the phone lines.* As concerned as Darrell was for Link and Brock, with contact lost he had a more personal problem. He glanced at the wrist of the NIP where an LCD screen indicated the time. It was a little after eight. The sun had gone behind the mountains, and the sky was darkening with clouds. Spending the night on the chaotic streets seemed unthinkable, but with no one coming to get them, it was a probability he might have to face.

Darrell glanced sideways at the man to whom he was attached. Failak would also be thinking, looking for a way out for himself. If Darrell nodded off in the night, he knew the terrorist would not hesitate to take advantage of it.

Listening for a moment, Darrell heard sounds of unrest but nothing close by. *Better keep moving while we still can.*

Darrell needed a better position, something high and hidden with an unobstructed view of all approaches. Hurrying from doorway to doorway, he kept an eye on the rooftops.

Far down the street, he could see several figures moving against what was left of the evening light. It seemed to be getting dark quickly. Darrell realized what was causing the perception—the streetlights weren't coming on.

Behind him, he could hear a noisy group coming their way. It looked like they were going to have to risk the alley. This time he looked above him carefully. The roofs were high and if they were quiet, the darkness could conceal them. He prayed it was not concealing others as well.

They worked their way through the alley. Down the street to the right, he heard angry voices, but it sounded like they were yelling at each other.

Across the street, the alley continued between two small parking lots. The concealing clouds parted for a moment to reveal the moon. Darrell looked across the lots. *That's a possibility.* Then the light was gone again. With his prisoner in tow, Darrell headed for what was now just a dark shape. The ground around them lit up, fixing their shadows to the street in front of them.

Behind him someone yelled, "Hey, there's a couple."

A quick glance over his shoulder to the alley from where they had just come showed figures already running in their direction, silhouetted against a blinding, handheld spotlight.

"Time to run again." They sprinted, trying to keep the rhythm of their linked arms synchronized.

"Shoot them." Failak panted.

"You deserve to die more than they do, and I haven't shot you yet." Darrell snapped at him.

"Then let me go. We can't outrun them with you holding onto me."

"This way." Darrell pulled Failak toward a three-story apartment building that grew more visible as the spotlight moved to follow them.

Darrell could make out what he had noticed from across the parking lots when the moon had been out—metal staircases and landings crisscrossed the outside of the building, the last one leading to the roof. If he could get up to where Failak could not safely jump off, he could release him and have both hands free to battle any attackers, one at a time, as they came up the stairs.

The men behind him were close enough now that Darrell could hear at least one set of feet gaining on them. As they reached the apartment complex, Darrell saw it was not as well suited to his strategy as he thought. The strange layout made it so they had to go down first, to the basement level, to reach the staircases to the upper floors. As they ran, Darrell told Failak. "We're going down."

"Are you crazy?" Failak yelled, looking down the narrow set of concrete steps that led into darkness.

Darrell had no time. He arrived at the metal railing that ran along the top of the sunken landing. Shoving Failak down the first couple of steps, he turned. The man that had the spotlight was still some distance away, using the light to illuminate the way for the others.

One man had outrun the rest and rushed to close the remaining space. Darrell leaned against the railing and shot his leg out in a well-timed kick. The man was already reaching out his arms to grab Darrell when the kick caught him under the chin. His momentum carried his lower body out from under him as his head snapped back where it connected with Darrell's foot. He flopped on his back and didn't get up. Two others were not far behind but slowed at the sight of the lead man hitting the asphalt. Across the parking lot, Darrell heard the shouts of more men coming out of another building and heading their way. Fire burned in an open doorway behind the men.

Darrell pushed Failak down the steps. One of the men arrived at the top and started kicking at Darrell's head. Darrell had no choice. He fired one round from his pistol into the meaty portion of the man's thigh. Crying out, the man dropped at the top of the stairs.

Out of the dark, a pair of hands grabbed Darrell's handgun. One of the attackers had reached through the metal pipe railing. He was a big man with a powerful grip. A second man bent down so he could put his leg through the railing to kick at Darrell's ribs. Two more men were climbing over the man he had shot. The spotlight, dancing around on the side of the brick building, lit the scene like a stage show.

With both hands occupied, he had no way to fend off the kicks, and he was losing the fight over his gun. In desperation, Failak was jerking to free himself and pulling Darrell off balance. Darrell released the NIP's grip on the terrorist. The man tumbled to the bottom of the steps, screaming in protest, but Darrell had no time to think about him.

Swinging around with the freed prosthetic, Darrell latched onto the ankle that was kicking at him. Driving the man's leg forward, he rammed it hard into one of the railing's metal support posts. There was a crack, and the man cried out. Darrell let go and continued the forward drive of the NIP into the arms that held his gun, breaking the man's grip and flinging the arms out of the way.

He continued through with the momentum, grabbing the ankle of the first man coming down the stairs. Darrell launched himself backward, jerking the leg out from under the man who flipped back hard into the legs of the man on the stairs behind him, taking them both down. Darrell spun around as he landed at the bottom.

The spotlight was dead-on Failak, who was climbing the metal staircase. Two of the men had run around and were grabbing at him from across the railing. Failak had nowhere to go but up.

Someone landed on Darrell from above. One of the attackers had jumped the railing, driving him into a set of wooden steps that led up to an apartment door. Darrell lost his grip on his gun, and it clattered into the darkness under the steps.

Using the NIP to push off from the stairs, Darrell brought his elbow around into the man's head, stunning him. He pivoted on his feet and followed the spin until the man was the one against the stairs. Darrell moved further back into the basement area. He saw the shadow of the man who had tried to take his gun roll under the railing, onto the concrete stairs, to join the other two who were back on their feet and coming down. Darrell moved backward as the four attackers poured into the cramped space.

Chapter 47

Failak managed to kick off the attacker that grabbed at his ankles. He rushed up the stairs with the spotlight both blinding him and illuminating his way. Glancing back, he saw one of the men climbing onto the stairs. The man with the spotlight finally trotted up and stood directly below the staircase. He moved the light off Failak and onto the scene in the basement. Darrell was being swarmed by the rest of the men.

Failak spent only a second in gratification as he made it to the top of the first set of steps. The next set ran up the other direction. He sprinted across the landing to reach them. The light flitted around below him, near the bottom of the staircase. He caught glimpses of it through the slits in the metal steps. The man with the light was climbing onto the stairs to pursue him as well.

Below, Failak heard the smack and thuds of strikes along with the resulting groans and curses. There was a cry of pain and the terrorist started to give thanks to Allah for deliverance, but the metallic rattling of stairs reminded him that he was not delivered yet. He started up the next staircase.

It had been too long since Failak had trained with his men. He was feeling his age. His intellectual talents had been far more important to the jihad. Now his heart threatened to come through his chest, and he labored for each gasp of air. Only his fear propelled him upward. He could no longer hear the battle beneath him. The only sound was the clanking footsteps chasing him, sounding twice as loud as they had before. Below him was all darkness. The light must have gone out.

His pursuer clanged onto the landing that Failak had just left. As he finished the stairs to the third floor, Failak heard a groan from the man below. Pausing to listen through his own panting, Failak prayed the one chasing him had met with an accident. The clanking resumed. His pursuer must have only tripped on something in the dark. Failak sucked in a desperate breath and took off again.

His night vision was returning. Failak could see the outline of the stairs to the roof at the other end of the landing. As he headed toward them, his pursuer started up the next set of steps, faster than before. Failak hit the stairs leading to the roof, not knowing what he would do when he got there. Perhaps he could ambush the man as he came onto the roof and push him off.

As Failak arrived at the top, clouds pulled back away from a bright moon just long enough for him to see his surroundings. Across the expanse of roof, he glimpsed the top of another set of stairs going down the other side, then the clouds plunged him into even deeper darkness. *Allah is with me.* He took off toward the other stairs as he heard the footsteps on the last flight of steps behind him.

Another gap in the clouds let a stab of moonlight through just in time to save Failak's life. He came sliding to a halt and balanced precariously on the edge of a drop off into darkness. The roof had two parts. It was divided in the middle by a thirty-foot gap that opened to the courtyard below – too far to jump across. To his left, at the other end from where he was, the building joined together and formed a horseshoe around the courtyard. Failak backed away from the edge and headed that direction as the moon slid behind the clouds again.

Failak's leg caught on something. "Uff!" he groaned as he hit the asphalt and gravel of the rooftop. He had tripped on a small wall running across his path.

The pursuing man came onto the roof, but a quick glance revealed only a dark outline of him to Failak. The man was searching for him in the dark. Failak was up and running again. He saw a second short wall in time to hurdle it. Another glance back revealed his pursuer starting across the roof toward him.

In the cloud covered blackness, Failak searched the roof in front of him for where the building wrapped around the courtyard. He kept away from the drop off to his right, which appeared as just a darker part of the roof. There!—the crossover section wasn't visible until he was right on it. He turned and ran toward the side of the building that was across the courtyard.

Out of the corner of his eye, Failak noticed the dark shape of the man heading at an angle in his direction. He was coming fast, aiming to cut across the roof and intercept him. What was he…realization hit Failak. The man didn't see the gap and didn't know he had to run around it. Failak held his breath. If he didn't stop, he…the man vanished. There was no cry, just a sickening *whump* when he hit the courtyard below. The shock made Failak stop and stare down into the darkness. He had no remorse for the fool, only for how close that had come to being his own fate.

When Failak looked up, another figure stood across the gap from him. They both started running at the same time. His next pursuer now knew about the gap and headed to the crossover section of roof. Out of the corner of his eye, Failak saw the man hurdle both white walls. Rounding the other side of the gap and starting toward the stairs, Failak risked a glance over his shoulder. The dark figure was already coming onto the crossover section. He was closing the distance between them. Failak focused on the outline of the stair rails ahead of him. His vision was beginning to blur, and his heart was pounding in his ears. He knew that even if he made it to the stairs, the man would be on him before he got far.

The roof around him again began to brighten. Then he saw his way out. The branches of a tree, as tall as the building, spread out from below so that they touched the edge of the roof just beyond the stairs. The leaves shimmered in the moonlight. If he leaped into the tree, he could go crashing down through the branches, letting them slow his descent to the ground. The pursuer was unlikely to follow. He would at least hesitate and give Failak the edge he needed to escape. It was a risk, but it was his way out.

Once again, Allah had made the way for him. His intelligence was always superior. No wonder he had been chosen. The man behind him was fast. He could hear his feet closing in, but still too far away to stop him. Strength and speed were no match for cunning and boldness.

The tree was just ahead, the branches like the open arms of his virgins in paradise. In a moment he would jump and…there was a *pop* and pricks and Failak's muscles seized. He twisted and fell onto the rooftop a few feet from the edge. His body slid to a stop, the gravel of the surface tearing into his arm and the side of his face. As he quivered from the painful waves of electricity, Failak saw Darrell striding forward, in the bright moonlight, with the fingers of the NIP forming the letter L.

Chapter 48

Darrell didn't sleep. In the dark, listening to screams from the street below, he was confronted by his helplessness. *Why do I have to listen when I can't do anything about it?*

Failak slept and Darrell watched, each cry making him want to re-charge the taser lines still attached to the man slumbering before him. Darrell realized that it was his police training, and not his own strength, that kept him from doing so.

As the hours passed, Darrell reached the end of himself, and God got through. When people complained to him about how hard it was to get justice and put criminals away, he would explain to them that the methodical procedure of due process was one of the costs of freedom. *I guess this is the same thing. This is what the world must sound like to You, and You sit and listen, waiting for us to make better choices.*

Darrell felt the answer form inside. *"Let Me handle the things that are too big for you. Worry about what I have called you to do, and I will work out the rest."*

Sinking to the roof with his back against the half wall that was near the stairwell, Darrell prayed the deepest prayer of his life. Occasionally he glanced at Failak who was lying near the middle of the roof, where Darrell had ordered him. His hands were bound behind him and fastened to his belt with a length of telephone cable Darrell had found. *Some evil is worthy of hate…isn't it?* The hours passed as Darrell wrestled with what he knew he had to do.

A noise tickled his senses as he said his amen. Distant and indistinct, it made him think of the baseball games his father took him to when he was a kid—the all-American sport. He wondered if the America he knew was ending.

Darrell contemplated the sound but couldn't identify it. A bird began to sing nearby. That must be what it was. All over the city, things were waking up with the dawn. The sound was hopeful.

Should he leave the roof? He eased his stiff body up the wall and scanned the streets. Here and there, he saw people wandering. Smoke rose from smoldering fires, giving the city a misty appearance. Through the night he had been unable to contact Link. How far had the violence reached, and was there anywhere for them to go? Darrell turned his attention back to the roof.

Failak's eyes were open, watching him. "What do you intend to do?"

How do I answer that? Did the man really expect a response? Darrell considered the taser.

Failak licked his lips. "I can understand your anger."

"I'm trying to forgive you like God wants me to. Don't mess it up. Maybe you shouldn't talk." Darrell examined the dark eyes hovering above cheeks bloody with roof rash.

Bringing his eyebrows together, Failak considered the statement. "I did not realize you were such a man of God. Perhaps I have been judging you incorrectly. You see, I suffered a great loss that never would have been necessary if it wasn't for the United States. I also struggle with being able to forgive. It is hard for me to get past that hurt when I deal with anyone from your country. Maybe we are not so different. Maybe it is time we truly got to know each other. If we could forgive, leave behind what we can't change, there might be hope for our two countries." Failak wormed around to move his body up and off the gravelly surface.

Darrell scrutinized the man. *Smooth. Very smooth. He must know I would have been briefed about his history. You want to play games? Let's see how much you'll admit about your part in all this. There's lots of evidence, but a confession is always nice for court.* Without moving, Darrell surreptitiously sent the order to the NIP to record the conversation.

Now he just needed Failak to know his rights. "We might not be so different as people, but we come from very different cultures. Take this conversation. In this country you don't have to talk about any of this if you don't want to. Because what you say might be used in court against you, you don't have to say anything you don't want to, and no one can make you. The United States is a free country, and even if you're not a citizen, while you're here you have the right to stay silent or tell your side of the story. It's your choice. We'll even give you a lawyer if you want one and pay for one if you can't afford it. We really aren't that bad if you get to know us." *Time to show some sympathy.* "I know that might be hard to believe after what happened to your father. I'm sorry. It was a horrible accident."

The terrorist paused his movements and inspected Darrell.

Returning the man's gaze, Darrell tried to read the face. He didn't see grief or resentment. *What's inside a mind like his?*

After a moment, Failak resumed his struggles, working his way to a seated position. "You say it was an accident, but in reality you could really know nothing about what happened. You weren't involved. You have heard the story your government gave, and you believed it."

Darrell kept the sympathy on his face. "The same would be true for you. That happened when we were both kids. It must have been hard."

Failak lifted his chin. "It is not the same in my country. At almost sixteen, I was old enough to be counted as a man if I had the strength to act like one."

Darrell imagined Failak being told his father was dead. How would he have handled it? "What did 'acting like a man' look like in your country?"

Failak turned away but not before Darrell caught something in his eyes.

The man shifted his position. He stretched his shoulders. "If you would be kind enough to untie my hands, they are asleep, and I need to get blood flow back into them in case you decide we need to leave this roof." As he made the request, Failak averted his gaze, examining his shoes.

Darrell's perspective shifted. *That was an avoidance gesture.* He had seen it hundreds of times during suspect interviews - movement to mask nervousness, a change of subject. Failak had let his body language slip. *What was in that question?*

Darrell's cop sense was nudging him. *There's something you don't want to talk about.* His father's death must be the right theme to hit on. *Your arms hurt? Let me make you more comfortable. I'm a nice guy. You can talk to me.*

Darrell walked to Failak. "I think we can work this out. Just don't try anything, okay. For now, don't take the taser darts out of your back. I'm doing what I can for you, but as a cop I need to be careful. I don't want to have to hurt you again." He bent down and untied the cord.

Failak rotated his shoulders and flexed his arms while making casual glances toward Darrell. "God is great to have given us an opportunity to talk. Despite the problems we have had between each other, I feel there is something bigger going on here. Do you sense it?"

Darrell took a seat on a large vent cap a safe distance from Failak. "I think so. How often do two people from cultures as different as ours get to sit down and lay everything aside and be honest with each other?"

Failak moved into a cross-legged position, making sure Darrell could see his hands. "Yes. We might discover that there are reasons behind each other's actions that we did not understand before. If we could work together, it might be the beginning of new relations between our peoples. But it would require forgiveness for many hard things. Do you think that would be possible?" Failak faced Darrell with a sincere expression.

Darrell tried to match the look. "Yes, I do. I always feel it's as important to know the why of someone's actions as it is to know the what. Understanding the reasons behind what happened can be the key to working things out."

Failak swayed forward and back like a blade of grass in a slight wind, giving Darrell a pleasant smile. "Your words give me hope that there might be a way out of all this for both our people. In war many things are done that must be overlooked if peace is to be pursued. Do you desire peace as much as I do?"

I see what you're up to. Your crazier than I thought if you think I'm letting you go to negotiate peace. "I think we all want peace, but if we're going to get there, we have to get past what some people are going to think about all that's happened. Others don't see this as war. They might look at it as crimes against innocent people. There are going to be those who say a person would have to be crazy to do something like this. But if we're going to be honest with each other, I have to start there—I don't think you're crazy. I've worked with a lot of cases over the years, and I'm amazed at how well this whole plan with the MEamps and the fake cops worked. That kind of plan had to come from a very controlled mind. It was genius. You have reasons for everything you do. That's what makes me think there is a reason for all this, a reason that most people could understand. It's your father's death that caused you to do this, isn't it?"

Failak's eyelids flickered a couple of times. "There are things more important than death. Just like there are things more important than revenge. The fate of a nation sometimes requires us to lay aside our desire to right wrongs. I think we are both faced with the opportunity to change the fate of millions who are still alive. Shouldn't we consider that more important than seeking some type of justice for a handful of people that can no longer benefit from it? Strong men of conviction have always been called on to seek what is best above their personal feelings."

Not quite a confession yet. He's a master manipulator. He probably knows what I'm doing. Darrell decided he had nothing to lose by continuing. "I might be able to rise above my feelings, but what am I going to tell those others that haven't been through the things we have? If they don't know what was in your mind when you were planning this, all they're going to see is that you attacked innocent people for no reason." Darrell gestured over the half wall at the edge of the roof. "I'm going to have to have an explanation before those people will get it."

Failak let out a sigh. "We haven't randomly attacked people. The MEamp does not create racial hatred or violence. It only capitalizes on emotions that are already there. It uses your own television and movies to bring out what is hiding under the surface. Your entertainment is full of sex and violence and blasphemies, so there is obviously a market for such sin in your culture. All we have done is brought the evil into the light."

There it was. The confession. But something else was needling at Darrell's mind. *He passed up every opportunity to accuse the U.S. of his father's death. Why?*

Failak kept talking. "There is no reason for you to answer to these people. It is up to you to do the right thing, Darrell. Let me illustrate the problem using something familiar. It is like the zombies that are so popular on your television. The people of the United States are spiritually walking dead. Your nation has no zeal, even for its own God. They care for nothing but their appetites." Failak dipped his head toward the edge of the roof. "Down there is the apocalypse that was naturally going to come. All we have done is accelerate the inevitable outcome of this culture. Down there is what this nation really is. America professes to be the moral leaders and peacemakers of the world, and yet all they do is export the same filth and violence that their own homes are full of. As a man of God, that must disturb you also. It is up to men like you and me to do what is right."

I see the theme he's using on me, but there's something that came out earlier. "I know there's a lot of sin in this country." As Darrell talked, he recalled things that Failak said— *never would have been necessary if it wasn't for the United States, counted as a man if I had the strength to act like one, there are things more important than death, strong men of conviction...called on to seek what is best above their personal feelings.* Darrell's mind put it together. "I guess I haven't really had the courage to face it, not like you."

Failak opened his hands in front of him like he was welcoming Darrell in. "I am sure you have the courage. You must step away from a culture that has weakened you. This wickedness is not where you belong."

Sighing with relief, Darrell smiled at Failak. "You must truly be devout to do such hard things for God. I understand now. I knew you couldn't have been as evil as they said. I mean, the evidence clearly showed what happened back then, but now I understand why you had to do what you did. Not even family comes before God."

Failak's nodding head faltered for a moment. "No, we must not let anything else overshadow our willingness to obey God, not even our own family. It can be painful, but it must be done."

Darrell leaned toward Failak. "I am sure it was hard at first. I mean he *was* your father. It took a lot of strength not to falter after having to do something like that." He recalled everything he knew about the Vincennes incident from the report he had done all those years ago.

The beginnings of a scowl developed on Failak's face. "What do you—?"

Darrell cut the terrorist off. "I knew there was a good reason. I mean he was the one that taught you the skills you used to hack into the ship-to-ship computer, but even if he did, it took a lot of talent to make the Vincennes think a fighter was attacking them."

Failak leaned back, looking stunned. "How did you…?"

Darrell made another motion toward the streets below. "But you're an expert at all this, and you have been since you were a boy. I knew someone who was intelligent enough to do all that wouldn't cause that ship to shoot down the plane his father was on unless he had to. You had to make a man's decision that day. You had to do a man's job, didn't you? I knew you wouldn't have killed your own father without a reason. What happened? What made you have to do it?"

Failak's eyes had gone to stone. He was staring past Darrell. "He was defying the Imam. He was defying God. It was better for him to die as a martyr of the holy jihad than to risk his soul. Every Iranian on that flight died honorably. The Imam knew our people were becoming tired, weak. They needed something to strengthen their resolve in the holy war and to be reminded of the evil your people represent."

It was unbelievable. Darrell felt like he was watching the scene outside of himself, hearing his voice coming from someone else, but he was being led to continue. "I wasn't smart enough to figure it all out. How did you do it?"

The terrorist turned toward Darrell as if just realizing what he had revealed. His face was calm. He straightened with resolve. "Our Iranian intelligence obtained one of the black boxes that your navy's computer system used to authenticate ship to ship communications. Infiltrating their system was easy. The Imam designed the plan to use the boghammar boats to lure them in and create an issue at the airline gate to delay takeoff until we had the ship directly in the flight path. I learned so much that day about leading people's minds. I couldn't change the IFF readings, so we had an F-14 sending out a signal from the runway at Bandar Abbas and hoped my manipulations of their system would cause them to focus on that signal. It worked perfectly. The crew of the ship believed the airliner was an attack fighter."

Placing his arms behind him to prop himself up, Failak uncrossed his legs and stretched them out in front of him. In his face was the little boy, long lost to time.

When Darrell spoke, his words were genuine. "I'm sorry you were involved in all of that."

The boy vanished. The terrorist drew up one leg and turned a hard face to Darrell. He let his hands drop in front of him. "I was honored to be chosen." His appearance grew more hardened as he seemed to realize the significance of the interaction. "I guess our peace negotiations have ended."

The NIP's phone rang. Darrell answered.

Link's excited voice came through. "Thank God, you're alive."

Darrell sighed in relief. "That's what I have been doing all night. I hope you're coming to get us out of here, 'cause I could use some sleep, and my friend here could use some bandages."

"Don't expect much emo from me on that last one. Sorry you're still solo surfing. The cell masters lost their grip last night so we couldn't connect with you. I guess everyone decided all at once to use their cell phones. When we lost contact with you, we had to back out because Brock said if we got toasted there would be no one to help you. The National Guard was finally forced to take control of the cell services. They're only letting top shelf traffic through. I can't reach the Cals, so I'm hoping she is all right."

That statement hit Darrell's heart. "Well, come and get me. The apartment she was at is too close to all this. We need to find her."

"The service I'm on is really first generation. I have no way to locate you and the camobacks…I mean the guard, are only letting primeware vehicles downtown to go to and from a warm woolly they've set up around Civic Center Park including the state capitol grounds. Can you make it there?"

"I think so. I can see the capital building about a block southwest of us."

"Good. Brock got a level up from the camobacks for us to go in on our own if we go directly there. We'll bust out of here in a nano and head that way." Link paused. "There's a new hack to the system I gotta warn you about. The Denver cop's skywhopper is reporting two mammoth human hordes moving around in that area. They started forming at day boot. One is whites only and the other is all black. If those two collide, it will be matter and anti-matter. You don't want to be anywhere around."

Leaving the roof still wasn't sounding good to Darrell. "Thanks for telling me that. We're already 'around.'"

"Full regrets, LoneDarrell. Keep treading. We'll throw you a donut soon."

Darrell stood up and stretched his stiff muscles. "I assume a skywhopper is a helicopter. Why can't we get that in here?"

"Sorry," Brock's voice came on, sounding regretful. "Denver won't risk it. They have already lost one of their air units on a rescue attempt. They are using what they have left on a limited basis to get their own people out and those unaffected who made it to the police station. They have been evacuating from the roof of the division headquarters east of you, but don't try to go there. I got word they are out of pepper spray and beanbag rounds. If anyone tries to enter that building, the officers in there will be shooting lethal ammo."

Darrell couldn't believe what he was hearing. "What about the military?"

"They're getting them staged, but the President is not going to take action until they can come up with a plan that won't result in a blood bath. The ones affected can't be reasoned with and they are not afraid of dying. The whole country is watching this, but the average person can't comprehend what we are dealing with. The conspiracy theorists are having a field day. Every racist of whatever color and any anti-government group is posturing, just waiting to use the outcome here to inflame the nation. It's not just about Denver. It's about saving the whole country and millions of lives."

Brock's voice changed. "But Darrell, ·if you hadn't stopped the broadcast and helped us get Failak's people, it could have been even worse. We're going to get you out. The military has shut down traffic because cars were being used as weapons, so it will take us a while to get through the checkpoints. Just be careful and stay safe. Gotta go. I'm driving."

Link came back on the phone, talking fast. "Okay, Darrelldown, we are in the stream. I'm at the end of our communication credits the camobacks gave us. We won't hit another power up for about 30 minutes, and then we'll check in again. When you get to the capitol, the camobacks are protecting that area. They're using their own sky…choppers to evacuate people outside of town, but there's a megabyte waiting in queue. Don't stroke, we're coming to get you."

"Okay," Darrell forced his aching body toward Failak, "we'll head that way. Just hurry. I'm worried about Callie." Darrell could tell the line was disconnected and was not even sure his last part got through.

Chapter 49

Failak's expression had become more triumphant the longer he had listened to Brock's report. He looked smugly at Darrell.

"Get on your stomach," Darrell made a rolling motion with his finger. "I'm going to take the darts out. Just remember, even though I have forgiven you, you're too dangerous for me to let you escape. There was only one cartridge for the Taser, so that won't be an option. If you run, I'm not afraid to do what I have to do."

Failak squirmed in pain, cursing and threatening Darrell when he pulled the Taser probes out of his back. Darrell didn't like to lose the control, but he knew the thin wire lines were too long and fragile to survive the trip down, let alone a run through the streets. Darrell freed Failak's hands and quickly clamped the NIP on his right wrist again.

The terrorist pronounced Darrell the worst of infidels using graphic terms. So much for the peace negotiations.

Darrell decided to go down the same way they came up because he knew it had good cover. As they approached the stairway, Darrell recognized the same sound he heard earlier. *It's not birds*. It was many mingled voices in the distance – like a sporting event.

"We better hurry," Darrell directed Failak down the steps.

When they reached the basement area, Darrell noted how differently the open basement appeared in the light of day. The area under the stairs where he had blindly searched until he found his gun was easily visible now. The men he had left battered on the concrete were gone. Perhaps they were now a part of the group that sounded closer all the time. Darrell picked out one voice calling out something about the police – it didn't sound supportive.

There was a loud shout. Drawing his handgun, Darrell whirled around, jerking Failak's arm. A man ran by on the street. He didn't notice them standing in the shadows of the staircase that surrounded the basement landing. There were other shouts from various directions.

Looking over the concrete wall of the sunken level, Darrell had a view to the end of the block where the source of the commotion came into sight. It was a group of dark-skinned bodies moving east on the street he and Failak had crossed the night before. The mob overflowed the curbs and sidewalks on both sides like a flowing river, spilling into the parking lot as they reached it.

Two men ran by the top of the concrete steps. They were so engrossed in reaching the rabble, they didn't spot Darrell and Failak. The men covered the block distance and became part of the tide of lemming-like human beings.

In the crowd, Darrell could see the fluttering of red. Looking closer he saw that many of the people had a red belt or ribbon around their waist. The red sash appeared to be simply wrapped around and tied, the ends fluttering. Other people that did not have the ribbons arrived from all around, but those that had the ribbons dominated the mass. The new arrivals were welcomed and drawn into the group with angry gesticulations toward the east. Occasional loud outcries came to Darrell's ears concerning killing and attacking whites.

Darrell glanced at Failak. "What is the red for?"

"What are you talking about?" The man showed disgust at the interaction.

Darrell pulled him forward and thrust him toward the mob. "Those red ribbons around their waists, what is that?"

Failak gazed for a minute and seemed perplexed. "Perhaps they have adopted it as some type of symbol. The MEamp does not render them mindless. It simply destroys their inhibitions and amplifies their aggression, focusing it to one subliminally suggested activity or target. But the seeds of this violence were already inside them." Failak turned toward Darrell, with contempt. "This is what your people are. All I have done is weaponized it. Look at the crowd that is forming. That is far more than the MEamps we had in service could have affected. It is as I predicted. The broadcasts have been a catalyst to create a movement under which the hatred of your people can flourish." He smiled again. "You might have stopped the transmission, but it was no longer needed. The brutality has taken on a life of its own, far better than I could have hoped for."

Darrell did not want to give him the satisfaction of conceding. But he was sick inside watching the mass of what should have been humanity pouring by. "We need to get to the Capitol."

There was too much open area to the east of the building, so Darrell took Failak to the west end where the cement wall dropped to ground level to meet a sloping driveway. The building next door concealed them from the mob. Darrell rolled under the metal pipe railing that separated them from the driveway and then helped Failak. Peeking around the southeast corner of the building, he examined the mob that still flooded the street.

"Put the gun down." The voice came from behind them.

Darrell knew the sound, the confidence, the forcefulness—the man had a weapon on him. He made sure he didn't provoke whoever it was but turned his head slowly to look over his shoulder. There were two of them, both Caucasian, both had shotguns pointed at him and both wore red ribbons around their waists.

"Listen," the first man said, "we know you want to get them blacks as much as we do, but if you try to take on that whole group by yourself, you'll just get killed. We're all getting together down that way so we can finish them off right. You'll get your gun back when you need it, but we don't want any accidents right now so put it down."

Darrell knew there was no way he could survive two shotgun blasts. Even if he was able to get off good shots with Failak tethered to him, he would likely be hit. He also didn't want to kill the men. It was not their fault; they did not know what they were doing. He decided his best chance was to put down the M&P and let them get confident enough to get in close so he could disarm them. He had the advantage of the NIP. He set the handgun slowly on the ground.

"Now move away from it."

Darrell prayed he was making the right decision. He began moving away, still holding onto Failak. Once he was far enough away, one of the men moved in and picked up the handgun and stuck it in his waistband.

It was apparently what Failak had been waiting for.

"He's a cop" he blurted out. "This man is a cop. Check him. He's got ID on him somewhere. Make him let me go and check him."

The first man got a panicky look on his face. "Shut up," he told Failak. Then he looked at Darrell, "You a cop?"

Darrell was trying to think. Silently, he unlocked his grip on Failak. "I used to be. Now I want to get them just like you do."

Failak felt the release and jerked his hand away.

The second man took a menacing step toward Failak, pointing his shotgun.

"He's lying to you." The terrorist sounded exasperated.

The first man snapped back at him. "Who are you and what do you know about this?"

"I was after the blacks, and this man was trying to arrest me. He's a cop."

"What's that on your arm?" the other man nodded toward the NIP.

Darrell paused. *Why not tell them?* "I lost my hand. It's a prosthetic." He saw a way to bolster his statement. "Why do you think I'm not a cop anymore?"

The first man eyed him, tipping his head back. "So now you're after the blacks?"

"What do you think I was about to do?"

Failak started to interject, but the man cut him off. "Okay, you both come with us, and we'll get this worked out. We got our own group, that way." The men began moving them away from the black group.

Darrell switched to Cmode and texted Link, **We've been caught by two men that are taking us to the white group. They both have shotguns.** He glanced at the NIP's screen as he walked. There was no answer. He queried, **You guys there?** Still nothing. The thirty minutes Link spoke of was long expired.

Chapter 50

The men directed them southbound, but once past the building, they headed them southeast across a parking lot. At the corner of Colfax and Grant they headed south again. The area seemed to have settled down. They came upon one black group as they moved down the street. There were five of them compared to their four. Three of them wore red ribbons.

"Get over to the side." the first man motioned with the shotgun barrel. "We'll get them later."

The shotguns had an impact because the Red Ribbons in the black group also moved toward the opposite side of the street saying, "Not now. We'll take care of them when we get there."

The first man with the shotgun sneered at the other group. "We'll see you soon."

In a few blocks they came upon a mass of Caucasians as large as the black group. They were pressed into the group by Red Ribbons who encouraged them with, "Come on. We'll take care of those blacks." The shotgun toting men left Darrell and Failak to be absorbed into the mass, as they moved to the edge of the crowd, guns pointed down, watching everything.

Darrell was surprised that the distance separating the two mobs was relatively small. At the moment, they were safe from the threat they had faced all night, but it wouldn't be long before the gangs met and made downtown Denver a battlefield.

They were headed toward the main police station at Colfax and Washington. He saw the same thing he had seen in the black group. More and more whites being welcomed in all along the way. The group swelled and Darrell knew no law enforcement, not even the National Guard, could contain such a mass without catastrophic bloodshed. The result would send shock waves across the nation. Perhaps it would even cause the civil war Failak wanted.

Darrell kept his eye on the terrorist, who seemed to be basking in it all.

The crowd of people, all shouting cries for violence, pressed together and pushed forward like blood through an artery. Failak's head swiveled, examining those around him. The man closed his eyes as if he was reliving something. Darrell moved toward him, pushing his way through the crowd. Tipping his head back, Failak was propelled forward by the press of bodies. A thin wicked smile came over his face as Darrell caught up with him and clamped the NIP around his wrist.

Failak's eyes snapped open. He gave an instinctive tug at the grip then conceded, glaring at Darrell. "You know we will die when the fighting starts. Where's the compassion you were so self-righteous about? Let me go, and we might both have a chance."

Darrell pulled him in close, inches from his face, where Failak could hear him over the crowd. "I might not be able to stop all this, but I can stop you. If I have anything to say about it, you're not getting away again."

"How loving." Failak's face displayed his contempt.

Darrell regarded the man then looked around at the group. Their hate-filled chants echoed off the buildings around them. "I know what love is not." He kept Failak close and paraphrased the Scripture for him: "Love is not happy with evil but rejoices in the truth. It always protects."

Easing the pressure on Failak's wrist, Darrell let the terrorist move to arm's length. *He's right about one thing, Lord. We are in a lot of trouble.*

Love always protects. What help was he to Callie now? Surely, she was wise enough to get her and Nandi out of the area before this started. He paused in his prayer and looked up. *Please watch over her. Keep her safe through what will come.*

The crowd continued its advance. The Red Ribbons mingled throughout the throng but a good number of them stayed on the outside— pushing the mob forward, encouraging them in their goal. Darrell looked for an opening to slip away, but there was none.

The Red Ribbons on the outside were intent on growing the ranks and keeping them together. They were building an army that would be unstoppable. The other side was doing the same thing. It would be a clash of titans, and the loss of life and the political fallout would likely cause race riots all over the country.

Please, Lord, give me a chance to get out of here and find the others. He hoped they could survive and see what was left after the dust settled.

The group snaked through the streets in and around downtown Denver for some time, but all too soon they were nearing the police headquarters. As they turned the corner to head west down Colfax, a helicopter lifted into the air a couple of blocks away, pounding sound from its rotors. It was the only thing louder than the crowd. The chopper was probably filled with civilians that had sought shelter at the PD early on.

Darrell knew cops. They would make a stand to get the innocent to safety. Unarmed, there was nothing he could do to help.

Over the heads in front of him, he saw the black mob. They were moving their direction. Darrell wanted to drop back to position himself toward the rear, but even on his own, it would be hard. Locked together with Failak, it was impossible. They were being pressed forward against their will.

Then Darrell saw him. Over the mass towered a tall gangly figure. Even hanging down as it was, his head was above the rest of the group so Darrell could plainly make him out. Link looked terrified. Darrell tried calling to him, but his voice was lost in the noise of the mob.

Darrell abandoned moving to the rear. Link was ahead of him and off to the right. It was easier to move forward and laterally. Gradually, he made his way toward the kid. They were going to make it.

The crowd stopped. Continuing to push forward just brought angry pushes back. Darrell fixed his eyes on Link, watching for an opportunity.

Someone tested a bullhorn. "Are you ready?" The bullhorn squealed from the volume of the announcer. There was something familiar…

The crowd spread out. The mass expanded as those on the periphery moved out of the street and into parking lots. The Red Ribbons waded through the group giving instructions, taking people by the arms and positioning them for the attack. They were organized, stationing themselves around those that did not have ribbons, strengthening the force, preparing to make sure no one broke ranks when the fighting started.

"This is it." The bullhorn-enhanced sound washed over the crowd. An angry cheer went up from everyone around. Even with the electronic amplification, Darrell recognized the voice. Stretching to get a look toward the black forces, he saw what he feared. Standing on a partition wall, elevated above the other dark faces, hanging onto the iron railing that topped the wall, bullhorn in hand, was Callie.

Why was she…how? He felt sick to his stomach. It couldn't be. *God, please, no.* Darrell's heart pounded.

Callie spoke. "We've put up with this long enough."

The blacks roared and the whites jeered back.

"You ain't seen nothing yet," someone nearby yelled.

I'm not going to let…I can't. If he could make it to Link, together they could get to Callie. They could get her away when the fighting started. They could get her back to BERT and Link could reverse the MEamp's effects. Callie herself said it was possible.

"Are you ready to put an end to it?" Callie yelled into the bullhorn.

The blacks shook their fists, yelling so loud that building windows shook.

The whites responded in kind. "Bring it on," a skinny white kid challenged, and a stocky red ribbon wearer stepped up beside him.

"They thought they could defeat us." The bullhorn thundered Callie's words.

Darrell started toward Link but felt the tug of the NIP. Spinning, he faced Failak's smug expression. Darrell wanted to break the teeth out of the man's mouth while he stood there looking triumphant. He longed to kill him, snap his neck. He could justify it. This terrorist was too dangerous to let live.

Not now.

It wasn't an audible voice. Call it an impression, but Darrell had never heard such a clear message inside. God was speaking to him—to him. It made sense. He couldn't risk attacking the man. If he caused the group to turn on him, he might never reach...but there was more.

For the one in authority is God's servant for your good.

Darrell never would have remembered the Scripture on his own, in the middle of everything. He couldn't help his anger. *What are You expecting of me now?*

"But they were wrong." Callie also sounded angry over the loudspeaker.

I can't stand here and let this happen to her. There was a chance...but not with Failak in tow. The terrorist was too dangerous to release, but he was in custody and Darrell had taken an oath. *You can't ask me to sacrifice her for him...or my duty, You can't.*

Trust Me. Another clear message.

Darrell couldn't. There were so many reasons. He couldn't do it...on his own. He gazed at Failak and everything inside...melted. Who was he kidding? Like anything he had tried to do on his own had worked out. His soul was ready to surrender. He was ready to try and pass the test. *Take it, God. You lead.*

The terrorist's expression changed as he watched Darrell's face. Was it curiosity or amazement?

Callie shouted again into the amplifier. "Are you ready?" Black and white both raised their voices. The mob braced itself.

Darrell did the same. He was stuck with Failak but he would still do what he could and leave the rest to the Lord.

Callie shouted, "Red Ribbons, now!"

As one force, the crowd moved and Darrell moved with it, his eyes locked on Link, his first objective. He felt someone grabbing at him. He ducked under and backwards, using his free hand to shove the person into another man that was moving in on Failak. The terrorist added his own one-handed shove, and the two attackers tangled and went down.

Darrell wove through the crowd, heading for Link, Failak running with him. It was pandemonium. Everyone was fighting each other. People all around were taking others to the ground. Soon it became a minefield of bodies. Link's head jerked as he went down like a tall tree falling in the forest.

Darrell ran and Failak kept up. *This is different.* Everyone was focused on someone else and ignored them. They were some of the few still on their feet, so the field of vision was clear. Callie was still on the wall, surrounded by supporters. That would be bad when it came time to extract her, but for now she was safe, and it allowed Darrell time to help Link.

The kid was on the ground with three guys sporting red ribbons on top of him. Darrell made it to him and gave the man that was kneeling on Link's shoulder a stunning blow to the nerve center in his neck. The man slumped over. A man in a yellow shirt with the distinctive red ribbon around his waist stood to take Darrell on. Darrell used Failak as a brace and delivered a kick to the man's midsection. Yellow shirt went down on his seat with the wind knocked out of him.

The last of the three, a smaller man, let go of Link's arm that he had been holding to the ground and jumped up. Both Darrell and Failak faced him as Link started rising. The man backed up with his hands in front of him, like he didn't want further trouble.

Darrell grabbed Link's arm to help him up the rest of the way.

The kid batted at him with his hand until he realized who he was. "Darrell!" He gave Failak a harsh look.

"No time to talk. We've got to get to Callie."

Darrell tugged Failak into motion and the two ran side by side. Link caught up and together they ran through a maze of bodies fighting on the ground. Leaving the street, they ran in the grassy border next to the sidewalk and sprinted the last of the distance between the two groups. Darrell heard feet slapping the ground behind them.

Callie's defenders saw Darrell, Failak and Link heading toward them. Two of the large men ran to meet them, both looked ready for the fight.

At the sight of them, Link slowed. Uff! Someone took him down from behind.

Failak lagged also, pulling on the NIP. Darrell looked at Callie, and she saw him, obvious recognition on her face. She jumped down from the wall. If Darrell could take out the two coming at him, there would only be one man between him and Callie.

Darrell was snatched sideways by a jerk to the NIP. Yellow shirt and the small guy had grabbed Failak. Darrell released the NIP, letting the men take the terrorist to the ground. *None of us are going to live through this if*

I don't have both hands to fight. He turned his attention to Callie's defenders who were coming at him from the front.

Someone hit Darrell from behind, grabbing his waist. As he went to the ground, Darrell quickly reversed the situation and applied a neck restraint. A glimpse of white skin was all he knew about his attacker. Darrell saw a dark hand grab for his arm. He released the hold and grabbed the incoming wrist with the NIP. A heavy body came down from the other side and encircled his shoulders pulling him backward. Darrell tried to twist out of the powerful grip, but another body added to the weight on the NIP and the combined force drove Darrell to the ground. More weight pinned his legs. Someone else added to the pile and Darrell felt the wind being crushed out of him.

Callie's voice broke through the cacophony. "Stop. Stop it. He's okay. I know him." Then she was there above him grabbing onto one of the big men's shoulders and saying. "He's okay. He's with me. It's okay."

At Callie's command, the men let go and stood back, poised to jump on Darrell again.

Darrell sat up, and Callie knelt and grabbed him in a hug – black on white. All the men around them, every color, relaxed.

Darrell looked up in the faces, which were all smiling down at him. Red ribbons were flapping around their waists. Callie finally let him go and grabbed his arm, attempting to pull him up. One of the men reached down a huge dark arm, offering a hand, and in a deep booming voice said, "You must be Darrell."

Chapter 51

As Callie brushed the dust off Darrell, she spoke to the man who had helped him up. "See if you can get through to the police. It may take some convincing, but tell them what we've done."

Darrell examined Callie. "You weren't affected by the MEamp?"

"No. Nandi turned the thing on without thinking, but the moment I heard it, I remembered what you did and unplugged it."

Darrell surveyed the scene around him.

Nearby, two men, red ribbons circling their waists, held down a young man who struggled and hurled curses. The older of the men spoke softly to the fighting youth. "Calm down. We don't want to hurt you."

The spectacle was similar all around. Black or white made no difference. Those wearing red ribbons were restraining the ribbonless. Sometimes three or four on one person, depending on the individual's size.

Taking it all in, Darrell spoke to Callie. "The people with the red ribbons aren't affected either?"

"No."

Darrell swiveled until he caught sight of Failak, under yellow shirt and small guy. He looked secure for the moment. Darrell spoke to the big man that had helped him up. "Can you help make sure my friend here doesn't go anywhere. He's the one that started all this trouble."

The man put his huge hands on his hips. "Really."

Darrell regarded the terrorist. "Thanks for working with me for a little while there."

Failak shifted uncomfortably under the restraint. "We both thought our lives depended on it. Do not take my expediency for weakness."

"I won't. I thought about killing you earlier, out of expediency. God told me no. Don't take His compassion for weakness either. It's a strength you might consider."

Turning away, Darrell saw Callie helping Link to his feet. He stood to tower over her, and Callie jumped to pull a twig from his hair. "You're a mess."

"What do you expect. I was mistaken for malware twice and got two hard shutdowns. And I've got further to fall." Link twisted his back and grimaced. "Nice rescue, Darrelldelivery. Next time, leave me on the ground."

The shotgun toting man that had taken Darrell's gun earlier approached with his partner and between them was Brock, brushing asphalt from the scuffed knees of his trousers. "This fellow says he's with the FBI, and that one," the man indicated Darrell, "said he used to be a cop. You know 'em, Callie? Are they both on the up and up?"

Callie clenched her teeth and shrugged sheepishly. "Forgive us, Agent Brock. Yes, Clarence, they both are legitimate. And Darrell still is a cop…a really good one."

"Well then, I guess you better have this back." Clarence handed Darrell his M&P pistol.

"Thanks." Darrell holstered.

Clarence's partner turned a handgun over to Brock as well. "Sorry, we couldn't take any chances."

Callie shook her head. "How did all of you end up in this group? Did you go under cover or something?"

Brock gave a shamefaced grin. "Let's stick with that story." He approached the grounded terrorist, taking a last swipe at his own arms to remove the debris.

Callie's gaze fell on Failak. She marched over to him, bent over, and pushed up her glasses. "Things didn't work out quite the way you planned, did they? We may have problems, but fear and hate still don't play that well in this country."

The terrorist glared at her. "Don't lecture me, woman."

Callie threw her hands up and stepped back. "Oh, I won't. By the look of your face, someone already expressed my point of view."

The mirth on her face angered the man further. "Your silly trick means nothing. Your country doesn't need me to destroy it. Things have already been set in motion and Allah will jud—"

Brock stepped between them, pulling a set of handcuffs from a case on the back of his belt. "Save us your speeches." He leaned in and took custody of the terrorist.

Darrell motioned for Callie to wait while Brock walked his prisoner away. Failak cursed them all.

As Clarence and the other men moved off to assist the team of Red Ribbons who were going around and securing the restrained with zip ties, Darrell followed them with his gaze. "How did all this happen?"

Callie glanced after them as well. "This is the physical equivalent of a prayer network. Where one person calls a group of people for prayer, and each one of those calls a different group of people, and it grows exponentially."

Darrell surveyed the Red Ribbons and their detainees up and down the street. "Put me on the list. I could use this much prayer, or backup depending on the situation."

Callie giggled. "The more Nandi and I talked about how crazy everything was, the more I realized that only God was big enough to solve the problem. We started praying, and I started calculating—how many people there were in downtown Denver, how many MEamps Failak could deploy in the time he had, how many would be watching TV that night. It had to end up with a lot more people that were unaffected. It's like always, it only takes a pinch of bitter to spoil the sweet.

"So Nandi and I started organizing a prayer network – both black and white, except when we were through praying, I realized that the Lord was calling us to battle. I explained that there were not enough cops to stop the fighting and unless we wanted the city to burn down around us, we better do something. It had to be the Lord because people started calling, and we had church buses turning up from everywhere. Unfortunately, I think we brought down the cell phone system but not before we had enough of a crowd to make it work. After that, it was just coming up with a simple strategy. God showed me the whole plan like a mural."

"Which was?"

"Failak wanted it blacks against whites so he could divide and conquer. We did it God's way—unite and defend. I took another cue from the way God does things and let our enemies think they were winning. We segregated for the common good and pretended we were against each other. Those of us who have a little more color to us," Callie gave a wink, "went out looking for black people who were affected, and the paler members of our group gathered up the whites. Some of us had to be armed in case we came across anyone with a gun but with God's help, I think we avoided any serious violence."

Darrell glanced around. "And the red ribbons were so you could tell each other apart from the affected?"

"Yeah, it was the quickest and easiest thing I could come up with at the 24-hour Walmart. Hey," Callie pulled the ribbon from her waist, "we created a new race. The red ribbon race." She waved the ribbon back and forth in her hands. "Where skin color doesn't matter." She interwove her arm with Darrell's and with a grin wrapped the ribbon around both.

Callie examined all the affected people. "Maybe he's right. We might be our own worst enemy. Maybe we've been listening to the real enemy too long." Callie's expression was pensive. "My daddy died to murder white Christians."

Darrell brought Callie's hand to his mouth and kissed it tenderly. "That's not you."

Callie smiled at him. "No, it's not, and I don't want anyone to judge me for what he did. I believe in fresh starts. God gave me one. I believe there's still hope. I don't have to let anything from the past define me or anyone else." Callie leaned against Darrell. "That is one of the things that made me think the plan would work. I come from a prejudiced family, but I'm not like them. And even though I have known people that are, I know a lot more who aren't."

Callie used her free hand to indicate the activity of the Red Ribbons. "We did all this by getting together as a Christian family, blacks helping whites and whites helping blacks. Nobody was worrying about who did what in the past. It was all about forgiveness, but I don't think anybody was consciously thinking about that. We just concentrated on what we needed to do for each other right now. It would be so nice if it didn't take something like this for that to happen."

Darrell brought the prosthetic across and gently patted the hand holding his arm. "You are one amazing lady, Calneshia Williams. That is why I love you so much, you help me get the important things right."

"God did it. Without Him I couldn't—." Callie faced Darrell. "You love me?"

Darrell looked in Callie's face and nodded. "With all my soul. You helped God make a new man out of me. You didn't get to see the old me very long, but that was probably plenty. I owe you more than I could repay in a lifetime."

The tears came freely down Callie's face. "You're wrong. I did know the old Darrell. I knew him when he saved an eighteen-year-old girl from a bunch of frat boys behind her college science building. My folks said no one would believe me because I was black, and the guys were white. They wouldn't let me cooperate in the investigation, and my name was never released to anyone. That night my clothes were torn, and I was a mess, so I hid my face against your chest until the female detective pulled me away from you. It's no wonder you didn't recognize me when we met at ATS. But I remember staring at your name tag just inches from my face—*D. Jacobs*. To me you were everything that was safe and secure, and I could tell when you held me and took care of me, color didn't matter."

In stunned silence, Darrell pulled Callie in for a hug. The red ribbon unraveled and fell away. Something stronger held them. Darrell rocked her back and forth and remembered. Callie, again, hid her face in his chest.

Into her ear, Darrell whispered. "Why didn't you tell me?"

"It just…never was the right time. Now it is."

Darrell admired her anew. "I knew there was something. I felt it that first day at ATS. God linked us together a long time ago. I just lost you, and myself, for a while. This time, with God's help, I'm not letting anyone take you away from me."

Chapter 52

Darrell rotated his hook in the steering wheel spinner. He didn't want to quit using the old prosthetic and lose his skill with it. As Callie had said, the NIP was dependent on technology that could fail.

Darrell pulled next to the curb in front of Pikes Peak Christian University, where earlier in the week Callie had helped Nandi enroll in the accounting program. The new student strolled out, enthusiasm gracing her countenance.

As Nandi settled into the backseat, she reached up and patted Antonne in the passenger seat. "How you do'n, baby?"

"I'm good, Mama."

"How you like'n your new school?"

Antonne shrugged. "It's okay. Lot different than public school. They talk about God a lot."

"Mine too, baby…and that's good. What you learn'n about Him?"

Another shrug. "Stuff."

Darrell cleared his throat and gave the kid a sideways glance as he pulled away from the curb.

Antonne began again with a more respectful tone. "I don't know. I guess I didn't know God was so…big. I mean, I thought He was for church and that but…they talk about Him like He's for everything. Even what I say. I have to watch what I say all the time."

Darrell chuckled. "You didn't believe me when I told you the devil had control of your mouth. You thought it was going to be easy, didn't you?"

The kid grinned. "Yeah, but I'm controlling it a lot more now. You gotta admit that."

"With?" Darrell cocked his head toward the kid and waited.

Antonne put up one finger. "God's help."

"That's better. Now I won't have to mop up the mat with you next practice." Darrell feigned a backhand strike to the kid's face.

Antonne blocked with a palm strike and captured Darrell's wrist, coming up with his other arm to form an arm bar to Darrell's elbow.

Nandi gave a sharp inhale. "Antonne. Don't do that when the man's driving."

Darrell grinned and with a push, rotate, and flip, he was out of the hold, giving a light swat toward the kid's crotch.

Too late, the kid sent his hands to guard the sensitive area. "Hey, you said groin strikes were only for the streets and not sparring."

Darrell steered the car. "We're on the streets."

Antonne reared his head back, and his face expressed that he had been cheated.

"Besides, those rules are for upstart apprentices, not the instructor."

"Ohhhh, I see how it is."

"That's good. Clarity is important." Darrell turned onto a side street.

Antonne started to protest further, but Nandi jumped in. "I sure appreciate you giving me a ride." The face Darrell saw in the rearview mirror said she appreciated other things he was doing as well. "Your bus schedule down here in the Springs makes a body walk a long way between transfers." Almost in the same breath, she said, "Don't think I'm complaining or nothing. Colorado Springs sure is beautiful. All those years I lived so close, can you believe I never seen the place? I'll never be able to repay Callie for getting us set up down here. Does she own a lot of houses like ours here in the Springs? I get the feeling she helps a lot of people."

"She would tell you it's God's house. He lets her help Him. Callie is happy to have you around. You're a good friend to her, and the ride is nothing. You're right on the way. I'm glad your class meets on the same day as practice."

Nandi displayed a big smile. "You and Callie are gonna to do great together."

Antonne held up his finger again. "With?"

Grinning, Darrell took the kid's cue. "God's help."

Nandi caught Darrell's eye in the mirror again. "When you gonna ask her?"

"I'm waiting for the right time. I want it to be special."

Nandi further questioned Antonne about his day as Darrell weaved through residential neighborhoods. In the mirror he caught her looking around in confusion.

"I wanted to show Antonne something." Darrell pulled to a stop and stared at the tidy yard that surrounded a well-kept home. He gazed at the structure, remembering it much differently. "We were doing a drug raid on a house. A man was selling dope out of it. A lot of elderly people were living in this neighborhood and were scared of all the drug users that were coming here to get their junk."

Darrell shook his finger at the structure. "This is a new house they built on the same site. There was nothing left here but a burnt hole in the ground after that night." Darrell glanced at Antonne then back at the house. "Three cops were killed that day along with the drug dealers when the dealers' boss blew up the house to destroy the evidence. The cops' names were Raul, Fraizer, and Steve. They were my friends. They had families that will never be the same."

Antonne looked at his lap.

Darrell made sure to speak calmly. "I wanted to show you this so no one could lie to you and tell you drugs don't hurt people."

Putting the car in gear, Darrell drove to the end of the block and around the corner. He got out and the others followed. "I chased the leader of the group here. He had friends in a van that came to help him. This is where they shot me." As Darrell walked to the curb, he took off his prosthetic hook. "I was hiding behind a car that was parked here, trying to hold my gun. I saw my hand all torn apart and mangled." He glanced at the asphalt. "I wonder how many rains it took to wash my blood away."

Darrell held his stump in front of his eyes. He recalled dangling fingers for only a moment. They were gone. He had no pain. He had no depression. In curious scrutiny, he examined the attachment that Callie had created to interface his stump with the NIP. He had no regrets, either.

Like Job in the Bible, God was not giving him an answer as to why he lost his hand, why so many died that night, why, after that, everything hurtled toward Pete's suicide. No answer, only an invitation to trust, and he did, and he would.

Antonne and Nandi stood in silent reverence.

Darrell smiled at them. "But it's okay now. The Bible says God makes beauty from ashes." He took a deep breath. "Actually, it's better than okay."

The monitor before Callie's eyes flickered. A message appeared on the screen. **Come to BERT. I have something to show you.**

"Oh." *Link must have made some progress.* The CIA wanted a lot of extra security features in the new Federal Law Enforcement Training Module. Maybe Link had completed them.

Callie made her way to BERT room. *Where is everyone? They should all be back from lunch by now.* She peeked into the R&D room. It was empty. Probably one of Raji's meetings. She hurried to BERT before someone could find her and tell her about it, forcing her to go.

The door was open to the training floor. Inside was a small table with a note and a BERT headset.

Put on the headset. I need your input on this scenario.

Callie looked up to the control room. Link was not there. *Okay, let's see what he's up to.* She positioned the headset and turned on the switch. The room transformed.

There were trees and a stream. Birds sang and the water trickled. As she neared the edge, she saw a dappled reflection of flowing white cloth. She examined herself and realized she was wearing a gown with a medieval design.

Across the water, a deer burst from the foliage, sweat-soaked and panicked. It leaped the brook in one bound and passed not ten feet from Callie. It was beautiful, and she turned to watch it.

A boom. Then a second. Spinning around, Callie watched as the forest parted, trees cracked and fell to the side as a huge body lumbered out. Stunned, Callie stared into a single yellowed eye fixed on her from the middle of a head that sat between hunched shoulders attached to a massive body with long arms hanging beside the creature's sturdy tree trunk legs.

Turning to run, Callie saw a horse and rider charging across the meadow. A knight in gleaming armor from head to toe straddled the pure white animal. The earth shook, throwing Callie down. She rolled over to see the cyclops had made it to the stream with one mighty ground rattling step.

The knight was upon her. The horse reared right beside Callie, and the armor-clad figure slid off its back and drew his sword in one smooth movement. The beast across the river snatched up a tree as a club.

The knight cast the sword at the monster. The whirling blade embedded in the single eye. The beast dropped its club and grabbed at the sword that had gone in to the hilt. The creature stumbled backwards and fell, flattening the forest and shaking the surroundings again.

The knight stepped toward Callie and lifted his visor.

"Darrell?"

Darrell knelt. "Never have I beheld a maiden so fair. My heart is stricken with love unquenchable. I claim my right as the victor to ask for your hand in marriage. Pray do not refuse me, for I live under a heavy curse, doomed to roam the land battling foul beings, and can only be freed by true love's kiss. Consent to end my suffering and be my wife."

Callie couldn't have suppressed her wide smile if she'd tried.

As if they were spirits materializing out of the ground, the ATS staff surrounded her. Nandi and Antonne were there, as well. They began to chant. "Say yes. Say yes."

Everyone froze as the Cyclops stirred and lifted its body from the flattened greenery. It stood to tower over the party. The single eye was gone, and Link's face replaced it. He was picking his teeth with the sword. He gestured with his hand for her to go on and do something.

Callie smirked and shook her head at the giant figure, then turned to gaze into Darrell's beseeching face. "No one should have to face something that horrible every day. I give my hand to the bold knight, and he has but to set the date."

Darrell rose, and the forest fled away into the walls of a massive church. Their audience made their way to the pews. A body-length looking glass stood beside Callie, and she found herself dressed in a gorgeous flowing white wedding gown and veil. At the other end of the auditorium stood her pastor at the pulpit. Link was now the best man.

Darrell gazed at her with stark admiration.

She knew her eyes must look like saucers.

"How about today? Will you accompany me to the beginning of the rest of our lives?"

Callie beamed. She stepped forward, taking his arm and they walked down the aisle together, like he was escorting her to the ball.

After this I looked, and there was an enormous crowd—no one could count all the people! They were from every race, tribe, nation, and language, and they stood in front of the throne and of the Lamb, dressed in white robes and holding palm branches in their hands. They called out in a loud voice: "Salvation comes from our God, who sits on the throne, and from the Lamb!" Revelation 7:9-10 (GNT)

Author's Note

Thank you for reading DOMESTIC ENEMIES. If you enjoyed the story, **please leave a review** on the platform where you purchased your copy (e.g. Amazon) and on any reader groups in which you participate. Next to prayer, this is the best thing you can do to support an author. Reviews help push a book up in rank so more people can see it and give other readers information to help them decide if they might like the story. Also, your like and share on social media and by word of mouth would mean a lot to us. Without reviews and recommendations, even well written books flounder.

How this story began

Thanks for reading DOMESTIC ENEMIES – a book that grew out of a short story I wrote in 2014 (though the seeds were planted much earlier). I was winding down my law enforcement career and fearing for those just beginning theirs.

It was the early days of the violent, destructive racial protests against law enforcement action (sometimes law enforcement mistakes—more frequently, it didn't matter). Even then, the various sources of media were exacerbating the hatred and violence. Instead of moving toward racial reconciliation, forgiveness, and healing—racial division was being weaponized for criminal, ideological, and political gain.

DOMESTIC ENEMIES was my first novel, but I chose to lay it aside for a few years. I feel the Lord orchestrated the delay because the story's time had not come. It began as what I call a Christian horror story to warn against horror stories. I wanted to convey the responsibility that falls on those of us who weave words and tell tales. Like law enforcement, we bear the burden of where each of our literary bullets land and their potential for destruction. The story grew into a novel. The theme about the hazards of the power of media became mingled with the story's call for racial redemption. Little did I know how prophetic it would be as evidenced by the last couple of years.

My second novel, EARS TO HEAR was like that as well. Long before anyone had heard of corona viruses or COVID-19 (outside of specific areas of research), I began writing a novel concerning genetic experimentation resulting in a virus that could wipe out the human race. The theme of EARS TO HEAR explored the meaning of life itself and what power individuals should have over the life of another, even if that person was instrumental in bringing the life into existence. Again, God had a far bigger plan for our books than we could see. Isn't He an amazing author?

<u>The story of the USS Vincennes shooting down flight 655</u>

During my research for the back story of the antagonist in Domestic Enemies, I came across the story of the Vincennes/flight 655 tragedy. It is a true event in history that some might remember.

When I read about the strange things that occurred that day, I knew I had a new twist to my story. The account of the incident in the book is well researched and accurate. I fictionalized some internal thoughts of the characters to add depth to the drama. Of course, Alireza and Failak are my own creation and not part of the original event. "Scenario fulfillment" was the actual term used to account for the bizarre mistakes made by the crew of the Vincennes.

For some time, both the United States and Iran accused each other of deliberate aggression and deception. Many Iranians still believe today that the Navy shot down the jet on purpose. Some in the U.S. speculated the Iranians loaded a plane with bodies and manipulated the Vincennes crew into shooting down the airliner to turn public opinion against the American military and justify their own aggressions.

While it is likely there was no human conspiracy on either side, we know we have a supernatural enemy whose aim is to kill, steal, and destroy and such a horrific tragedy bears his fingerprints. Some involved in the investigation speak with certainty about the final assessment, but the subjective nature of the reviews suggest that what occurred that day may never be fully understood in this life.

312

In this book, several characters have an encounter with God. Getting your life right with God is the most important decision you will make, the greatest experience you will have, and the most life changing event you can encounter.

It is not about religion; it is about a real relationship with your Creator.

Any serious historian recognizes that Jesus was a real person. But He was unlike any other historical figure. Jesus claimed to be God Himself come in human form. He was hideously executed for those claims because the corrupt religious and political leaders of the day feared and hated Him. None of this took Jesus by surprise and He warned his disciples about it ahead of time, seeming to embrace it, teaching about a spiritual kingdom that was not of this world and was completely upside down to what sinful man was used to. His death should have ended the influence of an obscure carpenter in an insignificant country. But, despite repeated attempts in the last two thousand years to eradicate His story, which never should have survived in the first place, He still changes lives today. Something occurred in connection with Him that reset history so that we record the eons as before and after Christ—an event so incredible that it altered the course of the world. That event was Jesus's resurrection from the dead.

There is ample evidence to believe Jesus is exactly who He claimed to be and if that is true, then our response to Him is the most important thing in life.

Without Jesus you are a slave to sin, it will destroy you in the end, and there is only one thing you can do about it.

When you truly give yourself over to God through Jesus Christ, everything changes. You will have the power to weather everything else this world and the powers of hell can and will throw at you. You can endure until the end and spend eternity with God.

The Bible is where to go for the answers. Start with these Scriptures and have a sincere talk with the one your soul has always longed to know.

For no one is put right in God's sight by doing what the Law requires; what the Law does is to make us know that we have sinned. But now God's way of putting people right with himself has been revealed. It has nothing to do with law, even though the Law of Moses and the prophets gave their witness to it. Romans 3:20-21(GNB)

We are made right with God by placing our faith in Jesus Christ. And this is true for everyone who believes, no matter who we are. For everyone has sinned; we all fall short of God's glorious

standard. Romans 3:22-23 (NLT)

They are made right with God by his grace. This is a free gift. They are made right with God by being made free from sin through Jesus Christ. God gave Jesus as a way to forgive people's sins through their faith in him. God can forgive them because the blood sacrifice of Jesus pays for their sins. God gave Jesus to show that he always does what is right and fair. He was right in the past when he was patient and did not punish people for their sins. And in our own time he still does what is right. God worked all this out in a way that allows him to judge people fairly and still make right any person who has faith in Jesus.
Romans 3:24-26 (ERV)

Brothers and sisters, my heart's desire and prayer to God on behalf of the Jewish people is that they would be saved. I can assure you that they are deeply devoted to God, but they are misguided. They don't understand how to receive God's approval. So they try to set up their own way to get it, and they have not accepted God's way for receiving his approval. Christ is the fulfillment of Moses' Teachings so that everyone who has faith may receive God's approval…If you declare that Jesus is Lord, and believe that God brought him back to life, you will be saved. By believing you receive God's approval, and by declaring your faith you are saved. Romans 10:3-4 & 9-10 (GW)

My friends, what good is it for one of you to say that you have faith if your actions do not prove it? Can that faith save you? Suppose there are brothers or sisters who need clothes and don't have enough to eat. What good is there in your saying to them, "God bless you! Keep warm and eat well!"—if you don't give them the necessities of life? So it is with faith: if it is alone and includes no actions, then it is dead.
James 2:14-17 (GW)

If this has led you to make a commitment to God, the Bible says it is important that you tell people about it. We would love to hear about your experience. Please email us at <u>copintheway@kentwyatt.org</u>. We have a free short story to share with you about someone who had the same experience and the difference it made in his life. Like all our writing, it is from an unusual perspective. It might give you a little idea of what to expect.

Acknowledgements

Thank you, Rebekah, my wife, friend, and best editor. As the years charge ahead, I fall deeper in love with you. I am grateful for the meticulous care you take in searching my manuscripts for those things that I can never find myself. You give your loving input so faithfully. Thank you for sticking with me as our story unfolds.

Calista Wyatt what a fabulous editor you have been. The way you have pored over this manuscript, and the sound writing advice you have given have amazed me. Bless you.

To Laura Coen: how we cherish your feedback. Your editing is worth more than we could afford—which is why you work for free. Your hearts and enhances our stories.

Thank you Billie and Kathy Thompson for reading and spreading the word about our writing. You have been such faithful friends and an encouragement to us. As a fellow author, Billie, your editing skills add an extra dimension to our books. We value your input in so many ways.

Thank you my son, Kwinn Wyatt, for the times you have come up with inspirational fixes for the sticky messes I have written myself into. Bless you for taking time out to pray with me and encourage me to keep on.

To Sharron Williams and Jeanie Nance: your keen eyes at the last minute saved us! Thank you for your support.

More About Kent and Rebekah Wyatt

Kent Wyatt was born and then he died. Wait a minute, I'm getting ahead of myself. (Whew! I'm glad I put that part in because, for a second there, I thought I was dead.) Now that you know the beginning and the ending of my story, let's go a little closer to the middle...

Actually, my novels are "our" novels, produced by the team of Kent and Rebekah Wyatt. My wife, Rebekah, will always be quick to tell you she is not a writer, but she contributes greatly to the finished product of our books. Rebekah (whose official title in the Wyatt Republic is Minister of Household and Finance) is a voracious reader of Christian Fiction. In the Wyatt writing world, she serves as (among other things) editor, researcher, manager, financial planner, contributor to the story board, plot, and characterization, and of course the final word on all things romantic. So, when you see our characters behaving like ladies and gentlemen instead of blowing snot, passing gas, and belching—thank Rebekah. (Disclaimer: the second half of this sentence was not Rebekah approved.)

Kent and Rebekah's novels have been semi-finalists in the American Christian Fiction Writers Genesis contest and a Finalist for the Romance Writers of America Daphne du Maurier Award for Excellence in Mystery/Suspense. Kent serves as Vice President of the American Christian Fiction Writers NW Arkansas Chapter.

So how did such a partnership ever get started? I mean really, a man and a woman, together, they're so different. Whoever came up with such an idea? Oh. Sorry, God. Great idea by the way. (Disclaimer: the preceding portion of this paragraph was not Rebekah approved). Of course, such an unlikely alliance could only begin in somewhere remote and mysterious— like the flatlands of Northwest Kansas.

I was born there. Rebekah was dropped there, like a tornado drops a rare orchid in the middle of a wheat field. Both our early days were, like most young lives, bizzare in their own ways. Mine full of the mundane misadventures of the son of a firmly planted fourth generation farmer, and Rebekah's comprised of the exotic escapades of a traveling evangelist's daughter. When we were in our early teens, we met and fell madly in opposite directions and both skinned our knees. For the few months that her family stayed at our farm, we rode horses and performed magic shows together, but then Rebekah's family was off to the next ministry opportunity. Over the years, we both strayed from God's plan in our own ways and then were thrown together again in our late twenties. In a few months, we were married. God has rescued us from our own imprudence, grown us in our understanding of His plan, and bound us together for His purpose. We love Him greatly because He has saved us exceedingly. Our prayer is that through our stories we might introduce others to THE ONE who longs to do the same for them.

To understand how this whole writing thing began, there is one thing you need to know about Rebekah: She is a faithful helpmate to her husband and selflessly supports his dream far better than he deserves.

There are two things that you need to know about me: I was born a writer, but I became a cop.

As a child on the lonely plains of Kansas, I always enjoyed reading and telling stories to the other kids. When I was thirteen years old, I read *R is for Rocket* by Ray Bradbury, and I decided I wanted to write stories like that, ones that haunted you and made you think. John Boy Walton became my hero, and I was going to change the world with my pen. Over the years, I learned that I wasn't Ray Bradbury, but God had given me a writing voice of my own and He could use that if I would let Him. The only problem was I didn't have enough life experience so...

When I was seventeen years old, a car almost ran my mother and me off the road. With my terrified mama holding onto the dash beside me, I pursued the other vehicle in my 1973 Mercury Montego and forced it to pull over. It was the town drunk doing what he did best. He came at me, and I knocked him down and picked him up by his belt and threw him in the back seat of his car to sleep it off. My mother decided that I should be a police officer. She knew that writing nonsense was never going to get me anywhere.

In 1983 my mother saw an ad in the paper saying a small town nearby was looking for a police officer. She convinced me to apply. But all the time I was being a cop, the bite I received from the writing bug became infected and grew septic. I fed the fever over the years with short stories, award winning poetry and a humorous newsletter that I put out for a growing email list. Another life changing event was when I read *This Present Darkness* by Frank Peretti. It helped get me back on track with my faith and introduced me to Christian Fiction. I had found the direction God wanted me to go with my writing. Foolish fans encouraged me by saying that they loved my newsletters and re-read them when they wanted a good laugh. Many even said I should write a book. With my law enforcement career and my family to raise, I could never commit to writing fulltime. So, I satisfied myself with learning the craft and producing short works. After 32 years, I ended my law enforcement career. I still have many friends walking the thin blue line, and I have a deep love for the profession. But God has told me it is time to fulfill my other destiny. Now, with His help, maybe my writing can change the world after all. Where are my old reruns of The Waltons? Look out, Ray Bradbury, something Wyatt this way comes.

You can find Kent and Rebekah at the following internet locations:

Website:
https://www.authorkentwyatt.com (free stories both real and imagined)
Facebook:
https://www.facebook.com/kentwyatt.org
Twitter:
https://twitter.com/authorkentwyatt
Amazon:
https://www.amazon.com/Kent-Wyatt/e/B07GSHF65Q
Goodreads:
https://www.goodreads.com/user/show/36911883-author-kent-wyatt
BookBub
https://www.bookbub.com/profile/kent-wyatt
Linkedin:
https://www.linkedin.com/in/kent-wyatt-b162b014a/
Instagram:
https://www.instagram.com/authorkentwyatt/
Youtube:
https://www.youtube.com/channel/UCW_AzksI3It_PSJQFt4oo4w
Pinterest:
https://www.pinterest.com/AuthorKentWyatt/